The Afflicted Saga
Defilement
Tale of the Fallen: Book III

Katika Schneider

ISBN: 978-0-9974268-4-7

For Amy
Thank you for holding my hand
through all of the Big Scaries.
You are what wonderful is made of.

ACKNOWLEDGMENTS

Thank you to all of my readers—from the brave souls who beta read for me all the way to my dear fans who are holding this finished book—for taking time out of their lives to make a place for Nes and Mathias.

Thank you yet again (and again) to Sarah Anderson for my covers. I literally could not have my books published without you.

Thank you to Felipe, Ayse, and all of the amazing artists to come who are helping my characters come to life through their artwork.

Continuous thanks to my fantastic street team for believing in me and reminding me to keep believing in myself.

And the utmost gratitude to the amazing staff, instructors, and fellow writers of the Superstars Writing Seminar for their expertise, encouragement, and inspiration.

ONE

Kol lay on his stomach, cheek pressed against the stone surface supporting him. He didn't have the strength to keep his wings erect—or even neatly tucked at his sides—and one flopped over the edge of the table, the other cast haphazardly atop his right arm. Breath came to him in weak, wispy strains, but he wasn't in the frame of mind to care about that right now. The only thought he clearly registered was that they were almost through.

Outside Kol's field of vision—not that it mattered, given his limited ability to focus—Annin clanked through the collection of medicinal components he'd used in the process of injecting life back into Nessix Teradhel. Demons were hardened, calloused creatures, and they often hid their fears well, but knowing his ally was near comforted Kol in the delirium he floated through. Annin made no other sounds besides the organization of his supplies, and Kol couldn't muster the will to speak. That didn't stop the questions from coming.

Had the procedure been a success? Would Nessix rise again? Would he recover from the foolishness he'd volunteered to endure?

That last question bothered Kol more than he'd expected it to. Several times, he'd boldly declared how he was prepared to die to bring Nessix into their ranks, but as he teetered on this obscure cusp between realms, he was no longer confident in that claim. It had nothing to do with fear of the unknown or what might await the twisted remains of a demon's soul in the afterlife. He was more concerned about the things he'd never see accomplished.

Kol had been here from the start. Him and Grell and Annin and... *Berann.* His lip twitched in a deeply ingrained desire to frown at that last name. It had been too long since he'd thought of *that* old connection. Longer still since it had been permitted for demons to speak of him. Kol blamed this lapse of judgement on his weakened physical and mental states.

Hauling his mind back to the present, Kol reflected on how hard he'd worked to reach this milestone. He'd been among the first wave of demons created and his rank at that time had secured his position within their hierarchy. He'd witnessed all the attempts at peace, at patience, at pleading. He'd been among those who had voted for war. He had observed every trial and error which led the demons to where they were today, and when his mind functioned correctly, he believed his new creations, the akhuerai, were the demons' key to finding retribution at last.

Abaeloth would have to listen to them now. *Etha* would have to listen. The world couldn't keep rejecting everyone.

Kol tried to smile as he stared at Nes's still form. It wouldn't be much longer until she was back in action, harnessed under the demons' control. Under *his* control. Kol blinked, the action demanding more effort than he appreciated, and groaned. He'd become so accustomed to holding Nes's soul over the past several months that an eerie hollowness engulfed him without it.

Thanks to Annin's magic, Etha's indirect blessing, and Affliction's binding might, half of Nessix's soul had been returned to her. A tiny ring protruded from her chest where the vessel containing that fraction of her soul was plugged into her, and Kol ached to know what Annin had done with the other half.

Mental clarity continued to develop and Kol identified the annoying rasp of a priestess's sobs as she huddled in the corner. Feeling dribbled back into Kol's limbs in the form of prickling tingles on the backs of his arms and across his face. He couldn't be too close to regaining his wits, though, because he swore he saw Nes's finger twitch. He stared a heartbeat longer and saw it again, then dragged his eyes to her face.

Her eyes worked slowly beneath their lids, and the priestess stifled her sobs. Had she seen it, too? Nes's lips pressed tight for a moment. This wasn't supposed to happen yet.

Kol drew a shallow breath to alert Annin, cursing how long it took, but all that left him was a prolonged groan unable to convey his urgency. His fingers uncurled to reach toward his belt to grab for his dagger, but his efforts failed him. This time, he released a sharp cough.

"I told you to relax." Annin's voice cracked with irritable fatigue. The words had been muffled enough for Kol to know the oraku hadn't turned around.

Nes's entire arm jerked, and Kol pushed as hard as he could to mobilize himself, straining his debilitated body back to the point of numbness. His head spun.

No. It was too soon for Nessix to awaken. He had to properly restrain her for the safety of them both. This woman, Kol's masterpiece, needed to be controlled from the start if he hoped to gain any use of her. He should have seen this coming and at last, too late, he wished he would have reconsidered his role in Nes's resurrection.

A startled gasp inflated Nes's lungs as her eyes shot open, and she launched upright to a seated position. Self-preservation engaged immediately, as it always did upon an akhuerai's awakening, only without restraints, Nessix was free to seek her survival. Terrified and desperate, remembering the threat of death and spurred by twisted impulses that were not entirely her own, Nessix groped for a weapon, fingers clawing at her naked hip.

Registering this vulnerability as a threat, Nessix shrieked her fury as Annin spun around with a curse. His reaction caught Nes's attention and her eyes darted to the oraku. Though she was unarmed, she'd found a target, one she longed to see dead.

Springing into motion, Nessix plowed over top of Kol's prone form.

Damn it all... the alar thought as his hands failed to obey his attempt to grab Nes's ankles when she passed above him. *Damn it all!* Nessix scrambled from Kol's field of vision. In the corner, the priestess ducked her head beneath trembling arms but otherwise

3

didn't move.

Kol tried to turn over, managing to drag his hand closer to his face, but nothing more. Annin hadn't exaggerated when he said this procedure would cripple him. Kol was so weak that his heart didn't even thump with an adequate intensity. Annin cursed again, followed by a belligerent growl from Nessix.

Don't end her... Kol thought, unable to produce the words out loud. *Whatever you do, do not end her....*

There was another clatter and the sound of glass popping against the stone floor. Kol failed his second attempt to shove himself upright. The scuffle escalated in grunts and growls, culminating in a crunch and a scream from Nessix.

"Nnn..." It was all Kol could voice, and it was too tiny of a sound for Annin to hear over his more pressing concerns.

A sharp hiss from Annin announced that Nessix found her second wind, which he dealt with by slapping her. Maybe he'd heard Kol after all.

"Stay down, you little bitch!"

The broken staccato of feminine gasps was interrupted by an occasional sharp wheeze and Kol let his eyes drift closed. Nessix would survive strangulation in the long run. Her little noises persisted longer than Kol expected her to hold out, though that could have been due to a faulty judgement of time on his part. Nessix fell silent before long, revealing Annin's panting in the relative silence.

Holding his breath, Kol waited for confirmation of Nes's fate. His eyes peered open with a touch more control than they had earlier as his concern built. Annin's respiration rate steadied and he rustled around, grumbling bitterly in hushed tones. Moments later, he grunted as he hefted Nessix from the ground and walked into Kol's field of vision.

Kol's eyes climbed past Annin's torn shirt and the runes scarred across his chest. Annin's sneer was directed just as much at him as it was at Nessix, and his bloodied arms dropped the woman unceremoniously onto her platform. He'd bound her arms behind her back, her legs secured at her ankles.

Annin met Kol's eyes flatly. "She's *damn* lucky I like you.

Understand?"

"Uhn…" Kol's attention drifted away from Annin and back to Nessix, and he blew out a relieved sigh, echoed more tersely by one of Annin's own.

"You keep recovering," the oraku grumbled at Kol. "It'll be my head Grell takes if you don't come through this." He spun toward the sobbing priestess in the corner. "Shut yourself up…"

Annin busied himself with releasing the priestess's tether from the wall to drag her to her cell, but Kol didn't pay attention to any of that. All he could do was stare at Nes's back, secretly thrilled that she'd been quick enough to catch Annin by surprise. He had an intense longing to see her eyes, dampened only by an unusual aversion to witnessing what sort of damage Annin had dealt to her face. Kol must have been less coherent than he thought.

A gentle smile tugged at his lips, and Kol closed his eyes to concentrate on recovering. They'd done it. They'd brought Nessix Teradhel back, and she was marvelous.

* * * * *

Kol had no way to gauge how much time had passed before he could sit upright again, and even that simple action winded him. His head swam, the muscles of his arms and legs pinching as he bent his joints. Annin had returned at some point to collect Nessix and take her to her holding cell. Kol allowed himself a prolonged groan while he still had the luxury of privacy.

As his breathing regulated and the pressure lifted from his head, Kol surveyed his surroundings. Annin hadn't cleaned up the mess made during his tussle with Nessix, an unusual thing for him to neglect and evidence of how upset he was over the current events. Where the oraku typically stowed his supplies sat a small wooden plate loaded with cured meat and stale bread, a cup of thick brown liquid beside it. The faint tremor beneath Kol's skin was backed up by an angry demand from his stomach, and he eased his feet to the floor.

Wings uncoordinated, Kol steadied himself with a hand on the table he'd been laying on, relieved yet again that he was alone. He hobbled around the platform to reach the food and found a note scrawled beside the cup.

You will drink this.

Kol frowned at the blunt instruction, and when he picked up the cup to smell what was in it, his stomach turned. Scowling, wishing Annin didn't care about him enough to want to see him pull through, Kol downed the contents in one gulp. He gagged before he managed to completely swallow, and again as he forced the liquid down his throat, gasping as soon as he was able. Wiping the tears from the corners of his eyes and shuddering off the sensation to try purging whatever he'd just drank, Kol gathered the plate, curling his arm around it to steady it against his chest. With a deep breath, he staggered to the door and opened it before he was convinced he was ready.

"Master Annin has moved her to the barracks," said the single demon who stood guard outside the laboratory.

Kol tore off a bite of meat and nodded. "Where are her belongings?"

"Already delivered to her location, sir."

"And her second soul vessel?"

"Master Annin didn't consider it safe left unguarded. He took it with him."

Kol frowned. Even before she'd attacked him, Annin was less than impressed with Nessix, and Kol didn't favor the idea of his oraku companion having control of any part of her soul. Trusting that Annin's commitment to their operation overshadowed his personal grudges, Kol strode ahead. The food calmed his stomach and physical activity awakened his systems. He was still far from feeling like himself, but at least he could function independently of assistance. Tightness in his right hip limited the length of his stride, pulling his leg up short the way it always did when he faced exhaustion. He took a break from eating to irritably knead the joint.

The few demons populating the cavernous halls watched Kol with dubious eyes, quick to whisper words he didn't care about when he passed. Whether they shared rumors spread by Grell or Annin, or simple fears of what Kol had involved himself with, was irrelevant. All that mattered was that he'd been successful and his new army would be functioning soon. Kol took another bite of meat and turned the corner.

Annin leaned a shoulder against a closed door, a nondescript cloak draped over his arm and a tidy pile of weapons and armor at his feet. He stood with his arms crossed and expression just as warm as Kol had expected. His old friend was always more cordial with him than not, and it had been quite some time since Kol had seen this degree of dissatisfaction flawing Annin's rugged face. With a pinch more of his wits, Kol would have smirked at the trouble he'd caused the oraku.

In typical fashion, Annin didn't lower himself to shouting ahead to Kol, which suited the alar just fine. Burdened by a lingering headache, he didn't particularly care for the idea of shouting. Instead, he weathered Annin's scowl as he walked closer, munching away at the final morsels of food before discarding the plate on the ground. All of this could have been much worse; Grell could have been there.

Kol cleared his throat as he stopped before Annin.

"Your limp is showing," Annin said coolly before Kol had the chance to open his mouth.

Kol frowned, pleased that he had the strength to keep his grimace at bay. "I hadn't noticed," he sneered. Quarrels among demons were not uncommon, but Kol preferred having one person he could consider a comrade. He flicked his gaze to the door, doubting Nessix would be included in his short list of pleasant company. He rubbed his hip again. "You have her vessel?"

Annin didn't move from his position. "I do."

Kol met the oraku's eyes and the two stared each other down. It was no great secret that Annin disapproved of Kol's obsession with Nessix, but he'd always submitted to Kol's orders. The alar extended his hand. "I'll relieve you of it."

Annin hesitated, holding Kol's eyes a moment longer before sighing and shoving his hand in a pouch to dig out the remaining portion of Nes's soul. "I respect the fact that you are the one who conceived the akhuerai, but remember that I am the one who understands divine manipulation." He pulled a slender, crystalline pendant out of his pouch and paused once more. "Be careful."

7

Expressing appreciation, especially for something meant to be concern, was beneath Kol. He reached forward and snatched the pendant from Annin. "I know exactly what I'm doing." He tucked the gem into his pocket. The familiar warmth of Nes's soul, even fractured as it was, pressed against his leg. Kol let out a relieved breath. "Has anyone told Grell yet?"

Annin worked his jaw slowly and bottled up the rest of his objections. "He's not here, is he?"

Kol snorted, an ache pressing behind his left eye now that his head was regaining normal function. "And do you have any updates on Nessix's recovery?"

Annin shoved his weight against the door to push himself upright and stepped aside. "She's woken at least once since the incident you know about and shrieked herself hoarse. No one has interacted with her yet, per your orders. Based on her previous actions, I advise caution."

Kol looked into Annin's pale eyes. They still bore the blunt truth of Kol's stupidity, but had been washed with the compliance Kol was accustomed to. As mad as Annin might be and as stupid a move as Kol might have made, Annin was just as anxious to see if their years of trial and error, all of those experiments and laborious research had paid off. He was as ready to punish the mortals as any other demon alive, and if their team reached that point first, they'd seize the most advantageous position when the new age dawned.

"I've taken her out once, I can do it again," Kol said.

"You took her out after she'd been exhausted by an assault and when you still had your wits about you." Annin raised his chin and tilted his head. "Do not forget the power you have allotted her. She is no longer some fragile fleman girl."

The warning burrowed into Kol's mind, sensibility telling him it was time to start making good decisions again. His heart, on the other hand, sang of eagerness to see Nessix with his own eyes, to behold the perfection he had created. Kol grasped the soul vessel in his pocket, hoping it was hidden well enough to evade Nessix's notice. Her tiny sliver of a soul would be drawn to it, he was sure—it was what allowed a handler to control his assigned akhuerai—but Kol planned to hide this from Nessix until he gained her obedience.

"She's unarmed?" Kol asked at last.

"Yes."

Kol smiled and gave his leg one last stretch. "Then there's little I should have to worry about."

Annin rolled his eyes, but didn't offer any further protest as Kol plucked the cloak from his arm, and opened the door.

The room was small, barely large enough for a pair of bunks, though it only contained one simple cot. Thin streaks of blood swept across the top and Kol's brows furrowed at the thought of Nessix being handled so carelessly. There were no other access points besides the doorway which Kol occupied, but Nessix was nowhere to be seen. His mind crept along with his recovery, preventing him from thinking to ask Annin if he was sure Nessix had been secured in this room.

Kol took a step forward and the door slammed shut behind him. Rough fibers of rope wrapped around his neck, followed briskly by a pair of nimble legs latching around his waist. Nessix made no sound as she struck, her breathing controlled and even, unfazed by this act of violence. Her heart beat steady against Kol's back with the confidence he expected from such a well-forged weapon. For a moment, he was so swept up by Nessix's effectiveness that he nearly forgot to fight back. Unlike Nessix, however, Kol couldn't afford to be neutralized.

His wings wouldn't allow him to effectively crush Nessix by slamming her against a wall or the floor, so he dropped the cloak and reached over his shoulders to grope for her wrists. One hand grasped the tail of the rope—close enough to buy him an extra breath—and the one that brushed against warm flesh was instantly pierced by Nessix's teeth. Kol didn't have the time to marvel at how little hesitation Nessix used to counter his defense as her teeth threatened to sever the tendons in his hand.

Howling in pain, Kol grit his teeth with determination. He'd hoped to win Nessix over without undue force, but she seemed to like things done the hard way. Sucking in a deep breath, Kol released his hold on the rope and it dug into him once more. This time, Nessix sawed its rough edges against the thin flesh of his neck, and Kol drew his dagger.

Four fingers still functioning, he grasped Nessix's ankle to ensure he didn't misjudge her location and plunged his knife into her calf. A scream tore from her, ringing in Kol's ears, and Nes's entire body cringed against his back. Kol gave her credit for her tenacity as she continued clinging to him, but his attack had momentarily weakened her enough for him to pull her off of himself.

Before Nessix had the chance to recoil and regroup, Kol ripped his dagger free from her leg. It would have done him no good at all to let her be armed with anything more substantial than a piece of rope.

"Do you need assistance?" Annin's bored voice drifted casually from the other side of the closed door, expressing a distinct lack of surprise that Kol had encountered difficulty.

Kol glared at the door. "We're fine," he seethed, casting his gaze back toward Nessix as she hunched over her injury. "Just in need of a little training."

"Am I free to address the lords?"

Through the perils of physical assault, Kol's heart rate had only climbed an inch. The thought of announcing to Grell and the other inoga that Nessix was alive nearly shot it straight from his chest. Having shown too much weakness to Annin and refusing to divulge it to Nessix, Kol bit down on the inevitable.

"Tell them what they need to know. I'll be by as soon as I'm through here."

Annin never gave Kol a verbal response, but he seldom did after receiving orders he didn't care for. The lack of reply didn't bother Kol; he was focused intently on Nessix as she pushed herself away, hands clasped around her bleeding calf. Kol allowed her to seek distance from him, in no rush to force her submission. After all, they had the rest of his life to work on that. He wiped his blade clean on the leg of his pants and shoved it back in its sheath.

Nessix kept her eyes pinned on Kol, her jaw rigid. She didn't pulse with the fear Kol expected from past trials, though given Nes's illustrious past, that didn't surprise him. Rather, her eyes swelled with an eerie loneliness, as if she felt betrayed by the very mechanics of life. It was a feeling Kol knew well.

"That wasn't a very smart move, you know," the demon said, crossing his arms as he studied Nessix's deepening glower.

She refused to answer him, though Kol gave her adequate time to do so.

Kol sighed and strode past her, smirking as she flinched away from him. He flicked his wings back and sat on the edge of the cot. "Do you know who I am?"

Silence still, not even a nod to allude at compliance.

"Your reaction to seeing me suggests you know *what* I am." He narrowed his eyes in careful consideration. The past few months Kol had spent bonding with Nessix's soul had led him to believe she'd been more aware of her circumstances. Was she playing him now, or had he misjudged her reactions due to his own aspirations? "Do you remember nothing at all about me?"

Nessix lifted the heel of her palm from her wound and grimaced at its severity before pressing it down again. "I am dead."

Kol cocked his head. "Are you? Do you recall how that came to be?"

Nessix ventured a fleeting glance at Kol's wily orange eyes. "You..." Her tone was bold and firm, riddled with no more fear than her daring assault had been, but that uncertain void in her eyes glowed of something else entirely.

"I what?" Kol asked.

"You killed me." The confidence in her voice shrank away at her statement. This demon had slaughtered Nessix Teradhel, leaving Elidae to struggle alone without her general. *No,* she thought. *Not alone. They still have Mathias.* Nes's eyes closed, her brows tipping in a melancholy relief, the faintest smile touching her trembling lips.

Kol raised a brow. Happiness was one reaction he'd never witnessed from an akhuerai realizing what had happened to them. "And it was an honor to do so."

A clipped chuckle beat its way free from Nessix and she opened her eyes. Feisty courage swirled about her now, deepening her eyes and raising her smile to a degree that bristled Kol. "I suppose it would be an honor for one of you pathetic beasts to be slain by Mathias Sagewind."

Kol blinked and straightened, his resentment of Nes's arrogance shuffled aside. "I wasn't—" He clamped his mouth shut and wrapped his fingers around the edge of the cot as he leaned forward. "What do you mean?"

Nessix's smile flashed her teeth, wicked validation illuminating her face. "I am dead," she repeated, "and this is the afterlife. I never imagined my heaven to be like this, but if you're here, Mathias couldn't have spared you. He destroyed you, and that's enough for me."

Kol erupted with laughter at Nes's determined claim, unable to witness her flicker of indignant confusion through the tears in his eyes. He covered his mouth with a hand, straightening his behavior with a drawn-out, mirthful groan. "Oh, Nessix, you *are* a gem."

She frowned at Kol's reaction, face contorted in rage over how little her declaration concerned him.

"Does your leg hurt?" Kol asked, wiping the dampness of tears from his lower eyelids.

Nessix's eyes narrowed and she shifted her grip on her calf to apply more pressure to the wound.

"Do you think pain is something that registers when you're dead?"

She didn't answer him this time, either, at least not with spoken words. Instead, she looked down at her leg as the pain dulled toward numbness, stared at the coating of blood which doused her hands. She had no idea whether or not pain like this could affect a soul, but her general understanding was that bleeding was a very mortal trait. A quiet gasp parted her lips and frightened eyes darted up to Kol's laughing gaze. The demon stood and retrieved the dropped cloak as he took a step closer to her. He crouched down, just as he had before he'd killed her.

"This is not your heaven, Nessix, and you and I are both very much so alive."

The fire dulled from Nes's eyes, the rate of her breathing picking up as instinct flailed between the need to run or fight and the terror of not knowing how to do either. "How... how did...?"

Kol smiled with a hum of satisfaction, pleased to see how readily Nessix accepted her fate. "I brought you here, brought you back." He draped the cloak around Nes's bare shoulders. Cupping the back of her head in one hand, he leaned forward and kissed the top of her head. "You are destined for great things, little one. Do not think of disappointing me."

He stood and crossed his arms, delighting in the confusion tumbling about his treasure's fractured soul. This was exactly where he wanted her, and as long as she remained timid and subdued, introducing her to Grell shouldn't be a problem.

"Let that breathe," Kol nodded toward Nessix's injured leg. "It will heal faster that way."

Kol strode to the door and pulled it open, hesitating briefly as he exited. "Do not greet me like that ever again," he said over his shoulder. "I do not like the idea of hurting you. I am your only ally down here. Do not make me regret that."

Nessix hadn't watched Kol reach the door, too stunned to follow his movement, and she didn't respond to his warning. The door fell shut with a dull thud followed by a lock thumping into place. Nessix drew her knees to her chest, huddling under the cloak's insubstantial warmth, and willed herself not to cry.

TWO

Mathias Sagewind stood on polished marble floors, staring at the closed door in front of him as if he didn't trust it to not reach out and pull his hair. Centered on the door was an elaborate carving of a kite shield laced in a ring of lilies—the heraldry which the Order of the White Circle had adopted after his resurrection. The constant reminders of his title and the greatness that was meant to accompany it wore on Mathias more persistently than usual today. Sucking his tongue, Mathias held his breath and knocked on the door.

He waited longer than he would for most people, but the room's inhabitant—one he knew was currently present—wasn't most people. He knocked again.

An exasperated huff, forced out loud enough to be audible through the door, preceded an entitled, feminine fuss. "Impatient, im*patient*!"

Mathias smiled tightly and took a step back, clasping his hands in front of him. The door flung open, accompanied by more spoiled prattle before a gasp interrupted the rant.

"Mattie!"

Mathias had thought he'd adequately braced himself, but a winded breath burst from his lungs at the impact of Julianna barreling into him for an enthusiastic embrace. Physically, she hadn't aged past her late teens. Nearly as tall as Mathias, she had his same blonde hair and green eyes. Beside himself, Mathias chuckled and accepted her embrace. Amidst the burdens in his heart and mind, such comfort was a welcome reprieve.

"Hi, Jules." The hug drew on longer than necessary, and Mathias tried without success to pry his way free of his sister's arms.

As much power and influence as Julianna had within the workings of the Order and in regards to the manipulation of divine energy as a whole, she had never grown out of her innocent reliance on Mathias. Always the little sister, not even the title of High Priestess was enough to sully her joy of their reunion after being apart for so long. Mathias was often less enthusiastic with his affection for her, but the tension that kept the muscles of his arms flexed and his breathing too regulated gave Julianna pause. When he refused to offer more of a greeting, she pulled back from him and frowned. She'd hoped he wouldn't carry business home to Zeal.

Julianna drew a deep breath. Mathias was closed to the notion of small talk, and the Mother Goddess Etha had given her enough insight to have an idea as to why. Foregoing all of her curiosity about the wonders of Elidae, Julianna released her brother, nervously running her hands down the stomach of her powder blue gown.

"Etha told me Shand was behind it?" She took a step to the side and gestured Mathias into her chamber.

Mathias stared at her invitation for a moment before letting his head bow through a nod and walking inside. Julianna followed him and quietly closed the door.

"And she said Shand was teaching the demons about necromancy?"

When Julianna turned around, Mathias still had his back to her, his posture hunched forward. There were many things Mathias did that frightened his sister—from foolish charges into combat to the glint of mischief that accompanied his boredom in political situations—but seeing him helpless and uncertain was something she'd never grow used to. Even before he was immortal, even as a *child*, Mathias had always had answers, had hope. Julianna bit her lip and grasped fistfuls of her skirt to keep herself from rushing forward to hug him again.

"And she…" The compassionate side of Julianna begged her to quit talking, scolding her over how badly her blunt words hurt her brother, but Etha had built him sturdy enough to handle the world's problems. And this was certainly problematic. "She said the demons are stealing souls?" Her words died out in a timid squeak.

Mathias remained silent, and when his stalwart frame shuddered, Julianna glanced away. She'd have preferred a spoken answer, even if it was raging and fierce. She sighed and tried to draw upon the diplomacy her title had schooled into her over the past few centuries, but as usual, it never quite reached its full potential when addressing Mathias.

"We've sent out task forces to investigate this claim," Julianna continued, voice shrinking.

Mathias raised his head, though he still didn't turn to face her. He wasn't ready for that quite yet. "There's no need. I've seen it myself."

Julianna gasped, taking an impulsive step closer to him. "Then you must report it to the Council. Tell them—"

"I don't have time."

Julianna sighed again, this one more irritated. Mathias *never* had time for the Council, even in situations when honor and duty bound him to report. Granted, even Julianna found sitting in on their meetings drudgery, but she respected that her station required some tedious responsibilities. "I think you just don't want to tell them."

"It's not that." Mathias stopped for a moment, thoughts identical to Julianna's flitting through his mind. "Alright, that's part of it, but more like an added perk. I seriously don't have time."

"Wait a minute. You're not implying you plan to run a one-man crusade to stop this…"

Mathias bowed his head at Julianna's scolding tone. He knew what was coming next.

Hands on her hips, Julianna marched around her brother and ducked low enough to peer accusingly up at his face. "Mattie, you need to quit trying to shoulder *everything* on your own."

"I don't intend to take on everything." He kept his eyes directed away from his sister. "Only matters concerning the demons."

"And that's why you came here to snatch Sazrah away?"

"Somebody had to keep an eye on Elidae after I left."

Julianna's brows furrowed and she straightened, cocking her head. Mathias reluctantly lifted his head to watch her reaction. "You didn't rid the holy land of the demons before you left?"

"Oh, we won the war," Mathias said. "Once Shand fell, it ended the demons' fluid passage to the surface, but Elidae's still recovering, and there are still demons running about."

"So... why did you leave?"

Mathias sighed and glanced around the chamber, locating a glass pitcher of lemon water sitting on a side table. He wasn't particularly thirsty, but would take any excuse to avoid looking at Julianna. "You know me. Too soft. Sazrah's better equipped to clean things up."

Even with his back to her, Mathias shivered and grimaced as Julianna's disapproval seared through him.

"Your mind is not in a soft place," she said. "Your twitchiness tells me that much. You want to tear out demon throats worse than ever, but you *left* before you had the chance to accomplish your mission?"

The grimace contorted to a sneer Mathias was glad he hid from her. Only his mind had registered protecting Elidae as his mission; his heart knew he'd been sent to take care of Nessix. He poured himself a glass of water and drank it slowly, mulling over his options. "I caused too much grief for the rising general." He omitted the fact that he and Brant had finally managed to find common ground. "Trust me, Jules, it was best that I left when I did."

Julianna didn't believe him one bit. Not from the tension in his embrace. Not from how reluctant he'd been to answer the heavy questions. And certainly not from how he aimed to keep himself hidden from her. Lips pursed, Julianna set down the dirty path of trying to trick her brother.

"It couldn't have *all* been doom and gloom over there. Tell me about Elidae."

"There's too much to say, and I don't have time for that, either."

Julianna spouted an offended snort and would have stomped a foot if she was a few years younger. "Etha said you met a girl?"

Mathias drew a slow breath, placed his glass down, and turned to face Julianna. As much as the two fussed at one another, disappointing Julianna often stamped an irritating ache in Mathias's heart, but right now, he was too preoccupied with the ache already in place. "I met a lot of people."

Julianna pouted and crossed her arms. "Then why'd Etha tell me it was a girl?"

He rubbed his forehead. "Julianna, I really don't want to—"

Mathias only ever used her full name in professional capacities or when he hoped to pull seniority over her, but that thought skipped right past Julianna. "Did Etha lie to me?"

"No!"

She raised a taunting eyebrow. "So why are you so ashamed? Did you sleep with her?"

"Jules…"

She laughed at the warning in his voice, mischief interpreting it to her will. "Oh, you did, you dog, you! Is she pretty?"

"She *was*," Mathias snapped, turning a shoulder from Julianna. "If you really must pry, she was the most beautiful woman I'd ever known."

It only now hit Julianna that Mathias's defensiveness hadn't come from modesty. Her arms fell to her sides. "She *was*… Oh, Mathias… What happened?"

He frowned tightly against the resurgence of sorrow and regret and rage he'd anticipated would accompany rehashing this tale, but he knew it had to be done. As Julianna said, the Order needed to know what the demons were up to if they hoped to stand a chance at stopping this blasphemy. What little information Mathias did have, he needed to deliver to Julianna. He closed his eyes for several heartbeats, commanding his chest to accept breath in a slow, even rhythm. Once he was convinced he had a firm hold on his emotions, Mathias turned to Julianna, recognizing concern on her face at last.

"She was the general of her people, a prime target for the demons from that fact alone, and she needed more guidance than even I could give." Mathias bowed his head. "The demons made no great effort to hide the fact that torturing me was their primary objective with that war. I can't help but think if I would have kept my distance from Nes, maybe they would have spared her... at least not have..." He couldn't finish, but Julianna's gasp assured that she understood what Mathias had been unable to say.

"You know what the demons are doing because they did it to her, didn't they?"

Mathias glanced up. Julianna always was one for blunt questions. "Yes."

"Do you know how they did it?"

Mathias shook his head. His knowledge of divine energy manipulation was driven by blind instinct, a trait relatively unique to him. Those who knew how to wield magic could see and access the threads of divinity that held life together, and Mathias was quite sure he'd have better answers for Julianna if he was able to see those secret workings. She frowned at him, but didn't criticize or question the shortcoming he had no control over.

"All I can tell you is that they bled her out until she was too weak to hold her soul. An oraku extracted it through her mouth and... *held* it. By the time I reached her, they'd already taken wing and there was *nothing* I could do for her."

As Mathias finished speaking, his mouth shrank into a grim frown, damp eyes lingering on the floor. He could count on Julianna to not pity him for his sorrow, but the tumult of her disgust and confused rage beat toward his heartache.

"An *oraku* flew?" she asked, pressing a knuckle to her lips.

Mathias nodded slowly, eyes losing focus. "Unusual for them to have wings."

"It is. Do you think his winged status had anything to do with his abilities?"

Mathias heaved a sigh, relieved that Julianna chose to pursue more practical matters. "I'm not sure. I hadn't seen this particular demon before, and to the best of my knowledge, he didn't surface again while I was there. He called himself the Spirit Binder. Ever heard that title before?"

Julianna's face scrunched up in concentration and she shook her head. "I'm not familiar with it, no." She tapped on her lower lip. "But if he was able to extract and contain a soul, he's strong in his magic. If he's ever made himself and his unusual talents seen in the past, it would be recorded in the archives. I'll task some of my students with seeing what they can dig out of research."

Mathias let out his breath, an artificial peace creeping over him. He looked up at Julianna, who smiled at him sheepishly.

"Now you get to go up to your room and sleep off the past year of worry and trouble."

And as soon as that peace had come across him, it fluttered away. "I told you, I don't have time for that."

"You said the war was managed and that Sazrah was keeping an eye on things. It's been quiet lately. Mattie, you have nothing else to worry about. Go get some rest." Mathias's jaw clenched with a determination Julianna had quit trusting some time ago, and when he pointedly looked away, she shook her head firmly. "Oh, no. No. You are *not* going to go looking for her."

Mathias leaned his head back and groaned. "I don't have any other choice. Her fate is tearing me apart. I need to save her soul, Jules. You know that."

She crossed her arms. "Do you know where they took it? Because I'm guessing you don't, otherwise you'd have already nabbed it."

"Etha says they have her tucked away deep in the hells."

"Which is why you can't go after her. Mattie, last time you thought it was a good idea to go gallivanting through the demons' realm, they captured and tortured you and *I* had to go down there to save you. No!"

Mathias paced an agitated stride, grasping for excuses. "I'm much more skilled now than I was then."

"No. I don't like this."

"And you think I do?" His roared response silenced them both. It had been some time since the urge to cry had threatened to overpower Mathias's resolve, but it hit him now. "Jules, please." His voice cracked with the doleful plea. "I need this. And I'd be grateful for any help you can give me."

The sight of tears glistening in her bold brother's eyes forced Julianna to look away. This was a stupid, dangerous plan he was concocting, and she forbid herself from having any part of encouraging it. "Mathias, I can't help you. I never met her, so I can't go fishing for her soul."

"But your students, your priestesses! *Someone* is bound to hear or read something. You'll task them with it. You said you would."

Julianna bit her lip and shook her head. "Mattie, this is new. You admitted it. *Etha* admitted it. There's only—" She stopped herself quickly, but not before Mathias extrapolated what she'd meant to say.

"There's only one way to get these answers, and that's to go find them myself. When the demons took Nes, they were too perfect, too aware of what they were doing. They've done this before, and I can assure you, they'll do it again. It's a filthy, blasphemous practice that we have to stop before they steal more souls from Etha."

His words made perfect sense to Julianna's practical side, the side which Mathias often approached when he wanted to get his way. She narrowed her eyes. "You'd head out to seek information on what they're up to?"

"Yes."

"And when you found that information, you'd come straight back here and report it?"

"I—" Mathias blinked, recognizing an intelligence in Julianna's eyes that he often forgot she possessed.

"So this is a selfish motive?"

Mathias froze, jaw hanging open. How could he tell her that it was? He wanted to scream that he deserved one selfish act in a lifetime of serving others, that he never took anything for himself that wasn't necessary for survival, unlike Julianna who pampered herself with fancy clothes and luxuries. Did he even intend to head out in search of answers, or would he stop once he found Nessix? Mathias hadn't considered his intentions selfish before, but since

Julianna so bluntly put it as such, there were few other ways for him to think of it. He needed to find Nessix so he could know what happened to her, and free her from whatever horrors the demons planned to subject her to. He wouldn't lie and say he didn't hope to be with her again, but he had to believe he was doing something right by wanting to protect her.

"It was a promise I made to her people, to her cousin who is struggling to lead in her absence. Plus, Jules…" He held out his hands, petitioning her for support. "The demons *torture* people down there. Badly. And they have Nes's raw energy. The things they might be doing to her…"

This time, Mathias couldn't shield his pride from the barrage of emotions, and he ducked his head from his little sister, covering his eyes with a hand. Julianna shifted her weight and a sigh flit from her as she tried to think of what to say to fix what she'd unintentionally dug out of him. If anything, she should have thanked him for having the decency to give her prior warning about his intentions.

"I will find her," Mathias vowed from behind his hand, voice cold and bent with a frightful determination. "With or without you, I will find her." He dropped his hand, comfortable enough with Julianna to let her see his tears as he strode to the door. He reached forward and grasped the knob.

"But will you do this without Etha?" she asked him quietly.

"I do nothing without Etha," he said. "And she understands."

Mathias hadn't expected Julianna, of all people, to be so against his quest. Worried about him, sure, but not intent on keeping him from finding out how and why the demons were snatching away souls. There was nothing else he could say to smooth things over, and so he shoved the door open and left the High Priestess to brood over his homecoming.

* * * * *

Julianna loved and respected her brother no less now than she had when they were mischievous children keeping watch over the other kids in their hometown. She'd always been the tattle tale, the one who went crying to the nearest authority when she saw someone about to do wrong, but Mathias, even from a young age, never hesitated to jump straight into action. He'd always been fair. He'd always sought justice. And he had never stepped back just because a task seemed impossible. Julianna had spent her entire life idolizing her brother for this bravery and strict code of ethics, but today, these traits frightened her.

She knew she wouldn't be able to talk him out of trying to find this Nessix he'd lost. He'd claimed Etha supported this quest, and Julianna knew from past experience that Mathias was well past the days of using lies in the goddess's name to get his way. No matter how determined either of them were to solve this new problem, the very thought of Mathias chasing after demons capable of stealing souls from Etha's grasp terrified the High Priestess.

Mathias had always dashed around being the hero, and Julianna had always been his snitching sidekick. It was time for her to use that talent against her brother.

The paladin had issues with the Council, a residual bad taste left from the way it operated upon his resurrection. That had been more than a couple generations ago, and Zeal had seen significant improvements in its governing body since then. Julianna regretted that her actions might rekindle some of that old hostility, but she had nowhere else to turn to. Hopefully, the officials would have some urgent task to assign Mathias, something important only he could accomplish.

Something like uncovering the fate of stolen souls?

Julianna stopped and sighed. The thought hadn't flowed to her in Etha's typical tone, but that didn't mean it was delivered by any less divine means. She rubbed her temples, wishing there was an easy answer. With Mathias and the trouble he frequently found himself centered in, Julianna feared easy would never be an option.

The Council had been built and torn down and rebuilt several times during Julianna's time as High Priestess, and she considered this particular group of elects more competent than average, a factor which would work in her favor. She had an unusual effect over the mortal members of the Council; while they all treated her with respect, it wasn't without the taint of bitter sneers shared behind her back. Well accustomed to these sorts of grudges given her station and influence, Julianna never let her opinion on this matter show. She was not, however, above collecting on such indiscretion.

Willard Aligoth had proven himself reliable and honest in the past, and his position as Minister of Petitions marked him as the best candidate to fulfill Julianna's scheme. She didn't make a habit of personally coming by Council members' offices, and her appearance reflected as much by the flustered haste which Willard's clerk darted into the more secure location of his private office.

Julianna waited patiently as the two men likely bickered over whether or not they should lie to her about Willard's whereabouts, speculating over why she had stopped by for a personal visit. She waited longer still while they probably tried to sort the pages of reports into some sort of formal order to give the illusion of a more tightly run ship. By the time the clerk returned to usher Julianna into the office with a suffocating degree of graciousness, she was certain Willard was convinced she brought word of a new war.

He wouldn't have been entirely wrong.

Willard was on his feet, face flushed and eyes pleading for there to be no problems on his horizon as Julianna entered. A thin smile stretched across his face, giving the distinct impression that he was about to be sick. "High Priestess. To what do I owe the honor?"

Julianna tucked her grimace behind a charming smile and folded her hands politely in front of herself. "I need you to find a problem for me, Master Aligoth."

His fear faded, replaced by a confusion that only enhanced his ill appearance. "A... problem?"

"Yes, please." Julianna's placid expression held steady and she showed no outward signs of distress.

Willard had never faced a request like this before. "High Priestess, my job is to make sure there *are* no problems." He gestured to his desk, cleaner than it usually was. "All pending complaints are being sorted by local jurisdictions and able-bodied task forces, and—"

Julianna straightened slightly, her brows tipping sorrowfully as her lips turned into a tiny frown.

"Oh. No. Please don't be... disappointed?"

As a child, Julianna had learned to capitalize on a proper pout. She'd grown out of the cute phase of such manipulative gestures, but her dismay had proven reliably toxic to those who held her in respectful regard. This time, the very real possibility that she wouldn't be able to secure leverage over Mathias enhanced her ploy. "You're absolutely certain?"

"I—" Willard's brows furrowed and he shook his head. "With all of the greatest respect, my lady, why would you *want* there to be trouble in our realm?"

Julianna's shoulders slumped and she flopped her hands to her sides. "My brother's back." She drew out her woe as though she'd just been told no cake would be served at banquet. "And he..." she caught herself, lacking enough information to risk blabbing her suspicions to a Council official quite yet. "He needs a mission to take his mind off Elidae. Badly."

Willard's eyes widened. Mathias was a masterful problem solver, efficient and quick, and he single-handedly maintained much of the realm's security. As many problems as he solved, though, he gave back to the Council two-fold due to his impulsive character and propensity toward making his own excitement. It would serve all of Gelthin best if Mathias was kept occupied on the back end of a campaign as impressive as the liberation of Elidae was rumored to be. There was just one issue with that concept.

"My lady, I meant it when I said times have been quiet of late. I don't have the authority to order other towns to stand down from threats they're comfortably handling and—"

"But do you really want him to get *bored?*" Julianna asked. She knew as well as anyone the headaches her brother seemed to thrive off causing. "Is that a risk you're willing to take?"

Willard rubbed his forehead with one hand and swept his stack of reports across the top of his desk with the other. "He'd be just as bored looking into any of these cases as he would be sitting here at the Citadel." Willard's eyes glistened, horrified by the thought of disappointing Julianna.

"Then find the most demon-y one and exaggerate it."

Willard's eyes widened further. "*Exaggerate* it?"

Julianna nodded, lips quirked and brows arched in satisfaction of her order. "Yes. That should do nicely."

A hollow laugh tapped from Willard and he took a step back from his desk, as if the physical distance between himself and his work would save him from whatever Julianna was trying to trick him into doing. "Are you… are you asking me to *lie* to your brother?"

Julianna crossed her arms and gave a short nod. "I am."

"Right. But to *Mathias Sagewind*?"

She raised a brow and nodded again. "That's the one."

Willard rubbed his forehead again, mumbling a quick string of something irritable which Julianna couldn't quite catch. He blew out a tight stream of air and began to sort through his pile of papers. "Lying to *the* Mathias Sagewind…"

Had Julianna not been too frightened for her brother's fate if he ran off to chase after his lost love, she'd have pitied Willard. Unfortunately, she was very worried about Mathias. "It's either that or disappoint me," she said. "I'm counting on you, Master Aligoth. Please do not let me down."

A ragged moan escaped the man as he looked up at the High Priestess, her eyes calm and swollen with expectations of obedience. "I'll see what I can come up with," he caved, voice quaking with defeat.

"And you'll make it your priority?" Julianna asked, relief trickling into her at last.

"If that is a direct instruction from the temple."

Julianna caught the gentlest hint of a challenge in Willard's words. He wouldn't go straight out and accuse her of abusing the power that came with her station, but he was sharp enough to identify a hidden motive lurking in the High Priestess's demand. His words gave Julianna pause. This request couldn't be delivered under the decree of the temple, as she was the only member aware of the imminent crisis. She was, however, appointed as the organization's head and just this once, she would take advantage of that title. At least Willard hadn't asked to know if it was Etha's will.

Julianna swallowed that tickle of guilt.

"It is," she said. "And I beg your haste in delivering whatever assignment you select for him. It is imperative his mind stays busy."

Willard couldn't shake the feeling that this was an elaborate trap, though he couldn't quite determine who it was designed to catch. Julianna had too much influence over Zeal and official matters pertaining to it, and she'd never shown a predisposition for cruelty. Instinct urged against it, but her pleading gaze and the desperate expectation spewing from her aura forced Willard's compliance. He glanced at his desk and cleared his throat, trembling hands sorting through his papers.

"I will see to it, High Priestess."

Julianna's stress fled her in a gushing exhalation, her eyes drifting closed as her entire face relaxed. "Thank you, Master Aligoth. You are serving both the temple and Zeal better than you'll ever know."

Willard delivered a polite bidding of farewell, one that came reactively and that he didn't hear for himself, and Julianna flit from the room, dragging her anxiety away with her. He sank into his chair and rubbed his forehead. If only she'd taken his, too.

THREE

Nessix breathed in the cool aroma of dirt, its scent taunting her with memories that seemed a lifetime away. She didn't know how long she'd been curled up on the clay floor of her tiny prison in the hells, nursing her wound. The earthen walls insulated the room against invading sounds, leaving Nessix with nothing else to listen to besides her own taxed breathing. Transparent orbs nestled in crevices throughout the cell and tucked among the corners of the ceiling cast a warm glow, obscuring her ability to track the time. Even if she'd been able to see the sun, Nes's mind spun too tightly around a fact she couldn't escape to concentrate on anything else.

She was alive, and the demons had captured her.

Nobody was around to hear Nessix whimper over her plight. She'd failed to defeat Kol, even when fueled by such hot determination and hatred. Unarmed and unable to overpower a single demon, her prospects of finding a way to escape seemed rather grim. Even if she did manage to hold her own against a kingdom of these beasts, she hadn't the vaguest idea how to navigate the tunnels of their realm. Nessix had witnessed the demons' cruelties on the surface, and Mathias had shared with her brief glimpses of the tortures they inflicted upon their prisoners. Brave warrior or not, this was not the sort of place Nessix wanted to be.

Her leg had quit burning, the pain dying out into a dull ache until she could no longer feel any evidence of injury. Afraid to look, not wanting to face the damage done to such a vital muscle, Nessix drew her hands back and braced herself to assess her wound. Blood coated her lower leg, soaking into the hem of the cloak Kol had given her, and had grown crusty over her knuckles. She blinked as she stared at her leg, certain she'd been maimed severely enough to face a permanent handicap, yet the gaping wound she'd expected to see was nowhere to be found.

Slowly, Nessix wiped at the blood on her leg, smearing it thinner across her flesh as she hunted for the jagged puncture that should have been there. Her fingers traced over a raised part of her skin as prominent as a scab, but far smoother. Biting her lip, Nessix twisted to gawk at her calf, her back protesting with sharp pangs as she contorted to find the wound almost completely healed. Her heart beat faster, mind not comprehending what had happened. Mathias had healed her more times than pride allowed her to admit, but he'd allegedly done so with the blessing of a goddess. A goddess Nessix had been assured wouldn't shine her smile into the demons' depths.

Nessix's brows furrowed as she ground her fingers against her newly healed flesh, trying to dig out some sort of reaction familiar to combat wounds. Her experience as general of the fleman army insisted that this was the sort of injury that would have taken a skilled surgeon and several weeks of healing to reach the stage of scarring. She hadn't fallen asleep—she hadn't allowed it—and she doubted she'd been hunched on the floor more than an hour or two.

She recalled Kol's words, instructing her to let the wound breathe if she wanted it to heal, and her heart beat faster still. This was not the natural way a body was meant to work. Demons were resilient and capable of an uncanny degree of regeneration, but flemans weren't. *Nessix* wasn't. She knew she'd died, and Kol told her that he'd brought her back. Her lower lip trembled over the implications this meant.

She couldn't be a demon. She *couldn't*.

Nessix curled her legs under her body, leaning forward onto

her hands to support herself on all fours. Her empty stomach twisted about, assuring her it was a good thing she couldn't recall the last time she'd eaten. When she had more faith than doubt that her body would comply with her demands, she pushed herself to her feet.

Gingerly testing her weight, Nessix's recently injured leg proved fully weight bearing. The discovery comforted her far less than it should have. She clutched the cloak tightly around her shoulders and looked around the tiny room, walking up to one of the glowing orbs embedded in the wall. A reddish hue pulsed through the crystal as she poked it, flaring an obscure objection to her touch. Pinching her lips between her teeth and blinking back a surge of tears she couldn't quite control, Nessix crept along the perimeter of her cell. The smell of damp earth and waste flowed in from a ventilation point she couldn't locate. The ceiling, though well above her head, was uneven and looked poised to crumble down on her with the slightest disturbance. Great wooden beams braced against sections of the wall, lodged into place by boulders sunken into clay floors.

When she'd first woken, Nessix had been too caught up in trying to free herself from her restraints for more than a quick appraisal of her surroundings to search for makeshift weapons. She'd heard voices on the other side of the door, voices speaking a language she didn't understand, and she'd cared more about survival than surveying. Now, as she paced the tiny room, she realized she hadn't missed anything. There was nothing of note, nothing to arm herself with, nowhere to attempt an escape. She stopped in front of the locked door. She didn't know what to expect on the other side, nor if she'd stand a chance making it through the inevitable challenges behind it. Certain she wouldn't be able to beat the door down without being heard, Nessix turned back to the cot and sank onto its flimsy support.

Pressing the heels of her palms into her eyes, Nessix racked her brain for what she should do, frantically flipping through all of the lessons Mathias had taught her about her captors. He'd held her hand through every demon encounter she'd faced to date, and she'd let herself rely on him so much that she couldn't formulate a sound tactic on her own. Beyond that, she wasn't the valiant hero he was. She couldn't face hundreds or even dozens of demons by herself. She hadn't even been able to face one. Nessix had been born into an army, had lived to be with that army. Her heart panged with a hollow wail and her tears flowed freely. She didn't know how to be alone.

Clipped words sprang up from the other side of the door, interrupting the mournful ringing in Nes's ears. She sprang to her feet and took two steps back to tuck herself behind the head of the cot, as if it would offer her protection. Another rustle outside the door and Nessix sniffed back her tears and wiped her nose on her shoulder. She shrank into the negligible protection of her cloak as the lock clunked and the door swung open.

Kol entered, carrying a bundle made of Nes's armor, and she slunk farther back, drawing an amused smile from the demon. He made a great scene of turning around to close the door, brazenly displaying his back to Nessix as he secured her only chance at escape. By the time he turned to face her again, Nessix had composed herself behind a clenched jaw and eyes that glittered with what she prayed passed for determination.

Fanning his wings open to act as a counter balance, Kol held the bundle of Nes's armor forward on a fully extended arm. "Get dressed."

Nessix stayed put. She didn't dare get within his reach again, though the pessimist inside her sang a warning about how that would likely prove impossible in the future. She eyed the armor cradled in her breastplate, unable to spot her sword belt or any of its accoutrements. Her eyes flicked back to Kol's, waiting for him to expose his game.

He heaved an irritated sigh and rolled his eyes. "Fine." The word popped from scornful lips and he dropped the bundle to the floor, jarring the tiny pile so it scattered about.

Nessix flinched at how disgracefully her armor was handled, instinctively wanting to tend to the plates and leather that had saved her life so many times. All the times but the one that had mattered. Her lips rolled between her teeth.

"You're going to want to wear something more substantial

31

than that cloak where I'm taking you," Kol said.

Nessix swallowed hard, ashamed by the volume which her gulp rang in her ears. She read Kol's words as a clear promise of danger ahead, but the fact that he seemed to care whether or not she was effectively protected frightened her nearly as much.

The truth was, Nessix's memories of her death were fogged from the exhaustion which had made her give up and distorted by the occasional flash of a terrifying man missing half his face. She remembered the demons surrounding her, remembered them picking at her until her strength couldn't sustain her anymore. Then, she remembered Kol's face. He'd been just as calm then as he was now, self-assured and expressing a degree of respect she hadn't previously imagined to find in his kind.

"What do you want from me?" Nessix asked at last, voice rasping against her dry throat.

"I want you to get dressed." This time, Kol's words were less patient, but he didn't make any signs of aggression.

Heart still thumping as it screamed for her to take any and all necessary measures to get past this demon and run, Nessix fought down her flight response and crossed her arms. "Where is it you're taking me?"

Kol tilted his head to assess the nature of Nes's rickety confidence. "It's best I don't tell you until we get there."

A quick breath shoved its way into Nes's lungs before she could stop it. Her suspicions grew readily and the desperate part of her mind, the one flailing about for anything that might point to safety, prodded her to listen to Kol's previous advice. She wouldn't be able to escape, at least not yet, and wherever he planned on taking her seemed to be less than safe. She still couldn't sort out why he cared, but figured she would be best off in her armor, regardless of any other circumstances.

Nessix let one arm fall to her side, the other gripping her elbow as she fought to keep a hold of her nerve. She took one slow step forward then hesitated, a gentle hum of reluctance fluttering in her throat. Kol took a step back, his lips playing with a smile, and Nessix walked forward again.

She felt like a dog, aware she had power, but unsure whether or not the man who called himself her master had more. Right now, Kol had exclusive control over the situation, of her future and her life. He hadn't shown her any unwarranted reasons to actively fear him, and as Nessix reached her precious armor and knelt down to sort through it, her tactical mind lit the kindling of her helplessness at last.

Her best—possibly only—bet was to play to Kol's whims until she had her bearings and found what few options she had. Let him care. Let him protect her, if that was truly what he was doing. That would buy her time.

Nessix pawed through the remnants of her previous life, nostalgia and desperation leaping at the chance to wrap herself in familiarity once more. She pulled out the strip of cloth used to bind her chest and a blouse with dirt ground into what had once been starched fabric, and frowned. Apparently, she'd been buried. She'd been found by Mathias, and somehow Kol had lived. She'd been given a funeral and the demons had dug her up, and somehow Kol had lived. The fabric hung heavy in her hands and she stared down at it until Kol cleared his throat.

Whatever had happened, whatever events had tarnished her past, Nessix had to stick to the only viable battle plan she had. Tucking away her confusion and despair to the best of her abilities, Nessix draped the two pieces of clothing over her arm and prepared to shrug the cloak to the floor. She froze as Kol stood there, staring at her. He seemed bored, disinterested by the prospect of seeing her naked body, and Nessix tried to console herself with the notion that he'd already seen her exposed. That realization didn't mean much to Nessix, and when it became apparent that Kol had no intention of turning away, she held her breath and turned from him. He'd had plenty of time to harm her if he'd wanted to do so.

Shrugging off her untimely bout of modesty, Nessix ran the length of her binding's fabric through her hands, rolling it up for a more manageable application. She worked as slowly as she thought she could get away with before frustrating Kol, mulling over how to approach this challenge. Would it be possible to befriend a demon? To win him over enough to aid her? Nessix had never known a time when she wasn't adored and respected, and that had cultivated an abundance of charisma. She glanced over her shoulder, instantly meeting Kol's eyes—now sullied with a bit less patience—and jolted her head back around. He didn't seem the kind to succumb to charm or showmanship, and he certainly didn't owe her any degree of respect after the actions she'd taken against his kind.

Internalizing her discontent strictly to deny Kol the pleasure of seeing her teeter on the edge of falling apart, Nessix let the cloak drop to the ground. Unrolling the first few feet of cloth, she moved to pass it behind her back when she lowered her eyes to discover a small metal ring protruding from her chest, centered just above the brands left behind by two gods who had failed her. No larger than the loop at the hanging end of a pendant, it was connected to a metal disk roughly the size of Nes's thumb nail and sat flush with her flesh. Her left hand dropped the end of fabric to reach for the ring, tentative fingers lifting it.

"You don't want to mess with that."

Kol murmured the suggestion in Nes's ear and she voiced a humiliating yelp as she scampered away from him. Flushing furiously at how lax she'd become, Nessix scolded herself for allowing Kol to sneak up on her. None of that discipline kept her fingers from returning to the ring.

"What happens if I do?"

"Bad things," Kol said, tone even.

Nessix narrowed her eyes, trying in vain to read the demon. There was still too much unknown to Nessix for her to risk recklessness, no matter how badly her rebellious side wanted to disregard Kol's warning out of spite. She pressed her fingers against the metal disk for a heartbeat, a comforting warmth pushing back against her fingertips, and then went back to work.

She wrapped her chest and, with increasing fortitude, retrieved her blouse from where it laid near Kol's feet. Breeches and boots came next. Base layers in place and confidence actively restoring, Nessix turned back to the pile of her belongings for her greaves, finding the first casually gripped in Kol's hand. Boldness fluttering away, Nessix froze as she looked up at the demon before her.

"Is there a problem?" he asked.

Nessix shrank away from Kol and lowered her eyes. "I can… um…" Reluctance was a foreign concept to Nessix when it came to matters of orders and combat, but that didn't erase the fact that she didn't have the confidence to address him. She cleared her throat, voice cracking as she spoke. "I am a general. I can dress myself."

"You *were* a general." Kol said. "And you're moving too slow."

A shaking breath rattled from Nes's lungs as Kol smirked and walked up to her. He knelt and wrapped the greave around her calf with a possessive tenderness. Nes's muscles twitched, instinct begging her to run, though she didn't know where she'd go. Slowly, she bent forward to retrieve the other greave.

"I'm not dead," Nessix said, her voice small and subdued. She didn't look up at Kol, but saw him straighten out of the corner of her eye to pull the bundle of armor closer.

"Not anymore, you're not." He handed her the next piece of armor to position in place and walked behind her to tighten the straps around her legs.

"And you never died, either?"

"Not even close."

Nessix pinched her eyes shut, willing those shameful tears away. They weren't tears of fear, not this time. They weren't tears of anger that she hadn't been avenged. These were tears Kol would have savored far more than that. These were tears of regret, of a hollow devastation she'd never be able to set at ease. "And Elidae…?" A stifled sob swallowed the rest of Nes's request.

Kol gave a final tug to the strap and stood, walking around Nessix to pick up her cuisse. He shot her a knowing look, catching the sorrow in her eyes. "Elidae thrives," he said. "Your people won that skirmish."

Nessix gasped and looked up, scouring his eyes for any sign of deception. No, he'd been honest. Bitter and honest. A flourish of pride swelled in Nes's heart, but she bit it back in this precarious moment. Bragging over the might of her mortal army while trapped in the hells and imprisoned by the beasts her people had overcome did not strike her as the best idea. Too stunned by Kol's statement, Nessix didn't take the armor from him, and his hands moved across her thigh as he worked on it himself, jolting Nes's mind from the prospect of relief.

"So now what?" Nessix asked. "If the war is over, what purpose am I serving? My men are too smart to come after me."

"Oh, we know that. None of them ever tried."

Nessix watched Kol as he walked around her again, still unable to read him. She'd once prided herself on her ability to judge her opponents, but she'd never before tried to negotiate with someone she hadn't grown up with or commanded the respect of. Demons were largely a mystery to her, and here she stood, hoping she'd find a way to manipulate the one who had slain her. She wouldn't react to his goading. She had no reason to. Her men, as she'd stated, were too smart to come after her. She didn't want them to try.

But Mathias? If Nessix wouldn't have been so uncertain and alone, she'd have chuckled. He was every bit the sort of fool to come after her. He was the sort of fool she *wanted* to come after her. Nessix repressed the notion that perhaps he hadn't wanted to. After all, he hadn't avenged her, hadn't killed Kol. She shook her head and drew in a deep breath. Dwelling on the past would not secure her present or lead her to the future. Right now, all that mattered was figuring out Kol's motives and trying to make an ally out of the most unlikely source.

"You never—" Nessix caught her boldness in a bout of self-preservation.

Kol didn't seem to mind what had begun to be a debate. "I never what?"

Nessix held her breath and summoned what courage she had at her disposal, muscles twitching rapidly as she turned to face the demon. "You never answered me," she said, equal parts proud and terrified of the commanding tone she'd mustered. "I asked you what you expect of me." She didn't dare throw out any mocking remarks in regards to Kol's implied desire to protect her from harm. Willingly opening those doors was dangerous and Nessix shuddered at the thought of what forms of torment the demons had mastered across the centuries.

"Of course I told you." Kol's smirk suggested some part of

him approved of her gall, and he cupped Nes's face in his hands and patted her cheek. "We've brought you to do great things. Behave yourself and you'll make it far."

Nessix gulped down her desire to tear free from his vile hands, eyes hardening. "And if I choose to misbehave?"

Kol drew his left hand away and struck Nessix across the cheek. "You won't."

Nessix winced at the sting of Kol's reprimand but held her ground, her previous assumption that he meant her no harm wavering. He left the threat open and heavy enough to keep Nessix from questioning him, at least for now. She didn't move to nurse her cheek and stood rigidly as Kol wrapped the plates that protected her torso around her.

"Where are you taking me that requires me to be dressed for combat?"

"Not combat," Kol corrected, his voice more amiable than before. "That would require you to carry weapons."

Nessix read that as a threat, as well. They were going someplace unsafe. She closed her eyes. Maybe wherever he was taking her would result in her death. A permanent one. Maybe that would be how she escaped the hells.

"I'm taking you to meet my lord and his peers." Kol spoke with no less confidence, but his words stretched thin with a bitter regret Nessix didn't recognize. "They are a temperamental lot and as I told you, I have no desire to see harm come to you. I've got even less desire to see harm come to *me*, and so you will come obediently and you will behave yourself. Am I clear?"

There might have been a time, buried somewhere in Nes's past, where she would have argued Kol's terms, but common sense developed through a war against demons silenced those obstinate whims. Death should have meant Nessix couldn't be alive. It should have meant that she found her eternal bliss. But here she was, alive and trapped in the domain of her sworn enemy, forcing herself to obey the actions of the man who had killed her, the one who allegedly brought her back to life. The flecks of venom in Kol's words stated his displeasure with the idea of talking to this lord of his. That should have stoked some amount of fear in

Nessix, but she'd quit registering her circumstances as tied to reality. All she felt was small.

Kol tugged the final straps of Nes's armor tight and walked around in front of her. Arms crossed, his stern orange eyes critically scanned her over before the slightest hint of a smile lifted his lips. He gave a brief nod, as though accepting credit that Nessix stood before him, and she shivered

"The way I see it, you'll never be ready for this life," Kol said as he grasped Nes's forearm, "so I won't bother asking if you are. Let's go."

Nessix swallowed her rush of objections as she allowed Kol to tow her from the room. Her experience negotiating with demons was limited to feigning attacks so she could kill them before they killed her, and her knowledge of their culture stopped at what she'd observed of their battle tactics. She followed Kol, not out of obedience, but out of not knowing what else to do. To the best of her understanding, physical strength determined one's ranking among the demons. If Kol recognized the ones they were going to speak to as his lords, they were stronger than him. And the past had proven Kol was stronger than Nessix.

Desperate to distract herself from the weight of impending doom, Nessix scanned the passages around them. Her fortress had been built with the main arteries a jumble, designed to thwart those of simple minds who didn't belong there. She was accustomed to nonsensical floor plans and considered herself above average intelligence, but this maze which Kol navigated with such ease emphasized how lost Nessix was. She drew closer to her demon escort.

Kol did Nessix the favor of not mentioning her timid move and ushered her along. Disoriented, Nessix couldn't tell if their path led them deeper into Abaeloth's core or nearer to the surface, and all of a sudden, the weight of the world sitting over top of her crushed down, squeezing the breath from her. Through all of her mortal tantrums of wanting things she couldn't have, of feeling trapped in her position, Nessix had only thought her duty had robbed her of careless bliss. She'd only imagined her station demanded she couldn't drop her guard. Not until now did she truly understand the value of freedom.

Nessix had never before been afraid to speak. It had been back when she'd been a little girl, restrained by respect for her elders, since she'd last been afraid to push her boundaries. She'd grown up forgiven of minor infractions, free to express her impulsive nature, to expect the admiration and tolerance of those around her due to her name alone. Trapped in the hells, that name was unlikely to receive the same regard.

They continued to wind through the halls, activity bustling through the wide corridors as they reached what must have been the main arteries. All around Nessix loomed the faces of twisted men and women she'd routinely struck down, the beasts who had tried to seize her home from her. Instead, they'd taken her life. They eyed her hungrily as she passed, warped minds twisting with varying whims of what they'd like to do to her, yet none approached beyond those thirsty gazes. Nessix flicked her eyes to her guide, finding his jaw clenched and his glower steeled with a firm warning for those demons to keep their distance. A single alar and his frightened fleman charge shouldn't have been much of a challenge against a mob this size, yet Kol managed them with nothing more than his stony expression. Nessix ducked her head, working furiously over how to make sense of that information.

She didn't get to dwell long over whether or not Kol's authority came from a latent physical power Nessix hadn't yet seen or a hierarchal structure she'd previously believed above demons before Kol pulled her to a stop and stepped in front of her. His expression hadn't changed from that rigid glare he'd used to fend off the other demons, and Nessix gave a fruitless tug against his grasp.

"You will *not* shame me," he said.

Nessix opened her mouth to try to answer, but the tumult of information she didn't yet know what to do with strangled her ability to form a reply.

Kol took a deep breath, let it out in a sigh, then reached up to stroke the stray hairs from Nes's face. "You will do exactly what I tell you and nothing more. These are demons you don't want to find the bad side of."

Trapped in the hells, Nessix was quite sure she didn't want to find the bad side of *any* demons. She was poorly equipped for following orders, but smart enough to realize doing so right now was in her best interest. She'd thrived in her role of general, had savored every rush that accompanied it. Even those aspects she'd hated had been considered privileges, and her entire adult life, Nessix had thought she'd done an effective job upholding justice and honor. As Kol made the final adjustments to her physical appearance, Nessix wondered what she'd done to land herself in this position.

"Come with me."

If Kol's voice wouldn't have been enough to pull her along, his rough tug on her arm would have seen to it, and Nessix staggered forward until she fell in line beside him. She rehashed the events of her past over and over again, trying in vain to determine where things had gone wrong. Should she have been more diligent about the troops patrolling the mountains? Would that have made a difference? Perhaps she'd opened the door for her nation's vulnerability when she'd agreed to give Veed half the kingdom after her father's death. Tears tickled their betrayal and Nessix bit down on the inside of her cheek, refusing to go too far down this path.

Ultimately, it didn't matter where she'd made her mistake. Time had played out the way it was meant to. Her father *had* died. She *had* made terrible decisions. One of them had cost her her life and resulted in whatever purgatory she was trapped in now. Kol threw his shoulders back an inch, glanced at her from the corner of his eye, and dragged Nessix through a broad hole in the wall.

They stepped into a large cavern furnished only with a long banquet table directly opposite the entrance. Another hole toward the back of the wall to Nes's right glimmered with firelight. The room was lit both by those unusual orbs and fires placed strategically beneath small openings near the ceiling to facilitate ventilation.

Kol spoke as Nes watched the smoke dance its way to a freedom she coveted, and when she failed to respond, he wrenched her arm and jammed his heel against the back of her knee. Nessix cried out as she crumbled to the ground, jerked just shy of falling on her face so she landed on her knees. Kol bent over her, his eyes flashing with a sharpness Nessix hadn't yet seen from him.

"I told you to listen to what I tell you," he growled quietly.

Nessix stared at the floor as Kol took a knee beside her. The two of them stayed there, genuflecting in this silence before the empty table, until an ache began to pulse in Nes's knees and she contemplated seeing if Kol would reprimand her for shifting her weight. A hollow gong sounded, followed by the brisk rhythm of dozens of marching feet, and instinct spurred Nessix to try to rise.

Kol's fingers crushed down on her forearm, holding her in place. He speared her with another scathing glare. "Stay. Down."

Nessix hunched her head lower. Kol's calm had wavered from where he'd held it during their previous interactions, betraying a few of the preconceptions Nessix had of who he was. Her survival and success depended on Kol having some amount of leverage in whatever system governed the demons, and for the first time, Nessix questioned how much of that he held.

The steps clomped louder and shadows passed across Nes's field of vision as dozens of demons obediently filed past the fires to take stations along the walls. Nes's heart beat faster, begging her to arm herself, to run, to do anything she could to find safety while so ridiculously outnumbered. But Kol's words, his gripping fingers, the glare he'd engraved in her mind, held her fast. At least until she could come up with a better idea, Nessix had to keep this demon happy. A second gong sounded and this time, Kol held his breath, rattling the meager fistful of calm Nessix clung to.

She spared the stoic alar a glance. He'd traded his scowl for a slightly tighter tuck of his lips, his eyes directed forward. Kol's muscles twitched in their hold as a fresh set of footsteps entered the room. Nessix licked her lips and lifted her gaze, head still bowed, to assess what it was that had pushed Kol so close to cracking.

Nessix was built small, even for a woman. She was well accustomed to being the least physically imposing person in the room. Training had given her the confidence to make up for that disadvantage, which was how she'd found the gumption to attack Kol when he'd first entered her cell. But the demons who lumbered into the room, swaying like ancient trees as they plodded down the length of the table, shot the hairs on Nes's neck erect and clenched her stomach.

While an average demon could easily blend in with the mortal populations they were derived from, the four monstrosities that filed in bulged with grotesque, unnatural mounds of muscle. The first to enter bore a massive scar that nearly cleaved his face in half and an impressive set of wings. Despite their gigantic span, Nessix doubted their capability to carry his weight in any sort of agile or effective flight. That one walked alone, but each of the other three were followed by an alar wearing the same grim resignation Nessix had just discovered on Kol's face. Nessix stared at these brutes until she couldn't stomach looking at them any longer, and then she hunched lower.

"Who are they?" she whispered to Kol.

He answered with an equally hushed bid for her silence. An instruction that, this time, no part of Nessix resented.

There was a tumultuous scuffle of chairs and stools and the single winged inoga barked out a statement Nessix couldn't understand. Kol's head snapped up and Nessix unconsciously leaned closer to him. He'd mentioned wanting to keep her safe. Wanting to keep *himself* safe. Nessix didn't know how she'd endeared herself to him, but she would capitalize on that boon now.

The largest of the inoga roared something back at the first, and though Nessix cringed at the tone and volume of their voices, Kol slowly released his breath, muscles loosening. Nessix tried to soak in his composure, to reassure herself that if he'd managed to relax, it would be safe for her to do the same, but fear reminded her that she was not—at least as far as she hoped—a demon. The debate which Nessix wished she could hide from continued for a few more exchanges before Kol cleared his throat to silence them.

Nessix had preferred it when these monsters had invested their attention solely in each other.

Kol stood and hauled Nessix to her feet. Her knees threatened to buckle from where pressure had sapped her strength, but she obeyed. Forget how filthy it made her feel to take orders from a demon; doing so would keep her safe... or at least as safe as possible.

Kol spoke more words Nessix didn't understand, and though every fiber of her muscles shook with the desire to run, she raised her timid eyes to the panel before her.

Nessix had never seen inoga in action before. She'd never witnessed their tantrums or the arrogance they threw against one another. Right now, all she saw was crude speculation, distinct sneers of dissatisfaction, nothing Nessix couldn't grit her teeth and handle. Just as her respiration began to slow, Kol's hand slid down her forearm and grasped hers as he led her forward.

Nessix didn't move with him immediately, waiting until both of their arms had extended in full. She hesitated a fraction of a heartbeat longer and it took nothing more than the twitch of Kol's upper lip before Nessix held her breath and took two steps closer to the table of beastly demons.

Confidence had reclaimed its position in Kol's voice and demeanor, suggesting to Nessix that whatever reservations he'd had of these massive demons had passed. Her guide was calm. These foes hadn't yet threatened to engage her. If Nessix was to capture any sort of political sway, she needed to prove her worth now. Heart hammering, Nessix pulled her shoulders back and raised her chin, hoping the tears stinging her eyes weren't as obvious to her audience as they were to her. Kol smiled at her change of posture and resumed speaking.

He released his hold on Nessix to walk a slow circle around her, making the occasional gesture in her direction and giving her the distinct feeling she was being offered up for sale. Uncertainty poured into Nes as she glanced at Kol and then back at these huge demons as they threw comments back against the alar.

Nessix caught the obvious words travelling between them. Elidae, her name... Mathias's name.

Mathias. Thinking of him drew the breath from Nes's lungs and threatened to crumble her into a pile of helplessness. Desperation flooded her resolve as the demons continued chortling, pointing at her and grunting their opinions as Kol delivered what sounded like patient answers. Desperation to escape. To find Mathias. He'd know what to do.

Nessix blinked as she realized the demons had fallen silent, no longer speculating over whatever they'd been discussing. Kol stood in front of her, arms crossed and head casually cocked to the side as he looked her over. Nessix reached over and grasped her elbow to stabilize her trembling arms. She shrank from their stares as she brought her mind to the present from where it had tried to wander. Kol sucked his teeth and shook his head, striding up to her.

"What's the matter with you, little one?" His tone suggested a firmly rooted degree of disappointment, but Nessix couldn't quite call it unkind. "You're making my superiors doubt you."

Nessix looked into those awful orange eyes, the last ones she remembered seeing in life, and she shivered. "The only expectation I was told to uphold was to obey you," she said, her lips numbly complying with her effort to speak. "I don't see what they'd have to doubt."

Kol chuckled and laid a hand on Nes's shoulder, prompting her to suck in a sharp breath as she waited to see what would follow. There was no attack, no aggression of any sort. Instead, Kol turned his head back to the massive demons he'd identified as his superiors and spoke again, a short question answered by a few indifferent grunts and one sharply spoken reply.

Kol stepped behind Nessix and grasped her arms, lowering his chin so he could whisper in her ear. "Don't yet look at him, but there's a pale haired demon to your right. He looks bored."

One hand let go of Nessix and after the gentle whisk of steel against leather, Kol's hand—strong and steady—pressed a dagger into her grasp. Her fingers wrapped around the hilt instantly, clutching it with a desperate familiarity, as though she'd be able to fight all of these demons with nothing else.

"You don't want to be here," Kol continued, "and we're willing to give you one shot at freedom."

The words stoked a flicker of hope back to life in Nes's soul as she straightened, back pressing against Kol's chest as she tilted her chin toward him. She had no reason to trust a demon, but if he *was* being honest, if they truly were giving her a chance, she'd be a fool not to take it.

"If you're smart, he won't even see you coming." Kol's words were smooth and enticing.

Nessix flicked a quick glance at the demon in question. He pressed his back against the wall, arms crossed and spear propped against one shoulder, out of his grasp. Confirming his boredom, he allowed himself a generous yawn.

"Kill him," Kol commanded. "Take him down for me, prove to these inoga that you've got noteworthy fight in you, and you will earn your freedom."

Nessix gnawed on the inside of her cheek. She'd come to accept that the demons put very little weight in concepts like camaraderie and the value of life, but Kol's casual disregard for one of his own sat poorly in her gut. She shifted to turn and face Kol in full, his eyes alight with a morbid eagerness, lips raised in the faintest hint of a smirk.

"What's wrong?" he murmured. "Are you content here?"

She glowered at him, though she knew she shouldn't have. He was giving her a chance—one which she was quite certain she was skilled enough to exploit—to fight her way to freedom. Back to Elidae. Back to Mathias. This demon had displayed some degree of honor in the past, and the optimist slowly suffocating inside of Nessix pled for her to not pass the opportunity by.

There were no furious shrieks, no battle cries or taunts, as Nessix wheeled from Kol's steady control. She cleared the distance between herself and her target in the span it took his eyes to widen and his lungs to suck in a quick gasp. By the time he'd moved to grab the shaft of his spear, Nessix had his forearm in her free hand. She gave the unfortunate demon a stout yank forward, sinking Kol's dagger into his gut in the same motion.

He sputtered, the reflux of blood choking out his attempt at a growl. Nessix knew from experience that this sort of wound was unlikely to kill a demon, and she withdrew the dagger to swat her opponent's polearm out of reach. By now, the inoga were yelling, but Nessix disregarded their concern. All she cared about was complying with Kol's orders, not because he'd told her she had to, but because she was holding on to the only hope she had at walking out of the hells.

The demon lurched forward, grabbing for Nes's neck, and she danced a quick retreat. Smaller in size, she effortlessly evaded his attempt to grapple her. From the corner of her eye, she saw one of her target's comrades grasp the fallen spear and take a step forward. In a flash, Kol swept overhead, tackling headlong into that interloper and slamming him against the wall. If Nessix would have been less committed to her principles, she'd have tried to remember to thank the alar for what appeared to be his assistance once this was through.

By now, the inoga were pitching a fit loud enough to catch Nes's attention as a potential complication. Even if she'd been confident in her abilities down here, she'd have identified those brutes as a threat, as she suspected these were the kinds of demons even Mathias was reluctant to engage. All the same, Nessix kept her target in focus, trusting Kol—trusting a *demon*—to have her back.

Her opponent lunged again and Nessix braced herself, squaring her shoulders as she hunched down to catch him in the gut. He sputtered a rough cough, hands wrapping around her waist. As the demon lifted her into the air, Nessix dug her knife into the inside of his thigh, dragging it up toward his groin.

Blood flowed rapidly from the severed artery and the demon howled as he dropped Nessix so he could crumble to the ground and make a desperate attempt to stop the loss of blood that would see him dead in minutes. Nessix landed on her shoulders, tucking herself to roll away from compressing her neck, and scrambled upright.

Moments later, Kol's voice filled the chamber, not with the sound of awe or praise, but with a frantic and firm demand which Nessix still couldn't understand. She lifted her head to see him dashing toward her, wings lifted as if to take flight. An unusual horror saturated his eyes. Halfway through his first stride, a massive shadow passed above Nessix, and she shrank beneath the inoga who raged over top of her, desperately trying to sink into the earthen floor as she raised an arm in a feeble attempt to block the incoming blow that would pulverize her.

The demon above her threw his arm in the air, roaring a curse that even their language barrier conveyed with petrifying clarity.

Loud crashes from the table and chairs toppling over, enraged screams from Kol and the clatter of weapons from the demons who'd been standing guard around the chamber inundated Nes's ears. The inoga's arm struck down faster than she imagined a body that size could move, and then there was nothing.

FOUR

Mathias liked to consider himself a tolerant, patient man. He'd seen—and been the cause of—enough suffering in his life to know the value of trying to forgive those who had wronged him. But as he stood in front of a second wooden door etched with a shield and lilies, a disgusting knot of loathing twisted and coiled inside him. The two guards posted on either side of the door said nothing as a pair of young priestesses lit lanterns to combat the evening's creeping darkness. Mathias stared at the door for several long minutes as he scratched around for the motivation to let himself into the room.

That motivation, now and always, was Nessix. He needed to know what happened to her and the other unfortunate souls the demons had targeted. There was only one place to start that search—with the woman who had inspired the demons' interest in necromancy. Mathias had made the executive decision to leave his sword in the safety of his chamber, taking the only measure he could think of to discourage himself from accidentally snapping and killing the now-mortal Shand Heltsa.

You wouldn't have killed her, anyway, Etha chimed, her voice prompting the gentlest sigh from Mathias. *She wants to die. You wouldn't dare give her that, not with the sentence she's yet to serve.*

While Mathias agreed with Etha and had cordially discussed

the matter with her prior to this visit, restraint was so much harder knowing nothing more than a simple wooden panel stood between him and the sweetest vengeance he could think of.

And if you take that vengeance, you'll lose one of the only chances at insight you might be able to get. Behave yourself.

Mathias closed his eyes and pulled his lips between his teeth. A slow breath grounded him, binding him just a bit tighter to Etha's side. He pushed the door open, striding inside in the same motion.

Visible by the dying light filtering through a narrow row of windows positioned high on the wall, Shand sprawled on her back across a simple cot in the middle of the room, one leg hanging off the edge and arms stretched out to either side as she stared at the ceiling. Mathias slammed the door shut behind him; the guards didn't need to know what happened in here. Shand blinked and flicked her gaze at Mathias's scowl, a smile creeping to her lips as she curled her limbs back in so she could sit up.

"Oh, my dear, *dear* Mathias." Her voice dripped with an ironic fondness that begged Mathias to punch her in the face. "It's so good to see you! When they told me you were paying for my room and board, I'd thought you'd be by to visit me much sooner."

Mathias worked his jaw to dislodge the sour taste from his mouth and sucked it off his tongue. "Don't think as far into it as you have most of your mistakes. Etha's the one who wants you alive; my funding was the only way to appease the Council."

"Oh, nonsense," Shand said. "A heart as soft as yours wouldn't *dream* of mistreating a lady."

Mathias clung to Etha's bid against him bringing harm to this woman, and he cast his eyes toward the ceiling. "For you? I've dreamt of much worse, believe me."

Shand tittered, an unusual sound to come from a goddess whom Mathias had once considered too proud for such expressions, and he dragged his glower down to scrutinize her. Shand had always been of fair skin and what Mathias considered exotic features. Too gaunt to be considered healthy, her time in confinement had not been gentle on her. Signs of mortal aging blotched her skin, flaws she'd previously been able to snap her fingers to dismiss. Her eyes were sunken behind puffiness born of weeping or insomnia or a mix thereof. The glint in those eyes had warped from menacing entitlement to a pathetic desperation, though her wearied smile suggested she was still prepared to try hiding that fact. Mathias should have delighted in finding such a haughty and terrible goddess torn down to the barest of mortal conditions, but not even this seemed worth a smile to him. He stretched out the fingers of his sword hand.

"Are you still interested in making deals for what you want?" he asked slowly.

Interest piqued, Shand sat more upright, her brows rising. "It depends on the conditions. Can you find me a new god shard?"

Mathias's lip curled at the simple innocence in which she delivered that question. "It was your greed for a god shard that landed you out of my graces to begin with, Miss Heltsa. You would be wise to forget they even exist."

Shand flinched at the incredibly mortal way Mathias addressed her, and she parked her fists against her hips. "If you want to bargain with me, you'll need something sweeter than an upgrade to my accommodations."

"Your treatment is the Council's decision," Mathias reminded her.

"But your funds are paying for my upkeep."

"And I am not the one in charge of preparing your fare. Consider yourself lucky for that."

Shand laughed again, though she didn't press a hand to her chest the way she would have in the past. "Such a vicious threat from such a just man! And if the Council heard how you spoke to me now?"

Each trill of laughter pulled at Mathias's patience and he took an aggressive step forward before it snapped completely, silencing Shand as she choked on a sharp gasp. "The Council wouldn't care. They want to see you punished. *Properly* punished. Publicly. Humiliatingly. Excruciatingly. I cannot say I disagree with them, but you still have someone who demands you're kept alive. Someone not even I dare to question. It's in your best interest to keep that in mind."

Eyes wide, it took Shand several breaths to coax her mind back into functioning. "So *Mother dearest* wants me alive?"

Mathias straightened and flung his glance aside, taking a step back to reposition himself out of striking distance. "She does."

Shand belted out an obnoxious groan of frustration, throwing herself back onto the cot as she pounded her legs against its stretched fabric. Mathias crossed his arms and waited out her tantrum. If he'd been in a slightly better mood, he might have found the fit entertaining, but as it was, it registered solely as an annoyance that stood between him and his objective.

"And Etha will see to it you stay alive as long as you have a purpose. She's the one who advised me against bringing my sword for our little chat."

Shand rolled her eyes and stared at the ceiling. "What makes either of you think I have anything I can give you? She's the one who ripped the divinity out of me. *Remember?*"

"Oh, I remember," Mathias said. "And if I could have my way, I'd shove it back in you so I could harvest it again for myself. Tell me where Nessix is."

Shand scoffed. "Are you *still* yammering about that little tramp?"

Mathias drew a sweltering breath, clenching his teeth to stuff his rage aside. Shand shot him a sly glance and smirked at his fragile resolve. Divine or not, an intoxicating rush still accompanied irritating Mathias and with his disclosure that Etha forbid him to harm her, Shand coveted the fun she could have with him.

"I don't know where she is," Shand continued, waving a hand through the air in front of her as though conducting some grand orchestra. "The demons have her, I know that much. They've got her body, too. And—" She dropped her hand to scratch her neck and turned her head to look at Mathias, a wicked smile lighting her face. "I *did* offer them my insight on necromancy, you know. I'm sure you'll see your little Nessix—"

Shand's taunt cut off in a sudden wheeze as Mathias rushed forward and grasped her throat. He crushed down on her with both hands, ignoring the bite of her nails as they dug into his wrists and watched her writhe the same way she'd tormented him. Fear seeped into her eyes. She thought just because Etha told Mathias not to kill her that he wouldn't hurt her? After the hell she'd opened Nessix up to?

Mathias waited until Shand's struggles grew frantic and panicked, and a little longer still until they tapered with a slow acceptance of her fate at which point he forced himself to uncoil his fingers and pull his shoulders back. Shand sputtered and coughed, scuttling away from Mathias until she toppled off the opposite side of the cot, where she then scrambled to the wall.

"This is what your Etha allows?" she rasped, rubbing her throat. "Is this the greatness and goodness she bestowed on you?"

"Etha bestowed on me the duty of tending to demons and the undead, atrocities which you have tied yourself to. Now tell me. Where is Nessix, and what have they done to her?"

Shand pressed her back harder against the wall. "I don't know."

Mathias struck another step forward and Shand cringed.

"I swear to you! I don't know!"

Mathias stared at Shand, burning with the desire to choke her again, to flail her until she was bloodied and pathetic. He wanted to peel Nessix's redemption from this woman's flesh in ways he'd never wished to subject demons to for their misdeeds. The first of Shand's tears rolled free and the ringing in Mathias's ears subsided to a muddled din.

"I don't know where they have her," Shand repeated. "I don't even know what they're *doing* to her. Not even deities can travel the far depths of the hells, you know that. I don't know what they have planned."

The stubborn side of Mathias that blamed Shand for this mess demanded that she was lying to him, but those tears... It had been lifetimes ago, but the only other time Mathias had seen Shand cry had been when he'd saved her from her insane master. She'd cried tears of pain, tears of terror, and at last, tears of relief. Shand was too proud to feign such a weakness, and Mathias had no justifiable way to doubt that the tears she shed now were more genuine than not.

"What did you tell them of your mortal studies?" he insisted, reluctant to admit that a fleck of goodness might exist in this devious woman.

Shand shook her head and held a hand out as if it would protect her from another attack, should Mathias make one. "Nothing more than what they could have figured out for themselves. I told them about the threads—they already knew about them. I told them about tying them to a phylactery or host to gain control of their servants—they seemed unimpressed. A full, sentient being cannot be raised from the dead without the direct intervention of divine grace, and you have my word—" Shand's eyes widened and she silenced herself in a gasp as more tears flowed.

These were tears of regret. Mathias's eyes narrowed. "I have your word of what?"

"You have my word that I wouldn't have assisted in bringing Nessix back to life," Shand murmured, pressing herself more firmly against the wall.

Mathias frowned. "Not even to torment me?"

"I—" Shand whimpered and looked around her sparse furnishings—a cot, a chamber pot, and a shallow wash basin—for anything she might be able to rely on for protection. She glanced at the door, wondering if the guards would bother rescuing her from Mathias. "I'd ordered her *dead* to torment you... why would I possibly want her alive?"

That was the confession Mathias had longed to hear, the one that would justify his retaliation against Shand. Well past her sins of opening a way for the demons to reach Elidae. Well past the elaborate plans she'd laid in place to see him cursed and blocked from Etha. Mathias now knew who had been responsible for Nes's death, and his heart ached to take vengeance for those actions here and now.

His throat constricted from the surge of bitterness, yanking him back to the concept of morality. Etha had stayed out of this conversation, trusting him to keep his head and conduct himself as the compassionate man she'd risen from the dead to act on her behalf. She'd relieved Shand of her godly duties, and there truly was no greater punishment appropriate for one of Shand's temperament. Mathias had already killed once over faulty accusations and hasty judgement, and it was a death which still weighed on his mind when he let his guard down. Etha had some purpose for Shand, whether or not she planned to disclose it to him. He had to trust Etha. He knew no other way.

Rigid stance trembling, Mathias took two slow steps toward Shand and she recoiled her arm to huddle behind it. "You have no other insight. None at all."

"None." Her hushed voice squeaked just past a murmur.

"But you can confirm they have full possession of her?"

"I saw her soul myself, harvested by an alar named Kol and his oraku, Annin. After that, I have no idea what they did with her."

As manipulative as Shand was and as badly as the demons had betrayed her, she'd have offered something more if she'd had it, not sobbing in terror of Mathias's righteousness. Perhaps in a year or a decade, he'd find a way to utter the beginnings of forgiveness for what Shand had done, but it wouldn't be today.

Mathias turned from Shand and her pitiful sputtering, and stalked back to the door. Yet again, he faced that simple panel of wood, wondering how he'd adjust to life on the other side of it and if he'd regret crossing through it without taking advantage of all of his options. This was Etha's will. Mathias bowed his head and pulled the door open.

The guards kept their focus trained ahead. Mathias didn't know if they'd received reports of his relationship with Shand or if their forced disinterest was rooted solely in respect for his station, but he pulled the door closed behind himself, took a deep breath, and walked off down the hall without a word.

The more distance Mathias put between himself and that cursed woman, the more ease should have washed over him. Instead, he dwelled over what Shand had told him. The Order's efforts to shield knowledge of necromancy from the demons had failed. He toiled over Shand's involvement in Nes's death, how it had been because of her that the demons thought to claim Nessix at all. Mathias's feet ground to a stop, fists shaking at his sides as he struggled against the urge to turn and run back to Shand's cell to complete the mission his heart screamed at him to accept.

You have names now, Mathias…

Etha's voice washed across him and pushed a slow breath out of his lungs, dragging the tension from his shoulders and emphasizing how badly his knuckles ached. He opened his fingers and shook his hands out to bring circulation back to them. *Names won't get me far, not up here.*

But they're a start, Etha said. *A better one than you had this morning.*

Mathias rubbed his forehead and sent one final glare down the hall before continuing forward. *They are,* he admitted. *But I doubt demons of this caliber will have ventured to the surface often enough to have made names for themselves in our realm. And that's assuming I have the time or patience to go researching for something so obscure.*

An alar closely aligned with an oraku, and an oraku with wings. I'd think that'd be something noteworthy enough to make it past obscure.

Mathias frowned. *If I go to the library…*

I know, Etha sighed. *You'll never get out of Zeal if you don't sneak away this second. I can drop a suggestion to Julianna and ask around the heavens about the matter.*

That was a much more appealing option than the one Mathias felt shackled to. *Thank you, Etha.*

And thank you for restraining yourself. You and your free will are enough to age even this goddess.

Mathias suspected that had been meant to draw a smile from him, but he couldn't quite find one. *This isn't hopeless, is it?*

Etha remained silent for several more of Mathias's strides, speaking only after she sensed his composure slipping. *Nothing is hopeless, Mathias. Difficult. Trying. Yes, both of those. But what makes you you is hope. Nes's soul hasn't come to me. They still have her, and that means she can be found again. If anyone can rescue her, it's you.*

Mathias nodded slowly and heaved a sigh as the stairs leading to his chamber came into view. All he had to do was pack a few necessities and he'd be on his way. *Have the demons stomped on your laws enough for you to bend them a bit in my favor?*

Depends on what you're asking.

Am I allowed to approach the new children to see what information they have? Shand's too boastful to have kept her plans completely silent.

Ask who you wish, but remember that I can't force them to comply with

55

you. You have my permission to travel where you must to seek your answers.

A breath away from thanking Etha for her assistance, the more ominous intricacies of her blessing crossed Mathias's mind. He could travel wherever he must. Mathias bowed his head, wondering if Etha suspected he'd end up trapped in the hells once again. That was an option he didn't particularly care to entertain.

I'll poke around where I can, Etha said softly, chilled by her chosen son's stony demeanor. *I'll let you know if I find anything of value.*

Thank you, Etha.

She didn't deliver any parting words, though Mathias didn't know what else he'd want to hear her say. He continued the rest of his walk in silence, Shand's confession echoing through his mind.

Mathias tried hard to stuff his frustrations and fury into that compartment where he hid all of his negativity, but Shand had cultivated so much that the box overflowed. In a year or two, his heart and mind would settle enough to come to terms with the fact that Shand was better tortured by staying alive than being killed, but for now, he longed to choke the life from her. He'd do it slowly, to allow her to reflect on how she'd tortured Abaeloth; her mortal strength wouldn't stand a chance against his retribution. Mathias's finger twitched in anticipation of that day.

Tears blurred his vision of the hall, a gentle reminder from Etha of who Mathias Sagewind was, and he bowed his head, releasing the rigidity of his clenched jaw. Perhaps this vile response to loss was one more reason to hate Shand. Whether or not she'd been honest, even if she knew where Nessix was, Mathias didn't, and he had to clear his mind of distracting impulses if he wanted to find that answer anytime soon. Sniffing back his regret, he irritably smudged his tears away as the patter of rushing footsteps bounced off marble walls. Mathias wasn't an evil man, nor was he in the mood to display his fragility to unexpecting passersby.

Unfortunately for Mathias, Willard Aligoth wasn't merely a passerby. "Sir Sagewind!"

Mathias jumped at the sound of his name shouted through the hallway. Unarmed, reactive, and ready to take his frustrations out on whatever target deemed itself most applicable, the last thing Mathias had anticipated was Willard hailing him so close to the safety of his quarters. Hadn't today been trying enough?

Mathias had an agreeable relationship with this particular official, a rare trait for one of those buffoons to claim. But Willard did his job well, without complaint, and was among the more efficient members Mathias could recall to date. That still didn't make him feel any better about being hunted down to deliver what promised to be an urgent address.

Partitioning his emotions behind the public façade Zeal often expected from him, Mathias stretched a smile across his face, eased his brows into something that passed for friendliness, and turned to see what the man wanted.

"Good evening, Master Aligoth. Is all well with Council business?"

The man's gait slowed at receipt of Mathias's full attention and a timid uncertainty flickered across his brows. "As fate would have it... no."

Mathias's frown returned and he narrowly stifled a groan. "That is most unfortunate. Do you need to discuss tactics?"

"I need *you*, Sir Sagewind."

This time, Mathias let the groan come out. "I'd hoped to have some time to myself. If you hadn't heard, I only just got back from a lengthy and very trying campaign defending Elidae."

"I am aware, sir." Willard gave a polite bow of his head. "But I'm afraid this is a matter we need you to investigate. We'd have sent the Shade, but she seems to have disappeared on us... again."

Mathias clacked his teeth together and shot a perturbed glance aside. Of *course* there was an emergency right now. He closed his eyes and quickly scratched the side of his head. *Nes, hold on for me...* "And what reports have you received?"

"Increased signs of demon movement, targeting the village of Haddenton," Willard reported promptly, as though carefully rehearsed.

"Haddenton?" Mathias asked, brows furrowing. "I thought the portals over there had been tended to years ago."

"They had been," Willard said. "Which is why I consider it a concern."

Mathias wanted to tell Willard to go away and busy some

other unit with this report. He wanted to shout that he had far more important matters to tend to than going to confirm that the access points between the hells and the surface had remained plugged. But what it boiled down to was that with Sazrah gone, Mathias was the most skilled demon hunter to investigate such a potential threat. If there was one thing he learned on Elidae, it was that the demons hadn't grown weary and were more than capable of throwing him surprises. Besides, there was a chance he'd be able to leverage weaker willed demons to give him information. If only it didn't come at the price of another day of torture for Nes's soul.

"I will... I'll look into it," Mathias said, though the declaration lacked conviction. It even lacked the grumpy resignation his acceptance normally held.

Neither of those facts seemed to bother Willard as he gave a deep bow and nodded enthusiastically. "Thank you, Sir Sagewind. Come by my office in the morning and I'll give you the maps and reports you'll need."

Mathias pinched the bridge of his nose and missed the way Willard actively avoided looking at him, as well as the relieved sigh that lightened the other man's stance. "Alright," Mathias caved miserably, aching over the time he'd lose to this task. "I'll be by early."

Willard left with generic words of gratitude and Mathias flopped his hand to his side. Just once in his never-ending life, he wished matters would sort themselves in a sensible manner. He aimed to avoid being selfish, something Julianna had reminded him of, but this quest for Nessix was every bit as much to save her soul as it was to satisfy himself.

I will come for you... Mathias vowed as he hung his head and climbed the stairs to his tiny slice of the heavens. *I will always come for you.*

FIVE

Warmth caressed Nes's torso, emphasizing the coldness of her extremities. The irritating hum of muffled voices pierced through the ringing in her ears. She felt as though she was suspended under water, not quite floating, but too comfortable to be drowning, and all external stimulus came distorted through a fluid weight around her. The warmth seeped from her chest and down into her arms and thighs, creeping closer to her neck. She tried to wiggle her fingers and toes, still too numb to gauge the effectiveness of her attempts, and a slow, deep breath inflated her lungs.

The dampness of the air around her and the musty scent of clay and rocks staked reality back to the forefront of her mind, sapping the euphoria from Nessix and stealing that pleasant sensation of drifting away. One of the voices said something sharp, there was an aggravated sigh, and then Kol's voice distinguished itself amidst Nes's confusion.

"Stay calm. You're fine."

Clinging to that confirmation and the twisted comfort of a familiar voice, Nessix zipped back to the present or, more accurately, what she believed was the recent past. She'd been fighting a demon, surrounded by those giant overlords, and then an inoga struck her down. Her eyes flashed open and she flailed to try locating a weapon, desperate to arm herself before the next strike came. Instead, Nessix effectively flung herself from the plush bed she'd been laying on. She thumped to an abrupt landing on the floor, the breath propelled from her.

"You are..." The rest of the words came out as an illogical jumble, but the scathing tone conveyed the insult's meaning.

Nessix rolled to her back and hauled herself upright by the bedside, scanning past the chamber's rich splendor and fine furnishings to see the demon she recognized from her initial recovery shaking his head at Kol, a refined sneer curling his lip. This demon turned and left the room. Nessix cast her hasty gaze to Kol.

The alar sneered after his departing comrade. "You are..." Kol muttered an identical insult to the demon's back and strode forward to fling the door shut.

Nessix climbed to her feet, a wave of dizziness nearly snatching her knees from beneath her. She slumped to the bed, head spinning violently. "What happened...?"

"Inek killed you," Kol said. "Impetuous brute..."

"Killed me?" This concept of surviving death still didn't add up to Nessix and if it hadn't been for her ability to feel pain and fear, she'd have insisted none of this was real.

Kol sighed and turned to face her, expression flat. "He did."

Nessix raised her head, trying so hard to read Kol's intentions. "I suppose the fact that a walking house killed me negates the fact that I killed my target. I didn't earn my freedom, did I?"

Kol cracked a smile and walked up to the bed, encroaching on Nessix until she shied away from him. "No, little one. No freedom."

"So what does this mean?"

"It means we keep you away from Inek until he decides he's been adequately compensated for what you did."

"What you told me to do," Nessix snapped.

Kol's focus shot to Nessix and her sharp tongue, the hint of whimsy wiped clean from his face. "You performed well for me, but do not think that alone will guarantee your safety. There are others far more important than you to please. You'd better get used to that."

The knowledge that her honor and legacy had been completely invalidated stung even the dead parts of Nessix, yet she found herself laughing at the ridiculous notion that she'd *ever* be safe. It was a hollow sound, one that rattled against her aching heart. She had no idea what Kol had done to her, but she'd just discovered one very convenient truth. For better or worse, it seemed she could no longer die.

It was a haunting feeling, but a liberating one. Nessix had seen the melancholy longing in Mathias's eyes when he spoke of how many pasts he'd seen come and go. She'd seen how tired and lonely he was the few times he dropped his guard. But she'd also seen him charge recklessly into battle without fear of falling. He commanded the rest of eternity to run his crusade and now the demons, the only foes Nessix would ever hate again, had given her that same advantage.

Kol's frown creased deeper at Nessix's laughter, but he didn't correct her for the gesture. "I'd watched you for some time while you were alive and hadn't pinned you as one to be relieved to lose her station."

The words weren't what silenced Nessix, rather it was Kol taking a seat beside her that stifled her laughter. She thought to lean away from him, but had nowhere else to go. This was it. She'd accepted her position and if she wanted to secure control over it, she had to strike where she found her openings. Today, Nessix Teradhel would engage Kol in the war for her life.

"You may have slain me, but that didn't take away my station. You told me yourself that the flemans won."

Kol furrowed his brows and looked Nessix over with a cynical scoff. "And you think they credited *you* for that? You didn't even make it halfway through the war. Your pathetic commander and your cursed lover are the ones who got songs composed of them. You reached recorded history, I'm sure, but the most noteworthy thing you did during that war was die."

Worn to her barest level, Kol's bluntness punched Nessix in the gut, but for some reason, she couldn't force herself to react. "Why should I bother to obey you?" she asked, her tone wearied and defeated. "I'm not stupid. I know I'll never be safe here, not by mortal standards. You just proved to me that you won't let me earn my freedom. I could have killed that demon, killed that Inek, killed *you*, and someone would have still stopped me."

Kol straightened and gave a dry chuckle. "If you were as smart as you think, you'd realize you don't stand a chance against me and you'll *never* be able to stand against an inoga."

The insult slid off Nes's back. "But what reason do I have to do anything you say? I won't be able to win. I have no motivation to try. I won't be free and I can't be killed, provided you've been honest." The irony of that statement left Nessix with a bitter scowl. Had she truly just entertained the idea of an honest demon?

Kol sighed as he stood to go rummage through a heavy wooden trunk adjacent to the bed. "I've been nothing but honest with you, Nessix. I've had no reason not to be."

"You would have truly let me have my freedom if I'd walked out of that chamber myself?"

He didn't turn back to face her. "I knew you wouldn't, so it was never a concern of mine."

All of a sudden, that plan Nessix had concocted to try to endear herself to this demon began to unravel. The only bits of demon history she knew had come from Mathias's stories, and she'd only listened to a few of them. While Kol had proven to know her rather well, she knew nothing about him. His steady temperament, the amount of control he commanded, and the certainty he maintained in his plans suggested he outclassed Nessix in ways she would never allow herself to admit.

Changing tactics on the fly was a skill Nessix had trained in since she was a child. Kol was resistant to her efforts to placate him, and though the idea of attempting to demand control forced her to cross her arms to mask their trembling, Nessix was committed to it. Kol had mentioned twice now that he'd been impressed by her performance in life, and if she wanted to continue impressing him, she had to tap into that boldness. Swallowing the horrified lump in her throat so it wouldn't choke her words, Nessix jutted her chin forward.

"You didn't answer my first question."

The firm delivery of her demand succeeded in gaining Kol's

attention, though with him facing away from her, she couldn't tell what he thought of it. All she saw were his shoulders draw back and his wings lift slightly from their neutral position. Nessix's breath caught in her throat as she sent up a quick prayer that his reaction wasn't a sign of aggression. He stayed still a moment longer, fostering Nes's dread, and then plunged his hand into the trunk.

"Your motivation to obey me"—Kol stood and faced Nessix, her fully equipped sword belt grasped in his hand—"is to limit the torment you have to face. Please be aware that there are far worse fates than death when you live in this realm. Fates that death is a welcome release from." Kol cleared half the distance between the trunk and his bed, watching Nes's eyes follow her weapons. "I have a generous sway over many of the demons in this region, but not all. And those who are above me are there for a reason beyond my physical control. Am I clear?"

Nessix lifted her gaze to Kol's, saw that same calmness, that unexplainable inclination to oversee her well-being, and bit her lip. There had to be a way to influence Kol, but her wearied mind couldn't quite grasp how. For now, he demanded her obedience, and though Nessix was quite unskilled at accepting orders, she would do her best to comply. "I believe so," she said at last.

The answer didn't prompt any sort of outward relief from Kol besides a brief nod. "Good. Get up. I've got someplace to take you."

Nessix stared blankly at Kol. Though she'd just agreed to accept his orders, she rightfully balked at his words. "Where are we going this time?"

A tiny frown crossed his face. "Nowhere you need to be afraid of. Come with me before this becomes a problem."

Nessix hesitated a moment longer, internally screaming about how many times she'd already misinterpreted Kol's motives. The thought of repercussions, though, of not knowing what these fates worse than death might be and in no hurry to uncover them, gave Nessix the necessary shove to rise to her feet.

The last time Kol had told Nessix to follow, he'd dragged her along with him, forbidding her the chance to try something as foolish as an escape. This time, the only restraints he placed on her were his watchful eyes and the psychological pressure that came from his superior insight about what was going on. Nessix hated him even more for that leverage he'd found. She'd quit thinking all demons were stupid midway through the war for Elidae, and she fully anticipated a hard battle of wits against this particular demon.

Nessix followed Kol willingly to avoid stoking his ire, focusing her attention on the path he led her down. They turned the opposite way from before, the ground clearly descending deeper as they walked. She stayed silent, letting Kol deal with the few demons they passed along the way, a smaller number than they'd run into on their last little trip.

Kol made no indication that this journey would end in potential peril as he had when he'd taken her to be gawked at by the inoga, but the fact that he carried her sword belt hung paramount in Nes's mind. She was coming to trust that Kol was disinclined to throw her into a situation without giving her adequate chances of survival, but dressed in her armor and with her weapons so near, Nessix had to wonder what awaited her. Kol didn't offer any additional insight on the matter, and Nessix didn't request any.

The arrangement contented Kol and suited Nessix well enough, allowing her to concentrate on the passage they traveled so she was confident she'd be able to find her way back to Kol's chamber if needed. The rumble of sullen voices crept their way, voices which Kol didn't acknowledge, and Nessix shot him a quick glance.

Wherever he was leading her, there was at least an entire village worth of people talking. Nessix was no stranger to this level of commotion and as her mind suggested they were approaching a room full of demons, she eyed her sword again, took a deep breath, and stopped walking.

Kol continued on three more steps, each slower than the previous, before he stopped and turned to face Nessix. "Is there a problem?"

"Where are you taking me?"

"Somewhere you'll fit in much better than a room full of

inoga."

He was still so casual, so confident, and a more naïve version of Nessix would have stamped her feet over how effortlessly he evaded her prying. She held her ground. "I cannot comply with whatever it is you want me to do unless I know your expectations."

Kol smiled and walked toward Nessix. She didn't cower or flinch from his approach, her jaw set firmly and posture fit for defense. Her eyes glistened, but Kol was not fool enough to think fear alone was responsible for that. He loosened his grip on Nes's sword belt, allowing it to uncoil and drop to its full length, the buckle dancing just shy of the ground.

"I *told* you my expectations," he said, stopping a hand's width from Nes's face. "You are to obey and you are to do great things."

Nessix drew a quick breath to respond, but Kol's free hand sliding to the base of her spine ripped that breath from her. He gave her a firm pull closer to him, his arm wrapping around her as the color drained from her face. Memories of an equally repulsive man bombarded Nessix, and she curled her arms to begin fighting him. The familiar rustle of sheaths and a scabbard falling into place whispered its comfort to her. Kol's deep eyes held Nessix's terrified ones, laughing at her assumptions as his hand grasped the opposite end of the belt. He took a step back to allow himself room to secure the buckle, and shook his head. Reaching his fingers up to Nes's throat, Kol rested his thumb against the scar at her jugular.

"Frightened you a bit, did I?" His grin broadened as Nes's growl vibrated against his touch. Slowly, her heart rate dropped, though her tension remained steady. "Don't flatter yourself, little one. I've got my eyes on you for different reasons. Now come on. I've given you both your sword and armor. There's nothing left for someone as competent as you to fear, is there?"

Nessix wanted to let loose on Kol, to throttle him for his clear disdain and choke out every last attempt at laughing at her he had in him. She'd thrown this sort of threat around freely in her life and was certain it reflected in her eyes, yet Kol ignored her fury and turned to continue down the hall, as if confident she'd follow him simply because he told her to.

His back turned to her, Kol was an easy target. Nessix had no reason to listen to him, except for the fact that he was so *relaxed* about walking away from her. He'd bested her in a flat-footed attempt to take him down once before, and there was a good chance he'd do the same if she tried a second time. Assuming she was successful in neutralizing Kol, where did she honestly think she'd go? She had no knowledge of how to navigate these tunnels and no idea where to hide as she attempted to find an exit. Even if she'd been blind, she'd have sized up those inoga as threats, ones she hoped to never run into again, and she could hardly imagine any escape attempt she made would evade their notice.

Kol was a more formidable opponent than Nessix had anticipated, and he was confident and secure in that position. Balling her fists at her sides, Nessix stalked after him as he worked his way closer to the commotion down the hall.

Several strides later, the hall opened to a massive pit. A narrow staircase hugged the wall into the depths of Abaeloth's core. Kol stopped at the edge of the chasm, his toes peeking over the edge. As Nessix neared, she thought of how easy it would be to shove him off the ridge. Of course, he had wings and would be able to save himself, and the fact still remained that he was her best bet at staying safe—or some form of it—down in the hells. Nessix stopped a pace behind him, waiting for her next set of instructions.

Voices echoed off earth and stone walls, though Nessix still couldn't see the bottom from where she stood. Kol turned just enough to ensure his words carried clearly to Nessix.

"I'd be happy to escort you down, unless you'd prefer to take the stairs."

Nessix glanced at the stairs. They looked fit to crumble at the slightest weight, so narrow she wondered how a creature as broad as the typical demon navigated them without falling. She suspected the higher ranking demons—those like Kol—wouldn't particularly care if they lost a few of their lackeys if they were forced to venture down, and though armed with the knowledge that she couldn't die in the permanent sense, the idea of falling to her death, of crushing herself on the floor below, was something Nessix hoped to avoid.

"I—" She didn't know the best way to thank a demon for this sort of consideration, and suspected Kol found great humor in her attempts to sort through it. "I would prefer the most timely and least hazardous method possible."

Kol flashed that suave smile of his and extended his open hand. His fingers rested against the air elegantly, as though beckoning a dance partner, and Nessix had to brace herself with a deep breath before stepping forward to take his hand. The concept of trusting a demon left Nes's legs trembling and her mind screaming over her stupidity, but what other choice did she have? Kol's fingers curled around hers with a deliberate feel of control, not enough to trigger a flight response, but with a firmness that convinced the reactive part of Nes's mind that running was not an option. He drew her closer, her bumbling steps contradicting the grace he seemed to expect from her, and pulled her in front of him, her back pressed to his chest.

"Do you have any recollection of the other times we've flown together?" he asked.

Nessix's eyes widened as she stared into the chasm. At least one hundred feet beneath them, milling bodies of dejected men and women wearing drab clothing hustled through the expanse in tight clusters. Nes's breath caught in her throat as pieces of this puzzle began to fall into place, and a surge of fury and terror welled inside her chest, choking her with a silent sob.

Kol's hands left Nes's arms to wrap across her torso and he leaned closer. "Do you remember?" he repeated.

Nessix blinked back tears and opened her tingling lips. "I…" She couldn't quite form the words to answer his question, as she was only vaguely aware of what he'd asked her. All she remembered was life. She remembered fighting for innocent men and women, the kind of men and women who were afraid of demons, who would cluster in tight groups, hoping to find safety in numbers. She remembered leading men who were frightened of an unknown enemy to what she'd been convinced was certain death. This pit below her was why she'd fought the demons. Kol wouldn't give her much more time to form an answer, she was sure, and so she batted aside her regrets. "I don't remember," she murmured.

Kol sighed, his breath pushing against Nessix in a way she swore felt disappointed, and his arms tightened around her. "Do not struggle and do not fight me unless you want to fall."

His leg moved behind her and Nessix held her breath as he pushed their weight forward and over the edge. For a moment, all Nessix saw was the ground beneath her and as a rush of air struck her face, she clenched tight to Kol's arms, clinging to him in desperation. Horrified eyes remained open, unable to pinch shut as the ground raced toward her.

Everything inside Nessix screamed at her to claw for something firm to grasp a hold of, but all she had was Kol. All she had was the demon who had killed and claimed possession of her. All she had was the demon she hoped to form some sort of working relationship with. A massive snap cracked behind her, and the breath fled her as she was drawn backwards, higher up into the air. Another snap and her body pulsed in flight. Nessix dug her fingers deeper into Kol's arms as he banked toward the perimeter of the chasm and began a slow spiral around the outer walls.

"You understand where we are now, don't you?" His question cut through the whoosh of air he propelled them through.

Drawing breath to respond as the air beat against her face was difficult, and Nessix tucked her chin toward her shoulder to try blocking its offense. "These are other people the demons have killed." She was afraid her voice had been too soft to carry over the rush of air around them, that Kol would consider her inability to deliver an audible answer as disobedience and choose to drop her.

Instead, his chuckle beat against her back, making her wish he'd go ahead and release his grip. "Very good. Do you understand why I'm bringing you to them?"

Nessix pressed herself closer against Kol as they spiraled toward the bottom of the chasm, the nearness of solid ground giving their flight the illusion of greater speed. "I don't even know why you bothered to bring me back to life," she said.

Kol shifted his arms, one and then the other, so he held Nessix closer. "These are *your* people, Nessix."

She tried to gasp, but ended up choking on her efforts, scanning the faces of people dashing for cover as they zipped by. These men and women were terrified of Kol's presence, cowering at the sight of a demon encroaching on whatever peace they'd managed to fabricate in these depths, yet none of the faces were fleman. Certainly, the demons had slain enough of her innocents and soldiers to have filled this cavern, but these people were not hers.

"I don't understand."

"What's there to not understand?"

They were dangerously close to the ground now, low enough that Nessix was confident she'd survive a fall, but moving too fast for her to risk it. "These are not flemans. They are not my people."

Another snap and Nessix was jerked upright, as though standing in the air. Several beats later, Kol eased their feet to the ground and loosened his hold around her. Nessix unclamped her knuckles to let go of his arms and took a slow breath in an attempt to steady herself.

"You are not a mortal anymore, little one," Kol said, holding Nes's upper arms firmly so she could neither bolt nor turn to face him. "And you need to quit thinking like you are. These men and women, these are your *new* people, and you will serve them every bit as diligently as you did those on Elidae."

Nessix looked through the cavern where men and women huddled in clusters against the walls, peering from behind mounds of dirt and protruding boulders. They'd given Kol a wide clearance and though he'd been so blunt about explaining the fact that none of them could die, the fear in their eyes conveyed their absolute certainty that he would kill them. Or something worse.

"I served the people of Elidae by leading them to war against your kind," Nessix said, finding her tongue at last as these terrified civilians looked at her armor and weapons, searching her face for some sign that she might have the power to resist.

Kol wrapped one arm across Nes's shoulders and pulled her back against him so he could whisper in her ear. "I cannot fault you for hating my kind for what we did to your homeland. I have been through similar trials in my past and understand the tears you've shed well. But I cannot understand what makes you so eager to continue fighting us. We're on the same side now."

Nessix's lip curled as she pressed her back against Kol's chest.

"We are not nor will we ever be on the same side."

His fingers worked through her hair to cradle her chin, his thumb brushing against her cheek as she shuddered. "What was it your dear Mathias told you to make you hate us so much? That we were beasts unable to be negotiated with?"

Thoughts of trying to negotiate with demons aside, that had little to do with Nes's hatred of them. "No. He told me you were wrongfully victimized. That the world should have done better for you. *You* taught me that you are beasts. That cannot be put on me or Mathias or anyone else."

"Now that's not very fair," Kol said. "To the best of my knowledge, you hadn't even known who I was before I claimed you. You're saying it took you until that point to form your opinion of my people? That all the actions you took against us until then were merely coincidence?"

Nessix's snarl grew, though she kept her growl at bay. "You know damn well what I meant."

Kol dropped his hand and laughed again. "Glad to see you're starting to find your tongue again. You're going to need that fire in you."

Nessix's shoulders slumped as the weight of her predicament fell onto her yet again. She still didn't know what this greatness Kol was after entailed. She didn't know how she'd get out of the hells, only that she had to. She didn't even know how it was that she survived her death. Kol wanted to see her fire, and she'd let him see it once she got all of this figured out. If she ever got this figured out.

"So these are—"

A shriek erupted from the far end of the cavern, interrupting Nes's reluctant attempt at compliance, and Kol shifted his weight to face the source of the sound. Nessix's hand instinctively flew to her sword, fingers wrapping around the comfort of its hilt. Kol placed a gentle hand on her elbow—a motion Nessix had felt several times through her life, delivered by men she'd trusted—and for a moment, she almost felt as though she was back home. As the shrieking man came into view, that sensation embraced her more tightly.

"You dare to show your face down here, you *bitch*!" the man screamed, tearing across the open expanse.

A fleman man wearing tattered trousers and barely half a filthy shirt raced her way, unarmed with anything other than shaking fists and an enraged snarl. Nessix's jaw dropped and it took her several heartbeats to register that the man must have been speaking to her and not Kol. She flicked her glance at the demon, and though his eyes glinted with amusement, his lips were tucked into a frown. He made no indication that he planned to intervene and so Nessix took a step forward, an action Kol readily allowed.

There was something different about this fleman compared to the rest of the men and women who hid from the sight of a demon. There was a fire driving him to face what the others recognized as terror. The clumsiness of his gait and the fact that he wasn't braced for combat assured Nessix that he hadn't been one of her soldiers, and she couldn't fathom what would have made one of her civilians this bold. She withdrew her hand from her sword and walked forward.

"I think you're mistaking me—"

The presence of an alar in his midst didn't thwart the man's charge, but Nessix taking a step forward did. He skidded to a stop, bent forward at the waist as if it would give him more power for yelling at her. "Where were you?" he screamed.

Nessix shook her head. "I don't know what—"

"You were the *general*! You swore to protect us! *All* of us! *Where were you*?"

All of that confidence Nessix had rallied, the nerve she'd salvaged to address Kol at what she hoped was a level comparable to his own, shattered at the worst insult she'd ever received. "I never stopped fighting for—"

"*The entire city...*" the main wailed. "All of it. All of *us...* Where... were you?"

A ragged breath struck Nessix and a wave of dizziness sought to throw her to the ground. If she'd trusted Kol even a hair more than she did, she'd have allowed herself a step back to try gaining his support. As it was, all she could do was shift her weight and pray she could keep her knees from buckling.

Sarlot. It was the first time one of Elidae's townships had been lost to war. It was Nes's greatest failure, one that had hung on her mind every day through the rest of the war, one that haunted her worse than reflecting on her own death. The entire city had been razed by hordes of aranau—the most twisted and insane subclass of demons—the citizens torn apart and brandished as a mockery against an army that hadn't yet learned how to fight this enemy. Even after all of that experience had filed into place in Nes's mind, memories of the city's fall still turned her stomach.

"I will never forgive myself for that," she murmured.

"Of course you won't!" the man shrieked. "You stayed safe and warm in your fortress, fighting your petty fights with Veed and that savior of yours while we were massacred!"

Chilled by the man's accusations, wondering how it was that he had been spared the brutal ending which had claimed the rest of Sarlot's citizens, tears rolled from Nes's eyes. The truth was, a good part of her had died in Sarlot, too. Her innocence. Her sense of hope. Her belief that the world was not rife with evil intentions. None of those truths could be spoken to this man. Not now. Not ever. She'd never make it up to him, and she wouldn't insult him by trying.

Nessix had no response to this man's sorrow or rage. She had no way to tell him he wasn't wrong to hate her for how her inexperience had betrayed him. It had been Nessix's job to protect her civilians, and this man had watched his family and friends, the shopkeepers who he dealt with every day and the children who lived on his street, die. And somehow, *somehow*, he had been unfortunate enough to end up the sole survivor of that massacre, enslaved to the demons, unable to find peace even in death. That same twist clenched around Nes's stomach now as it had then, and she longed for Mathias to tell her that this wasn't her fault and that she'd done all she could. All she had was Kol.

"I am so sorry..." she murmured, knowing those words wouldn't fix anything, no matter how badly she wanted them to.

The man didn't offer her another snipped remark or brutal insult. He chose instead to launch himself at her, hands extended as he grabbed for her face and neck. Nessix was rooted firmly in the moment and didn't feel the need to react with violence. She'd have let the man attack her, relying on her experience with hand to hand combat to subdue him as gently as possible, but Kol took a brisk step in front of her before the man had cleared half the distance between them. He intercepted the fleman with ease by grabbing his arm. A trio of demon guards appeared from someplace Nessix hadn't yet identified, rushing toward the man with spears raised. Kol gave a sharp jerk to the man's arm, flinging him aside and then shoving him to the ground. The man cried out in terror and agony, trying to hide himself beneath weak arms.

"Stop!" Nessix shouted as Kol gave the man a sharp kick to the gut. "He wouldn't have hurt me. Leave him alone."

Kol spun to face Nessix, blocking her path with wings fully extended as the three demons jumped on the fallen man, bearing spears down on him over and over again until his screams filtered down into tortured moans and then silence.

Nessix had seen several sides of Kol up to this point, always calm, always commanding, but never with this sort of coldness about him. "Assaulting an authority figure is unforgiveable," he growled. "Let this be a lesson to you and all of your people. You will be kept safe, and you will lead them."

Nes's arms shook at her sides as she fought to restrain herself from attacking Kol here and now. She had no idea how many reinforcements Kol had down here and she couldn't count on any of her so-called people to serve such a role for her. Kol's words rebounded through the fury in her mind. This was meant to be an example to her, as well. She swallowed her desire to help the fleman man, realizing as his groans died into silence that there was no longer anything she could do for him. Raising her chin with the last bit of confidence she could conjure, Nessix met Kol's eyes.

"Lead them to what?" she asked.

He stared at her a moment longer, his diminutive smile slowly lifting across his face. "That's not something you need to worry about right now."

"And what if I refuse?"

Kol lowered his wings to allow the spectators to get a good look at Nessix trying to make a stand against him. "You won't," he said, "because you care too much about the innocents to do so. Go get yourself good and cozy with these people. Give them that confidence you're so good at fostering."

Nessix gasped and turned from Kol to look around the chamber full of bodies. Hundreds of bodies. Possibly thousands. She was to lead them. To build their confidence. She spun back to face Kol. The demons weren't scooping up mortals and twisting them into whatever creatures they'd become for pleasure. They were building an army.

Kol's patient smile confirmed that he knew the conclusion Nessix had just reached. "Teach them well," he said. "I'll be back to check on your progress soon. Do not disappoint me."

He launched himself into the air, leaving Nessix stunned and silent below.

SIX

An ocean away from Elidae and back in the relative safety of Zeal, the same sweet memories Mathias never had the chance to make lurked in the realms of sleep. Warmth he coveted filled his dreams, a life he'd have traded his immortality to experience. The pull of Nes's laughter and charm harbored in these unobtainable moments comforted him until his mind grasped a hold of the bleak aspects of reality and reminded him of the entire reason he had to escape to his psyche to experience such happiness.

These dreams no longer distressed Mathias, and when he woke after this last one, he did so calmly, though disappointed. Sitting up in bed, he slapped himself on the cheek and swung his legs to the floor, coming face to face with Etha. They stared at each other for a moment, sharing a silent sense of duty and resignation before Mathias sighed and stood to head over to his wash basin.

"Good morning, Etha," he said as he dipped a cloth into the blessedly warm water to wash the sleep from his eyes.

"I take it you slept well?" She turned to face him, meeting his eyes in the mirror as he scrubbed his face.

Mathias glowered at his reflection as he ran a hand through his hair where it stubbornly stood out of place. He gave up on taming it flat after a few failed attempts. "I rested well and am ready to get back to work."

75

Etha quirked her lips to the side, gaze drifting downward. When she'd first brought Mathias back to life, she'd never intended for him to be tied to this sort of life. Mortals and gods alike had the chance to find rest, to find happiness. They had the luxury to seek their hearts' desires and be able to walk away from responsibility once their objectives were reached.

Neither mortal nor god, Mathias hadn't enjoyed rest since Etha plucked his soul from its paradise and shoved it back into his corpse. His luxury was life unending and uncanny strength and wisdom to facilitate his quests, but the tasks he was meant to complete were a responsibility he'd never be able to fulfill. There was always one more urgent request, another plea for help only Mathias could tend to. Etha had never wanted this for him.

"Can you tell me anything about what I'm heading into this time?" Mathias asked, turning to face his goddess with the same warm smile he always tried to give her.

Etha's brows furrowed. "Mathias, we don't have enough information for you to head *anywhere* yet."

The smile faltered with an air of grumpy disappointment. "Not that. The demons in Haddenton? The sooner I tend to them, the better. I'm in no mood for—"

"Oh, that?" Etha batted a hand to disregard Mathias's apparent concern. "There aren't any demons in or near Haddenton. You have my blessing to ignore that assignment."

Mathias narrowed his eyes and shook his head. "Ignore...? What would possibly motivate Willard to lie to me?"

Etha opened her mouth, the nature of Julianna's treachery on her tongue before she snatched enough sense to keep quiet and spare Mathias the frustration. She pulled her lips between her teeth and scratched the side of her nose. "Maybe... um... Maybe he's overworked? Stress. He must have misread a report due to stress." Etha gave a satisfactory nod, face twisted as though she'd be sick at Mathias's flat expression.

"Jules said Gelthin's been quiet while I was gone. What sort of stress could Willard be facing?"

Etha's face scrunched up tighter and she groaned. She didn't like hiding the truth from Mathias. She hated blatantly lying to him even more. The thought of trying to claim ignorance on the matter crossed her mind, but Mathias knew there were very few instances—those involving conflicting gods and demons snatching souls—Etha was genuinely in the dark about.

"Is there or isn't there something I need to know about?" Mathias asked, reading Etha's internal conflict plainly. "If the Council is disorganized right now, I'd appreciate hearing about it so I can know what sort of headaches to expect."

"There's no more demon activity on Gelthin than normal, no signs of anything greater pending, and the only threat in Haddenton is a group of bandits that the local authorities have been combating for the past month. Combating successfully, I'll add."

Mathias pressed his hand to his forehead, wishing he could go back to bed. "So why did Willard lie about the conditions?" He walked past Etha and opened the doors of his armoire to begin packing for a quest that may have no end.

He pulled out the most durable of his shirts and most comfortable pants, tossing them behind him to land on his bed. He dug out his weathered pack and deposited it in the same manner. He contemplated the most practical footwear, considering he didn't know where his journey would take him. When Etha still hadn't answered him, Mathias heaved a sigh, straightened, and turned to face the little goddess.

"It was Jules, wasn't it?"

Etha wouldn't look at him and her face caved in with a guilty wince as she nodded. "You have to understand, she's worried about you, Mathias. The last time she saw you try to take on the demons with this sort of determination it... well... it didn't exactly go as you'd planned."

Mathias rolled his eyes as he crammed his clothing into his pack. "I've grown since then, both physically and mentally. I know what I'm doing."

"Not... really."

He glanced up at Etha's cocked eyebrow and sighed. "No, I know exactly what I'm doing. I just don't know how to go about executing it." He flipped the pack's flap closed and secured it, leaving it sitting on his bed as he rummaged through a dresser drawer to locate his coin purse. "I'd like to think you'd be a little more confident in me now than you were back then."

"I am," Etha said, drawing that second word out longer than necessary. "But you're still rather heated up."

"Heated up!" Mathias slammed the drawer shut when he found the purse missing and opened the next one. "Are you telling me you aren't?"

Etha frowned at the gentle bite of Mathias's accusation and wondered if she should speak up that he'd left his pouch in his desk, not his dresser, before his growing mountain of frustration caved in around him. "I've spoken to Zenos," Etha said softly. "He confirmed that the balances are off by much more than Nes's soul alone."

Mathias paused his search and stood to gape at Etha. Zenos was the most diligent of the new children gods, an avid scholar and bookkeeper with too much interest in records and accuracy to manipulate facts for anyone's benefit. Etha's decision to speak to him over this matter was astute, and Mathias was ashamed of himself for not thinking about it sooner. Maybe Julianna's concerns were valid. Maybe he *was* too caught up in his emotional flood to safely take on this quest.

"How much is 'much more'?" Mathias asked. He briefly turned back to his dresser, but the urgency of this information tugged him back to face Etha.

The goddess's shoulders slumped, her expression falling pathetically. "Thousands of souls," Etha said. "Due to her station, Nessix was the only one demanding unusual attention, but Zenos reported nearly a kingdom's worth, taken from all reaches of Abaeloth. The demons have to have been practicing this for years now..."

Mathias struggled to accept his disbelief, unwilling to process the report for what it was. The demons were supposed to have only taken Nessix. This was supposed to be a simple rescue mission against an act taken solely against him. Etha didn't need to voice her suspicions that the demons were planning a more drastic move than simply infuriating a heartbroken Mathias for him to know it was on her mind. He turned back to his dresser and Etha sighed.

"Your desk," she murmured.

He looked back at Etha.

"Your purse is in your desk."

Mathias swallowed hard and dug his money from his desk, accepting Etha's assistance as orders to see him on the road. She wouldn't tell him directly how she depended on him to uncover the demons' ulterior motive, but he didn't need her to. He'd been the implement of her justice for centuries, the only man alive with the ability and obedience to take on the impossible. Hearing that thousands of souls had gone missing—more to follow, if Mathias knew the demons half as well as he thought he did—suggested that this issue was one he alone could safely investigate. He tucked his coin purse in a side pocket of his pack.

"What's the plan to get me out of here without Jules and the Council finding out?" Mathias didn't look at Etha as he spoke, feeling her reluctance and fear radiate against him. She didn't want to ask him to do any of this, not even the parts he was self-motivated to take on.

"Sneak out during morning prayers. Julianna will feel a disturbance if you teleport, and the Council will hear if you order a horse to wait for you. Ceraphlaks will make too much of a scene. You'll have to move on foot until you distance yourself from the Citadel."

Mathias looked at Etha now and allowed himself a smile. "It wouldn't be one of my adventures if it wasn't hard, now would it?"

She tried to smile back, but failed. "I do mean it when I say I never intended for this to be the life you lived."

Etha's eyes brimmed with a crippling regret, her tiny hands clenched together and tucked beneath her chin. The truth was, Mathias often wondered what it was Etha *had* expected would find him once the world discovered they had an immortal champion to guard them and the demons learned Etha had an avatar to torment. She was an intuitive goddess, armed with a sharp mind. She had to have had at least a vague suspicion that eternity wouldn't be gentle for one in Mathias's position, yet here he was. Mathias had felt Etha's pain and regret before, felt how badly she wanted to offer him the chance to retire to the heavens and let a new hero save the world. But there was always one more task, one more concern, one more demon who needed to be stopped. As much as Mathias relied on Etha and her might, Etha had come to depend on his loyalty and valor, his absolute foolishness. Etha kept Mathias around because she loved him and couldn't bear to lose him, but also because she was afraid.

He sighed and walked over to Etha, kneeling before his tiny goddess. "Maybe not," he murmured, "but it's the life you gave me, and I'll do what I must to make you proud. If I have to walk clear across Gelthin and swim the oceans myself, you have given me the power to do so. I'll find this answer for you and for me, for Nes and Brant and all of Abaeloth. See me through one more mission and we can discuss options after that."

Etha's hands eased over his shoulders and Mathias raised his head to smile at her. "Sending you into certain danger and suspected torment was so much easier when you resented me."

His smile broadened. "I do aim to exceed your expectations. You'll placate Jules for me once she discovers I'm gone?"

"I doubt I'll have a choice in the matter."

Mathias eyed Etha keenly. "You're going to tell her running off was my idea, aren't you? That I fled from official Council orders?"

Etha allowed herself a smile now and caressed Mathias's cheek. "How is it that a man can know a goddess so well?"

He chuckled and stood, stretching out his arms and turning back to his armoire to find fresh clothes to change into. "I only have the powers which you have lent me. I'm sure you can come up with that answer yourself."

Be quick with your preparations before Julianna grows suspicious.

Mathias smirked and shook his head, glad he had Etha to cover for him.

SEVEN

Nessix stood and watched as the three spear-wielding demons dragged the body of the fleman man away, never before so crushed by self-loathing. Kol's words echoed through the chaos in her mind. She was supposed to teach these people, to lead them. She was supposed to turn this collection of terrified prisoners into an army.

The demons discarded the mangled body against a wall, scattering several timid onlookers with gleefully mocking snarls before they grunted and trudged off in separate directions. Nessix tracked their movement as they tucked themselves into secluded alcoves carved into the perimeter of the open void. Scanning the walls, she spotted several more of these posts where demons monitored the expanse from hiding spots surrounding this prison. It was no wonder the people lived on edge. Craning her neck, Nessix searched the lip of the chasm for Kol, but he had left the scene as far as she could tell.

Lowering her gaze, Nessix gave up on identifying where demon assaults might sprout from to investigate where she was meant to live. The lighting wasn't nearly as good here as it was in Kol's chamber, but it wasn't the relative dimness that made Nessix shudder. What struck her as she stood alone was how, for the first time in her life—or whatever this existence was meant to be—she didn't know what to do and had no wise mentor to turn to. She'd always been able to find a solid heading, but now all she saw was a bleak future trapped in the confines of the hells as she attempted to coax ferocity out of men and women who cowered behind rocks from those she needed them to stand against.

Nessix had hoped these people would relax after the demons cleared out, and though faces peered more completely from their hiding spots, nobody approached her. That wasn't much of a surprise, given what happened to the first man who had done so. Nessix shivered and folded her arms across her chest.

Sighing away her gloom, she walked forward, her boots crunching against the dirt floor the only sound audible above the thumping of her heart. She walked to where the demons had abandoned the fleman and crouched to look over his wounds. A compassionate killing, if there could be such a thing, would have struck through his throat or chest. Instead, this man bore dozens of gaping punctures in his gut, his previously filthy clothes dyed with the colors of his blood and fluids from his vital organs. Nessix wiped her nose, both to staunch her tears and shield herself from the stench of death. She forbid herself to look at the man's eyes.

Head bowed, Nessix pushed herself to her feet. She'd failed this man when they'd both been alive, and she'd failed him now. The horror he'd seen and continued to live through—neither things he'd volunteered for—haunted Nessix. She pressed a hand to her eyes, wishing she had a way to fix this.

There is one way, she thought grimly. *Make Kol proud of you. Teach these people. Earn your position, and you'll be able to slip free.* The demons couldn't have a use for an army in their realm, so there must be plans to unleash them on the surface. At that time, Nessix would lead them. Even if it meant causing death and destruction, she'd leave a trail for Mathias to follow. He'd know what to do. He always had. But in order to get to that point, Nessix had to please Kol.

She took a deep breath and moved into the main body of the chasm. The braver of the people had crept forward to gawk at her, whispering to each other from behind hands shielding their mouths, timid fingers pointing her direction. Nessix had been the object of the public eye her entire life and was used to the attention, but a distinct eeriness tarnished the way these men and women observed her.

None of them ventured to meet her eyes, legs braced to launch them back into safety at a moment's notice. This fright wasn't due to respect, as Nessix had experienced in her previous life, but perhaps an uncertainty of who or what she was. As important as Kol liked to act, Nessix could only assume it wasn't often a demon of his stature visited this lot, much less while expressing any degree of civil discourse with one of them. Nessix stood among these people—*her* people—wearing battle tested armor and a fully equipped sword belt. She prayed they'd think better than to form a mob and try to overtake her for the latter.

A few of the gawkers seemed more awed, glistening eyes turned toward her as though she was some sort of savior. With the exception of the one dead member of this community, Nessix doubted any of them had the insight to connect her to the glorious life she once lived. Perhaps these few brave individuals with their pitiful strains of hope thought she would be able to rescue them with nothing more than her armor, her sword, and the feisty tongue she used against the demons. How many times had Mathias been on the receiving end of such pathetic eyes? Nessix gulped down her reservations. The difference between her and Mathias was that he'd always been able to deliver on that hope. Nessix doubted her ability to even save herself.

She took her time looking back at the crowd. Old men and little girls averted their eyes as her attention neared them. Plump middle-aged women and gangly farm boys shuffled along as though they had business to attend to. Every one of them lacked confidence and even the desperation to fight for survival. Without such a basic drive beating inside these hearts, how was Nessix supposed to draw military discipline from them? No matter what Kol said, they'd never be her people and she had no idea what to do with them. As frightened as they were, they weren't suited for combat, and as far as Nessix could tell, no soldiers were in the group. That last realization was a heavy slap to the face. The demons hadn't snatched any soldiers, but they'd managed to seize a general. Nessix's heart sank a little more.

"My name is Nessix Teradhel," she called at last, needing *something* to change in the situation. She knew trying to communicate with them was a lost effort. Besides the few demons who had picked up her language over the extent of the war, she couldn't understand anyone else down here. With only one other fleman in the population, Nessix had no reason to expect them to understand her.

Her words might have slipped past them, but her soothing tone seeped through their reservations. Those still in hiding poked their heads out and the clusters hunched together for security took steps apart. Even if Nessix didn't feel confident or strong, her diplomatic presence hadn't died.

"I'm here to help you stand up to your fears," she continued. They wouldn't understand these words, either, but speaking them made her feel better at the very least. "I will do what I can to give you the strength to do the same, and vow to protect you when you can't."

Skeptical glances and rolled eyes were exchanged within the cliques and the first few bodies milled away from their throngs. Nessix's smile faltered as her audience drifted away to resume the same drudging socialization she'd heard when Kol first led her here.

Heart falling, Nessix watched these dejected people wander through the crowd. How was she supposed to win them over and train them if she couldn't even speak a common language? She sent another heated glare toward the top of the cavern, wondering if Kol had tucked himself away up there to laugh at her failure. It seemed unlikely; he'd never bothered to mask his presence, and as many times as he'd told her she was to do as he said, Nessix suspected he genuinely wanted her to condition these people for war. She looked again at those derelict stairs, wondering how high she'd be able to climb before one of the demon guards took her out or the steps crumbled beneath her weight.

Loneliness cascaded around her through the hundreds of bodies filling the chasm, mocking her for the glorious past she'd once lived, and Nessix crossed her arms again, shoulders hunched as she trudged around what she assumed would become her home.

Speculative glowers continued to follow her, more curious now that she'd quit trying to communicate, some of them judgmental, and the boldest eyeing her weapons. Bold or otherwise, those last looks didn't do much to bother Nessix. Her previous observation stood that there were no trained combatants in her vicinity, and she'd be able to take on a small assault if she had to. She frowned at the thought. She never wanted to control others through fear.

The group of mismatched civilians weren't the only ones keeping tabs on Nessix; a much colder presence watched her as she made her way through the area.

Working her jaw slowly, Nessix slid her eyes away from her path of travel and to the walls of the cavern. Tucked away among the orbs of light and rocky outcroppings that jutted from the walls were more guard posts, all equipped with watchful demons. They followed her movement like ravenous wolves waiting for the herd to move away from their young. Nessix wondered how often these demons got bored with their jobs; this group didn't seem like a crowd of rabble rousers, yet the intensity with which they were monitored assured Nessix that their guards longed for physical contact. Her plans to stir up a rebellion, even if she somehow motivated these people to fight, looked increasingly grim.

Sighing, Nessix tried to brush off the demons' attention, a notion her instincts insisted was a terrible idea. These demons were tired of watching people shackled by fear. Here she strode, more confident than most, efficiently armed, and bearing a history she was sure even lesser ranked demons were aware of. Nessix would put up a good fight, a fight they might have spent weeks yearning for. She'd avoid instigating them as long as she could and bank on the hope that Kol was as influential and respected as he claimed to be. Maybe that would convince these demons to leave her alone.

Nessix walked on with no further complications, given a wide clearing when she neared anyone else. Never before had she experienced crowds scuttle away from her, and she tried to ease their minds and hers with gentle smiles and polite waves. Her efforts failed to yield results, and so she sighed and followed her nose and growling stomach to the smell of cooking meat.

The area was set up similar to a war camp. There were no solid structures, though a few of the people closer to the feeding station toted around simple wares, calling out to those they passed to try drawing attention to whatever it was they peddled. Off to the side, others sat and stitched clothing back together or tacked the soles onto worn shoes. Nessix watched to see what they used as currency, but hadn't caught any formal transactions being made. Suddenly, her masterwork armor and ancestral weapons weighed three times as much, and Nessix was struck with a sickening blow of guilt. It was no wonder these people sneered at her.

A long stone slab stretched alongside the wall to her left, strategically placed rocks guiding smoke toward the top of the cavern. Nessix paused and watched it travel upwards to where it disappeared into the darkness above, and her frown crept lower. It seemed as though the stairs were the only way out of this hole without wings. She returned her attention to the food station and walked closer.

As dismal as the population was, Nessix had expected food to be a limited commodity, but the people appeared in good flesh. There wasn't much of a crowd around the stone slab and as Nessix approached, those who were present shuffled away, filthy hands cupping their food as they went to take seats well out of Nes's reach. Her heart ached at their reactions and with her desire to plead for their trust. That would be a campaign in itself, and Nessix sighed and turned to the cooks.

Two men and three women stood behind the stone slab, and they were not afraid to meet Nes's eyes. Despite their leery glares, Nessix considered this progress and smiled at them. "Nessix Teradhel." She pressed a hand to her chest before extending it to prompt the same from the man she faced.

He grunted, stuck his hand into a large metal cauldron, and slapped a handful of shredded meat into Nes's open palm. She flinched as the juices it had marinated in splashed up her arm and across the stone beneath her hand, but nodded her appreciation, still held hostage by this language barrier. At least lax handling of food suggested nutrition was in abundant supply.

The other four servers watched Nessix impatiently, and so she walked down the line. A steamed root vegetable was stacked on top of her pile of meat and a warm roll shoved into her free hand. The last woman barked a gruff statement and jabbed her finger over Nes's shoulder. Nessix turned to find a wide cistern situated against the opposite wall, a slow trickle of water draining into it from above.

Attempting one last smile that went ignored, Nessix carried her handfuls of food toward an unclaimed spot on the wall. These people clearly didn't want her company, and she wouldn't impose on them before she knew how to assure them of her intentions. She abandoned her smiles, feeling the grimness in her eyes, and stared down at the food in her hands.

Nessix was no stranger to eating on the move. In her past, she'd had a rough mess kit, a spit to hold her meat at the very least, but she'd make the most of what she had at her disposal. Glancing at those around her, she saw some of them holding their food in the fronts of their shirts or designating one member of their group to hold it all while the others picked at it, and Nessix sighed. There would be no dignified way to eat, and she knew better than to approach any of the surrounding demons to ask if they'd be inclined to bring her proper dining utensils.

She sank her teeth into the roll. It was bland in flavor, but soft, and she had to restrain herself from tearing into it more ravenously. Her stomach groaned again, reminding her that she had no idea the last time she'd eaten. Hollowing the bread to form a bowl, she dumped her handful of meat inside of it, staring at the mess left behind on her hand before resigning herself to simply let it be dirty. Unlike those around her, she couldn't soak up the residual juices with what she wore, and she wasn't quite desperate enough to lick her hand clean.

She dug the root vegetable out from under the pile of shredded meat and took a bite. Its bitter flavor choked her, but she was too hungry to not finish it as she continued to survey her location. The wandering vendors were gaining attention now that the demons had vacated the immediate premises and Nessix had removed herself from their concerns. A steady flow of people moved through an opening in the wall opposite the feeding station, but that was the only other apparent source of interest. The life that the demons had carved out for this sorry lot had no purpose, something Nessix suspected they'd done intentionally. When bored enough, anyone would be willing to learn to take up arms. She shoved the rest of the vegetable in her mouth and stood.

Carrying her little bowl of nourishment, Nessix made her way to the portal and peeked inside to discover crude sleeping quarters. Hundreds of worn cots were tucked along the walls, an abundance of hammocks hanging around them. Piles of filthy blankets were strewn across the floor. There was no privacy in this massive barracks and nowhere to store personal possessions, though Nessix doubted many of the people had any belongings to worry about. Her fingers twitched and she had to restrain herself from nervously reaching for her sword. For people who had nothing, the weapons she carried would hold an even greater value.

Nessix slopped her fingers into her food to grab another bite and backed out of the barracks to resume exploring. She turned away from the feeding station, setting course for the more sparsely populated side of the chasm. The people parted readily for her, and it didn't take Nessix long to figure out why.

Two demons, heavily armed and wrapped in fiercely tooled plate mail, stood guard over a pair of narrow pathways that twisted into the wall and wound out of Nes's field of vision. She stopped a dozen paces from the sentries and met their eyes in turn. Both held themselves with a rigid confidence, but their quiet eyes suggested they were much less opportunistic than the guards packed through the rest of the chasm.

Once Nessix was convinced these demons wouldn't try anything if she didn't, she shifted her attention to the paths they guarded. Well packed by foot traffic, it was unlikely they led to any sort of freedom, no matter how badly she wanted them to. Hoping that her connection to Kol was known and respected through the demon ranks, Nessix swallowed her next bite of food.

"Can you understand me?" she asked the guards.

They stared at her in silence, expressions unchanging. Nessix gave a brief gnaw to the inside of her cheek, debating whether or not to press her luck by demanding an answer. The creak of wagon wheels crept down the right-hand passage and saved her from such foolishness.

Nessix longed to sneak a glance over her shoulder to see if the locals were concerned of whatever was approaching, but she kept her attention schooled on the tunnel. Without knowing where it led or why the demons guarded it, she refused to open herself up to potential danger. She flexed her fingers, muscles waiting anxiously to rip her sword free from its scabbard.

One of the demon guards swayed his mass sideways to turn and face the path as a shadow stretched across the walls and Nessix held her breath. She didn't move yet, well aware of how closely the second guard watched her, but braced herself for whatever was coming. A voice called ahead of the creaking wheels and looming shadow, all of the words but one escaping Nes's comprehension.

"Home."

She had ironically understood that single word, a word that meant safety and comfort. A word that described nearly any place but here. And then there was the unusual fact that she'd understood the word at all. It had been so clear, instantly registered, that she struggled to brush it off as simply misinterpreting a different word spoken in a foreign tongue. Her confusion came to a jarring halt as the shadow filled the entire wall and a wooden cart stacked high with those bitter root vegetables pulled by two sweating men came into view.

Four other men walked on either side of the cart, all of them shirtless. From the centers of each of their chests glistened tiny metal rings identical to the one Nessix had found in herself, and her fingers timidly pressed against her breastplate. Those rings had something to do with what the demons had done to them, and whatever that something was, Kol had warned her against investigating it. As far as Nessix could tell, she was the newest member of these ranks, and if those who had trudged through this life had chosen to ignore them, there must be a valid reason.

The demon stepped forward to investigate the load of vegetables and glanced over each of the ten men. They didn't balk at his authority the way those from the main cavern had, and they shot Nessix suspicious glances. Once the demon was satisfied with his inspection, he waved the men forward, and they pulled their cart toward the common area.

It looked as though Nessix had been mistaken. Some amount of structure did exist for these people and, no matter how strongly she disbelieved it, their welfare was of some concern to the demons. They were kept nourished. The most innovative were allowed to practice their trades. Though it was kept guarded, some sort of agricultural development existed. To Nes's observation, the only thing these people lacked was a benevolent leader to stand up for them, and that, the demons had provided in her.

Sweeping a final gaze over these two guards, deciding it safe to show her back to them, Nessix turned to follow the cart toward the main gathering. All she could do was pray that the people wanted her leadership.

EIGHT

Among the trivial benefits of being a god was the ability to alter one's physical appearance. Etha and Inwan had taken to experimenting with different bodies to suit their changing whims. The gods of natural forces permanently altered their forms in manners to best compliment their elements. The vain tweaked their mortal features to enhance the strengths they'd been born with and smooth over their less desirable traits, as Shand had. Each of Abaeloth's deities had taken at least a few measures to distance themselves from their mortal pasts, except for the sensible Azerick and Drao.

In Azerick's case, Mathias couldn't blame him for maintaining his mortal appearance. Ascending into the position of the high god of good as a young knight and hailing from a family of nobles, Azerick had never been an unattractive man. Built sturdy and capable with warm, welcoming eyes, Azerick must have received his fair share of admirers even when he'd been nothing more than another body in the Order.

Drao, on the other hand, could have benefitted in every way from a little bit of vanity.

The high god of evil had disconcerted Mathias from the moment they met, and the paladin often wondered whether or not Drao preserved his mortal form simply to spite his elegant and arrogant peers. Drao was marked by gray hair thin enough to reveal the age spots on his scalp and a face as withered as a rotting apple, and Mathias often suspected the god maintained respect more from his frightening appearance than any amount of true devotion. When Drao stood and crept along, he held himself hunched over and with a hand braced at the base of his back, but Mathias had seen this decrepit façade disappear when necessity demanded it. Such as in times like this.

"Having a good game, my lords?" Mathias asked.

Azerick dropped the ivory pawn in his hand and Drao jolted against the modest table, sending it and the game board toppling to the floor. The good god's flush filtered away as he recognized Mathias, but Drao's eyes—the only part of him that had always maintained a youthful glow—simmered as he glared at the pieces now scattered across the floor of their divine chamber.

"I was *winning*, you clod!"

Mathias bit into his smirk, knowing better than to accept Drao's unspoken invitation to engage in debate. They'd hammered out an amicable relationship over the centuries, but Mathias was eager to keep the god in his favor, at least for now. "Cheer up, Drao. A blind ogre could beat Azerick at a game of Etha's Gambit." Mathias walked over to the mess he'd caused, righted the table, and set to work gathering the pieces off the floor. "You'll win again, I'm sure."

Azerick, as good natured as ever, allowed Mathias that gentle jab, well accustomed to the paladin's subtle way of placating Drao. The god crouched down to help collect the pawns. "Not to imply you're unwelcome, but your presence here often means something's wrong."

Mathias pursed his lips and nodded grimly. "Yes, that seems to be my pattern."

Drao snorted and leaned back in his chair, crossing his arms as he looked down at the two men cleaning up the mess. "Not sure what you want from us. Word's gotten around about you quickly. You're in even lower regard than usual among our peers, you know."

Mathias glanced at Azerick, who kept his eyes tactically

averted and jaw set. "Either of you mind telling me how that happened?" the paladin asked.

Azerick heaved an irritated sigh at Drao's exaggerated scoff. The more youthful god answered Mathias, though he didn't look up from his work. "Rumors have traveled through our realm about what you did to Shand."

"What *I*—" Mathias laughed shortly, though he didn't find the accusation funny, and sat back to look between the two gods. "*I* didn't do a damn thing to her. She brought her punishment on herself, and Etha's the one who dealt it."

"And you think any of the new children are stupid enough to accuse *Etha* of overstepping her bounds?" Drao asked. "Especially after what she *did* do to Shand? No, Mathias. They're blaming this one on you."

Mathias groaned and slapped his handful of pieces onto the table so he could gather more. This quest was heading in a direction he didn't want to travel and it had only just begun. He needed compliance from the children gods if he hoped to extract whatever insight or theories they had on Nes's whereabouts or the demons' nefarious plans.

"So, friend, why are you here?" Azerick asked, depositing the pieces he'd gathered on the table as he stood. "What are you after?"

"Information," Mathias said, scooping up the final piece and pushing himself to his feet. "Has the reason *why* Shand was punished made it to the heavens?"

"The report that's been floating around says she commissioned the demons to attack Elidae." Azerick busied himself resetting the board to avoid needing to look at Mathias.

More stubborn and skeptical than his counterpart, Drao leaned back in his chair, sneering as though a rambunctious child had just tracked mud through his parlor.

Mathias chuckled. Of course Shand's devastation would have stayed that simple in the divine realm, at least when he was a viable candidate for blame. "She did," he confirmed. "But it went deeper than that. A lot deeper."

"Are you referring to her curses?" Drao sat forward, one corner of his withered lips lifting in a mocking smirk. "Because the story I heard, she was quite clever with how she pulled them over you."

Mathias closed his eyes and rubbed his forehead. He didn't have enough of his wits about him to play with Drao right now. "I'm talking about how the demons have been stealing souls as they depart for the afterlife."

Azerick's hand fumbled with his game preparations, knocking the nearby pieces over once again, and Drao snapped to attention. Both wore strict expressions.

"*How?*" Azerick asked.

"I wouldn't be here asking for information if I knew," Mathias said. "I'm on a quest to find out, and I wanted to know if either of you had any ideas where I should start. Etha knows you're the only gods willing to work with me."

"Willing may be a bit of a stretch." Drao sighed—a labored expression which did everything to convey how inconvenienced he pretended to be over Mathias's alarming report—and leaned forward. "What *do* you know about what they've been doing?"

"An oraku extracts the souls just before the final breath and physically carries them away. All Shand could tell me is that she'd informed them about necromancy, but that's as far as I could get with her. Etha can't track these souls, and it took her consulting with Zenos to confirm how many have gone missing."

Drao rubbed his chin. "This is most interesting…"

Interesting was one of the last words Mathias would have chosen to describe this crisis. As a mortal, Drao had been a diligent student of the magical arts in every way but one—he'd never been able to manipulate threads. Despite this, he knew more about the art than the most accomplished practitioner Mathias had met, save Julianna, devouring every nuance and practice he could through whatever means he had to employ. Mathias frowned and closed his eyes. He'd been the one to select Drao to balance Azerick in the divine realm in the first place. He had to put some amount of patience and faith in him.

"If Etha can't track these souls, what do you expect either of us to do?" Azerick hadn't resumed resetting the board, kneading the meat of his palm instead.

Mathias shook his head and peered his eyes open. "I don't know. I don't know where to start, I don't know who to talk to. I don't even know if there's a way to find answers. I was hoping one of you would have heard or felt something, but I suppose your reach is too encompassing to register something as small as single soul."

Azerick nodded, his frown matching Mathias's.

"Well," Drao said, pushing himself to his feet—much more erect than such a feeble old man should have been able to achieve. "This has given me all sorts of ideas and theories to play with. Azerick—" He nodded to the god of good. "As fierce a game as ever. Care for a rematch in… oh… whenever I get bored with my theorizing?"

Azerick nodded. "Of course, Drao." His voice was absent as he toiled over what this report could mean for the longevity of Abaeloth and the sanctity of life. As Drao enthusiastically bustled from the room, no sign of aches or pains present in his buoyant stride, Azerick turned to Mathias, eyes wearied in a manner the paladin knew all too well. "You're going after these answers, no matter where the path leads, aren't you?"

Mathias stared at the game pieces, wishing so badly that his mind could settle enough to entertain something as frivolous as a game of Etha's Gambit. He sighed. "I have no choice. I'm Etha's shield. Whatever poses a threat to her and her creations, I must stop."

Azerick walked around the table and laid a hand on Mathias's shoulder. "There was a time when I looked up to you as an infallible hero, but the longer I've known you, the more I wish you didn't have to be one."

"Then forgive me for misleading you. I am far from infallible."

Azerick stared at Mathias's empty tone and the hollowness in his eyes, hurting for his old idol on a level exclusive to the divine. "Mathias, even gods make mistakes. You aren't blaming yourself for this sacrilege, are you?"

Mathias clenched his jaw until his temples ached, pride doing its best to rally him against the urge to surrender to the burning behind his eyes. "I'm blaming myself for not catching wind of it sooner."

Azerick chuckled and slapped Mathias's shoulder. "There *are* other powers on Abaeloth. You're not her sole shepherd. If Drao and I—if *Etha*—hadn't been aware of this, how would you have known?"

That was the same question Mathias had posed to himself for several months now. "I don't know," he said, voice soft and submissive. "But I *should* have."

"It's a good thing Etha gave you eternal life or stress would have killed you long ago. I'll keep alert for anything that might point to answers and promise to send any discoveries Drao makes your way. In the meantime, be smart about your search. Even a blind ogre can see you've got deeper ties to this mission than you're admitting."

Honesty was a trait Mathias valued immensely, one he tried his best to uphold, but his shame as it related to letting Nessix be slain, of letting the demons take her, begged him to avoid full disclosure. Too many people knew about his affection for Nessix, and Mathias didn't know how far that knowledge could safely travel before someone else used it against him.

"Etha walks with me," Mathias murmured, flicking his eyes to the tender, concerned gaze of the god of good. "She will see me where I need to go."

Azerick's smile shrank, a frown gleaming in his eyes. Mathias could never be bargained with once he set his mind, always ducking behind Etha's favor when concerns for his safety were raised. The Mother Goddess wouldn't let her paladin fall, but she couldn't protect him from every danger lurking on Abaeloth. Mathias knew this from harrowing past experiences, yet ceaselessly threw himself back in front of the blade. Azerick would never talk him out of this course of action, especially if Etha truly did back his mission. Mathias was who the foolish, mortal version of Azerick had admired enough to emulate in the heat of battle with the undead, and Mathias was every bit the foolish hero Azerick knew Abaeloth needed now.

"Good luck, my friend," the god said softly. "May Etha hold you close."

Mathias bowed his head, his gratitude caught in his throat. His visit with the last reasonable gods residing in the heavens eased part of his mind, but he'd wasted too much time on simple pleasantries. If he kept talking, he risked diving into truths Azerick would have patiently listened to but been unable to remedy. Mathias closed his eyes and stepped into the divine pathways before he had the chance to crumble.

NINE

Kol didn't need to look in Grell's direction to know the inoga was dissatisfied. Of all the traits becoming a demon had lent him, both the most irritating and most convenient was his heightened perception of energy. Even if he'd still been mortal, Kol suspected he'd have felt the ripples of irritation shedding from his lord. Then again, if he'd still been mortal, Grell would have been of a more pleasant nature. And he wouldn't have been Kol's superior.

"This plan of yours is falling apart in the most spectacular way," Grell growled.

Kol bit down on the snappy retort his own flaring doubts urged him to spit and regrouped his thoughts. "Give her time. She's got the charisma. She's got the experience. She'll have them performing soon."

Grell grunted and crossed his arms as he looked down at the pit's floor where Nessix strode off by herself, carrying her handfuls of food as the other akhuerai scuttled out of her way. It had been a week since they'd tossed Nessix in the chasm to claim her rule over them, and she'd yet to connect with a single one. Kol had sworn she was the only viable candidate for the job—had risked his life more than once over this conviction—but all Grell saw was an unmotivated and detestable woman carrying around weapons she was unworthy of.

Where Grell registered failure that the akhuerai weren't openly throwing themselves at Nes's feet and professing their undying loyalty to her, Kol still saw that air of intrigue that had first drawn him to her. She didn't rush off to be by herself, no hunched posture or twitchy glances. Though she kept her attention active, she held her chin high, her shoulders erect as she passed through the crowd. She sat alone and ate slowly, sharp eyes always watching how the others interacted, using that tactical mind of hers to sort out how to approach this problem. Nessix had been bred and raised to serve the masses, and as soon as they accepted her, Kol was confident she'd ease back into that role.

Nes's soul, or at least the fraction of it in Kol's possession, radiated warm against his chest, pulsing with determined passion Kol so badly hoped wouldn't die. "She *will*," he repeated. He needed her to.

Grell turned his back to the chasm so he could focus his glare on Kol alone. "I've let you play along with this fantasy for quite some time now, and I'm beginning to think it's not going to amount to that great payoff you seem to expect."

Kol didn't look away from Nessix as she continued to survey the crowd, studying their behavior and patterns. "She wasn't a general without reason."

"Yeah. She was a general because she was lucky enough to be born into it."

Kol bit down on the inside of his cheek to keep from grimacing. "Whether it was her birthright or not, it's the only life she knew. Even you have to admit that she controlled her army impressively."

"You don't think Mathias Sagewind had anything to do with that?"

Ever since the days of their mortality, Grell had shamelessly pressed for information Kol didn't always have. It just so happened that the demon version of the same man had a shorter temper and greater physical strength to make those demands more frightening. At this point, Kol was too committed to Nessix, and his only option was to hold tight to his course, whether or not it still looked like the safest path to take. He clenched his fist at his side to keep from wrapping his fingers around Nes's soul vessel.

"He had a lot to do with how quickly the flemans adapted to our attacks," Kol admitted. "But Nessix was the one who led them. She was the one who kept them functioning. She doesn't know anything other than receiving respect, and if it wasn't for how slowly she's overcoming the language barrier, I'm sure she'd have already gathered a close-knit group of would-be officers."

Grell rolled his eyes. "So she's dull?"

"Not dull," Kol said with a sigh of frustration. "She lived her whole life on one secluded island. She never had a reason to learn any other language."

"There are means we could take to hurry that along."

At last, Kol was able to pull his gaze from Nessix, spearing Grell with a caustic glare. Creating an akhuerai involved crossing mortal souls and demonic essence, an essence which carried that demon's memories. With their souls contained within blessed vessels, an akhuerai's life would continually be restored, their soul unable to depart the mortal plane, but the spark that brought them back to life came from the resiliency of the demon blood and spliced threads which held them together. Each time death neutralized an akhuerai, the demon side of them gained more influence on their mentality, deepening their insight of the world they now lived in.

Kol didn't know how to explain that he was afraid of Nessix gaining a deeper understanding of the demon she'd been bound to. Not all of Kol's memories were the kind Grell would want anyone else to know.

Grell hadn't cared for Nessix or the interest Kol had shown in her from the start. He considered her puny and ineffective, and Kol's faith in her usefulness reflected poorly on him. "Look at yourself..." Grell sneered, shaking his head. "That woman's making you weak."

It wasn't often Grell expressed concern for anyone, but he and Kol had known each other since they were mortal children and this was the closest Kol would get. Uncomfortable receiving such consideration, the alar crossed his arms. "She is not," he said, still believing the statement well enough. "She's exactly where we need her to be. Give her time."

Grell stared at Kol longer than the alar felt was necessary, making him second guess his assumption that his lord might genuinely care about him. When the first flicker of doubt crept toward him, Kol set his jaw and turned his gaze back to where the akhuerai actively avoided making contact with Nessix. Growing bored at last, Grell spat and left Kol standing there without another word.

As Grell's footsteps crunched away, Kol breathed out his regrets. He'd taken the risk of binding himself to Nessix because he knew to the depths of his own twisted soul that she was the right general for the job. The problem wasn't with her, but the subpar men and women she was meant to rule over. Maybe using aranau for their conversions had been a bad idea. Maybe they'd been foolish for discouraging a unified social structure. Maybe they should have kept the trials they'd sourced from soldiers.

Or maybe, Kol *had* been wrong.

Nessix had told him herself that these weren't her people and that she felt no obligation to them. Kol was running out of options to gain Nes's compliance and reluctantly opened his mind to the idea of taking more drastic measures to secure his control over her. Nessix was his masterpiece, his brilliant legacy, but in the end, his own survival mattered more.

"Do not force my hand, little one… It won't make either of us happy."

Turning before the urge to fly down into the chasm to confront Nessix overwhelmed him, Kol tramped back down the hallway. He had a few more days left before Grell's patience ran out. He'd give Nessix half as long to prove her worth.

* * * * *

What must have been a week passed as Nessix tried to adjust to life among the people who routinely rejected her. She gauged the days the best she could by watching the rate at which the demon guards relieved each other. Every four changes, they'd leave their hiding spots to herd the frightened once-mortals into the sleeping area, allowing Nessix to assume it took four rotations to account for one day. The orbs glowed constantly with their warm light, but within the sleeping chamber, several men would throw their shirts over them to dim their brightness.

Everyone had claimed their own designated spot for sleeping in the massive chamber, and their wary eyes followed Nessix as she walked among them, as though expecting her to use the remaining wisps of her pride or the weapons at her hip to force herself into the highest range of comfort and take that last bit of happiness from them. Their paranoia exhausted Nessix, but even so, she didn't want to sleep. She couldn't afford to relax. She needed to keep herself just on the fringes of discomfort to stay alert for intelligence that might benefit her plan to escape the hells.

She'd spent three of these days trying without success to integrate with the crowd, always met with more sneers and rude gestures. Despite having lived her entire life on Elidae with limited reason to explore linguistic studies, more words were beginning to make sense to Nessix—simple nouns and common verbs and what she picked out from the parent tongues of the fleman language. Nessix had no way to explain this trickle of comprehension, nor adequate means to communicate her desires to those she was meant to serve.

The more of these comments Nessix deciphered, the worse she felt; it was far easier to simply know snide remarks were made about her than it was to understand them. She heard through broken comprehension how the others judged her, sneering about how she must have thought herself above them and that she was there to infiltrate them on the demons' behalf. She heard the men say she needed to be knocked down a peg—though none made any indication of wanting to do so themselves—and the women accusing her of whoring herself out to the demons to gain their apparent favor.

These words might have hurt Nessix in the past, but they disheartened her on a different level now. These people were frightened and clearly overpowered by their oppressors. They had nothing left to hold onto except for memories they couldn't possibly want to relive. If they had to strike against someone,

Nessix would bear it.

Pity was an ugly emotion as far as Nessix was concerned, and she chose not to dwell on it. Instead, she focused on her desire to help those who couldn't help themselves, just as she had in life. If it took her years of this wretched existence or routinely challenging the demons through public, self-sacrificing displays, she would find a way to gain their trust. She couldn't consider herself a hero after what had become of her, but she was still a warrior.

Nessix held this sentiment close as she settled against the wall for the night. Without a cot or hammock or even a tattered blanket, she'd taken to sleeping near the room's entrance. It was a convenient arrangement for everyone; nobody else ventured that close to where the demons patrolled, and it allowed Nessix to feel as though she contributed to their safety.

Weighed down by her armor, Nessix never meant to fall asleep while posted on her watch, yet sleep always lured her away in those quiet hours. The past three nights, she'd dreamt of things which made her cry with longing; dreams of past innocence, dreams of glory she'd never embrace, dreams of Mathias. The fourth night, she dreamt of terror.

The rumble which shook the ground was familiar to her, as was the pain pulsing in her right hip. Nessix grit her teeth, wishing she wouldn't have known that joint was crushed—it was easier to ignore pain she didn't know the cause of. Lightning strobed around her, popping its curses through the sky and Nessix sat up, screaming as the weight of her upper body compressed her shattered bones. This time, she'd escape this horror. She'd drag herself the other way and find safety on her own.

Cries of devastation scratched at her resolve, chasing her heart to beat so fast it nearly made her vomit. Blinking back tears, Nessix frantically scanned her surroundings, looking for her best escape route and finding none. Gasping against her pain and choking on air thick with the smell of burning flesh, Nessix flung herself to her belly. The ground beneath her was scorched and cracking, too dry and compressed for her to dig her fingers into. Swallowing the pathetic sob that trembled in her chest, Nessix used her good leg to shove herself away from where she'd been hauled last time.

Her progress was slow and excruciating, and it wasn't long before her ears rang from exertion and her fingers grew numb. Nessix panted at her efforts, silently screaming at adrenaline to give her just a little more of a push. The entire world spun, bodies collapsing to the ground around her as the sky flashed with malice. She had to keep going. She had to escape.

Mind channeled solely on survival, Nessix screamed as a strong hand gripped her forearm. Panic suppressed sensibility and she whipped around to grope for anything she could use as a weapon. Nes's shattered bones scolded her promptly for the hastiness of her actions and her attempt to mute her scream behind clenched teeth failed. Tears squeezed out of her eyes as she gasped against the pain and recognized the war-torn man who had come to her aid before.

"Come on!" he encouraged with a strained voice which made Nes's heart beat faster. He finished his statement as he had before, though the rest of his message escaped her comprehension.

The man grasped Nes's other arm, and she struggled against his hold. "Please don't," she begged. Exhaustion and shock bound Nessix to weakness, and the man reached his arm around her and pulled her to his chest.

More words were murmured as he hefted Nessix to her feet and turned her toward their demise.

Tears rolled freely down Nes's face, their salt seeping into nicked flesh and her open mouth, tickling her tongue. "No!" she demanded. Dragging her broken leg behind her and forced to lean against this man for support, the greatest fight Nessix could put up was pulling at a leather strap which crossed his chest. "Not this way. We have to turn around. *Please!*"

His arm slid farther around her, raspy voice repeating his affirmation as he kept his focus trained ahead.

Everything inside of Nessix screamed at her to find a way to convince him that they were heading into danger. Conveying her intent with spoken words was useless and she struggled against the man's grasp, flinging her debilitated mass against his superior strength. Sapped by agony, shaking too hard to control her body, Nessix was powerless as the man clutched her against his side and returned a plea of his own. He spoke in a heartening tone, one laced with grim reservation. Nessix whimpered and pressed her eyes closed, tears still flowing as the bolt struck down before them.

In the first moments of waking, Nessix didn't have the luxury of attempting to safeguard her pride. She choked on her gasp, flailing for her sword with her right hand and doubling over to grip her hip with her left. She jerked violently and slammed the back of her head against the wall before her mind accepted that she was as safe as a demon's prisoner could be.

Panicked breaths assaulted her in humiliating bellows, and Nessix opened her eyes to find a young woman no older than her late teens sitting cross-legged beside her. The girl looked down at Nessix curiously, drawing the first wave of self-consciousness from her. Heart still racing, Nessix cleared her throat and sat up, swiping a rogue strand of hair from her eyes.

Before Nessix had the chance to cover for her pathetic jump back to the waking world, the girl held out her hand, presenting a chunk of that terrible root vegetable. This time it was uncooked, and Nessix wondered if that would change the way it tasted. Hopeful speculations weren't enough to make her anxious to find out.

The girl spoke, her voice melodic. The language barrier still obstructed parts of the message, but Nessix grasped enough to understand the instruction to eat this root called dream stop in order to forget her nightmare.

Nessix blinked and looked from the root up to the girl's face. She was tempted to blame her comprehension on exhaustion until she slowly and brokenly crafted a reply in the same dialect. "No dream," she said, wiping the sweat off her brow. "I'm fine."

The girl rolled her eyes and fit Nessix with a stern glare, shaking her head. "*All* of us dream." She gestured to the deeper reaches of the cavern where hushed sobs and panicked gasps drifted toward them. "Hmm..." The girl spoke another brief explanation and when Nessix shook her head, she pouted and glanced around before pointing at Nes's sword and swinging her arm as if attempting to use it.

"A war?" Nessix asked, reverting to her native tongue and

shaking her head as she tried again. "Hurt. Pain?"

The girl nodded. "Afraid, yes?"

Nessix was without her army, trapped in a foreign realm by enemies that overpowered and outsmarted her. The one shot she had at obtaining a wisp of influence relied on gaining the loyalty and trust of people who viewed her as a traitor. She'd never known a time when she wasn't adored and obeyed, had never been an outsider or faced the prospects of eternal torture at the whims of demons. She lowered her eyes and stared at her hands. Afraid summed up her current situation quite well. "Yes."

The girl's tiny hand reached forward and grasped Nes's wrist. After an initial, defensive resistance, Nessix allowed it to be pulled forward so the girl could press the root into her hand. "*Eat*," the girl instructed again, shoving Nes's hand back toward her. "It helps the… the afraid."

On the cusp of full comprehension, this language barrier frustrated Nessix more than ever, but at least she could piece her way around it. This was the first kind gesture shown to her since Kol had dropped her in the pit, and the longing to help which streamed from this girl's eyes suggested she wasn't after any mischief. Grimacing, Nessix put the root in her mouth and bit down.

"Kavita," the girl said, distracting Nessix from the root's offensive flavor. She pressed a hand to her chest and nodded warmly.

Though the root's taste pulled at Nes's lips, she managed a smile. "Nessix," she said.

"They say you're a general?"

Nessix blinked at how clearly she understood that statement, and her heart ached for a time when that was true. "I *was* a general."

Kavita frowned, eyes travelling once again to Nes's sword belt. "Why did your"—the last word was still foreign to Nessix—"let you keep those?" Kavita gestured toward Nes's weapons.

Nes's hand drifted to her sword's sheath, the surge of comfort which normally accompanied the action missing. Had Kavita referenced Kol in that last statement? Was he considered her master now? Nessix had never known what to think of the concept of being owned by another, though she'd had an attempt at such made on her in the past. She'd fought that instance, but only with the backing of men able to keep her safe. This time, her only confirmed support was this young woman who she could barely speak to. Nessix had tried to fight Kol in the past and failed. She'd been killed by those he claimed were above him. She didn't want to surrender to his possession, but what choice did she have? She couldn't fight. She didn't have an army anymore, and one comrade who had taken pity on her for having a nightmare wouldn't be enough against the entirety of the hells.

Nessix gagged as she swallowed the root. "I'm to..." She glanced at her sword and closed her eyes, wondering how to convey Kol's intentions with her limited vocabulary. "I'm to make you..." She furrowed her brows, scraping at what she'd picked up so far and finding none of the words as fitting as they needed to be. "Make you be strong."

Kavita's gasp opened Nes's eyes, and the girl scooted closer. "To be strong against *demons*?" Her voice squeaked on a breathy whisper filled with hope Nessix hadn't believed existed down here.

"Not yet," Nessix said. "But someday."

Kavita held her breath, eyes wide as she nodded. Nessix glanced at the room's entrance, wondering if she was stupid to verbally confirm her intentions of using these people to try to overthrow the demons. They were all so submissive, and pulling the necessary aggression out of them would be a battle in itself. If word of her scheme reached her enemies before she convinced this would-be army to hold its own, she didn't know what sort of punishments they'd meet. At the same time, the eagerness and innocent hope that illuminated Kavita's face was motivation enough.

"You can't... the demons can't..." Nessix growled at her struggle and settled for holding a finger to her lips.

Kavita nodded again and mirrored Nessix by pressing a finger to her own lips. Moments later, she sprang forward, wrapped her arms around Nessix's neck, and whispered words that held the intent of gratitude in her ear.

Nessix had never been terribly outgoing with displays of

physical affection, and she tensed on the other side of the embrace, but didn't fight it. Once Kavita released her hold and scampered off into the crowd of sleeping bodies, Nessix leaned back against the wall and loosened the straps of her bracers.

Her heart had quit racing. Her breath came slow and steady. For the first time since she'd been in Kol's possession, she felt like she had control over something. Now, she simply had to pray that she'd be able to hold onto it.

TEN

Mathias had a long history with demons, one which had taught him to forgive those who sought it. After all, they weren't that different from him—forcibly touched by the divine realm, endlessly searching for their definition of peace. Mathias sometimes wondered if he'd have taken a similar path had it not been for Julianna speaking in his defense when he'd burst from his grave. There had been a time when he'd thought himself far too good to fall from grace, but he'd acted out of passion enough times to realize even the best of men were capable of blurring the lines between right and wrong. Fortunately for Mathias, the goddess who touched him had permanently nestled close to his heart. The deities who struck the demons were long dead. It was no wonder they'd lost the strength to fight for moral integrity.

Despite lifetimes of battling the demons, Mathias had fostered a limited amount of good in a few individuals and showed them how to incorporate into a world that shunned them. His attempt to end this constant state of chaos by bridging the demons with the mortal realm had given rise to the town of Heiligate. It was a controversial move, one which the brunt of the Order—Julianna and Etha included—frowned upon, but Mathias had unique perspectives above them all. He knew what it was like to be alone, to be ridiculed and feared simply for being different from the mortals around him. He knew what it was like to be engaged in deadly combat against foes who, deep in their core, longed for death and the salvation that should come with it. Only the demons didn't receive salvation, driving them to pursue eternal misery over purgatory. Mathias knew the excruciating pain that came from being trapped in the hells. And it had been while enduring the tortures wrapped up in that dark realm that Mathias had first found good in a demon.

Heiligate and her safety were controversial topics in the Order, indeed, but Mathias had vowed to protect the city himself, should anyone challenge her growth or prosperity. Now that nearly two thousand demons populated it, they were able to stand in defense of the haven themselves.

Mathias trusted these demons as much as he figured any demon could be trusted. They'd each denounced their connections to the legions which sought vengeance, personally swearing to Mathias that they'd willingly and peacefully incorporate into Abaeloth's more conventional societies if given the chance. Over the three-hundred and fifty-eight years since Heiligate's founding, Mathias had only needed to eradicate three individuals for betraying those vows. The modest town wasn't much, but Mathias believed it was a step in the right direction.

Though the demons who called Heiligate home had been shunned by their kin, it was the only safe harbor for the occasional parties of wandering demons, and Mathias hoped for the first time ever that some of those fiends had stopped by for a recent visit. Heiligate's tavern was a rumored hot spot for the most nefarious foes, and demon brews had a reliable knack for loosening even the firmest of tongues.

There wasn't one demon who called Heiligate home that didn't understand Mathias's role in keeping them alive, but that didn't make them hide behind that bitter pride of theirs any less. Sneers meant to convey the tenacity which demons were renowned for and the passive rattle of weapons that did anything but intimidate Mathias greeted him at the gates. He gave the guards a proper smile and lifted his empty hands to his sides to imply he meant them no harm. He liked to think they didn't expect as much from him, but didn't blame them for the reaction.

Word of Mathias's arrival traveled fast through the streets of Heiligate, preceding his passage toward the heart of town. Shop keepers came out to shake their fists at him and accuse him of being bad for business. The females—save the town's one succubus who cast him an alluring gaze from beneath full lashes—warned him to keep his distance. The children, though, peeked at him with wonder, confirming that the town hadn't lost its appreciation. Stories were still woven about Mathias and the sacrifices he made for everyone, demons included, and the children hadn't yet been sullied by encounters with the less tolerant reaches of Abaeloth.

All was as it ought to be in Heiligate, and Mathias found peace in that. He ventured his way to the center of the ramshackle town to a dilapidated courthouse held together by a patchwork of planks and bent nails. Mathias shook his head and smiled. The tavern was kept in immaculate order. As was the butcher's shop and the seamstress's. But the city's central fixture stood in such disrepair that even Mathias, with Etha's blessings, was reluctant to enter it for fear of it collapsing around him. He followed the rickety building around its east side to approach the house slumped in the midst of a thicket of thriving brambles.

Mathias picked his way down the narrow path which led through the thorny yard, careful to lift his feet high enough to not catch a toe on the uneven stones which lined the walkway. The flutter of a tattered curtain from a window beside the door confirmed that the occupant was home, though Mathias knew better than to think simply being armed with that knowledge would make gaining entry any easier.

He hesitated at the porch to scrutinize the integrity of the structure before testing his weight against it with a firm shove of his foot. Despite missing boards and the uneven plane it sat on, the porch suggested it would hold, and Mathias stepped up to the door and knocked. As expected, he wasn't greeted, and he carefully eased over to the window to rap on it with a knuckle.

"I saw you in there, Mehalco," he called. "Let's not make a scene, shall we?"

No answer came and Mathias huffed a sigh as he craned his neck around the side of the house. Mehalco always took his time accepting the fact that he was the head of Heiligate and the demon Mathias had the closest connection to. The paladin suspected being in his pocket wasn't something most demons prided themselves on, but he also knew of no other demon he could trust quite the same way.

"I'm not here to cause trouble," he called again. "To the best of my knowledge, all of your citizens have been behaving themselves. Zeal has her eyes turned away from you. I'm just here for your help."

Mathias strained his ears to listen for any sign of movement, and the door popped open. Giving himself a second to tuck his smile away, Mathias turned to face the head peering through the insubstantial crack.

"Help from me?" Mehalco was small for a demon, pasty skinned and with a distinct lack of concern for his personal hygiene, but Mathias was content to overlook such matters. "Not sure what you think I can do for you."

"May I come inside?" Mathias asked.

"You can talk from right there."

Mathias nodded slowly. It wasn't as though these matters would be hidden from the town for long; Mathias had only known Mehalco to keep one secret, and besides, the more ears and eyes he commissioned to gather intelligence, the better.

"Have any of your more vile brethren stopped by in the past few months?"

Mehalco grunted and slipped out of the door to stand on the porch and crossed his arms. "They're here all the time. Busting my city up. What of it?"

"Have they mentioned anything that's going on in their realm? Anything to do with the war I'd been fighting?"

Mehalco laughed. "The war on Elidae? Yeah. They had a lot to say about that, or rather, about *you*. You've really done a fine job making them hate you, you know?"

"Feeling's mutual, friend." Mathias watched Mehalco's eyes dart around the bland scenery and how he couldn't keep his fingers from fidgeting with the tail end of his belt. "You said they came and busted up your town? What was the cause of the trouble?"

"Same story as always... they wanted a free ride, tried to stiff us on their tabs. Demons being... well..." He shrugged and fit a sheepish glance at Mathias. "You know."

Mathias allowed himself a smirk. Even the best behaved of the demons knew the destruction they were capable of. "Had any of them talked about how they gained access to Elidae in the first place?"

"Not that I heard. You could ask Bronte at the tavern to see if any of them slipped any information, but as far as I know, they were all tight lipped about it."

Mathias nodded. That was for the best. Whether or not the demons of Heiligate were trustworthy—or their rendition of the virtue—Mathias didn't relish the idea of it becoming common knowledge that the demons could potentially manipulate gods.

"I trust Bronte didn't hear anything. The information I'm after is big enough that he'd have told you if he heard anything about it."

Mehalco narrowed his eyes, fingers ceasing their twitching as Mathias's words hooked his curiosity. "You're not just asking about their movement, are you?"

"No. They've set their sights on disrupting Etha's realm now, and in ways I can't elaborate on at this time."

Mehalco cocked his head and leaned closer. "Interfering with Etha?" His lip curled at the use of the goddess's name, but in light of the demons' history with the divine and Etha in particular, Mathias overlooked the rude gesture. "*Your* Etha?"

Mathias nodded.

"*How?*"

"I told you, I can't elaborate on that yet."

Mehalco crossed his arms again and jutted his chin arrogantly. "You're trying to peel information from me, but won't share what you've got?"

"So you *do* know something?"

Mehalco's arms fell to his sides as he glanced from Mathias to his cracked door and back again. Mathias's brows were arched with a demanding patience and the demon growled at his own ineptitude. "You've got nothing you can tell me and I've got nothing I can tell you, and that's how it's got to be."

Mathias crossed his arms. "Do you want to step inside to finish this discussion, then?"

Mehalco sprang forward and grabbed Mathias's arm to pull him closer. When he spoke, it was on a rattling breath. "Rumor has it they'd mentioned something about an inoga named..." He squinted and snapped the fingers of his free hand. "Brell? Mel. Something."

That familiar knot in Mathias's stomach that showed up every time Mehalco tried to give him specifics pulled a bit tighter. Precision was far from Mehalco's forte, but Mathias did believe his intentions, if for no other reason than how desperately the demon's fingers dug into his arm.

"Alright, so what about him?"

Mehalco sighed, a flighty and almost frustrated expression, and he drew Mathias inside the house after all. "He was stationed beneath Elidae and has a troop of alar trying to build an army."

Mathias's heart stopped at the mention of alar. "Alar. Yes. What about building an army?"

Mehalco rubbed his nose and looked at Mathias through the sides of his eyes. "You're asking a lot of questions without giving much in exchange, *friend*."

Even protected in part by the Order of the White Circle, Heiligate would crumble in an instant if any of this information leaked to the greater demon population. "How long have we known each other, Mehalco?"

The demon jerked his shoulders back, brows falling flat. "Huh? What's that got to do with anything?"

"Long enough for you to know you can trust me, right?"

Mehalco grunted. "Trusting you is a bit of a stretch."

Mathias chuckled. "I'll keep that in mind the next time the Council wants to send some bodies to investigate the integrity of your beautiful city."

Grumbling curses, Mehalco narrowed his eyes even further. "I never should have led you to find that blasted succubus..."

"Maybe not." Mathias planted his hands on his hips and

stretched out his back. "But you trusted me then, and you trust me now."

"Fine," Mehalco snapped. "What of it?"

The whimsy wiped clean of Mathias's face in an instant, drawing Mehalco out of the defensive. "This inoga and his alar are up to some very bad things. Things that could mean danger for you and yours if they suspected you knew of them. You deserve the truth, more than most anyone else, but demons from the hells pass through your city too frequently, and it would do neither of us any good if they got suspicious. Trust me, Mehalco. Please. I'll tell you everything when it's safe."

Mehalco gnashed his teeth together and peered at Mathias from between narrowed eyelids. It was true that Mathias hadn't given him many reasons to distrust him. Mehalco could have refused to help the paladin when they first met all those years ago, and the sight of the human covered in blood and poised to defend himself still frequented Mehalco's dreams. Mathias had spared him then, and Mehalco often took for granted that he continued to do so.

"Bah, I'll never understand you." Mehalco swatted his hands in Mathias's direction as he trudged off to get himself a drink.

Mathias followed slowly, hoping to keep frustration from raising his voice. "What else do I need to know? How are they building this army?"

Mehalco uncorked his bottle and drank straight from it. "How would I know? You've seen how I run my town. I hardly know how to manage security forces, much less an army."

Mathias sighed and pressed a hand to his forehead. At least he had something resembling another name, and an army supported Zenos's report of multiple souls being seized. His chest filled with a sweltering rage that propriety barely kept contained. Nessix had been targeted for this reason, he was sure of it. However this army was being built, she was meant to lead it.

At least that means you're likely to see her again?

Not even Etha could salvage optimism from that prospect. She knew, just as Mathias did, that the next time he saw Nessix, she may not be the same woman he'd known.

115

"Hey, you alright?"

Mathias shook his head and drew in a slow breath, refocusing his attention on the demon in his company. "Yeah," he said, voice gruff. "Thank you for what you could tell me. I'll return when I can to see if you hear any more gossip, but don't go fishing for it, and don't speak a word of this to anyone but me. Am I clear?"

Mehalco clasped the bottle to his chest as if it would give him comfort in light of Mathias's atypical demeanor. "Yeah. I got it."

Mathias ineffectively tried to sort out a smile and settled for a silent nod. Mehalco deserved more of an explanation. He deserved a greater show of gratitude, especially in light of the danger he'd face if it leaked that he was funneling intelligence to the Order's strongest operative. Neither of those efforts could be mustered from Mathias right now, and so he showed himself out of the run-down house and away from the city of demons, wishing just one of them deserved a beating today.

ELEVEN

The morning following her dream, Nessix hardly recognized the people around her. As a whole, they no longer sneered at her or tried to avoid catching her attention. Most bitter glares had warped into prying, curious eyes, the tones of their whispers accented with admiration. They still fidgeted nervously and were quick to glance away if Nes's eyes wandered too close to theirs, but she was content to attribute that to the universal lack of courage which affected them. She sought out Kavita to serve as an ambassador to facilitate her fresh attempt at integration, but couldn't locate the girl through the crowd. Nessix hadn't thought much time had passed since she'd last gone drinking with her troops after a successful mission, so it baffled her why taking the initiative to approach common folk bothered her so much.

Nes's sword nudged its comfort against her thigh and the gentle creaks and clanks of her armor adjusting to her stride suggested the most obvious answer. These people were not her troops, no matter how badly Kol wanted them to fill that role. They were average civilians, the sort of people Nessix had never quite learned how to associate with. For all of the boldness she'd thrown about in her time, Nessix had no idea how to talk to normal people.

Nevertheless, walking through the chasm no longer carried an air of gloom now that the population quit watching her for signs of danger. Nessix didn't know how her discussion with Kavita had spread so quickly, but a sweeping appraisal of the demon guard posts suggested her intentions hadn't reached any ears she needed to avoid. The demons on duty waited day in and out for any infraction they could justify pouncing on, but they didn't put forth the effort to watch Nessix with any greater intensity. She breathed out a tense sigh, trying to relax into the irony of the concept of leading a rebellion.

Reflecting the previous night's progress, Nessix understood more words from passing conversations. Fewer insults were pushed her way, and hearing her title spoken without ridicule elated her on a level she'd forgotten existed. As the day progressed, she grew so comfortable with this mysterious comprehension that it startled her to a stop when she passed a cluster of tall young men speaking quickly in a language she couldn't begin to grasp. This was the first time she'd heard this tongue, and she stared at these men as she tried to come up with a valid reason for them to hide their discussion from their peers. The bliss Nessix had spent the entire morning gathering began to sift away.

One of the men glanced up as Nessix stopped in contemplation. His cheeks drained of color, jaw sagging as he lifted his arm and pointed toward her. Nessix straightened her shoulders as the man's three companions turned to face her. A cloud of reluctant confusion passed between general and civilians before a chuckle from one of the men drew broad smiles from his comrades.

"Bless you, General!"

"We stand with you!"

"My loyalty to you!"

Had Nessix not been so stunned by their enthusiasm, their willingness to fold to her motives without debate or question would have concerned her. After the past several days of facing bitterness and blame from these shattered people, it should have taken more than one display of vulnerability and a promise conveyed through broken dialect to win them over. That was, of course, if they'd had the heart to fight her. As it was, these people hungered for a leader who harbored the skill and political mind and courage to defy unjust authority. Defeated by their circumstances, they were desperate for a champion. Their hope tossed kindling on the dim embers in Nes's heart, their words blowing gently until they caught fire.

"No," Nessix said, heart swelling with purpose she'd resigned to never feel again. "I stand with *you*."

The cluster of men erupted with excited talk at Nes's reply, and she smiled before turning to continue appraising her budding kingdom.

There were still many factors Nessix was uncertain of—the only thing she did know was that they couldn't permanently die. That in itself should have given her some amount of reassurance. Combat wouldn't be less dangerous, but with death off the table, the risks were far less severe. Her mind flicked back to Kol's promise, that there were some fates worse than death. Nessix didn't know the alar well enough to think she could read him, but wasn't in a hurry to test that theory quite yet, least of all with unskilled bodies. One thing was clear, though. Nessix would eventually need help if she planned to stand against the demons.

Toiling over her resources and limitations, Nessix walked toward the food station, catching more pockets of lively chatter spoken in foreign tongues. Awed glances and humbly bowed heads accompanied the gossip, and Nessix realized that these people were talking about her plans, shielding them from the demons in the only method available to them. Nes's tactical mind hooked on an idea she should have caught the moment Kol divulged her situation to her. She hastened her pace.

Due to Elidae's remote location, Nessix only had a very basic knowledge of the rest of Abaeloth, but this colony of people—*her* people—hailed from every continent. She'd already determined that this army she was meant to raise would be tasked with attacking the mortal world, which meant she'd reach the surface eventually. She'd committed to the idea of personally launching whatever mayhem necessary to gain the attention of Mathias's Order, to leave clues behind that she was alive, but it wasn't until hearing the wealth of cultures the demons had submerged her in that Nessix realized she could be more proactive.

As she reached the food table, she unbuckled her right vambrace to use as a plate and held it forward to receive the first portion of her meal. Unlike mornings in the past, she was met by a welcoming smile and reverent acknowledgement of her station from the server.

Nessix returned the smile. "Where is Zeal?" she asked, hushing her voice to evade the reach of any demon ears.

The man furrowed his brows, but held back from commenting on Nes's apparent stupidity. The rise of Zeal and its Order of the White Circle was common knowledge across every reach he'd ever heard of. "Gelthin." The man stuck his serving hand into the vat of meat.

"Is anyone here from there?" For the first time since Nessix had woken on that slab, she felt content. Not yet happy, but at least like she had something to hope for.

Once again, the man pursed his lips and contemplated Nes's intelligence. "Where are you from, General?"

"Elidae."

His eyes widened and the meat plopped from his hand and into Nes's extended bracer. "You're... you're *that* general?"

Recognition was an intoxicating sensation after having surrendered to the notion that all she'd done in her life was destined to be forgotten. It seemed as though Kol's claim of her role in the war had been a bluff. Even if Elidae had forgotten Nessix, the people who needed to know of her courage the most had heard enough.

"I am," she said.

The man laughed—a giddy sound Nessix hadn't expected from one of his stature—and he moved farther down the line to tug on the arm of one of his friends. Words passed briskly between them, attention directed Nes's way, and the second man flit off in a hurry. The first gathered up two rolls and one of those terrible root vegetables Kavita had called dream stop, and returned to where Nessix waited.

"Forgive me," he said, voice still ticking eagerly. He deposited the remaining food in Nes's bracer. "The demons haven't snatched anyone from Zeal, but if you can give me until third meal, I can gather men from Gelthin for you."

As far as Nessix figured, she had all the time in the world. Waiting a few hours wouldn't put her any more off pace. "That will be fine."

Nessix spent the rest of the day working her way through the masses, doing her best to see as many faces as possible. As the hours passed, word of her promise and identity reached more and more ears, and she kept a wary eye on the demon guards. They either hadn't heard any of these rumors or didn't invest concern in them, allowing Nessix to mingle with increasingly few concerns.

The excitement was catching and in the brief moments when Nessix dropped her guard, she nearly forgot about the dire straits she'd been dumped in. Without fail, though, one of the guards would leave his post or a particularly bedraggled child would scamper up to beg for her protection, and she remembered all over again. Fostering good will with these people was the first step to gaining their loyalty, and she'd need loyalty without hesitation to build an army effective against demons.

As Nessix casually made her way through the crowd, she kept her eyes open for anyone who looked at her weapons with a wistful familiarity or who carried themselves with the confidence of a combatant. All she got were gawks of wonder, and sometimes fear of her sword and knives, and though several of the men were well muscled, they didn't move with the grace Nessix expected of soldiers.

The easy way to find out what she had to work with would have simply been to ask; this morning's change of affection suggested Nessix had a good chance of obtaining answers. In order to get those answers, though, she'd have to ask these people to revisit memories of the happiness that had been stolen from them. Nessix was well versed in diplomacy, but her desire to heal the wounds dealt by the demons forbid her from being so forward. She'd only just begun gaining ground and aimed to keep her influence positive. These battered men and frightened women would open up to her in time.

Allowing her plots to steep in the back of her mind, Nessix

devoted her energy to studying how this society functioned. The services provided by the skilled laborers were done free of charge. With no means of currency and a greater desire to simply survive than accumulate any sort of wealth, they'd developed an effective bartering system to keep the community running. Resources harvested from agricultural plots accessible by those guarded tunnels satisfied the needs of those skilled at mending clothing and tending to minor wounds. The most emotionally resilient of the population provided entertainment and distractions through talents of voice and storytelling.

No formal societal structure existed, which didn't surprise Nessix. Without wealth or feats of physical strength, there was no way for one man to maintain power in such a society. The concept of the masses running around without a leader chilled the disciplined parts of Nes's mind that had thrived on structure, but the thought of trying to claim such influence over a group that had gone so long without order chilled her more. Nessix had never been good at taking small steps toward her objectives, preferring to leap into them with all her might. These tiny steps forward grated on her patience, but she vowed to endure.

Evening pulled Nessix away from the task of trying to relate to and raise the morale of the civilians, and she approached the food station eagerly. As she unbuckled her bracer to gather her next meal, the server motioned her close with rapid sweeps of his hand. Heart leaping, Nessix quickened her pace.

The server leaned far over the table upon Nessix's arrival, handful of meat at the ready. "I've found some men from Gelthin." He kept his voice low, but his eyes were alight as he plopped the food in Nes's armor.

Nessix couldn't keep her grin contained and briefly glanced around to see if she could guess who these men might be. "Are they willing to speak with me?"

"General, *every*one is willing to speak with you after the hope you've brought us."

Modesty should have threatened to claim Nessix at this point, shaming her for being so frightened of something as simple as a nightmare, but the excitement of seeing her plans falling into place overcame embarrassment or anger that her vulnerability had been revealed. History told Nessix that the first general of Elidae had been the human captain of the fleet which had brought her ancestors to the island. Eager to escape the elven heritage which had rejected them, the elven king had married his daughter to this captain, encouraging the others of his kin to engage in similar arrangements with their own children. This line hadn't been challenged in Nes's lifetime and the closest she'd seen a kingdom built from scratch was when Veed parted ways with her. Whether or not she knew what she was doing, building this nation seemed right.

Born into leadership, Nessix had never had to worry about how to win people over. The flemans as a whole had been so conditioned to follow her family line that she hadn't fathomed the idea of needing to earn trust that hadn't been openly given from the start. Overcoming these people's doubt, proving to them that she was every bit as vulnerable as they were, was a worthy challenge. She'd have to show them that she was a normal person, just like them. That she had been forced into this hell, just like them. She'd show them the way to find the courage to stand up and ultimately take arms, and that they were more like her than they thought. Nessix would be the first of the Teradhel line to build a new kingdom. She'd been adored in her past. She could foster the emotion again.

"Thank you..." Nessix's gratitude tapered off uncertainly as she realized she hadn't ever been given the serving crew's names.

"Sten." The man held out his hand—his clean one—and gave Nessix a warm smile.

"Thank you, Sten." She tucked her bracer beneath her arm to accept the man's gesture.

"There'll be four of them," Sten said, "gathered near the sleeping quarters. I've already sent them off with their dinner, so they'll be eating."

Nessix thanked him again and hurried to gather the rest of her evening meal so she could meet the men who she hoped would open her door to Zeal. She had clung to the concept of hope for the past few weeks, doing everything in her power to convince herself that there was still a reason for her to keep fighting. This was the first time she truly believed it.

With this confidence, Nessix approached the indicated men, unable to keep her excitement from growing. The rate at which she'd been able to pick up languages that weren't her own encouraged her further. All she had to do was learn Gelthin's common tongue well enough to inquire about Mathias once the demons released her army to the surface and she could lead them away from this misery. The demons would have no reason to suspect her of devious intentions simply from her learning a new language. After all, she needed to be able to communicate with her army.

The first of the men looked up as Nessix approached, eyes widening as she met them and smiled. His friends were quick to turn, but before Nessix could address them, the color drained from their cheeks and their mouths turned from gaping in wonder to frowns of terror. Nessix stopped abruptly, confused as to what she'd done when the darkness of a shadow passed over top of them, followed by a burst of air.

Nes's loose hair stirred in the artificial breeze and she dropped her bracer of food as battle sense prompted her to draw her sword and step in front of the startled men. Turning her eyes to the air, she found Kol completing one last circle before he landed and stalked up to her. He kept his wings extended and his shoulders relaxed, wicked eyes gleaming from the reaction he'd pulled from the group.

That he derived so much pleasure from tormenting such fragile minds sickened Nessix. She held her ground positioned before the cowering men as Kol stopped two paces away from her and crossed his arms. The men and women who had been dining around them fell silent and tucked themselves into their hiding spots.

"You'd best put that away, little one." Kol nodded at Nes's sword. "You could hurt someone."

Nessix so badly wanted to growl at Kol, to assure him that hurting someone had been her intention, but her objective of winning him over forbid such rashness. Weighing the risks of her precarious position with the people she was responsible for against the risk of offending Kol, she kept her sword at the ready.

"You're interrupting my men's dinner," she said.

Kol puffed out a short snort of a laugh. "So you're claiming them now?"

He strode forward, walking past Nessix so closely she could have launched an attack on him without trouble. Her arms ached with the desire to do just that, but she would put neither her ultimate objective nor the safety of the men behind her on the line from such insubordination. She monitored Kol from the corner of her eye until she was forced to turn to keep him in view. All but one of the men had dropped their food to the ground, and they all braced their legs in preparation of jumping to their feet. Kol stopped on the fringes of their flight zones and turned his head to Nessix.

"I suppose they do look an awful lot like the army you left behind on Elidae."

Muscles trembling at the limits of her restraint, Nessix stitched together the last of her calm with a deep breath. She raised her chin, forbidding to let Kol win this time. "Thank you," she said, her voice schooled firmly against the sneer that fought to surface at those words. "It's a relief to hear you see the same potential I do."

Kol's cunning eyes lit in delight at Nes's restoring feistiness. He struck an aggressive step toward the group of men who Nessix sought to protect, flaring his wings forward and jerking his hands toward the knives on his belt. The men who Nessix had just proclaimed her faith in yelped at the threat and scrambled away. Kol chuckled and turned his head back toward Nessix, eyes dancing with a vile challenge.

"Oh, yes. Just like your men on Elidae."

Nessix ground her teeth so hard they hurt and sucked back her fear. She'd have to assert herself eventually, and now was an opportune time to start. "What is *wrong* with you?" she demanded fiercely. "You want me to make an army out of this lot and think it's *funny* to intimidate and insult them before they've even found their confidence?"

Kol blinked and straightened, humor swapped for intrigue.

Despite himself, he kept half an eye on Nes's sword in case she was as angry as she sounded. "They'll face far more intimidating things than me in war." He trailed his attention on Nessix as he walked ahead to sit down on the boulder her previous audience had occupied. He patted the spot next to him. "And they couldn't have understood the insults, anyway; there aren't many down here who can understand your tongue. Now, put that sword away and come sit down."

Nessix watched Kol warily as he unclasped a pouch from his belt and pulled out a palmful of deep red berries. He popped one in his mouth and, at Nes's continued noncompliance, shoved it into his cheek to talk around it.

"I suppose I should ask what's wrong with *you*," he said, chewing and swallowing the berry before tossing in a second one. "You promised me compliance and are only now integrating with the rest of the akhuerai? My superiors are growing concerned. I specifically instructed you to avoid doing that."

Nessix could have continued arguing with Kol over which of them was supposed to be in charge down here. She could have laughed over the irony of him being afraid of what demons would do to him. But something more immediate caught her attention.

"Akhuerai?" she asked.

Kol stopped chewing and looked up. "Yes," he said. "Your people."

Nessix shook her head. "No. They're from all over."

"Right." Kol resumed eating. "But now you're all from here. They've accepted it. It's about time you do, too."

The thought of letting go of her identity stalled Nes's heart, a chill running through her torso until a tiny pinch of warmth brought her back to the moment. "I am a fleman," she said.

"You *were* a fleman," Kol corrected.

Nessix shook her head again, baring her teeth. "If you want the general in me, you've got to take it all. You cannot separate me from who I am."

Kol rolled his eyes. "I'm not going to tell you again. Put that"—he nodded toward her sword—"away so we can sit and talk."

The fact that Kol was so adamant that Nessix disarm herself should have amused her, but her mind was still with the men Kol had just frightened away, and the demons he had available to call on for backup, and memories of the fleman man who had first approached her. As it was, Kol was harmlessly sitting on a rock, eating, and if she complied with his demands, he seemed inclined to stay that way. Nessix glanced at her food where it laid splattered on the ground and back at Kol's sly expression. Frustrated at how effortlessly he toyed with her, Nessix slammed her sword back in its sheath and stalked over to the demon, grudgingly sitting beside him.

She glanced over to where these people—the akhuerai, as Kol had called them—peeked toward her. Fear engulfed their eyes, though she couldn't tell if it was fear of Kol in general or fear of what Kol would do to their general. That thought solidified Nes's commitment to them; they'd accepted her as their leader. The station she'd feared she'd lost was still hers, and these people depended on her claiming it. General Nessix Teradhel would *not* be defeated by demons ever again.

"So what do you want?" Nessix asked, perhaps a bit more boldly than was prudent. When the corner of Kol's lip lifted in the beginning of a smirk, she added, "And I want more than 'brilliance' or 'your obedience' this time."

The snappiness of Nes's tone and the arrogant way she attempted to mock his voice wiped the smirk from Kol, and he slowly turned to face her. In the past, she'd been quick to recoil from such silent warnings, but the clamp of her jaw suggested a much stronger determination. Kol had no taste for insubordination, but he was unwilling to dampen the fire she'd found at last.

"I came down here to ask you where my army is." He popped another berry in his mouth. "But it seems you've found it."

Nessix watched Kol chew and glanced at the pouch that was still stuffed with fruit. Her food was bland and barely palatable— not to mention she'd dropped her dinner upon Kol's intrusion. his eyes glittered as Nes's hunger worked across her face. She huffed irritably and cast her gaze aside. Longing for sweets would neither help Nessix secure her position nor satisfy Kol's demands, so she focused on their mutual objective.

"I'm doing my best with what I've been provided," she said, pleased by the amount of confidence she conveyed with her words. "But it's difficult to convert civilians into soldiers. The closest I've got to experienced men is a handful of game hunters. If you expect me to train an army, why didn't you populate my ranks with people who know how to fight?"

Kol quit chewing as Nes's question hit him. He might have been the head of this operation, but he didn't know how much he could safely share with Nessix. He didn't know how to tell her that his superiors didn't cope well with ranks that were unafraid to challenge them.

Nessix trilled a brief laugh at his confused expression, disregarding the potential risks of doing so. She savored this rush of confidence. "You mean to tell me you and your hordes couldn't harvest actual soldiers?"

Kol bristled. "We harvested you."

Nessix leaned back. She'd faced that same insult several times now and had come to terms with it. "That was what? Forty to one odds?"

Kol's fist clenched around his little bag of berries, crimson juice seeping through the fabric and from between his fingers, and the tiniest tremor of reservation fluttered in Nes's heart. She hadn't meant to push him to the point of anger, especially when he had such easy access to those she'd vowed to protect. It seemed he'd accept insults to his kind and personal character, but the operation he backed was not safe fodder if Nessix wanted to keep him cordial. Kol turned his head from her with a chilling purpose, and Nessix held her breath, flexing her fingers to grab her sword if she needed to rush to the defensive.

"Does it matter how we took you?" Kol's voice was hushed and strict, prickling at the hairs on the back of Nes's neck. Slowly, he faced her again, the curl of his upper lip baring his canine teeth and his eyes glistening on the cusp of losing that calculated calm Nessix often took for granted. "Because if you're keeping score, *you* were the one who gave up. Every man in my unit survived that assault, but you... you were the one to fall."

He didn't raise his voice, and that made his reprimand that much more frightening. The overwhelming urge to retreat from the unknown promises burning in Kol's eyes flooded Nes, but she recognized a wolf prepared to pounce the moment she offered a chase. Letting go of the insult soured Nes's stomach, but doing so was her safest bet. Swallowing the impulse to argue, Nessix took a deep breath and forced herself to move along.

"If you want a functional army, I'm not the important one, anyway. Disciplined, experienced men are needed to fill the roles of officers and to guide exercises. Though I'm flattered by the notion, you can't possibly expect me to do it all myself."

Kol stared at Nessix a moment longer, the disapproval of his glare pressing against her confidence until she feared it would crack. Just as she was about to cave under the disgusting notion of apologizing to a demon, Kol sighed, flung the pouch of crushed berries to the ground, and wiped his hand on the leg of his pants. "Careful there, little one. It almost sounds like you want us to go catch these dream soldiers for you. If you doubt your talents so much, I suppose bringing you a few more bodies could be arranged with little trouble."

Nes's gasp slipped from her before she had the chance to catch it. The last thing she wanted was to encourage the demons to harvest more innocents. She didn't know how much of Kol's words were a bluff or how easy it was to craft a mortal into an akhuerai, but she refused to be the reason even one more body joined her ranks. Horrified by the thought she'd placed in Kol's head, Nessix stumbled over trying to find her tongue.

"I'll take it you're content finding a way to work with what we've given you," Kol said.

Nessix snuck a glance at him. His eyes were back to laughing and she hated him that much more for it. Kol didn't need to resort to force to control her; he'd managed to uncover all those little strings she couldn't bear to have plucked. It dawned on her now that he might have been completely aware that she was attempting to use him. After all, Nessix was clever, but Kol had played this game far longer than she had. If he'd caught on to that most basic of her intentions, there was a chance he'd already deduced her aim to reach Zeal. Tactical mind in full swing, Nessix hastily buried her doubts beneath ignorance and the obedience Kol craved.

"Can you at least tell me what I need to train them for? How long do I have to make them a functional force?"

Kol cocked his head and leaned back, supporting his weight with arms braced on the stone behind him. "You're a smart girl. What do you think you're training them for?"

There was the evidence Nessix needed. Kol *was* on to her. Now her struggle would be to avoid letting him know she knew that. "The only purposes an army has are protection and war. I'm quite sure your kind doesn't need to hide behind anyone for safety, so I'm not raising this force to be bodyguards. That means you're planning to go to war."

Kol chuckled. "We've been at war our entire existence."

"And you still remain," Nessix said. "What need could you possibly have for us?"

"That's a fine question, isn't it?" Kol swung his weight forward and stood, taking two steps from Nessix.

He stood there with that arrogant nonchalance of his, daring Nessix to take a cheap shot at him. Kol was a smart man, smarter than Nessix wanted to admit, but it seemed as though he'd gotten accustomed to addressing simple minds. A lifetime of dealing with Veed had taught Nessix to see through no end of deception, especially when it came to a confident man's doubt. Kol's action of hiding his face from her, of answering her question with one of his own, confirmed exactly what she needed to know. This army was meant to strike on the surface, a move he suspected she wouldn't be pleased about. The demons felt cornered and were hiding behind a shield, after all.

With Kol's back to her, all Nessix had to do was keep the tone of her voice believable. She allowed her smirk to surface just a bit. "It's because your kind have gotten too strong, isn't it?" She murmured the question meekly, as if admitting the demons' superiority for the first time.

Before her, Kol didn't move. "We are stronger than any of you could fathom."

Nessix couldn't decide if that was a threat or a reassurance that the demons had grown gluttonous on confidence. "Which means the surface isn't even a concern for you. There's a war brewing down here in the hells, isn't there?"

This time, Nessix caught the slightest shift of Kol's shoulders and a contemplative tilt of his chin. She'd tricked him into opening his mind to the idea of her ignorance. Nessix bit back her smirk and veiled her eyes with stifled horror in case he turned around.

"Why would you suspect that?" Kol asked.

Unable to read whether Kol was trying to play her or if he was honestly attempting to understand her reasoning, Nessix cleared her throat. "I've seen the rise of power and how it seeks to devour those it considers inferior. My limited experience with your kind has shown that your soldiers hold loyalty to their generals and nobody else. Alliances may have been made, but only a fool would assume all demons were united. Your Grell and that Inek and whoever those other monsters were are seeking to dominate the rest of the demons, right? It's a very mortal dilemma, cast in a setting where an immortal army would be very beneficial. It's not a concept I'm unfamiliar with." Nessix spoke her declaration so concisely that she nearly believed it, herself.

Kol answered two seconds too slowly for Nessix to accept his reply, but that confirmed her suspicions adequately. "You are an astute woman," he said. "So now my question is, do you hate my kind enough to help me?"

Nessix narrowed her eyes at his back. Kol might have been playing her just as hard as she played him, but that question sounded like a request for allegiance. "Provide for me and my men what we need, protect me from those monsters you call your lords, and I will overthrow your kin."

Kol stretched out his arms and turned to face Nessix at last, a keen smile sharpening his features. "I've admired you since I first saw you on the field, little one. You haven't made me proud quite yet, but you're well on your way." He hesitated a moment then unclasped a flask from his belt and tossed it to her. "Do your best to keep me from waiting."

Nessix fumbled with catching the flask, having not expected any sort of offering. Her awkward receipt of Kol's untimely gift prevented her from objecting to his departure, so she missed her chance to ask if the demons would provide her men with weapons to train with. Either way, her first objective had been completed. She knew that her army was to strike the mortal world, and she was one step closer to gaining Kol's trust.

Opening the flask, she smelled the sweet aroma of wine and smiled. She wasn't the only one trying to win someone over. Confident in her ploy at last, Nessix recapped the wine to secure the flask to her belt and set off to reassure the frightened akhuerai that she could handle a couple demons.

TWELVE

Mathias didn't send a written message back to Julianna to share the limited insight he'd gathered in Heiligate. Granted, her temple full of diligent priestesses would have been able to do more with that information than he could on the road, but the chance of a physical message being intercepted was too great. Even speaking to Mehalco—trustworthy or not—was a risk Mathias wouldn't have taken if he'd been less invested in the case. He buried the two morsels of information in his mind and trekked down the road to the nearby town of Chilton.

He didn't enter this city with the intention of seeking more answers; sandwiched between Heiligate and Zeal, it was much easier—and far smarter—for any visiting demons to steer clear of it. Instead, Mathias came to stock up on supplies for a long flight.

His mind hadn't ventured far from Nessix in months, and given that she was his greatest motivation to carry out the quest of uncovering the demons' plans, he didn't expect her to leave any time soon. But Mehalco had confirmed his worst fears. The demons were building an army. They'd taken Nes's soul and her body. Shand had told him they had adequate insight on the nature of necromancy. A demon hunter by trade, risen from the grave to fight the undead, Mathias had put off thinking about what this meant for long enough. A dull throb pulsed behind his right eye as he continued to fight the truth.

Mathias purchased his rations, distracted from the shop keeper's attempts at small talk by the thoughts of Nessix being forced to lead the demons' army. The Nessix he knew would fight her captors, refusing to carry out a single order given to her, if not to keep true to her ethics, then out of spite. After all, it had taken Mathias months to convince her to comply with his guidance and suggestions, and he'd been trying to save her nation.

This was all assuming Nessix would still be the same bold and stubborn woman who put the needs of those she felt responsible for above her own well-being. The most basic of the undead functioned as mindless drones, flailing their way through what passed for life with only rudimentary, brutal instincts. At the top of the spectrum of the risen were the vampires, the corrupted individuals who pulled these puppets' strings. Their intentions, no matter what selected individuals claimed, had never been pure. But it was those servants that hung in the middle that truly frightened Mathias.

He had no qualms with cutting down risen corpses. They didn't think or feel, and releasing their bodies from function allowed their souls to flutter free of that final thread that tied them to the mortal plane. Neither did Mathias regret doing what he could to harm the vampires—they'd brought punishment on themselves through their acts of blasphemy. Though the Order had yet to find a way to permanently slay these juggernauts, Mathias and the blessings he carried had proven effective at thwarting them.

It was those poor souls trapped in the middle who Mathias wept for, even as he attempted to smite them. Typically seduced by the lies of eternal life, many entered their agreements without fully understanding the sacrifice of losing possession of their souls. Their masters would harvest them, draw on their energy for their own power, and dribble just enough of that essence back to keep their minions compliant, loyal, and deluded into not realizing they'd made a mistake.

Etha's creations were not meant to function without their souls, without that sacred tie which bound every living being to divinity. And the longer body and soul remained disconnected, the less stable the entire being became. Good people warped into reactive beasts, passive men would be provoked to murder over a simple misunderstanding. Even on her best days, Nessix had been prone to excitability, and Mathias feared how that would translate in her new existence.

"So you're convinced that's what happened to her?"

Mathias's tension seeped from him in an instant and drew his pain away. He closed his eyes and breathed in the first relaxed breath he'd taken in days before turning to face the young woman beside him.

"Everything points that direction," he said. The immediate weight had lifted from his shoulders, but that didn't stop the tick of guilt telling him that his worry ought to overcome even Etha's blessings.

She pawed through a curtain of hanging scarves, pulling a pink one from the bunch and cocking her head as she contemplated its hue. "You know… we do know someone who understands these kinds of terrible things much better than you do." She dropped the scarf back on its hanger and resumed sorting through them.

Mathias curled his lip and grumbled his opinion on the matter. "Before anything else, I'm heading to Elidae."

Etha frowned and tugged free a rich yellow scarf. "What do you expect to gain there?"

"Insight on how Brant's coping with his new position. Fulfillment of my promise to let him know when I've caught a scent."

She flung the scarf around her neck and twisted her shoulders about as she scrutinized herself in a mirror. "The information you've got is awful grim," she said. "Unless you plan to lie to him, in which case it'd serve you just as well to skip the visit altogether."

Irritation bubbled past that calm Etha had brought with her. An aching inclination to return to Elidae had plagued Mathias ever since he realized that the demons had been targeting Nessix for a greater purpose, and with Etha keen on pressing her agendas on him now, he was even more determined to distance himself from Abaeloth's main continents.

"Inwan's been regaining his might beautifully, hasn't he?"

Mathias smirked when Etha quit her twirling to glower at him. "Getting this information to him might allow him to investigate a few of his own avenues. Besides, I miss Sazrah."

Etha's brows fell flat. "Any other excuses you want to come up with? Do you suspect you left your favorite tea cup behind, too?"

Mathias heaved a sigh and cast his eyes toward the ceiling. He understood Etha's stance, truly he did.

"Then you should put on your brave paladin pants and go," she muttered to his internalized objections.

He lowered his gaze to her. "I will exhaust every last option that might exist before I go to Ceredulus for any sort of help."

Etha snorted. "You truly think anyone other than the god of the undead"—she lowered her voice and squeezed those words from the corner of her mouth, as not to draw alarm from surrounding patrons—"will be able to find you answers in a timely fashion?"

The smart side of Mathias, the part that calmly and rationally sorted through tedious politics and crucial battlefield tactics, agreed whole heartedly with Etha. The side of Mathias that had been the personal ragdoll for the god in question while the Veil was erected to contain his abominations longed to tell Etha that he didn't care *what* Ceredulus knew. Even if that last part wasn't entirely true.

"I think I'm following my instincts and the trail that's been laid out before me. Ask Jules to go talk to the old bastard."

Etha balled her fists and planted them on her hips. "She's frustrated enough with the two of us as it is."

Mathias cocked an eyebrow. "Jules is frustrated with *you*?"

"Well…" Etha twisted her lips and resumed digging through the scarves. "She hasn't openly admitted that part yet. But she's quite displeased with you. Besides, do you really think *he* would talk to *her*?"

Mathias frowned, no longer enjoying the humor of imagining Julianna's struggle to not appear disrespectful. It was through subduing the undead—their god included—that they had discovered how powerful Julianna was. Far more powerful than Mathias. The children gods had made note of this early on, likely one of the reasons Shand had targeted Mathias instead of the High Priestess to get even with the Order. Mathias could be ridiculed and scoffed at. He was Etha's shield, meant to take a good battering. Julianna, though, was Etha's sword, and none of the gods were quite ambitious enough to test how sharp she was.

"My heart says I need to go to Elidae," Mathias said at last.

"What does your head say?" Excitement sparked in Etha's eyes as she found a scarf that matched the one she'd previously selected. She tossed this one around her neck, too.

"My head says it wants to wake up from this nightmare."

Etha gasped, her eyes widening at Mathias's honesty, and she momentarily lost her desire to debate logistics with him. Mathias's long-standing rivalry with Ceredulus aside, Etha had almost forgotten how broken her paladin truly was. He'd faced death at the hands of a demon army. He'd endured tortures locked away from her in the hells. He'd witnessed the dead forced back to life, innocents claimed in the name of immortality. Mathias Sagewind had persisted through horrors greater than a goddess could ever hope to see her chosen go through, yet it had been the breaking of his heart, losing the one mortal whom he'd found himself kindred to, for him to feel so hopeless and lost. If Mathias had to return to Eliade for some sort of closure, Etha couldn't stop him.

"And how will you get there?" she asked gently.

Mathias closed his eyes, hoping that question marked the end of Etha's current debate. "I'd intended to take Ceraphlaks. Since I still don't know what I'm up against or where this quest will take me, I want to conserve my energy as much as possible." He opened his eyes and looked at the determination chiseled in Etha's firm jaw and strict brows. "Unless you're going to insist I find another way. If I'm to believe the rumors, Inwan's found a way to placate Havoc and open sea travel, though I'd prefer to avoid the time and attention that route would cost me."

Etha didn't debate the last, confirming its validity in doing so. "That, at least, is a very sound plan." She sighed and with a single blink, that fierce gravity flashed from her face, replaced by the glowing warmth Mathias preferred to receive from her. "It's just that—" She reached forward and grabbed his hand, glistening eyes looking up at him tenderly.

"I know," Mathias murmured. "I'll be careful. I'll be smart."

Etha bit her lower lip for just a second. "And you'll think about my suggestion?"

Much as Etha had few coping mechanisms for seeing Mathias helpless and desperate, he had very little immunity to his goddess's hope. She wouldn't have asked him to consider speaking to Ceredulus if she didn't think an audience with him would be worthwhile. That didn't make Mathias appreciate the idea any more.

"I'll remember you mentioned it," he said. "But let me play with this free will concept of yours a bit longer. Please?"

Her lips pursed and brows drooped lower over her eyes, though she didn't pursue the matter. She squeezed his hand once and let it go. "Safe travels, my love. I will only be a call away."

Mathias watched Etha turn and exit the shop, her air of comfort departing with her. Tension crept back into his shoulders as he contemplated whether or not he'd actually be able to find Nessix again. Even if he did, at the rate which demons broke their possessions, would he be able to save her? Mathias took a step forward, but was halted by the gruff bark of the shop keeper.

"Hey. Mister. You gonna pay for those?"

Mathias hesitated and turned to face the grumpy man.

"You know. Your girl's scarves."

The pain seeped back behind Mathias's eyes, and he turned to exchange coins for Etha's mischief.

THIRTEEN

It had taken Nessix nearly two weeks to integrate into the general population, but now that she'd found a common thread between the other akhuerai and herself, she made rapid progress with them. A sizeable group still resisted Nes's encouragement to learn how to fight, and she routinely directed the children to more innocent pastimes, but the majority of the men and women looked to Nessix for the guidance only she could give them. She'd gone from being sneered at and avoided to greeted with warmth and gestures of respect Kol had never seen even the most subservient akhuerai display to a demon. There had been no clear sign of what prompted this change, and while Kol longed to consider it a blessing, he couldn't stop the nagging concern that this rapid turn around had happened perhaps *too* abruptly. Grell, Ehsmil, and Annin breathing down his neck as they watched Nessix patiently put a group of eleven men through basic combative drills may have had something to do with his current degree of concern.

The four demons viewed the session in silence. If Nessix knew of their presence, she made no indication of it, too absorbed in her teaching to glance toward the top of the chasm. Her soul burned warm against Kol's chest and he fished it from where he kept it buried beneath his vest to interpret the message Nessix unwittingly sent him. The haze within the crystalline vessel glowed a pale and pure blue, brilliant sparks popping about in what Kol had learned to identify as confidence.

Ehsmil glanced at the vessel and tilted his head. The akhuerai intrigued him, but he'd never received insight on how to read souls. "That mean something important?" Ehsmil asked Kol, nodding toward the vessel.

Kol jolted back to his senses and cleared his throat as Grell turned his curled lip at him. "She's happy," he said. "Or as close to it as we can expect her to be."

Grell coughed. "Of course she's happy. She's teaching these undying creatures of yours how to kill us."

Kol laughed at the comment, but straightened himself when nobody in his company found the same absurd humor in the thought. "How to kill *us*?" Kol asked. "She's training her officers so the rest of the army can be formed. They're progressing exactly as we'd hoped. It just took a little longer than we'd expected."

Ehsmil raised a brow and glanced back down at the sparring. He scanned the greater area surrounding the modest training grounds to observe the groups of akhuerai sitting with each other as they watched the combat with varying degrees of interest. These noncombatants pointed at their engaged peers, leaning close to one another as they made observations and speculations of the tactics employed. Ehsmil glanced back at Kol, whose eyes were still locked on Nessix as she flung one of the men to the ground before she heaved a sigh and helped him back to his feet.

"Grell made a reasonable observation," Ehsmil said. "A week ago, she couldn't even engage these people in conversation. Today, she's trusting them enough to let them play around with her weapons. She's giving them orders that they're following without question." He slid his cunning eyes to Kol, watching closely for the alar's hidden thoughts on the matter. "She's gained a strong influence rather quickly. That couldn't have happened by luck, and they aren't following her out of fear, which means she either figured out a way to manipulate them or has given them a promise they've been waiting to hear."

Kol held his breath as those bold sparks popped about in Nes's vessel, then closed his hand around it before shoving it back in its place. "I've told you before, she's charismatic. These wretches have been waiting for a competent, benevolent leader for years. They've got one now, one who knows how to get people to love her. If you'd seen how she works those she's responsible for, you'd understand."

Grell spat and rolled his eyes. "She gets those she's responsible for to wage war against our armies," he said. "Ehsmil has a point."

"This is the entire reason we created the akhuerai," Kol countered. "We *want* her to train them. She's doing exactly what we told her to do."

Even as Kol spoke, Nessix called in her group of trainees, keeping the gestures that accompanied her explanations close to her body before nodding and sending the men out again. She beckoned them to charge her, and Kol watched in silence as she rushed to meet them, throwing her right shoulder at the nearest man and pointing at him. He openly scoffed at his failure and strode from the group, and Nessix flung her left shoulder forward, sending the next man away. At the end of her advance, she held both of her arms out to her sides and pulsed them forward. The remaining men stopped where they were and shook their heads before she lowered her arms and drew her would-be troops in to correct their mistakes. Both Grell and Ehsmil turned to Kol. He swallowed hard.

"Looks a bit like wing strikes and gusts to you?" Ehsmil asked.

The warmth drained from Kol's cheeks. Ehsmil, quite possibly the most reasonable inoga alive, didn't frighten him as much as Grell did, and so he didn't hesitate in delivering his excuse. "She thinks we're going to battle our kin from other regions," he said smoothly, his stance on the matter not quite firm enough to slow the thump of his heart. "It's reasonable for her to assume her troops would need such defenses in place."

"Did you tell her she'd be fighting our own?" Ehsmil asked.

"No," Kol said. "Our agreement was to keep her as unaware of our motives as possible. She reached this conclusion herself and I let her run with it. She's sworn fealty to me. I'm telling you, we're fine."

Ehsmil was as slow to anger as Kol could ever expect an inoga to be, but that alone didn't stop him from expressing his shrewd dissatisfaction. With a sharp tsking sound and pitying shake of his head, Ehsmil turned to leave. Alone with Grell and Annin's condescending gaze scratching at his back, Kol almost wished the other inoga would have stayed.

"You promised us an army," Grell said.

"I did."

"You told us they would be obedient out of fear of us."

"Yes."

"You swore they needed this Nessix to be their leader and that your obsession of keeping her close to you would ensure her loyalty."

Kol readily agreed with the first half of that statement, but found himself hung up on the last. He truly *had* believed Nessix had given him her obedience. She'd proven she trusted him as much as a once-mortal could trust a demon. Though she continued to snip at him when given the opportunity, she didn't debate his orders. For having been the ruler of an entire nation, Nessix had fallen into the role of subordinate with relative ease. But watching her guide her men through another feigned assault made Kol's insides roil with self-doubt.

"When was the last time you spoke to her?" Grell asked.

Kol lowered his head, realizing his error. Nessix was a beautiful creature of power, one that would seize it in full without consistent reminders that she couldn't have it. "Three days after your last assessment. I'll correct that immediately."

"See to it you do," Grell said. He cast a glance at Annin, whose dull expression suggested he was just as displeased with this new development, and turned to follow Ehsmil down the hall.

"For two weeks, you left her unchecked?" Annin asked in that casual, accusatory way of his.

Kol pressed his lips together and breathed out a brisk sigh. "I thought it would help her gain her people's trust," he said. "You know as well as I do that there's no way they'd have warmed up to her if they thought she was in my pocket."

"Yes, but was it worth the price of *her* forgetting she belongs in your pocket?"

Kol turned his head to glare at Annin, but the oraku kept his contemplative gaze directed at the scuffling men below. "I told Grell I'd make this right. I'm not stupid enough to lie to him."

Annin looked at his friend, eyes speculative as they judged him. "Are you sure about that?"

Patience burned to ashes from the recent interrogation, Kol was reluctant to address Nessix right now, afraid he'd do more damage than good in the process. What he feared even more, however, was how closely he danced with receiving one of Grell's beatings. Determined to prove that Nessix had no rebellious notions—or to put a stop to any she might be cultivating—Kol stepped off the edge of the chasm and shot toward the group of trainees without another word to Annin.

Sharp, startled screams from her audience were the only warnings Nessix and her men received of Kol's rapid approach, and even Nessix failed to save herself from the gust Kol shot at them with his wings. Dust and dirt rising up off the floor, the entire group was choked and momentarily blinded. Those with the weakest fortitude toppled to the ground and scrambled to distance themselves from the alar's arrival.

Taken by surprise and embarrassed by it, Nessix composed herself more quickly than the others. Shaking off the shock and spitting out a mouthful of dirt, she squared her shoulders and took a step forward to place herself between Kol and the men she'd only recently begun to cultivate confidence from. The fingers of her left hand rested against her scabbard, prepared to steady it for a hasty draw.

Kol smiled at Nes's reaction, a friendlier version of the gesture than she typically received from him, and he spoke to her in her native tongue. "You're settling in nicely."

Nessix bit down on the insides of her cheeks for a moment. "You told me not to disappoint, and I've always aimed to please."

He chuckled and swept his eyes across the men who struggled to hold their ground behind Nessix. They shifted around like frightened livestock, but didn't flee. It was an improvement from where they'd been the last time Kol came by for a visit. "And it looks to me and my colleagues that you've been making strides in their training. Have things been progressing smoothly?"

Nessix swallowed hard. Kol's body language suggested his pleasure with what she'd accomplished, but keen suspicion tainted the tone of his voice. Nessix would have been a fool to think the demons wouldn't recognize the tactics she'd been teaching her troops, but she'd already put in place the lie she hoped would protect them all from retribution. "They're eager students," she said evenly, "but all we've covered is some basic brawling. I won't allow them the risks of training with my weapons, and none of my requests for training arms seem to have gone through."

Kol's eyes twinkled at the subtle tremor he felt against his chest. "Ah, yes. But would we have a reason to trust the masses with arms?"

Nessix drew in a slow breath. So he *was* suspicious of her. "You told me to lead them. Told me to raise an army. Unless you're afraid of us, if you want this force to become even remotely functional, they'll need weapons eventually."

"And the tactics you've given them so far?"

"Basic hand to hand maneuvers."

"Huh," Kol mused. "It looked rather specific to me."

Nessix grit her teeth, heart beating faster. It had been years since she'd had to answer to authority, and grasping at excuses was much more difficult than she remembered.

Kol smirked as Nessix floundered for an explanation she didn't have. Seeing her rebounding confidence had elated the alar until Grell so rudely pointed out how rapidly she was becoming a threat. Witnessing her nervous tells as she struggled to confront him assured Kol that he hadn't lost her obedience. He turned from Nessix and her trainees, keeping an ear focused on her in case she decided to rush him from behind, and strode over to one of the crude benches on the sidelines.

The three akhuerai occupying the seat vacated it in a rush. One tripped in his hurry, grabbed by a friend and dragged away faster. This, too, pleased Kol, and he hoped it would alleviate Grell's bout of paranoia. Nessix could display every last deadly skill in her arsenal, but if her soldiers were too afraid to get close to a lone demon, they were unlikely to be a threat. Satisfied, Kol took his seat on the bench and looked up at Nessix.

"You didn't have to stop on account of me," he said. "These men still need so much work to meet my expectations; feel free to get them in order."

Nessix bit back the snarl that brewed at Kol's patronizing tone. He evidently suspected exactly what she was up to and was poised to put her plan to a firm stop. She stared at that patient gaze, delving as deeply into intellect she couldn't breach as he'd allow. This was a test, Nessix knew, but it was one she didn't know how to approach. Displeasing Kol meant losing the small margin of protection she had. Betraying him could mean something far worse.

In life, Nessix had been afraid to disappoint those around her, but in life, she'd understood the rules of the game. Few who had witnessed her failures had been bold enough to mention them, and those who were did so subtly and privately. Fewer people still had openly opposed her. Frustration boiled inside of Nessix as she faced yet another limitation she'd been unaware of. Through her inner turmoil, Kol watched patiently, his silent challenge irritating her even more.

Nessix cleared her throat and turned back to the men in training. They huddled close to each other, eyes wide and minds running rampant with an open panic that devoured every lesson they'd spent the past week learning. Nes's heart fell. Tactics wouldn't carry them far if they didn't have the courage to face the threat she was training them to stand against. How had Mathias raised Elidae's peasant force so quickly? Nessix sighed and lowered her head before turning back to face Kol.

"I'm afraid your presence has rattled them," she said. "Your men have embedded a deep fear in mine, and we've only just gotten to the point of physical assaults. Give me another week, and I'll have them willing and able to perform for you."

Kol stretched his shoulders and nodded slowly. "Are those men behind you your officer candidates?" His tone was mocking and cruel.

This time, Nessix let her sneer come forward and she jumped at the occasion to protect her men and her pride. At least Kol had the decency to speak his criticism in a tongue the trainees wouldn't understand. "They are," she said, chin raised.

Kol smirked and shook his head. "They're the best you could find?"

The intent of Kol's question slapped Nessix across the face. He *wanted* her to snap at him, looking for an excuse to punish or humiliate her before her men. Determination blossoming, she refused to give Kol that luxury. The akhuerai had overcome so much to get to this point. Kol didn't have to believe in them, because she did.

"There is no best in my ranks." A vague swirl of her old confidence rippled about inside of her. "We train and fight as equals. Different strengths, maybe, but none without value. That is the way of my people."

"Fleman or akhuerai?" Kol asked, hiding his impression of Nes's words more carefully than he'd previously done.

She crossed her arms. "Does it matter?"

Kol shrugged and stood, prompting another nervous shuffle from the crowd. "You tell me."

Nessix didn't understand much about how akhuerai functioned, so she was completely oblivious to how clearly Kol felt the nervous flutter of her heart echoed in the pendant he wore. She had no way to know that he was aware of her fear and doubt. Any attempts she made to hide her feelings would fail her, but that was exactly the way Kol wanted it.

Ignorant to this intimate insight Kol had of her inner workings, Nessix voiced an indignant hiss. "I pity you."

Kol blinked and gave an abrupt shake of his head. Neither the message nor the timing of its delivery matched the sensations ricocheting through Nes's vessel, and she had taken the liberty of delivering the sentiment in the demons' tongue—a language the akhuerai were all fluent in. Heat welled up inside of Kol, anger and humiliation stacking on top of the agitation Grell had previously dug out of him. It would be beyond satisfying to tear into Nessix for the remark, but the subtle part of his self-control threw sand on that fire, suppressing it before it had the chance to fully ignite.

"*What* did you say?"

The bulk of the population gasped and cringed at the danger

in Kol's words, and tears stung Nes's eyes as she forbid herself the same response. Swallowing the tremor that tried to climb up her throat, Nessix repeated herself. "I pity you. Sir."

The curtness of the final address muddled Kol's ire, towing his urge to snap at Nessix back to the instinctive side that he'd long ago trained to behave. He'd given up on the idea of gaining the whole of Nes's respect and suspected pride would have kept her from dropping such a title lightly. He revisited the message sent from her soul vessel, still feeling that thread of uncertainty, but perhaps he'd misinterpreted its cause. Either way, Kol suspected he didn't know Nessix half as well as he'd convinced himself he did.

"And why is that?" he snapped.

"The structure of your hierarchy is so broken that you have no choice but to live in your position. There's no true merit to your rank besides brute strength, forcing you to serve reactive imbeciles whose rashness would see them dead if not for their muscles. Value, to your kind, is based solely off one trait, the ability to control and repress those weaker than you, and you've *all* deluded yourselves into thinking this is the only way to live that those of lower rank readily throw their lives away for the benefit of those at the top. It's no way to live. Not even for demons."

Kol stared at Nessix, eyes wide and holding his breath for several heartbeats. A good ruler would have a firm grasp of how societies functioned, even ones that weren't her own, but Kol hadn't expected Nessix to fling such honesty at him. The simple truth was that Nessix was right. The much more difficult truth was that Kol had always been happier forbidding himself from thinking about how his own authority, gifted to him by a long-dead goddess, had been stolen from him by something as trivial as someone else's war. The tremor of Nes's soul had calmed, suggesting she'd spoken her observation with certainty and for the briefest moment, Kol brimmed with enough hatred that he wanted to launch a one-man assault on Grell. All he had, though, was a chasm full of frightened akhuerai and the annoying confidence of the woman who had pulled the truth into the light.

Nessix was well armed and protected by the bulk of her armor, promising Kol would not have an easy time of taking his frustrations out on her. She'd be bound to fight back and had been watching him with such expectations since he landed. Not to mention how a senseless act of frustration would complicate her future obedience. Arms trembling with the desire to wring Nes's neck for reminding him of his position, Kol stalked forward until Nessix was just outside of his grasp. The fact that she held her ground with the stalwart fearlessness she'd learned to employ against entire armies of demons only enraged him further.

"You speak awful boldly of matters you know nothing about," he growled, voice quiet and eyes commanding her to reply in kind.

Nessix respected the order, going one step further by slipping into her mother tongue. "I've pushed you since the moment I woke up and this is the first time I've seen you fight so hard to not lose control of yourself. I suspect I know more about it than you'll admit."

Snarling with a wave of agitation, Kol slapped Nessix across the face before she registered he'd moved. Several startled yelps and gasps shot up from the lingering crowd and Nessix—unmoved by the offense, save biting back a startled cry of pain—held out a hand to instruct them to stay back. She met Kol's eyes calmly, silently stating that she knew she was right, and Kol could not deny her honestly. He didn't know where she had come up with these conclusions, but that unnerving tick of apprehension that tumbled throughout Kol told him that this was the exact sort of thing Annin and Grell wanted him to put to an end.

Kol nodded slowly, eyes narrowing as he came to terms with what he had to do. Nessix was far too valuable to risk losing over what was ultimately a minor offense, but ignoring her play for authority would only prompt more attempts in the future. Besides, the idea of Nessix being harmed left a hollow spot in Kol's stomach that he was afraid to address. Steadying the small amount of diplomacy he had to work with, Kol took two steps back and looked over the crowd.

"Your general has been teaching you well." His voice carried easily through the hushed expanse as everyone tried to figure out what to make of a demon's compliment. "And I trust your desire to learn how to protect yourselves has made you diligent students."

Nessix tilted her head, watching Kol keenly. She hadn't anticipated him crediting the akhuerai for anything.

"You—" Kol pointed at Auden Clement, the nearest of the men he'd watched Nessix schooling. "She tells me you're one of her officer candidates?"

The man stood rigid, jaw clenched and limbs twitching as he contemplated how best to use his adrenaline. No inkling to fight or need to run could force his tongue to wrap around an answer, and he sent a pleading gaze to his general.

Nessix met Kol's unspoken challenge smoothly. "You are safe to answer him, Auden," she said. "Better off for it, in the long run."

Auden gulped, rasped a vague sound, then cleared his throat. "It's what she told me."

"Do you consider yourself competent in what she's taught you so far?"

Nessix narrowed her eyes at this, prepared to leap to Auden's defense if the need became apparent. Since Kol had relaxed his stance, she considered the risk low and nodded to Auden.

"I... suppose so?"

Kol twisted his lips in a mild disapproval at the man's lack of confidence. "I guess that will have to be enough. Congratulations, you've been promoted to commander of this army."

As Auden's jaw sagged, eyes wide as he frantically looked between Nessix and Kol, Nessix turned her full attention to the demon. "What is the meaning of—"

Kol held up a hand to draw a stubborn and offended silence from Nes's rebuttal. "Your general has just informed me that she's in need of a better understanding of my kind in order to fully benefit the lot of you." He walked forward and grasped Nes's elbow, his grip crushing down on her until she gave a subtle squirm to try to free herself. "Unfortunately, this means you'll have to continue training in her absence."

Nessix longed to scream at Kol and try to fight him, considering she had no idea what he was talking about, but she refused to risk the young army's safety. Neither did she dare to make demands of Kol to ensure none of his colleagues chose to mess with them while she was gone. It was best not to put ideas in his head. Auden was a good, competent man who Nessix had related to Sulik from the very start, and he'd taken to her lessons well enough. Even if Kol kept her away for days, she'd given her army a foundation to stand on, provided they mustered the courage to do so.

"All will be well," Nessix told the group amid their concerned murmurs. "You've come so far and once I've got my answers, I'll be back to pick up where we left off." Lying to people she cared about made Nessix feel like a monster. All she could do was hope that they assumed she was going to gather information to use in the future. And that Kol truly intended to bring her back.

Let them think this was my idea, she thought to combat the nervous flutter of her heart. *It beats whatever Kol likely has planned...* She shuddered at the thought, assaulted by no end of speculations of the potential torment he had in mind.

Kol didn't wait for farewells or extra guidance. The longer he allowed Nessix to linger, the greater her chances of growing noncompliant or the akhuerai discovering their nerve. Tucking Nessix in the security of his embrace, pleased that she didn't fight him, Kol lifted off from the chasm floor so he could teach Nessix the workings of demon society.

FOURTEEN

As Ceraphlaks and Mathias approached the island of Elidae, weariness demanded the paladin rub his eyes to make sure he comprehended the scene ahead of him. The mountainous coast clawed at the horizon, but a sinister cluster of obsidian clouds loomed low over the peaks, fierce bolts of lightning striking against the mountainsides and tracing dangerous webs through the clouds. Ceraphlaks didn't need the subtle shift of Mathias's weight to alter his course from that ominous display. The pair had flown to the sacred island twice before and hadn't caught so much as a scent of Havoc's storms either time. Mathias prayed this didn't have anything to do with the sea travel he'd heard rumors about.

The closer they flew, the stronger the wind pulled, dragging Ceraphlaks toward the torrents of rain and deadly bolts. As the pegasus fought against the gusts, Mathias squinted into the storm's heart. Visibility skewed by sheets of rain and the strobe of lightning, in the brief moments Mathias could see past the after images of each flash, he swore he caught a steady golden glow floating above the churning water.

"You're going to hate me for this..."

Ceraphlaks swiveled an ear back to his rider and wrung his tail. Nothing good ever followed those words from Mathias.

"Yeah," the paladin sighed. "I want you to fly into that."

Ceraphlaks groaned a weary snort and contemplated the consequences of dumping Mathias into the ocean before resigning himself to bank toward that blasted light.

The closer they neared the storm, the less control Ceraphlaks had over his flight. Even backed by divinity, the strength of the gales buffeted him in the sky. It wouldn't be the first time Ceraphlaks questioned his rider's sense of judgement. At any second, any slight misplacement of balance or orientation, he risked losing control and plummeting them both from the sky. A brief glance at the churning water below unveiled a great whirlpool spinning so fiercely it gave the illusion of baring teeth. Water soaked through feathered wings and saturated Mathias's clothing, forcing a greater effort from Ceraphlaks. The pegasus questioned why he still trusted his rider.

They progressed slowly through the darkened sky, pressing closer to that golden glow. Enveloped by the storm, they had no choice but to move forward, and after excruciating minutes, the glow brightened to reveal a massive metal dock jutting nearly a mile from the mountainside, suspended in the air. Mathias smirked and shook his head. Mortal hands never could have built a structure such as this. A few more beats of Ceraphlaks's wings and the silhouette of a man dancing blithely in the rain became visible. A few more, and Mathias distinguished peals of laughter cutting through the storm's howling. Mathias closed his legs around Ceraphlaks to ask for another burst of energy.

"What is the meaning of this madness?" Mathias called.

The roaring wind devoured his words from mundane ears, but they flowed with clarity to the divine. Inwan ceased his dance and spun to face Mathias, crossing his arms defensively. The god didn't lower himself to shouting back and waited in the pelting rain for Ceraphlaks to land. Hooves slipping on wet metal, it took the pegasus two attempts to safely ground himself and the moment Mathias dismounted, he spun his haunches to the wind.

Neither Mathias nor Inwan were particularly fond of one another, grudges for past transgressions not yet forgiven, but they'd cultivated what passed for respect. Either way, Inwan's crossed arms and stony pout suggested he was more than simply embarrassed that Mathias caught him acting like a fool.

The platform vibrated against Mathias's feet as he sized up the god, no more intimidated now than he had been when Inwan first staggered back to Elidae. Mathias brushed off the tremor as simple strain against the storm until the distinct sound of a large chain clanking in the wind squeezed through the driving rain.

"I repent!" The voice which called from beneath the platform was shrill and horrified, raked raw from a prolonged bout of screaming. "Mercy! I beg you, mercy!"

Mathias furrowed his brows and looked sideways at Inwan. Last he'd checked, Inwan had leaned far more to the light than this behavior suggested. The paladin's scrutiny didn't bother Elidae's guardian, and he met Mathias's suspicion with an authoritative gaze.

"Oh, shut up, whelp!" Inwan snapped to the voice's cries.

Below them, Havoc belched a hearty spray of briny water.

"I repent! I'll do anything! I swear it!"

Inwan rolled his eyes as Mathias identified the guilt in the voice at last. "Is that… Renigan Falk?"

Pride swelled Inwan's chest as he smirked, eyes glittering. "Sure is."

Mathias nodded slowly. He wasn't the kind to promote torture, but the weasel in question owed Elidae much more than a few terrified moments dangled above a man-eating sea after the pain he'd caused. Mathias stamped a foot against the platform and craned his neck to try gaining a glimpse of how Renigan was contained. "Will this setup hold against Havoc?"

Inwan shrugged. "It has so far."

"And this is how you opened Elidae's ports?"

Inwan's smirk broadened to a boastful grin as Renigan continued to sputter for help. "Havoc leaves the ships alone as long as she thinks she's getting fed. I can't be sure how long it'll take her to get wise, but I'll take advantage of her while I can."

The concept was cruel and unusual, something a man of justice shouldn't have tolerated, but Mathias couldn't argue. "A brilliant use of resources, and a fitting sentence for the wretch."

Inwan's pride inflated even further at Mathias's compliment. He opened his mouth and flourished a hand, prepared to brag of his cleverness when he realized Mathias wouldn't have made the trip to Elidae without good reason. The smugness drained from his face, replaced with a childlike longing. "Have you brought news? Of my Nes?"

Mathias's eyes drifted from the god to study the splattering rain at his feet. "I've got a couple flimsy leads, but that's it."

Inwan's scoff pulled Mathias's attention back up, though the glistening in his eyes assured that he desperately wanted to avoid offending the paladin. "Then why did you bother coming?"

"Mind reeling that dog back in so we can talk someplace dry?"

Inwan looked from Mathias to the sea churning beneath them and twisted his lips in dissatisfaction. "I have to secure safe passage for the ships," he grumbled, not meeting Mathias's eyes.

The paladin cocked his head. "How long ago were they scheduled to set sail?"

"Does it matter?"

The bitterness in Inwan's voice spoke clearly of how hot his drive for vengeance burned and Mathias realized they'd waste the entire day if he didn't give first. "I know you've got good intentions," Mathias said, careful not to incriminate himself with any other commendations. "And I know you would never do anything to betray your alignment. I'll leave you to your job of distracting Havoc. For Elidae, of course."

Inwan blinked in laughable confusion, having thought he'd have to work harder to fend off Mathias. "Where are you going?"

"To meet with the general—"

"That would be unwise."

Mathias furrowed his brows. He and Brant had a cordial relationship at best, but they'd parted on good terms. Or so he thought. "Has something happened?"

Inwan rolled his eyes and turned away from Mathias so he could behold the raging storm that flung Renigan around so helplessly. "You've got no news of Nessix. You made Veed's troops *very* unhappy with the old Teradhel force. And you were the one who brought that demon hunter here, right?"

Mathias pinched the bridge of his nose and nodded at Inwan's back. "Yes…" he groaned. What trouble had Sazrah made for

Elidae…?

"Then you'd be wise to skip visiting with Brant."

Everything about Inwan's words raised Mathias's suspicions and motivated him more to venture inland to seek information on Elidae's status. "Sulik?"

Inwan hummed his contemplation. "A much safer bet if you're adamant on reports of current affairs."

That was precisely what Mathias was after. Inwan had made no indication that he was ready to relieve Renigan from his punishment, and Mathias no longer felt it was his place to scold this particular god. "Very well. Try not to let Renigan die yet. He's still got a lifetime of suffering in him."

Inwan grunted a reply and waved a disinterested hand in Mathias's direction in a farewell gesture. Eager to get out of the rain, Mathias turned without complaint. He dismissed Ceraphlaks, who departed readily, then spent a pinch of energy to whisk his soaked self to Sulik's dry chamber.

The commander occupied one of the suites in the Teradhel fortress, with multiple chambers to house himself, his wife, and previously his two sons. He kept his quarters tidy, no obvious hints at the wealth that accompanied his station present.

Dripping everywhere his soggy steps took him, Mathias dragged a plain wooden chair to a strip of floor left uncovered by rugs and sat to wait on his friend's return. Too many memories lurked about this fortress, hardships and delights Mathias continued to regret having experienced. He glanced through the room and contemplated looking for something to read to keep his mind from traipsing down the roads of happiness that should have existed within these walls.

Mathias used the excuse of avoiding damage to the books from his soggy status as to why he never rose to select one, but the truth was that he coveted these memories too much to distract himself. He'd stood with Elidae through her hardest trial. He'd fallen in love with this land, with her people. Mathias had spent lifetimes travelling the reaches of Abaeloth, questing on those impossible missions reserved for him, yet Elidae was the first place to keep a piece of his heart. He'd wanted so much more for this country. Mathias hung his head; he hadn't needed a reminder as to why he was on this quest. Perhaps he'd been a fool to come to Elidae so soon and with so few leads.

The door to Sulik's chamber swung open, yanking Mathias from the dismal path he crept down. So wound up in the treacherous ways of demons and gods, he jumped to his feet, hand flying to his sword, just as Sulik cursed and reached for his own. Within the same breath, the weathered commander recognized his old friend and chuckled warmly, rushing forward to embrace him.

"Sir Sagewind! Please tell me you're here with good news."

Heart easing with Sulik's gentle smile, Mathias relaxed and returned the chair to its spot. "It's not with bad news, at least. I've got a couple leads on my quest—names only, but that's a start—and wanted an update on the situation here to see if there was anything that might help me tie them together."

Sulik's shoulders drooped and he glanced away from Mathias, bustling off to dig through a trunk tucked toward the back of the sitting room. "The situation here..." He rummaged around a bit longer and produced a towel, which he tossed to Mathias. "It's... it's chaos, sir. Packs of demons are hiding in the wilderness and the abandoned townships. Civil rebellions—increasing in force by the day—have sprouted up while everyone's trying to sort out their loyalties again. Our own kingdom is in distress, calling for funds we don't have so they can rebuild. And that Sazrah..." Sulik blew out a slow breath and shook his head.

Mathias's heart dropped and his brows furrowed. That was the second time she'd been mentioned as a potential problem. Sazrah was a strong personality to be sure, but her heart was good and Mathias had never known her to bring trouble to anyone who wasn't a demon. "Has she been causing problems?" Mathias vigorously rubbed the towel through his hair and patted the residual moisture from his arms.

"Not... directly." Sulik scratched the back of his neck. "She's the one who encouraged Inwan to find a way to open the seas." Sulik's explanation trailed off with a grimace and a pathetic squeak in the back of his throat.

Mathias cocked his head. There had to be more to the issue

than that. "I'd think that would be considered a victory."

Sulik picked at his cuticles to avoid looking at Mathias. "For the country, it is. We desperately need the resources to rebuild and the skilled labor and soldiers from your homeland."

"So how is it a problem?"

Sulik walked closer to Mathias so he could lower his voice. "These new laborers and soldiers are bringing their religions with them. Religions that have nothing to do with Inwan."

"Ah." Mathias nodded in understanding as he tried to wring some of the extra water from his pants into the towel. "I take it the citizens are showing interest in these new religions?"

Sulik nodded. "Inwan hasn't even been back with us for a year, and after you brought Etha to Elidae, people's minds have opened. Inwan's not handling their curiosity well."

At least the god's decade-long detention seemed to have stuck with him. "But he's still keeping the seas open? I'd have thought he'd do anything to save his influence and reputation."

"By keeping the ships sailing, he *is* saving his influence and reputation. Elidae is in too great a need for resources for him to bar transportation. Brant, Etha bless him, has done his best with what Elidae had, but the needs were too urgent and too great. This was the only viable solution."

Mathias finished drying off. "Is Brant doing well?"

Sulik coughed and shifted his weight to look over his shoulder around the otherwise vacant room.

"Easy, Commander. I'm not an officer here anymore. You can tell me things I don't want to hear without feeling disobedient."

The reassurance allowed Sulik to face Mathias again, but he only reluctantly met his eyes. "Brant is doing everything *but* well. I feel it'd be best if you avoided him until you have good news to deliver."

Given Inwan's blunt suggestion, Mathias had figured as much. The idea disappointed him, as he'd hoped to see firsthand how the young man was faring in his role as general, but those who knew Brant best advised against it. Mathias would honor their judgement. "Sazrah, then?"

Sulik's reluctance disintegrated into a nauseous wince and he shifted away from Mathias. "That's the biggest reason Brant's..." He scratched behind his ear and averted his eyes. "Sazrah... Well, she left, sir."

Mathias shook his head to scatter his exclamations of disbelief, the towel plopping to the floor. "What do you mean, she *left*?"

Sulik peeked at Mathias from beneath uneven brows and inched closer to retrieve the towel. "She cleared out half our vacant cities, organized an elite force, and helped integrate some members of the Order into our ranks. Things were going great until about a week ago when she quit talking to anyone. A few days later, she left a note stating only that she'd return, and was gone."

The concept of Sazrah abandoning an assignment couldn't quite register to Mathias. She was the most reliable warrior he'd ever known, far more reliable than he was, himself. For her to simply walk away was unheard of. Unfortunately, she'd left no details of her whereabouts, which meant not even Mathias would be able to track her down, assuming he had the time. In the end, he trusted Sazrah explicitly; she must have had a sound reason to leave.

Mathias pressed his fingers to his temple and sighed. "When she returns, can you give her a message for me?"

Sulik relaxed at Mathias's ready acceptance of the report. "Of course."

That was better than nothing. "Tell her we're looking for an alar named Kol. Have her ask around. She'll know what you mean."

Sulik nodded and tucked the name away safely in his mind. "Do you plan to come back to receive her reports?"

Mathias mulled over the idea. This civil unrest Sulik had mentioned was undoubtedly tied directly to Mathias's assassination of Veed. Brant didn't deserve the complications that would come from his return. Paramount, though, were the bittersweet memories that whispered their unfulfilled promises to him. Etha, as always, had been right. It was best if Mathias kept his distance for a while. He sighed, dissatisfied.

"She'll be able to get word to me," Mathias said.

Sulik had long ago quit doubting Mathias when he mentioned

a feat that sounded improbable, and accepted his answer smoothly. "It was good to see you again, sir. Keep your head down."

Mathias twisted his lips. He fully intended to disregard Sulik's gentle request for him to avoid peril, though Sulik was likely well aware of that. "You too, Commander."

The paladin saw himself out of Sulik's quarters and left the Teradhel fortress behind once again.

FIFTEEN

Kol didn't release Nessix when they reached the top of the chasm, as it wouldn't have fit his objective of reclaiming the frightened respect of the akhuerai for them to see her walk away on her own free will. She kept still in his arms, her soul overtaken by such a deep chill that it forced a brief shiver from Kol. Unlike the delightful tremors of fear, the radiant glow of bliss, or the elating jolts of rage, this cold was not an emotion Nessix had succumbed to before. Curiosity was what prompted Kol to land and let go of her at last.

Any other demon releasing anyone else would have expected their captive to run, but Kol didn't fear such a response from Nessix. She was too proud to run from him, too smart to think she could escape. Both that pride and intelligence kept her from turning to face him, and he allowed her that privacy for now. She didn't tremble with fear or reluctance, and she held her shoulders loosely.

"What are you feeling?" Kol asked, a creeping need to warm the chill seeping into him from her vessel, urging him to remedy whatever problem Nessix struggled with.

Kol had come to expect little fights from Nessix when he pushed her for insight. He considered it part of her charm. What he didn't expect was her to spin on him, fearless eyes blazing with demands. "Out with it. What are you planning?"

"You don't get to ask—"

"I'll ask whatever I damn well please!" Nessix said. "You wanted the general in me? You wanted me to find my confidence? Well, you've got it. And you will tell me where you are taking me and why."

All of Nessix's outward signs pointed toward rage, yet that numbing chill remained. If she hadn't been standing in front of him, Kol would have pulled her vessel from hiding to see if her soul had somehow leaked free or perished, but it was a risk he couldn't take. In the early phases of their research, Kol and Annin had been careless and allowed the akhuerai full awareness of the other halves of their souls, thinking the information would leverage good behavior from their creations. Instead, it had triggered an obsession with obtaining completion, causing senseless acts of violent desperation from the akhuerai as they tried to reunite their broken souls. Nessix, as powerful and sharp as she was, could never find out that Kol carried any part of her soul with him.

What Nessix showed now wasn't anger, Kol realized. It was a righteous entitlement, the strictness that came from a leader who had forgotten how to fear her opponent. Unlike her previous fits of obstinance, she didn't clench her jaw or make twitchy moves toward her sword. Kol could have tried for the rest of the day to reestablish fear and respect in Nessix, but she'd entered a dangerous frame of mind where she freely accepted that her safety no longer mattered. Like every brave warrior who had fought before her, Nessix was prepared to die before fleeing or submitting to an unjust hand. The next cold wave that coursed through Kol hadn't come from Nes's soul, but the thought that Grell had been very right to be concerned about the direction she was heading.

Meeting Nessix's calculated confidence with anything other than patience promised an altercation Kol preferred to avoid, so he looked past the disgusted curl of her lip and the haughty lift of her chin. Somewhere, she had to know the gamble she made by taking this stand—evident by the fact that she tried to talk her way through her concerns as opposed to fighting or running. Kol's control over Nessix was becoming increasingly slim, but as long as even a pinch of uncertainty repressed her, she still belonged to him.

"As I told you, little one, I'm taking you to have a history lesson. It'll do you good."

Nessix crossed her arms. "I know everything I need to about your kind. I'd rather be taught the how and why behind me and my people."

Kol sucked his tongue and shook his head. "That's something I cannot do for you."

"Of course you can." Her words carried a most tempting challenge, begging Kol to prove himself capable of that which he'd just claimed was impossible.

Kol had received an abundance of begging and pleading in his time as a demon. He'd been promised goods and services far beyond the capabilities of those more terrified of him than Nessix had ever been. He'd conned dozens into doing his bidding under the guise of some sort of friendship, but he'd never had anyone he outranked attempt to give him an order, let alone with the genuine expectation of his compliance. Kol gripped the hilt of his dagger to keep from reaching for Nes's vessel to gauge how sure she was of herself, and that action was enough to draw a brief ping of doubt through the chilly steel of Nes's determination. She kept her arms crossed, but shifted her left shoulder back, prepared to grab for her sword. It hadn't been Kol's intention to put Nessix on the defensive, but he'd capitalize on the opportunity.

Breathing out his tension on a slow breath, Kol slid his fingers to a more effective position around the dagger's hilt, a warm tingle of anticipation caressing his chest. He still had her. "You're right," he said. "I can tell you everything about the akhuerai. But I won't. Knowing your history won't mean a thing without first knowing mine."

Nessix let her arms drop to her sides, trying to appear casual as her left hand drifted closer to her dagger. "Then you'll teach me both."

Kol narrowed his eyes. He'd grown accustomed to the stubborn side of Nessix, and he often found pleasure in the feisty arguments she offered him. This time, though, she was making an indisputable stake for control. He didn't like the surge of disgust and disappointment he felt toward Nessix any more than he liked thinking about what would happen to him if he couldn't control her.

"This is not a debate we should be having," he warned her coolly, aware of her eager preparations to strike.

"Then let's not debate it," Nessix replied in kind. "Have I not served you as you've asked me to?"

Relief soaked through to Kol's bones. She'd opened this door herself. "No, you haven't." He smirked at Nes's defiant tremble of indignation. He trusted she wouldn't jump him until he explained himself just as well as he knew she wouldn't be able to dispute his evidence. "For the most part, you've surrendered to me, and I do have to give you credit for that. But the mission I assigned you was to raise an army. You've had plenty of time to do so and absolutely pitiful results to show for it."

A steady flow of prickling warmth from Nes's soul tickled Kol's chest, and he smiled. It had taken some prodding, but he'd uncovered her doubt and shame at last. This debate was nearly behind them.

"I've done the best I can with what I've been provided," Nessix said.

"I didn't tell you to do your best. I told you to raise an army."

Nessix clenched her teeth behind pursed lips and for a moment, Kol wondered if she'd snap and draw her weapon. He'd never considered her a woman of noteworthy restraint, but even through her frustration, her political mind plodded steadily on. She wouldn't jeopardize the safety of her people, not after she'd worked so hard to connect with them, and Kol hadn't once made an effort to suggest that he wouldn't use them to force her compliance. Nessix couldn't afford to fight Kol, and she knew it.

Erupting with an entertaining growl of aggravation, Nessix spun from Kol and marched down the hall, tight fists swinging rigidly at her sides. Kol allowed himself a chuckle loud enough to bounce off the passage walls, and strolled behind her.

"Where are you going, little one?"

Those swinging fists shook at the ends of trembling arms. She had no idea where she was going, only that the sooner she learned this history Kol was so concerned about, the sooner she could return to her budding army. "To learn," she spat.

"Do you plan on storming the halls until you stumble upon a history book?"

She bristled at the amusement in Kol's voice. "I'll interrogate the first underling I find until I get what I need to know, since you don't have the decency to help me."

Kol smirked. "An indecent demon. I never would have thought."

Nessix didn't respond, continuing on with her irate stalking until Kol got bored with her tantrum. As much as he enjoyed toying with Nessix, he wouldn't forget that he was being watched.

"What happens if you don't run into an underling first?" he asked. "What if you go raging around the next bend and run into an inoga?"

Nessix snapped to a quick halt at the mention of those brutes. On her good days, she wasn't quite afraid of Kol, but she shivered when she thought back on Inek's massive fist crashing down at her skull. Kol had proven himself influential and able to easily boss around lesser ranked demons, but he'd already proven that couldn't protect her from the temper and might of inoga.

Kol stopped a pace from Nes's back. "I take it you're inclined to follow me, then?"

Shaking with a storm of mixed emotions, Nessix shifted her weight to turn and glare at Kol's irritating smile. Still so patient. Still so confident. Still claiming possession of her. If Nessix hadn't surrendered to the fact that she needed Kol, she'd have wished him dead.

Kol met her eyes, silently telling her, *That's right. You're mine.* He strolled past her, catching her behind the elbow with the gentle touch of two fingers to draw her forward. Burning inside with hatred from this helplessness the demons had forced onto her, Nessix stalked ahead with an obedience rooted in her desire to keep her people safe and to avoid a second encounter with an inoga.

They walked in silence, as Nessix didn't know how much further she could push Kol before he retaliated against her demands. She was well aware of how much confidence the past couple weeks of training had returned to her, and she easily recalled how often that confidence had led her to make poor decisions in the past. This was the first interaction she'd had with Kol since the time he stopped by to insult her troops, and Nessix had to weigh the fact that it had been that long since she'd been able to work on winning him over. Sliding back into the submissive role of trying to please this demon did not come with the grace she'd hoped for.

Before long, Kol and Nessix reached a more populated passageway and the alar shed his posture of casual cockiness. He squared his shoulders, pressed his wings back and lifted the tips ever so slightly—his subconscious way of making himself appear a fiercer opponent. A quick glance at his expression showed that the mirth had left his eyes, replaced with strict instructions to give him and his charge space. The smirk was gone, hidden behind a strong jaw that sharpened Kol's lean features with a frightening edge. His hand, strong and protective, braced high between Nes's shoulder blades. Nessix might have forgotten that she was trying to use Kol as a safety net, but it seemed he'd never let it slip from his mind. Beside herself, Nessix soaked in the comfort of Kol's protection and that tightly coiled ball of tension that hung at the base of her spine relaxed just a bit.

"Where are we going?" Nessix asked again, this time in a more subdued tone.

Kol clenched his teeth in several small bursts of contemplation, gaze steadily sweeping across the demons they passed by. "I'd planned to lock you in the library until you learned what you need to." His voice no longer mocked Nessix as she'd grown used to, and it would have raised the hairs on the back of her neck, had his hand not slid there. "But it seems this confidence you found has been readily observed."

On a normal day in the mortal realm, Nessix would have taken those words as a glowing compliment. She glanced through the crowd Kol kept such a wary eye on, and the compliment instantly lost its value. Lustful eyes followed her, the throaty rumble of threats and challenges and promises leaving the boldest of the demons. They hungered to test her, to seek retribution for her part in their defeat on Elidae. Those greedy gazes drank up Nes's courage as though it was an elixir that would cure them of the curse they carried, eager to claim rights to her.

Fortunately, Nessix had Kol.

As long as he held his aggressive posture and speared these underlings with his warding glare, Nessix was safe. The timid flutter of her reluctance beat against Kol's chest and she bowed her head to mask the boldness that so badly enticed the masses.

"So if you're not leaving me in a public location, where are we going?" Knowledge no longer seemed worth the risk; all Nessix wanted to do was return to her chasm, where she was safe and respected—not coveted—for her confidence.

"My quarters," Kol said simply.

Nessix balked at his words, but only for a fraction of a heartbeat before Kol's touch reminded her to keep moving. Kol liked her, at least as much as she could expect a demon to like a mortal, but he'd done a terrible job hiding the fact that he considered her his property. On the receiving end of so many vile leers, Nessix loathed to think about what a demon who was actually *fond* of her might do to her.

"I will arrange for your safety," he said, voice low though he still pressed close to her. "You'll retain nothing if you're constantly waiting for an attack."

Nes's entire plan revolved around gaining Kol's favor, but the concerns flitting through her now made her wonder whether or not that had ever been a sound plan. "And after I learn what you want me to?"

"You'll be returned to your army. They can only do so much with what little you've taught them and will need you back to finish the job."

If Nessix wouldn't have been so determined to keep from looking up at the beasts around her, she'd have glanced up at Kol. His terse words had been delivered as both a promise and an insult, and Nessix accepted them as such. After all, Kol was all that stood between her and dozens of predatory demons. This was not the time to doubt his good will or test his patience.

Burdened by this fresh dose of certainty, Nessix was content to allow the remainder of their journey to carry on in silence.

Before long, a vague recognition of her surroundings did its best to comfort her. Kol stopped her before a closed door, pressed her back against it, and turned to face the few demons who had prowled behind them. He slowly spread his wings and folded them back so the tips touched the walls on either side of Nessix.

"This akhuerai belongs to me," he told the group, "and as such will not be claimed by any of you. Any attempt to do so will result in your death and will be considered an act of aggression between your lord and mine. Whoever wishes for me to forget the intentions you have for my property will find Annin and send him to my quarters."

Nessix couldn't see the reactions of this group of demons from where she shrank in the shadow of Kol's wings, but she did hear the hiss of bitter curses and the eventual shuffle of feet as the crowd dispersed. Long moments after silence reclaimed the hall, Kol folded his wings and turned to her.

The coldness had left his expression, replaced by an unusual weariness Nessix was too smart to mention. Thanks should have been in order for his protection, but his public claim of her barred any outward display of gratitude. Nessix suspected the bulk of the demons already knew she belonged to Kol and, on a level she actively suppressed, she'd come to terms with it herself. But hearing it spoken to witnesses and having them accept it dealt her an unexpected blow to her pride.

Kol reached past her and pushed the door open. "You'll want to avoid leaving without a guard I've appointed."

Nessix backed into the room as the door opened, her fingers pressed against the smoothness of the door's worn wood. Every one of her instincts waved warning flags that this as a trap. Kol was making more specific demands of her, the most paramount of them something she couldn't accomplish while locked in his chamber. If she tried to leave this haven—if it truly proved to be one—she doubted it would take long before the more reckless of the demons would find the courage to assault her. She watched Kol as he walked into the room to sit on his bed and remove his boots.

"If I wanted to hurt you, I'd have done so by now, little one," he said, tossing her a glance and a smirk. "You're safest distancing yourself from the door."

Nessix cast one more glance into the empty hallway and gulped down her reservations before turning to Kol. Drawing on her shaken nerves, she walked deeper into the security of this demon's private domain. There *had* been plenty of opportunities for him to lead her to harm, more than a few times when he'd overlooked how she'd probably earned it, yet Nessix couldn't shake fear's hold on her. Working her tongue through her mouth to combat its dryness, Nessix spoke, her words even, but small.

"Who were they?"

"Hmm?" Kol stood to unbuckle his sword belt.

"The demons in the hall. I recognize the look of hunger when I see it. The guards in the pit watch us, hoping for an excuse to take action, but never with that lust."

Kol closed his eyes and when he opened them, that cold jest burned alive and well yet again. He strode past Nessix, deeper into the lavishly furnished chamber, and up to an immaculately kept shelf of ancient tomes that spanned half of the back wall. "What did you learn of the Divine Battle as a mortal?"

Nessix grasped at memories of the stories Mathias had told her. Her heart ached for him now; she'd been so absorbed in training the akhuerai that thinking of Mathias had become a luxury often passed by from necessity. As her heart beat with pain, Kol's brows furrowed and he straightened, pulling his desired reading selection from its place on the shelf.

"It was a war between the first children gods, right?" Nessix asked. "The event that gave rise to your kind and ultimately the new children gods?"

Kol rubbed his chest where Nes's soul quivered against it, shook his head, and turned to face her. He slid the book onto the nearby desk. "That's the basics of it, yes. Is that all you know?"

Nessix chewed on the inside of her cheek and nodded.

Heaving a sigh, Kol turned back to the shelf and ran his fingers along worn bindings. "Thousands of young, mortal nations fought for their gods in that war, and thousands of young, mortal nations fell to those gods' cursed divinity." He pulled a second book from the shelf, briefly acted as though he was going to turn around again, then tucked the volume under his arm and resumed scanning. "Those of us unfortunate enough to survive the Divine Battle rose from that final battlefield as demons, but that wasn't enough to unify all of these nations. To this day, we're loyal only to our original clans."

"Loyal sounds like a bit of an exaggeration."

Nessix leapt at the growl that came from the open door behind her, and she shamefully scampered closer to Kol and the safety he'd promised to provide her. The oraku who she'd attacked on her first day as an akhuerai glowered past Nessix from the hallway before stepping inside and flinging the door closed. Nessix had nothing but frantic, terrible memories of this demon, but Kol seemed to trust him. She attempted to do the same, though the scowl in this newcomer's eyes promised her that he hadn't warmed up to her after their introduction, either.

"What is *she* doing here?" he asked.

Kol pulled two more books from the shelf and put them beside the first as he met Annin's eyes. The oraku hadn't so much as glanced at Nessix, disregarding her as a threat, a consideration, even a person. "Nessix, this is Annin. In my absence, you will answer to him. Annin, I've decided to give Nessix some perspective into our kind. Hatred comes from fear. Fear comes from ignorance. Ignorance has a simple fix." He tapped the stack of books.

"And what need do you have of me for this waste of time?"

"The others' underlings are too anxious to play with her, and I'm not yet convinced our own recognize her worth to trust anyone else keeping an eye on her."

Annin fired a poisonous glare at Nessix, one that shot straight for her soul. Nessix didn't flinch, catching that arrow just before it struck between her eyes. Annin frowned.

"And you think *I* care enough to not throw her to them myself?"

"Of course," Kol said, as relaxed as ever, despite the silent blows thrown between his oraku and his akhuerai. "You know what we had to go through to get her better than most. No simple grudge would make you forget it. You're too clever for that."

Annin snorted and turned to raid Kol's wine rack, leaving Nessix caught with trying to piece together the implications of their brief exchange.

"What did you have to go through?" she asked, craving that answer more than she'd expected.

Annin selected his bottle, turning to face Kol expectantly. He uncorked the bottle with his teeth, and spat the stopper to the floor. "Yes, Kol. Do remind me what we went through for your little pet."

Nessix should have known better than to hold her breath waiting for the answer, but knowing better didn't stop her from casting hopeful eyes to Kol. The alar's gaze was narrowed in good humor, and he shook his head with a gentle chuckle. Nessix glowered at Annin, who smugly smirked at her. He had no interest in keeping Nessix happy, and she discarded any thought of trying to endear herself to him.

Kol walked around the desk, grasped Nessix by the forearm, and kissed the top of her head "All you need to know, little one, is that you're alive."

"And apparently your people's history."

The snip of Nessix's retort brought a smile to Kol's lips. "And my people's history," he agreed, leading her around the desk.

Nessix hesitated at the stool, waiting for Kol to huff out a short sigh and pull the seat back for her. Outside of war stories, Nessix had always found research tedious and dull. This, however, would likely be her only chance to get a valuable inside look at the demons. Plopping down into the seat, she pulled the first book from the stack in front of her.

Bound in leather that had once been painted blue and embossed with a faded emblem on its center, age had chipped a generous amount of the color from the book's cover. Untold years of age, use, and conditioning mildew from the leather had worn it down so all Nessix could make out of the seal was the top of a half circle and a few faded lines beneath it. Tiny flecks of gold remained embedded in the deepest crevices, but it wasn't enough for Nessix to tell what it depicted.

From his stoic position of feigning boredom and disgust

halfway across the room, Annin choked on his wine and coughed his airway clear. "Kol, is that—"

"It's our clan's history," Kol interrupted seamlessly, spearing Annin with a glare meant to silence any other concerns. "We've wanted her to work with us, but we'd neglected to teach her how to do that. This is where she starts."

Nessix had missed neither the shock in Annin's exclamation nor the strictness in Kol's reply. This book hid something she wasn't supposed to discover, something Kol thought she wasn't smart enough to find. Her fingers curled around the cover covetously.

"A word with you, *sir*?" Annin said.

Kol rolled his eyes and left Nes's side for Annin to drag him to the corner farthest from the desk. The two bickered in hushed tones, emphatic gestures punctuating their points as they shot quick glances Nes's way. It was obvious Annin wanted to keep her from reading this book; there was no other reason he'd be so impassioned about preserving her ignorance. His desire succeeded only in making Nessix crave whatever secrets lurked inside even more.

Her orders had been to obey Kol. She was not to disappoint him, and he wanted her to read this book. Savoring the thought of Annin's rage, delighting in the idea that he seemed to have no power to stop her from absorbing whatever it was he feared, Nessix smirked and cracked the cover open.

An abrupt silence choked out the demons' debate after Annin swore sharply at Nes's actions. The oraku's teeth were bared, but Kol watched Nessix hopefully. And all she could do was stare down at the first page.

Nobody had taken the time to explain to Nessix how she'd picked up spoken languages so easily. She'd assumed it had something to do with her transformation from fleman to akhuerai, but Kol had made it clear that information regarding that was not important. Nessix now spoke nearly half a dozen languages to near fluency and could functionally find her way through a handful of others. But that didn't mean she could decipher foreign script.

Elegant characters swept across the page, filling the book with a steady stream of gibberish. If she concentrated hard enough, every third or fourth word almost made sense to her, but the rest was nothing more than a jumble of pretty lines meant to thwart her mission. Annin had no reason to worry after all. Nes's head began to ache.

"I... can't read this," she said.

Kol uncrossed his arms and straightened, brows furrowing. "You can't read?"

She fit him with an irritated frown. "Not *this*."

Nessix had spent the past few weeks imagining how much she'd enjoy seeing Kol disappointed in himself, but the fall of his features as realization struck him didn't please her nearly as much as it had in her fantasies. His mouth gaped in a tiny frown of horror and he glanced at Annin, orange eyes petitioning for help with overcoming this unforeseen hurdle. The oraku raised his brows and shook his head, extending a hand toward Nessix as if ushering Kol to finish the job he'd started.

Patience was something Kol had trained into himself, a tedious trait he worked at daily to maintain. As with any demon, it didn't come to him naturally, and Nessix routinely tried what little of the virtue he did command. His stomach flopped. "Open one of the others," he instructed.

Nessix loathed the idea of pushing aside this tome Annin feared, but did so to select the next book from the stack. This one had held its red lacquer well and didn't entice the same refined panic from the oraku, though Nessix didn't know if that was because of the material it contained or because he no longer feared her ability to learn it. She opened the cover to find a different script, this one blockier and running vertically down the page. At a quick glance, Nessix thought she could read about a quarter of it, but not enough to comprehend full sentences. She twisted her lips, raised her eyes to Kol's, and shook her head.

Fear abated, Annin laughed heartily and slapped Kol on the shoulder. "Have fun with *that*!"

That flop in Kol's stomach spun into a knot as he grumbled, "Go find us something to eat," to Annin, and trudged toward the desk. He snagged a stool on his way over and dragged it behind him as Annin chuckled his farewell and left the room. Kol shoved his seat beside Nes's, lip curled like he was about to be ill. He sat, staring at the simplicity of the scripts he'd known for thousands of years.

A small noise that Nessix was reluctant to label a whimper left Kol as he reached across the desk to pull the first book to himself. He ran his hand through his hair, sighed as though he was a messenger relaying a petty argument between two fickle noble women, and put his finger to the text.

"This alphabet has thirty-three characters..."

SIXTEEN

Mathias lurked through the townships of what had once been the Teradhel kingdom, avoiding Brant per the unusual requests of both Inwan and Sulik and brooding over Sazrah's untimely disappearance. He was surprised to see a handful of stout, non-fleman men bearing the Order's crest assist with hauling lumber, even more surprised to stumble upon a perturbed looking human smith hammering away at a makeshift forge. Inwan's ingenious method of opening the sea had been capitalized on, no doubt thanks to Sazrah's insistence; she had a knack for motivating people to work together for the common good. New construction speckled the towns, relieving the landscape of the damages left behind by snow loads and war. Industry thrived as demand for supplies and services surged, but a distinct aura of bitterness hung around many of the civilians, and Mathias's offers to help were rudely shrugged off.

Disheartened, Mathias respected the survivors' wishes and abandoned his attempts to do good. Stepping away from a responsibility that wasn't his freed him to continue pressing toward his own goal—one that potentially held a greater benefit for Elidae than mere physical labor. He left the clamor of the recovering towns, seeking the melancholy sweetness of the Great Spring.

A longing for peace he feared would never be his drew

Mathias to this place. The Spring had been Nes's favorite spot to sit and think, a reminder of what it was she fought for. Water bubbled up from indigo depths, the sun dancing blissfully on its ripples. Birds sang their chipper melodies to Mathias, thanking him for his part in returning peace to their home. Sweetness from thick patches of purple flowers filled the air. All of this should have soothed Mathias, reminding him of what he'd done to save Elidae, but all he could think of was how he'd failed the one person he'd most wanted to save. This sacred spot which Nessix had so adored wept over the distinct lack of her ghost, and Mathias had no way to hide from that fact.

Ceraphlaks drifted down beside his rider, his wings stirring Mathias's hair and battering the tall grass at their feet. He plunged his nose into the forage, snapped up a hearty mouthful, and raised his head to monitor the paladin's musings, chewing contently.

Mathias reached an absent hand out and patted the pegasus's shoulder, thankful for the companionship that saved him from his more destructive thoughts. He'd hoped Mehalco would have had more information for him and that Inwan would have felt some sort of flicker from Nes's soul, but nothing was ever easy when trying to out maneuver demons.

He didn't turn to Etha for advice on where to go next, actively avoiding the answer she'd give him. Instead, he turned to the Spring. He turned to the calm caress of the breeze and the songs of the birds. Most of the new children gods had declared themselves custodians of specific mortal concerns and there were two in particular that would have better knowledge than anyone else of an alar's passage from the demons' realm to the surface. Deciding it best to avoid lingering any longer, Mathias turned to Ceraphlaks.

"Standing around isn't getting me anywhere," he told the pegasus. "Let's head to Cardova and get back to nature, shall we?"

Ceraphlaks sighed a great breath, ravenously overstuffed his dainty muzzle, and steadied himself for Mathias to mount. Once his rider had settled, Ceraphlaks launched into the sky, wisps of grass fluttering free from his mouth.

* * * * *

The gods of nature's elements resided in a secluded valley on the continent of Cardova. Entering the forest which protected their sanctuary was never difficult. Navigating it, on the other hand, could prove quite deadly. Protected by the fierce brambles of Thausch's forests and the carnivore-riddled swamps maintained by Gilandia, one had to carry the blessing of the gods to survive the journey. In Mathias's case, not even his blessing coaxed compliance to his efforts. They were all gods of neutrality, coveting the ideals of balance possibly more than Etha did, herself. Mathias's impulsiveness had the annoying tendency to complicate their workloads. They wouldn't forbid him entry into their domain as long as he carried Etha's favor, but they had no issues making his journey to the valley as difficult as possible.

Mathias swatted a mosquito that came to feed on his neck and glowered down the dim path he traveled. Scattering a swarm of gnats that attempted to fly into his nose and eyes with an undignified flailing of his arms, he stopped and studied the trail. It appeared straight at first glance, but several yards ahead, it gradually curved to the right. Mathias turned around to look behind him, confirming that the path had curved all along. He'd been walking in a subtle circle for hours now.

"I appreciate your efforts, Thausch, but you won't thwart me today. I've got urgent matters to discuss with you and Xiral." Mathias waited a moment for the groan of trees resituating to open a path for him, but it never came. Heaving a sigh, Mathias trudged ahead. "If you won't believe me, you're choosing to disbelieve Etha, as well. If our words aren't good enough for you, ask Zenos how serious this is. You know *he* isn't capable of deception."

Still nothing. Mathias glanced off the path at the swamp filled with curious eyes that awaited his foolish decision to enter their reach. He peered up at the sky to see if he could borrow the sun's wisdom to guide him, but the canopy entwined too thick above his head. Grumbling, suspecting even more complications between himself and the gods if he opted to engage the swamp creatures, Mathias continued down the only path available to him.

His patience held out another ten minutes, ample time in his opinion for this quartet of gods to consult with Zenos. Trying to convince Xiral and Thausch to assist him through conventional means was doing him no good, so Mathias threw out his shame.

The children of Abaeloth were taught the importance of honoring the gods from a young age. Unfortunately for the fickle deities who demanded tribute and respect, the enthusiastic mortal world expressed these sentiments through song. More unfortunate still was the fact that Mathias had it on good authority how the simple rhymes raised on cheerful voices irritated the gods less playful than Etha. He cleared his throat and grinned wickedly.

> "Great Mother Etha, wise and true
> Gave the gods to me and you
> To guide us every night and day
> And so it is to them… we… pray…"

Mathias drew out the last line, giving his audience time to respond. Nothing changed on the wooded path, not even a glimmer of divine presence to suggest they lurked nearby. Mathias shrugged.

> "We must thank the goddess Xiral
> For the air we breathe
> For guarding all our skies
> And giving us the breeze
> Great goddess Xiral, here's to you
> For the air and the breeze and the sky so blue!"

The swarms of biting insects assaulted Mathias in droves now. Smirking, he tapped Etha's might to repel them, prepared and unafraid to continue this battle of wits.

> "We must thank the earth-god Thausch
> For the trees so green
> For the earth and the animals
> And the crops we need
> Great earth-god Thausch, here's to you

For the forests and the animals and the food!"

Mathias drew in a deep breath for the next verse as a great stag stepped onto the trail. It stared at him, head held high and left ear twisted to the side in irritation. Mathias ceased both his walking and his song. Clouds of insects were nothing more than an annoyance, but this stag towered over him larger than the greatest warhorse, its antlers sweeping as broad as the entire path.

"Is this an invitation or a challenge?" Mathias called, not particularly looking forward to the latter.

The stag snorted, gave a haughty shake of his head, and turned to step into the thick forest. When Mathias didn't follow, it looked over its shoulder and speared him with a filthy glare exclusive to divine beasts. Mathias chuckled to himself at the animal's dull humor and walked forward. The stag led him through the swamp, and Mathias made sure to step carefully in its tracks. Just because Thausch had sent him a guide didn't mean he was safe to drop his guard. After a short journey, sunlight flooded the pathway and the stag bounded off into the woods.

"Thank you!" Mathias shouted after its retreat. Of course, it didn't bother to acknowledge him.

Mathias took the last few strides into the clearing, a sense of wonder washing over him as the forest opened into a bright, lush paradise of a valley. The air was sweet and clear, speckled with a rainbow of butterflies that bobbed along on a subtle breeze. Several yards off, a crystalline pool glittered with the reflection of sunlight. A small island rose from its center, its sole occupant a brilliant flame that danced and contorted with the grace of a ballerina. Mathias stood transfixed to watch the flame's show until it appeared to turn and face him, froze for a heartbeat, then extinguished in a plump plume of smoke.

"Oh, come on," Mathias said. "You invited me here. There's no need to hide; I've got no qualms with you."

"We didn't *invite* you." A feminine voice manifested smooth and melodically through the air, tinted with the pompous disdain Mathias had expected. "We found the quickest way to rid ourselves of you and silence that... *insolent* singing."

Mathias swallowed his chuckle, figuring it was a bad time to pursue mischief. "It's good to hear from you, Xiral." He refrained from trying to visually locate the air goddess; she often hid in her element, though the gentle shiver across Mathias's skin confirmed her presence.

"I know nothing of these missing souls you seek."

An arrogant snip delivered those words, but Mathias knew how to defeat it. "I didn't think you would."

A stiff burst of air slapped Mathias across the face, burning his nose and chapping his lips. By the time he blinked, an ethereal, near ghostly woman stood mere inches from his face. Fathomless eyes so pale the irises barely showed glowered at him, thin lips tucked in a disapproving frown. Despite what recent experience had taught Mathias about tangling with gods, he held his ground.

"Are you doubting my might?" Xiral asked her question carefully, giving Mathias the chance to beg for forgiveness.

Mathias had never been keen on begging. "Of course not." He smirked at the glimmer of confusion that passed across Xiral's smooth face. "Keeping track of souls isn't your concern."

She didn't let Mathias enjoy her confusion for long, scoffing as she inclined her chin. "Then why are you bothering me with your drivel?"

"Because you are the keeper of the skies."

Xiral lowered her chin to look evenly into Mathias's eyes. He held her gaze confidently, cunning which Xiral hated to attribute to humans glistening back at her. Tantrums were beneath one of her stature, but that didn't stop her urge to have one.

"And?" she spat.

"And I want to know about the activity of a certain alar."

Xiral shook her head, luminescent hair flowing about her shoulders. Perhaps she'd been wrong. Perhaps there *wasn't* any cunning left in Mathias. She chimed a burst of laughter, letting the insult slap Mathias before she opened her eyes. "A single alar?"

Mathias shrugged off her response. "The skies *are* your domain. I figured you'd monitor them more closely. I suppose if it's too difficult a task for you, I could go ask Kenin what he—"

A second burst of air ruffled Mathias's hair and nipped his

ears as Xiral's eyes narrowed. "Which alar?"

Having found the closest thing to compliance he figured he'd get from Xiral, Mathias retained his smirk. "An alar named Kol. I encountered him while on Elidae and would like to know his flight patterns." Xiral didn't move at his request, and Mathias bargained with his pride to add, "Please."

Xiral twisted her head to the side to scour Mathias from the corners of her eyes. "Your most recent trip to Elidae or that first one we all heard about?"

"The first," Mathias said. The willingness dwindled from Xiral's expression, but not in the stubborn way she'd previously thrown against him. "Is that a problem?"

Xiral rolled her eyes and tossed her hands in the air. "Is that a..." A brisk, humorless laugh puffed from her. "You ignorant, *ignorant* man. Any traces of that demon's energy will have dissipated on the winds months ago." She held up a strict finger the moment Mathias's lips parted. "Yes, even to me. If you'd have asked within the hour of meeting with him, I could have helped you."

Mathias's mouth sagged the rest of the way open, a strangled fuss of disbelief leaving him. "Are you joking?"

Xiral's brows flattened above her pale eyes.

Any other time, Mathias would have been eager to poke at Xiral's apparent limitations, but Shand had more than exhausted his patience for entitled goddesses. "So he's lost to you?"

"He was never *found* by me."

Mathias twisted his lips in a pout. "Well. It was worth a shot, I suppose. You wouldn't be able to drag Thausch out here to talk to me, would you?"

Relieved from the threat of Mathias's criticism, Xiral scowled and drifted across the air currents, eager to leave Mathias's irritating company. "Using *me* as a messenger for your pathetic whims?"

"Pathetic? Huh." Mathias scratched his ear. "You know, Etha keeps a close watch on the trouble I get into and is particularly interested in this quest of mine. Souls are quite sacred to her. I doubt she'd be pleased to hear one of her elemental gods speak of this tragedy so dismissively."

Tiny storms of resentment swelled in Xiral's eyes and she

yanked her shoulders back. Just as she began to raise a shaking finger at Mathias, a noisy rustle of underbrush interrupted her. Mathias smiled smugly, gaining a tight frown from the air goddess.

"Quit lettin' the whelp get ya worked up, Xiral."

Thausch was a squatty bear of a man with thick eyebrows and a full beard. Grandfatherly wrinkles warmed his expression, even when facing the likes of Mathias, and he trundled into the clearing with all the grace of an overweight wombat. Common sense reminded Mathias that he still needed to petition for assistance, preventing him from asking the god of the earth which of them was truly the whelp.

"Thank you for coming to see me, my lord."

Xiral rolled her eyes dramatically and disappeared in a flurry of wind and chattering birds that forced Mathias to stagger to keep on his feet. He chuckled softly, relieved to have concluded his meeting with Xiral with so little trouble.

"You can quit with yer manners, boy. I heard Zenos's report and have nothin' to give ya."

The pinch of peace Mathias had just enjoyed fluttered from his grasp. His search for information was not going as well as he'd hoped. "You've got no news on the scars in the earth? You, of all people, should be able to feel when demons pass through their portals."

Thausch crammed his hands in the pockets of his worn trousers. "Isn't watchin' demon portals yer Order's job?"

Mathias opened his mouth, a debate fresh on his tongue, but stopped. His features fell. "I don't want to fight with you, Thausch. I came for help. I just want to stop the demons."

Thausch leaned forward and studied Mathias with narrowed eyes before waddling up to peer even closer. Breathing deep the scent of pine and damp earth, Mathias watched the god carefully, but didn't object to the scrutiny. Thausch leaned in closer and gave Mathias a few rapid sniffs before straightening, eyes glittering with a keenness that slowed Mathias's blood.

"Yer not either after just stoppin' the demons. Yer huntin' after yer mate."

The heat seeped from Mathias's cheeks and he snuck a quick

glance across the open valley in search of the other three gods. Not that trying to protect this vulnerability from the likes of the divine would do him any good. "Of—" His voice threatened to crack, and he cleared his throat. "Of course I want to stop the demons."

"Yeah, so you can sow yer seed."

The heat flooded back to Mathias's face in a rush he subtly cringed from.

"Livin' things, boy," Thausch continued, oblivious to—or simply not caring about—Mathias's clear discomfort with the direction he'd taken this conversation. "That's my territory. Ya can't hide this."

The god wasn't wrong. Mathias leaned closer to Thausch, keeping his voice low. "What do you know of Nessix?"

The god's lips played at a smile.

Mathias grasped his own elbows to keep from grabbing the god and shaking him in frustration. "I am *begging* you, Thausch. Help me. Please."

"Not usin' Etha's name this time?"

"No. This time it's for me."

Thausch crossed his arms and gave Mathias an approving nod. "All I know is what ya just told me. You'll stop at nothin' to find her. Same as Xiral, though, I can't track somethin' that moved about months ago. The demons are churnin' about in their halls, active as ever, but I've got nothin' on where this mate of yers might be."

Mathias's shoulders sagged, arms dropping to his sides. The elemental gods had domain over the physical world; he couldn't fathom how they wouldn't be able to tell when mischief was made within their domains. He'd never gone out of his way to gain their favor and he hadn't expected them to readily throw themselves at the opportunity to assist him, but he'd been confident they'd have had some sort of information he could weasel out of them. After Inwan, they'd been his most logical option. A meaty hand patted Mathias's upper arm with gentle condolence.

"It's hard needin' to see 'em go, isn't it?"

That flare of rage that had spurred Mathias this far stoked to life once more and he pulled his arm from beneath the god's touch, lip curled. "Do not pity me. I will find her, and I will stop the demons."

Thausch closed his lips in grim speculation and lowered his hand. "Not sure how ya plan on doin' that, but if it's what's in yer heart, may Etha watch over her reckless son."

The words should have offered Mathias some amount of peace, a compassionate reminder that he had the greatest power in all of Abaeloth on his side, but they only succeeded in bristling him further. "She does," he snapped.

Thausch cocked his head and narrowed his eyes. "I believe yer inquisition here is through." As he spoke, the trees creaked as they shifted to open a direct path to usher Mathias from the blessed valley. "There's yer door."

Mathias clenched his teeth and fists, struggling to remind himself that he was a guest here and that any bouts of anger or frustration directed toward the valley's inhabitants would be dealt with in unpleasant ways. Unable to voice any appreciation for how little he'd accomplished, Mathias stalked down the path, leaving the reclusive gods behind.

SEVENTEEN

It took Kol three tedious days and grinding his teeth to the point of muscle fatigue thanks to Annin's ceaseless goading to teach Nessix how to wade through the scripts of his people. She'd proven a more willing student than Kol had expected, her only debates rising from concern over how her army fared without her. On the fourth day, she finally convinced Kol to check on their progress, and he returned with a report of Auden's competent fulfillment as Nes's second in command. This reassurance put Nessix in a more compliant mood, and Kol made a point to observe the akhuerai ranks on a daily basis.

Though troubled by the distance between herself and her fledgling army, Nessix settled into this new arrangement gracefully. Kol had ordered a modest cot for her to sleep on, tucking it against the wall opposite his own plush bed. After months spent living in relative filth, wanting for physical comforts, the simple bed and woolen blanket seemed a luxury for the wealthy. Kol's rank had earned him the privilege of private bathing facilities in the form of a spring-fed water source located in the convenience of his chamber, and Nessix was given adequate privacy to bathe away the sweat and grime of the chasm. Three times a day, peons delivered meals far more savory than what the akhuerai foraged for themselves. If Nessix would have been asked a year ago if demons had any interest in mortal comforts, she'd have laughed. Now, this chamber seemed perfectly fitting for Kol.

Among this combination of unexpected benefits, Kol still demanded Nessix soak in the demons' history and inner workings. She'd resigned herself to an eternity of foul luck until this fortuitous change of pace. The circumstances could have been much worse, a fact Nessix remembered each time she caught Annin's judgmental glare. She could have been beaten for disappointing Kol. She could have been used for pleasure or tossed to be an inoga's plaything. She hadn't yet settled on what these fates worse than death might be, but here she was, playing Kol as smoothly as he thought he was playing her, keeping an inch ahead as long as he continued to deny Annin's concerns.

Nessix gnawed on her cuticle and squinted harder at the text before her. Even with Kol's guidance, reading the languages she'd learned to speak was a struggle she feared would never get easier. Easy or not, these tomes held the information she needed to effectively combat the demons from the inside, and her foolish captor was adamant that she absorb all she could. She learned of the Divine Battle—or at least the details relevant to Kol's ancestors. His people had served the goddess of the skies, Kalina, and marched down from the mountains. Strangers to combat, simply ordered to defend their goddess, it was a wonder any of them had held out long enough to make it to the demon-spawning climax of the war.

Despite the richness of the demons' history, Nes's quest for knowledge was actively compounded by the frequency of partially missing pages and blotted out passages. Kol and, to a lesser extent, Annin were quick to fill those gaps, and Nessix began to appreciate the mental reprieve offered by receiving spoken answers to her questions.

With her goal of discovering the vital information that must be hidden in these books not yet thwarted by frustration, Nessix flipped the page with a sigh. Taking a moment to rub her eyes, she pressed a finger beneath the text of the top line as the door of Kol's chamber flew open, slamming against the wall with such force that the hinges buckled. No matter how badly Nessix wanted to deny that she shared anything in common with demons, she and her two custodians were warriors, and they all leapt to their feet, prepared to take action.

Grell blustered through the doorway, teeth bared in a menacing snarl and eyes locked on Nessix. Perhaps if the inoga wasn't four times her size, Nessix would have charged at his challenge. As it was, that humiliating tickle of self-doubt wriggled in her heart, and she flinched at Grell's steady approach.

"Is there a problem—"

Grell interrupted Kol by grasping the edge of the desk and flinging it away from where it had provided an insubstantial barrier between him and Nessix. "*This* is what you call obedience?" Grell spat his demand with such ferocity that spit flecked across Nes's cheek.

Nessix had never had anything but bad experiences when it came to facing inoga, and despite her blossoming confidence, she cringed from Grell before the thought of answering him even processed in her mind. A mere cringe wasn't enough to remove her from the gigantic demon's grasp, and he struck like lightning to snag Nessix by a fistful of hair. She yelped as he jerked her head to the side and reached frantic hands up to try prying his fingers free.

Neither instinct nor common sense prevented Kol from stepping forward in Nes's defense, but Annin's hand catching his forearm did. "Sir, what problem do you have with her?" the alar asked.

"What problem!" Grell shook the hand which held Nessix and she cried out and grappled for his wrist. "Do you know what she's done?"

Kol's heart raced between his desire to protect Nessix from whatever peril Grell had planned for her and his fear of where trying such a rescue would land him. The frantic burning of Nes's soul against his chest clenched him tightly, threatening to choke him. Nessix was unarmed and in a plain blouse and slacks, unprotected by her armor. Even if she'd been prepared for combat, it was unlikely she'd survive Grell's tantrum. Kol had worked too hard gaining Nes's compliance to not step forward now. Terror was such an ugly look for her refined face.

"She's been confined to my chamber for weeks, under constant watch of either myself or Annin. She couldn't have done anything."

"Confined... Anything!" Grell sputtered through his raging mania. "I warned you, Kol! *Warned* you!"

Spinning sharply, Grell kicked Nes's legs from under her with his first step, and stormed toward the open door. Pain pried Nes's hands from her grip on the inoga's wrist and she clawed desperately to regain her grasp. Tears streamed down her face, and against all sense and logic, she brokenly cried out Kol's name. Grell cleared the doorway.

"Kol..." Annin's voice ticked with a warning that spoke of fear stronger than his desire to see Nessix harmed.

Still framed in the doorway, Nessix gave a valiant struggle against Grell, shrieking in the desperate throes of a snared animal, and she screamed for Kol again. Grell roared an unintelligible reprimand and jerked Nessix forward, pulling her from Kol's view.

The alar had faced certain death in the past and had survived on all accounts, and he'd meant it when he'd proclaimed his ownership of Nessix. Orange eyes ablaze, drawing on a time when his words were obeyed, Kol dashed ahead. Grell had no right to any of this.

Annin rushed forward and stopped him again. "Do not be fool enough to intervene. Grell is not in a mood to compromise."

Hot breaths heaved in the bellows of Kol's lungs as his past authority and present caution swirled around him. He didn't meet Annin's eyes, focusing instead on the open doorway and where Nes's cries of fury and terror and pain rushed down the hallway. "Grellandier has gone too far."

Annin hadn't heard that coldness in Kol's growl in centuries, and his own heart began to race. "And as our lord, that is his right," he said. "Do not be foolish—"

Kol spun with a speed defiant of his calculating demeanor, backhanding the last demon he considered an ally in the same motion. "*I* am your lord! Do not forget that."

The strike was powerful enough to repel Annin's hold from Kol's arm and as Kol stalked out of the room to chase his death,

Annin had to force himself to stay put. The battle ahead was not one he wished to enter. Obedience and loyalty were one thing. Stupidity was another entirely. Nursing the sting on his cheek, Annin sat on his stool and waited on the report to come.

* * * * *

Nessix was a tough woman, resilient in mind and conditioned to withstand physical pain, but as Grell's sweeping stride dragged her down the hall, legs scrambling in failed attempts to support her, her stinging eyes stayed trained on Kol. The alar marched rigidly behind, fists clenched and jaw set in a manner that prevented him from speaking any of the furious demands that actively spun in his flaming eyes. He focused on Grell's back, tendons in his neck twitching, and refused so much as a glance at Nessix despite her gasps and whimpers. Kol's attempt to ignore her distress was one of the clearest ways he displayed concern for her, but right now, she'd have killed to have him actively step up in her defense.

It was difficult to concentrate on anything other than pain and her racing heart, but as a mutinous roar lofted through the hallway, Nessix put together where Grell hauled her. They were heading toward the chasm, and that roar came from the raised voices of hundreds of soldiers in combat. Half delirious from pain, a swell of adrenaline surged through Nessix. She'd longed to hear those voices ever since she first woke up in the hells. They were the song she'd yearned for this entire time. It wasn't until Grell came to a stop that reluctance hit Nessix.

Kol had been diligent about delivering reports of the state of affairs in the akhuerai's pit, leading Nessix to believe that the situation had been relatively stable. The akhuerai were loyal to her, and she'd instilled the basics of honor in them. A civil dispute—at least one that would reach this volume or attract the concern of an inoga—seemed unlikely. Gasping, Nessix looked up at Kol as he stopped behind her. What hadn't he told her?

The answer came to Nessix quickly as Grell raised his arm, lifting Nes's feet from the ground. She convulsed against the pull on her hair, and Grell grasped her arm to spin her around to view what raged in the chasm below.

"Does this look like obedience to you?"

Nessix barely heard the sound of Kol walking up beside her as she gazed through her tears at the ragtag group of civilians who had at last organized into an army. The akhuerai rioted in a vicious manner neither Nessix nor Kol had fathomed they'd reach. Hundreds lay maimed or neutralized on the makeshift battlefield, but a noteworthy number of demons sprawled on the bloodied ground, as well. Weapons were salvaged from the fallen demons, and though the akhuerai weren't skilled with arms, they flowed through the techniques Nessix had given them with all the vigor of cornered people making their last stand. Kol turned his eyes to Nessix.

She'd quit squirming in Grell's grasp, though tears flowed silently down her cheeks, her mouth gaping in horror as she stared forlornly at her people. It took no more than that glance at her terror-stricken face to realize that Nessix had never wanted this sort of rebellion. She was every bit as alarmed by this violence as Kol was.

"Sir," Kol held his voice low and steady, prodding for the thin line of Grell's logic. No matter how badly he wanted to challenge Grell's authority, finesse was needed to rectify this situation. "Did we get any reports on what caused this?"

"This!" Grell shook Nessix by the grip he had on her hair, pulling a fresh scream out of her as his jostling flung her hands from his wrist once again. "Your little wench caused this, but you were too smitten with her to see it!"

"That's impossible," Kol countered, shuttering the memory of Annin's admonishing eyes from his mind. "She hasn't even spoken to them in nearly two weeks."

It had been decades since the last time Kol came this close to telling Grell he was wrong, and it was something he should have thought about, considering the inoga had his masterpiece in his hands. Grell was tired of correcting Kol for his foolishness, tired of seeing Annin's sound advice blown off. The inoga had been beyond patient with Kol, more lenient than he'd ever been with any other living being, and it was time to punish him.

In one fluid motion, Grell raised his arm and launched Nessix into the pit.

Whether or not she'd been praying to escape Grell, Nessix hadn't been prepared for this sort of ending. Her shriek of terror as she tumbled through the air pierced through the chasm, severing the focus of her green troops as they disengaged to gawk at their plummeting general. Their demon opponents leapt at the opportunity to annihilate the distracted masses, cutting them down as rapidly as they could swing their weapons.

"You see what you made me do?" Grell asked Kol, his voice searing with disappointment.

Eyes wide, it took the stimulation of those words to engage Kol's mind, and in that moment, he forgot how much he resented Grell and his stolen station. Nessix would come back to life after her collision with the ground, but how would that damage her progression? Grell was too enraged for Kol to stand even a flimsy chance against him. That left Kol one option.

Peaking the upper tips of his wings, Kol dove into the chasm, slicing through the air toward Nessix. Grell hadn't tried to stop him, an observation Kol didn't know what to do with. Nessix flailed through the air and as he neared her, he reached out and grabbed her left arm. Snapping his wings open, Kol stopped their fall in a rapid jerk. Nessix's scream of agony as her shoulder dislocated from the abrupt stop echoed off the stone walls so shrill Kol cringed and nearly dropped her. Throwing his weight to the side, the alar swooped beneath Nes's body to scoop her against his chest. So overcome with shock and pain, she clung to him fiercely, face buried against his chest. She missed seeing the great shadow pass overhead.

Grell flew infrequently, preferring to use the massive span of his wings as means to intimidate as opposed to travel. His flight was appropriately graceless and awkward, lacking the aerial dexterity Kol had mastered. That didn't stop it from being effective.

Kol had been too focused on rescuing Nessix to notice Grell's departure, robbing him of the chance to attempt an evasive maneuver. The only warning he had was the flash of Grell's shadow, and even without looking back, he knew the inoga was too close to avoid. Too near to the ground, he didn't dare twist around to assess Grell's position, and so Kol beat his wings against the current path of travel to halt his forward momentum.

Trembling, Nessix peered up at the sudden stop and her eyes widened, memories of Inek's assault flashing before her as she caught Grell's tight grimace of disapproval. The pain on her scalp had subsided, overshadowed by the agony in her shoulder, and the way Kol's arms locked around her assured Nessix of one thing. He doubted they'd escape this just as much as she did. There, pressed against Kol's chest, sharing this mutual dread, a strange completeness washed over Nessix, twisting honor in a way she'd never experienced. She and this demon had something in common, something far greater than the desire to walk away from this assault.

An instinctive understanding, an innate draw to ensure no harm came to Kol seized Nessix to her very soul. It consumed all of her hatred and her daydreams of revolt. Nessix could die and rise again, but she'd cut down hundreds of demons. They could die. *Kol* could die. Her jaw trembled at the thought, heart preemptively mourning his loss, brain screaming above the rush of air around her that she must keep that from happening. Gritting her teeth, Nessix shoved her functioning arm against Kol's chest and kicked at him. Grell was angry with her—for whatever reason—and her tedious efforts to make Kol care about her had endangered him. If Nessix could free herself from the alar's grasp, he might be able to escape. He might get to live.

Too many burdens distorted Kol's ability to think clearly, and the last thing he'd been prepared for was Nes's struggle. Focus tugged away from the most direct path to safety, Kol fumbled to keep his hold on Nessix, rebalancing his flight to make a hasty landing. They were no more than thirty feet from the ground, close enough to make the drop in the matter of a couple heartbeats, but that was still longer than Kol had. The distraction cost him dearly as Grell's iron fist slammed into the side of his head.

Bursts of light exploded across Kol's field of vision, blinding him of his surroundings. The sharp ring of the concussive strike dulled all other sounds. Blood trickled from his nostril, accompanied by a metallic wash across his tongue. His wings wouldn't flap, rippling limply from his back as strength failed him. Biological responses trumping even the strongest will, Kol's arms relaxed their hold and Nessix fell once again toward the chasm floor, trailed by the dazed alar.

The accumulation of bodies on the ground and a few less fortunate combatants broke Nes's fall. She gasped as the wind was snatched from her, losing her breath a second time as Kol landed on top of her. Her pain abated as she slipped closer to shock. On top of her, Kol groaned and flopped over to his side, pressing a hand against his right temple. Barely aware of her surroundings, Nessix rolled to her stomach and used her good arm to push herself to her knees. All around her, sharp curses and terrified screams sprang from her scattering army. She looked up to see that Grell had landed and now marched toward her.

Her mind latched on to the safety of her people as Grell prowled closer. This group of civilians, men and women and children who had lost their mortal lives to the demons, had shown more bravery than Nessix had thought they possessed. Brave or not, she was certain that those who still stood would flee from Grell's imposing aura. The rage sputtering from his eyes ensured that he wanted to see her suffer, and if he had any sense at all, he'd know that would come from taking out her army.

Grell was close now, tramping over fallen bodies as casually as he'd stroll across his bedchamber. Nes's wheezing breath and racing heart skewed her measure of time, but she guessed Grell would have his hands around her throat in the next five seconds. She grit her teeth, absolutely determined to rob from him the chance to hear her beg for mercy.

Beside her, Kol shuffled on the dirt floor as he rose to his feet. Nessix didn't take her eyes from Grell, even when the inoga cocked his head to look at Kol, and she wanted nothing more than to scream at Kol for drawing attention to himself.

"Stand down, Kol," Grell rumbled.

"This akhuerai belongs to me." Kol's subdued voice wavered with the weakness of shock, but the same finality glazed his words as the last time he'd spoken them.

Grell sucked his teeth and shook his head in disappointment. "Do not make me do this."

Kol took a step forward, raising his wings with an effort that outwardly taxed him in an attempt to shield Nessix. "It would be your actions, not mine."

That same annoying fear beat in Nes's heart as she heard Kol's words, and she stood up behind him. Neither of them would be able to touch Grell by themselves, especially in their battered conditions, but perhaps together they could humble him before they were killed. Nessix was convinced to the depths of her soul that she couldn't let Kol face this alone.

Grell charged, and Nessix braced her stance, hand already reaching for the knife hanging at Kol's right hip. In that same moment, Kol shouted, deliberately throwing a wing back to toss Nessix to the ground. Grell was on Kol now, arms reaching above the alar's shoulders to grab the base of his wings. Too close to draw a weapon and too dazed to gather the strength to grapple, Kol leaned against the agonizing support of Grell's grasp and slammed a heel into his lord's kneecap. He hadn't done so with the expectation of breaking free from his peril, but to buy time in hopes that any of the surviving guards—all demons who resented inoga nearly as much as Kol did—would be foolish enough to help him.

No demon reinforcements rushed to Kol's defense, but as Grell roared and lifted Kol by his wings, the alar felt a subtle tug at his hip. *Not you, little one...*

Nessix had never been particularly good at following instructions and only truly respected lessons that were laid on her the hard way. She'd yet to understand why she needed Kol to live, but she acted on that need boldly. She'd charged in to rescue allies from thriving units of demons in the past, and Grell was a single foe. Despite common sense's shrieks of caution, Nessix opted to believe that this put her and her opponent on even footing. She sprang forward, armed with Kol's dagger.

Mind disturbingly calm and focused, Nessix ducked under Grell's raised arms and drove the knife through the webbing of his wing. The inoga bellowed as the dagger pierced the membrane. He dropped Kol to spin on Nessix, the action drawing the knife through his leathery hide.

Nessix should have been afraid. She should have contemplated fleeing, crying at the sentence bearing down on her as she trembled in fear and begged for forgiveness. But all she felt was cold, clinical duty to engage this threat. It was different from the rush of battle she'd enjoyed in life. There was no burst of adrenaline as she savored the reminders of mortality, no satisfaction from Grell's flowing blood. She doubted she'd feel satisfaction at all until Grell's blood ceased to flow completely.

The inoga swung his trunk of an arm to try grabbing Nessix, but she was smaller and quicker, pressed too close to him. In a flash, he couldn't see her at all. Distracted and blinded by rage that needed to be satisfied, Grell spun to face Kol, who was once again pushing himself to his feet. Before Grell managed his first step toward his rebellious subordinate, the dagger bit into the bulging mass of his overdeveloped right trapezius. Tiny feet kicked upward, using his belt as a foothold as Nessix climbed his back. Grell spun wildly in his attempt to fling her from him.

Nessix rode Grell's thrashing with the same skill she'd withstood Logan's fits of youth when he'd been a colt, anchoring herself by sinking the dagger deeper into muscle and wrapping her toes around his belt for stability. With her left arm unserviceable, she hadn't yet figured out how to restrain her target for a proper execution, but as with Logan's explosions, Grell soon tired of his thrashing and Nessix uncoiled her toes to climb higher up the demon's heaving back. She pressed her right foot against the base of Grell's wing and launched herself up to latch her left leg around his neck, then jerked the knife free to clear a path for her right leg.

Sensibility flooded back to Nessix in a mad rush as Kol screamed her name. Not "little one" this time, but her given name, carried on a burst of terror. Before the next beat of her heart, the bones of her left ankle groaned in Grell's crushing grasp and he yanked her from her deadly perch. He discarded her on the ground as he turned to swat Kol back, and roared with maniacal laughter as Nessix tried to scramble away. He grabbed her with little effort and flung her between his legs to straddle her waist.

"What the *fuck* do you think you're doing, whore?"

Nessix couldn't speak, and it wasn't just because Grell's weight crushed her diaphragm.

"I was told you were smart," Grell seethed. Gripping Nes's shirt by the collar, he tore it open to expose the brands of the two deities who had failed her in life. His fingers pinched the tiny metal ring protruding from beneath them.

"Sir, *no!*" Kol's voice ached with panic, though remained at a distance implying he hadn't attempted another charge.

Nessix's heart beat so hard that the tiny ring pulsed in Grell's fingers and a tingling numbness spread across her lips.

The inoga leaned forward, blood from his punctured muscle running over his shoulder to drip on Nes's face and hair. His breath beat hot against her flesh. "You're lucky your master found his respect. I could end you here and now and would sleep better for it."

"I'm begging you, sir," Kol continued, voice trembling. "I'll make this right. I swear it!"

Grell's eyes narrowed as he stared down into Nes's increasingly blank ones. "Don't let him become a liar, now," he growled.

The strength had seeped from Nes's fingers, and the dagger that could have saved her weighed her hand down helplessly as Grell's fingers lifted from the metal ring. His hands wrapped around her neck, closing down with a steady pressure. The thought which carried Nessix to darkness was that she'd succeeded in safeguarding Kol's life.

EIGHTEEN

After his attempts at interrogating Xiral and Thausch had failed in the most spectacular ways, Mathias was in a poor frame of mind to cope with Etha's goading. She hadn't let up on the notion that he needed to speak to Ceredulus, but Mathias was no less stubborn than his mother.

Demons would forever be Mathias's mortal enemies, but the god of the undead was the reason he'd lost his chance at a peaceful eternity. The act of perverting souls began with Ceredulus, and he remained one of the few beings who Mathias suspected was more clever than he was. The god of the undead had launched Abaeloth into a mad age of darkness and was the only deity besides Shand who didn't balk at the idea of engaging Mathias in physical combat. Half a world away from Affliction's righteous security, there was quite literally nowhere Mathias wanted to be less than in Ceredulus's field of vision. Or his debt.

Motivated by these misgivings, when Etha had demanded to know where Mathias planned to go next, he blurted the first thought that came to mind.

Kenin was the youngest of the new children gods. Worshipped for his carefree love of adventure and propensity for mischief, he and Mathias had more in common than the god wanted to admit. He'd established his base of operations in the bustling trade town of Corrsik, which suited him and his patrons well. Mathias's entry into the city did quite the opposite. Though he doubted many people recognized who he was, they easily identified his crest, hushed their conversations, and gave him a wide berth as he passed. Representatives of the Order seldom condoned much of what Corrsik dealt in.

Their revulsion didn't bother Mathias. In fact, he preferred the lack of complications that resulted from their grudging avoidance. He followed the trail of divine energy past a row of seedy taverns until he reached a not-quite-as-seedy tavern at the end of the street. Well lit in the evening hours and with a lively melody played on pipes and a squeezebox drifting through the open windows, it was exactly the sort of place Kenin felt most at home. The boisterous crowd didn't quiet as Mathias entered, but the more sober patrons pinned him with shrewd glares. Sighing, praying this didn't mark the beginning of trouble he hoped to avoid, Mathias squared his shoulders and strode inside.

Unlike those in the streets, this crowd shot him mocking jeers and cryptic warnings to keep his distance. The notion that they didn't know who he was confirmed by this behavior, and Mathias allowed himself to smirk. He granted them all the favor of ignoring their threats and followed Kenin's steady glow to the back of the tavern where a closed door waited on the other side of a hazardous maze of barrels and crates. Mathias squeezed through the clutter and stood in front of the door for a moment, wondering if it would be wisest to knock. Figuring gossip from the divine realm had reached Kenin when Mathias first began his search and that the god knew of his pending arrival the moment he set foot in Corrsik, Mathias shrugged and opened the door.

A slender man with smooth, dark hair pulled back in a tight ponytail sat behind an ornately carved desk, counting golden coins into an even more elaborate chest. His dark eyes didn't lift from his task as Mathias entered and, unlike the reception he'd received from the other gods he'd recently visited, Kenin didn't greet him with a sneer. From Kenin, that could mean something worse than noncompliance. That could mean he was in the mood for entertainment.

"Rumor's gotten around that you're hunting for something. I *do* love a good treasure hunt."

Mathias stood still in the doorway for a moment, the levity in Kenin's voice raising both the hairs on his arms and warning flags in what remained of his common sense. He'd already piqued Kenin's interest, so it was too late to play with the idea of trying to slip away. At least the god of mischief seemed more willing to talk than his peers. Mathias stepped forward and closed the door. "Do you know why I'm here?"

Kenin arched his eyebrows, lips moving silently as he counted the last few coins in his hand. He snapped the lid of the chest closed, rested his forearms on the lid, and raised his narrowed eyes to Mathias's wary ones, a sly grin creeping across his face. "Oh, the divine realm is simply abuzz with your troubles."

Mathias didn't bother to hide his grimace, regretting that he hadn't taken the time to earn the respect of Xiral and Thausch years ago. Either way, he'd work with what he was given. "Then you've had time to snoop around for more information."

"To—" Kenin straightened and pressed a hand to his chest. "To *snoop*? What sort of god do you think I am!"

Mathias had learned how to read mortals with relative accuracy, but sorting through the emotions of the divine often posed annoying complications. His blunt tongue was about to offer the fact that Kenin was well known for his shameless deception and tenacity when hunting after interesting treasures, but his quickly dwindling patience begged him to avoid the insolence such an accusation would convey. Mathias rubbed his lips to keep his opinions to himself. He simply couldn't afford to offend anyone who might be able to help him.

The god laughed at Mathias's awkward reaction and waved a dismissive hand. "No, no. You're right to assume. I've done a great deal of snooping. Lots of interesting rumors floating around the great wilds of Abaeloth."

Mathias's hand slipped to his chin as he looked up, hope igniting his eyes and his heart. "I'll take any rumors you've got, my lord."

Kenin's eyes narrowed into tiny slits that barely revealed the glimmer of his jest. "You'll *take* them?" he asked, voice hushed and striking like a viper. "How would you possibly manage that?"

If Mathias had been speaking to almost anyone else or not so desperate to hear whatever information Kenin alluded to, he'd have berated the god for his cruelty. The intention of his request had been apparent and it was Kenin's flippancy which intentionally misinterpreted it. Struggling to maintain an air of respect, Mathias fumbled for an answer, stammering a string of sounds that were meant to begin an apology.

Kenin threw his shoulders back with an arrogant huff and crossed his arms. "That's what I thought! You couldn't take *anything* from me."

Mathias's flapping jaw sagged wider in a tiny, despondent gasp. It wouldn't be out of character for Kenin to bluff and know nothing at all, but hope and helplessness continued to demand that he had another piece to this puzzle. Mathias's heart fell. "I wasn't intending to *take* anything…"

"That's right you weren't!" Kenin slapped the lid of the chest and leaned forward. "So what do you have to offer me in exchange for what I know?"

Mathias floundered again, Kenin's confidence tearing his own apart. Too weary to stand a chance at a battle of wits, Mathias let his shoulders sag. "I don't have much to give, you know that. I'm Etha's bound servant. Neither my sword nor my armor nor my mount are mine to own, and I don't accumulate wealth." He shook his head, never before feeling as cornered as he did now. "What do you want?" he asked, defeated.

Kenin's sternness swapped out for a smile the moment Mathias surrendered. "You could start with a shard of Affliction, swearing yourself to complete a quest of my choosing and, if you're wanting the *good* gossip, you'll talk that sister of yours into a date with me."

Humor lost amidst his tension, a gutted breath wheezed from Mathias's open lips, his heart sinking further until righteous anger grabbed it by the scruff and hauled it back into place. If Kenin planned to withhold anything that would get him closer to Nessix, he'd fly back to Elidae to hunt down Affliction again and force an explanation out of the god.

Kenin sighed and shook his head, mischief continuing to spark in his eyes. "Oh, for the sake of all that's divine, Mathias. You are in a *foul* mood today."

Mathias clamped his jaw tight, determination setting his features. Intimidation wouldn't work on Kenin, but it felt just as good to express it.

"I know you've got nothing appealing to offer me," the god said.

"You need payment?" Mathias snapped. "I'll find a way to get it. A piece of Affliction, my service and… Jules are what you want? I'll promise you two of them and can attempt to work on the last as soon as I see the demons punished. But to do that, I need information."

Kenin rolled his eyes and walked around the table to lean against its edge. "You *are* in a foul mood. I'm just messing with you. You want the rumors I've got?"

Mathias carefully regulated his breathing and gave a curt nod, reluctant to show any more desperation to the devious god than he'd already leaked.

"All I need is your word that you'll never do me in the way you did Shand."

"Never give me a reason to and you've got it."

Kenin cocked his head from side to side, quirking his lips as he considered the value of Mathias's words. "Alright, then. Rumor has it, these souls that have gone missing are from all reaches of Abaeloth. Single snatches at a time, and no mortal witnesses. Well. Until you, I suppose."

Habit urged Mathias to correct Kenin's casual dismissal of his immortality, but sensibility snagged the remark before it made it halfway up his throat. Keeping Kenin on topic was more important than setting him straight over such a trivial matter. "Has it always been the same pair of demons?"

"That"—Kenin snapped his fingers—"I cannot confirm. The oraku's been the same, assuming he really is the only one with wings and no visible runes, but it's been unclear if the alar's the same one who subdued your girlfriend."

Mathias would have frowned at how fast news of him and Nessix had traveled, had he not caught something important. He'd been too distraught at the scene of Nes's demise to study the oraku in such careful detail, but now he knew the beast didn't possess any obvious runes. That was unusual for their class, nearly as unusual as bearing wings. Trying not to let his hopes run away with him, Mathias nodded.

"Where did you find these rumors? Not even Etha's heard this much. How could—" He stopped abruptly to avoid offending the first helpful god he'd found.

Despite Mathias's hasty effort, it was an offense Kenin found great delight feigning with a haughty gasp and slight widening of his narrow eyes. "How could a small fish like *me* have heard it?" He laughed heartily at Mathias's flush. "This isn't coming from other gods; there are a whole lot more eyes and ears in the heavens than us, you know."

Mathias shook his head to scatter away a distracting bombardment of thoughts. "You're getting this from souls?"

"Mmm. Those who haven't quite been able to let go of their pasts. They watch over their loved ones and estates, and they see all of Abaeloth's wonder and treachery, perpetually unable to do anything about it."

It was such a logical explanation, Mathias was embarrassed to admit that he hadn't thought of it sooner. "Is there anything else you've heard?"

Kenin crossed his arms and watched Mathias through the sides of his eyes. "Out of your streak of dead ends, you can't appreciate the first bit of progress you've found?"

This time, the dissatisfaction in Kenin's eyes assured Mathias he was through with the jokes, and part of the paladin was ashamed of himself. Though he'd never cared much for the children gods, Kenin *had* provided him new and valuable insight. "Forgive my lack of manners. I suspect those who've been taken had their bodies grabbed, as well?"

Kenin's expression never warmed. "As far as I know."

Mathias nodded, feeling dirty that he found pleasure in that fact. At least now he knew Nessix wasn't the only one, and he'd be able to inquire about missing persons and grave robberies in his search for a potential pattern in this madness. Having worn out his welcome, Mathias stepped backwards to grab the door's handle.

"Thank you for your assistance, my lord." After a brief moment's consideration, Mathias released the handle and gave Kenin a respectful bow. "I'll leave you to your mischief now."

Kenin didn't reciprocate a farewell gesture, but Mathias hadn't expected him to. As the god flung open his chest of coins once more, Mathias turned and left the room.

NINETEEN

Nessix recognized the rumble around her, the way the earth beneath her shuddered, and though she comprehended it was a dream, her heart still screamed of the danger she was in. She pinched her eyes shut, humming against the stabbing pain in her hip and the cries of the doomed warriors around her. Flashes of that terrible lightning strobed through the darkness. The smell of waste and blood and burned flesh turned her stomach.

Doomed to face this nightmare yet again, Nessix had one grand advantage this time around; she knew it was a dream. Scholars theorized that dreams hid clues of the waking world, and Nessix was determined to find out what this one meant to tell her. So many questions raced through her mind that she didn't know where to start, but she clenched her teeth and sat up, leaning her weight onto her left hip to spare her broken right one. She focused past the wounded and the weather, turning her mind from tormented cries.

Mountains rose far in the distance, clouds hanging low over their peaks so Nessix couldn't see their caps. What might have been a forest at some point spanned out from the foothills, though the remaining trees were little more than charred timbers reaching toward the sky, stripped clean of their leaves and branches. The ground was packed hard and bare. Was this Elidae? Kol had assured her that the flemans won that war, but Nessix couldn't fathom where else she could be. Drawing a deep breath, prepared to brace against the pain she knew was coming, Nessix pushed herself fully upright.

Her ears rang as her nerves fired in protest, and she grimaced as tears rolled freely down her cheeks. Biting her lip to muffle her scream, Nessix dabbed the tears away to study the men scrambling madly around the battlefield.

Those around her who weren't dead either ran in blind panic or huddled in helpless, shocked lumps, unable to muster their courage. There were no in betweens. The residue of combat masked these troops' physical features, and even Nes's own hands were so blotched with blood and dirt that she could hardly recognize them. Elidae had never mourned like this, and Nessix had to entertain the thought that this wasn't meant to be her home.

But if it wasn't Elidae, where *was* it?

More rumbles in the distance reawakened Nes's urgency to try to find shelter. She flopped over to crawl along with her three good limbs.

The weapons scattered on the battlefield were unlike any Nessix had ever seen. Forged of a metal that gleamed an iridescent white even through the blood, the blades were small and curved with blunt spikes protruding from the bottom of the hilts. She picked one up, finding it nearly weightless, and tucked it into her belt. Most of the men in her vicinity wore remnants of leather armor fashioned of thick straps woven across their chests with no obvious binding point. None of them wore helms.

Nessix dragged herself past two more bodies before a nearby bolt shot so close it stirred her hair. She flattened herself against the ground, wondering why she was repeatedly subjected to this war that had nothing to do with her. Once the ground quit trembling from the impact, Nessix hefted herself up again and continued to crawl forward into what appeared to have once been the front lines.

Blue banners lay crumbled in the dirt among the warriors. Determination blunting her pain, Nessix pulled herself close enough to tear the nearest one from a dead man's grasp. Easing back into a modified sitting position, she opened the banner to study its heraldry. The image of a winged man standing before a silver sunburst was emblazoned across the rich fabric. It was a crest Nessix couldn't fit to any country she knew, but a swell of melancholy pride filled her heart as she gazed down at it. She reached trembling fingers forward to trace the embroidery, just as a wad of bloody saliva struck its center.

"It's lost."

At every other meeting, Nessix had feared her savior on some level, but this time, she suffered a fleeting hatred for the shredded man. It was an uncomfortable, counter-intuitive reaction, and her loathing for him passed with the next ominous rumble. She turned her face to him, seeing the same tension and terror as always.

"Come on, get up!" the man urged, voice no less strained than every other time he tried to rescue her. Only now, she understood him. "Berann and Annin should have a barrier raised."

Nessix stared at him, eyes wide and mouth gaping dumbly as her heart stilled. Annin? He couldn't possibly be referring to the bitter oraku Nessix knew?

"We have to get moving," the man insisted, strong hands gripping Nessix by the upper arms.

Unable to respond as her mind grappled with this newfound information, Nessix wrapped her arms around the man's shoulder as he hoisted her to her feet. She screamed when the weight of her leg pulled on her hip, but she'd expected the pain and the rapid stream of insight washing over her was too vital to lose over a simple, mortal response. Nessix ground her teeth together and pressed closer to the man. There wasn't much time left to prod for information, and she had to use every available second.

"Who's Berann?" she asked, shouting above the crashes and crying around her.

The man spared her a pitying look and kept pressing forward. "You know. Magic-flinging Berann."

That didn't help Nessix nearly as much as she'd hoped it would, but it was a start. A fresh question struck her, one which she hadn't thought to ask in any of the previous nightmares, even with the language barrier. Nessix drew a deep breath, not quite sure what she hoped for. "And who are you?"

This time, her guide jarred to a stop and turned his shredded face toward her, eyes pooling with tears of disbelief. "How hard were you hit?"

Nessix opened her mouth and shook her head, unable to concoct a reply. It was a wasted moment, as her quest for information had distracted her from counting the heartbeats to that first deadly strike. The bolt lacerated the sky and struck Nes's companion before she had the chance to dig anything else out of him.

Startled by her lapse of focus, Nessix woke before she got struck, promptly curling her knees to her chest in a defensive huddle as reality closed in around her once again. Her initial gasp for air left her in a fit of coughing, and her loose hair stuck to her neck and cheeks from a cold sweat. She was no longer in the luxurious comfort of Kol's quarters, but on the hard clay floor of the chasm. Memories of the final moments of her fight with Grell rushed up to her two steps ahead of how the event had ended, and the steady feed of adrenaline from her dream spurred her upright.

"Take it easy. He's gone."

Nessix abandoned her instinct to find something to arm herself with as she heard Kol's miserable voice. He sounded tired, defeated. He sounded as pathetic as Nessix had once hoped to hear him.

She remembered; she'd jumped into Grell's attack to save Kol. Gasping, Nessix spun to see Kol propped against a boulder behind her, wings drooped at his sides. The right side of his face was swollen and turning a deep purple, and blood stained what little Nessix could see of the white of his eye. Posture slumped and unblemished side of his face sagging with exhaustion, Nessix couldn't decide if she should be relieved to see Kol breathing or dreading how he'd respond to the actions she'd taken once he felt more like himself.

"Eat this." He tossed a chunk of dream stop her direction.

Following that order was among one of the last things Nessix wanted to do, but she craved how the dream stop would help soothe her mind. She retrieved the vegetable off the ground and wiped the dirt from it on the leg of her pants. Biting into it gingerly, she pressed the fingers of her free hand against that little silver ring that had caused Kol so much distress. She suspected explaining that reaction would be more than Kol was willing to divulge at the moment. Her foolish disobedience—whether or not Kol ultimately appreciated it—in mind, Nessix waded into conversing with him carefully.

"You know about the dream stop?" she asked, heart rate reeling though she couldn't quite motivate herself to look at Kol.

"The what?"

Nessix swallowed her bite and waited to take the next until after she'd spoken. "The dream stop." She waved the remaining root. "It makes the nightmares less—" She coughed at how close she came to admitting this particular vulnerability. "Makes them more tolerable."

On any other day, Kol would have smirked at Nes's apparent distress, but he didn't have any humor left in him today. He turned his attention to the lip of the chasm. "It's used for much more than that. I was a fool to not bring any for your stay."

Nessix furrowed her brow. "Why is that?" She hadn't expected Kol to care whether or not she slept well.

"At the core of all akhuerai is raw chaos." Distracted by watching the upper level, Kol's words fell slowly.

A shiver raced across Nes's exposed flesh at the thought of him watching for a potential assault. She tugged her torn blouse more completely across her bound chest. "There's nothing chaotic about any of the akhuerai, besides the means that were taken to kill us in the first place."

Kol pulled his gaze from its position to study Nessix. "What were you thinking when you chose to attack Grell?"

Nessix blinked and snuck a quick look at Kol. The side of his face that still resembled the alar she knew wore the patient expression that always frustrated her so much. Reading his intentions was twice as hard when he only controlled half of his face. She swallowed the final bite of her dream stop and hastily looked away, trying to figure out how to tell him she'd been trying to save his life.

"I recognized him as the greatest threat," she said. "He was assaulting us both, endangering my people, and I knew I had to stop him or die trying."

To Nes's relief, Kol gave a short nod of acceptance. "But you must have known you *would* die trying."

Nessix opened her mouth to reply, but left it hanging for some time. She'd known when Grell first grabbed her to haul her from Kol's chamber that she'd been likely to die. She'd known it as she sailed through the air toward the chasm floor. She'd known it the moment she realized Grell was chasing after her and Kol. But shortly after that, all she remembered was resolve.

"I... I don't know," she said at last. "I should have known better. There's no way I can stand a chance against such an overwhelming opponent without the benefit of my sword and armor..."

"Yet you faced him, anyway. You faced him when I'd done everything possible to thwart your efforts to do so."

Nessix shot another hasty glance Kol's direction, afraid that was a reprimand. He'd turned his gaze upward again, expression as placid as he could manage, and Nessix blew out a sigh. "Yes, I did."

"And while you were engaging him, you weren't afraid?"

Nessix doubted Kol expected her to openly admit her fears to him, but he'd posed this question for her benefit, not his own. She distinctly recalled common sense telling her to be afraid, yet she'd charged anyway, and she'd done so in defense of a demon she routinely told herself she hated. It was an irrational action made from irrational decisions. This was what Kol had meant by her being based in chaos.

"So, my army..." Nessix murmured, eyes sweeping across the mangled bodies on the ground. "They were acting from that same chaos?"

Kol's shoulders ached too much to shrug. "I wasn't here to see what catalyzed their actions, but based on the observations I made, they weren't acting with sound minds."

Guilt pounded a fist into Nes's gut and suddenly, she wished she hadn't put the dream stop in her stomach. If she'd have denied Kol and refused to train the akhuerai, maybe they would have stayed timid enough to be spared such horrific combat. Then again, maybe if she'd trained them more carefully, they'd have been better equipped to defend themselves. Nessix couldn't change the past, so she tried to find its hidden benefits. At least this catastrophe had succeeded in getting Kol to talk about how the akhuerai functioned.

"Will they be okay?" Nes's voice was little more than a small squeak, carrying to Kol only because of the chasm's relative silence.

"Of course. Akhuerai cannot be killed by simple combat. Grell neutralized you by strangulation, so you had no grievous wounds to mend. Your army will rise again; their healing process will simply take a bit longer."

Part of Nessix relaxed at Kol's words, reassured of her people's safety, but the other part still trembled with fear. The demon guards were unlikely to forget this rebellion. Grell was unlikely to forget her defiance. She'd been so careful, working the appropriate angles and sidling closer to the key players than she ever wanted to get. Had this one event destroyed those efforts?

Nessix had grown used to the instability of the hells, but she couldn't see a clear path anymore. The demons would watch for the next infraction. They'd expect the akhuerai to rebel again. Nessix didn't know what had inspired them to strike without her guidance, but her loyal army had complicated matters for her. She looked up at Kol, matching his contemplative grimace. He'd proven his devotion to her yet again, and though their alliance was frowned upon, it was all Nessix had. She didn't look forward to what this meant for her future.

"What does that have to do with the dream stop?"

Kol's open eye softened in relief and he stood, grabbing the stuffed leather satchel that had been at his side. "It helps balance that chaos," he said, though clearly distracted. "Helps calm your wild impulses. Get up."

Nessix furrowed her brows and followed the order. "So you've been drugging us."

"Essentially."

"And I snapped because I'd gone too long without it?"

"That's what I'm hoping."

Nessix hoped it was that simple, too. She wasn't keen on the idea of having risked her well-being for a demon. Storing this information away, Nessix followed Kol's gaze to the top of the chasm where Annin stepped forward to glide toward the ground. The oraku took his time sweeping across the expanse, bright eyes soaking in the scene of destruction. After getting his fill of the carnage, he turned and flew toward Nessix and Kol, glare darkening the closer he got.

Berann and Annin should have a barrier raised.

Nessix shivered at the coincidence of those words and shook her head to scatter the thoughts aside. She rubbed the sensation away from the back of her neck with a clammy hand.

Half of Kol's face relaxed in a smile as Annin landed, the other half too puffy to lift his lips. "You made it back."

Annin didn't return the smile. Stalking past Kol, he dropped a small pouch on the boulder and began plucking supplies from it. "No thanks to you. Grell hasn't been like this in some time, and he's not letting anyone forget it. You're *lucky* I made it back."

The smile fell from Kol's face. "Is it wise for me to even try getting us back to my chamber?"

"Us?" Nessix asked.

Annin ignored her interruption as he uncorked a jar filled with a milky substance. "Wise?" He shoved a wad of dressing inside the jar to soak up the contents. "No. Safe?" He flung a scathing glance at Nessix and sighed. "It should be, as long as you keep yourselves unseen and unheard. Grell's calming down in the holding cells and I've brought escorts. If you want to get back to your chamber, now is your best opportunity."

Kol nodded, even as Nessix firmly shook her head. "My people need me," she protested. "You have to see that!"

Annin wrung the excess fluid from the dressing and flung the dampness off his fingers. Shoving past Nessix, he slapped the compress to Kol's cheek, grabbing the alar's hand to force him to hold it in place.

Kol winced as the bruised and broken skin on his face burned at the dressing's healing bite. "Your people have learned their lesson, and I've learned mine. You haven't finished your studies,

210

but I'll make sure you're able to return here daily to maintain order." He turned to face Nessix, functioning eyebrow dipped downward with menacing command. "You *can* maintain order, I presume."

In all honesty, Nessix didn't know anymore. It had been weeks since she'd last commanded her troops. The last time she'd spoken to them, she thought they'd agreed to hold their actions until she could coordinate a proper assault. Kol had reported that Auden led the akhuerai competently in her stead. He'd been the boldest of the akhuerai from early on; could he have declared himself their leader and ordered this attack? Did the akhuerai even respect her anymore?

Nessix was relatively confident she'd be able to stand against Kol in their current conditions, but she flicked a glance at Annin. He had his back to them as he quietly packed away his medical kit. The oraku had been searching for an excuse to humble Nessix from the start, and with her mind already tangling around how he might play into whatever was happening in her dreams, she didn't think she'd be able to best him.

"I'll maintain order," she murmured.

Kol gave Nessix a brief nod and turned back to Annin. "You said we've got an escort waiting for us?"

Annin secured the last of his items, looking no more pleased than normal. "You do if you hurry."

Placing a hand on Nes's stiff shoulder, Kol pushed her forward. Annin's wings snapped as he took flight, and Nessix cringed from recent memories linked to the same sound. "Aren't we going with him?" she asked.

Kol set his jaw in a manner Nessix balked at. "I'd love to go that route," he snipped.

Nessix blinked. Flight was the only way to leave the chasm besides… "Do those stairs even hold weight?"

"I hope they do." Kol spared Nessix a glance as he strode forward, fingers digging into her shoulder to discourage her from trying to escape from him.

Nessix wanted to debate the soundness of this decision—maybe Grell's strike had rattled the alar more than he'd let on—but

Kol's stony demeanor warned her against it. She peered at him from the side of her eye, trying to decide if this was a punishment for her prior behavior. He'd positioned her on his blind side, implying he trusted Nessix's good will toward him more than anyone else's. Apparently, her actions in his defense had made an impact.

Unable to decode Kol's thoughts by his expression, Nessix concentrated on the alar's posture. Strong strides carried him forward, suggesting he was of sound mind, and he kept his head raised with the authoritative pride he wore so well. Nessix had initially interpreted the hunch in his shoulders and droop of his wings as humility delivered by Grell's beating, but the longer she watched the incline of Kol's chin, the more she doubted that assessment. If he'd felt any sort of shame in his defeat—a defeat directly linked to Nes's perceived insubordination—she'd have been reprimanded for it. The fight with Grell had progressed faster than Nessix could easily recall, but she did remember Grell lifting Kol by his wings.

Kol didn't fly them out of this chasm because he couldn't. Nessix swallowed her discomfort in this realization, knowing better than to bring it up. A pile of guilt stacked on her shoulders, Nessix bowed her head and walked forward.

When they reached the stairs, Kol discarded his compress and gestured for Nessix to begin her climb. Shallow handholds had been dug out of the wall every other step, but the stones themselves looked even more dangerous up close than they had from a distance. At least Nessix had been spared the added weight of her weapons and armor.

"You charged a raging inoga, and you're telling me you're afraid of stairs?"

The sly humor in Kol's voice calmed Nessix. At least *something* had returned to normal. She heaved a heavy sigh and tested her weight on the first step. "Raging inoga have a whole heap of blind spots." She wedged her fingers into a handhold, relying more on the strength of her arms to steady herself than her legs. "If I'd had both of my arms functioning, I could have killed him."

A hand snatched the back of Nes's waistband, pulling her

reluctant progress to an abrupt stop. Cramming her other hand into the next hold, Nessix pressed herself against the wall and turned to face Kol. His right eye had swollen completely shut, but his left glinted with the strictness of a parent warning their child to not stick their hand in a fire.

"That is the last time you speak of such fantasies."

His tone raised the hairs on Nes's arms and her jaw trembled at the silent implications that came with it. He released his hold and gave her a gentle nudge on the small of her back.

"Keep going," he said, as though he hadn't spoken such dire misgivings seconds before.

Nessix resumed her reluctant creep upwards. Progress moved slowly, more so from fear than difficulty. When Nessix had first been brought to the chasm, she'd recognized these stairs as unsound. The demon guards must have used them to change shifts, though she'd never seen them do so. It was such a precarious structure that even left unguarded, none of the akhuerai had ever tried to scale them. And now, Nessix was being forced to be that first fool—followed by an equally foolish demon—to surmount this impossible barrier. She was about to laugh at the absurdity when Kol's voice pierced the silence.

"Why did you fight me?"

Nessix wiped the sweat from her forehead with her shoulder and inched tighter against the wall. "You're going to have to be a little more specific than that."

"After I caught you, you fought me. You must have known I wasn't Grell. Why did you do it?"

That was a question Nessix was unwilling to give an honest answer to. Kol was unlikely to believe the truth, anyway. Nessix moved ahead. "You'd just dislocated my shoulder," she said. "I figured a fall would let me start over, maybe make Grell give up his pursuit."

"And what was your plan if you survived?"

"Fight. Obviously."

Kol chuckled, a response Nessix hadn't expected given their pathetic conditions, perilous positions, and grim futures. She looked up the flight of stairs. They'd made it halfway without mishap. Comforted that Kol seemed to have forgiven her for the trouble she'd caused him, Nessix pressed the luck she knew was running thin just a little bit further.

"I can't help but think that this entire mess could have been avoided if you'd let me know how the akhureai were meant to function."

"I did," Kol said. "You function in chaos and do as you're told. That's all you need to know."

Nessix would have stopped to demand a proper answer if not for how close she was to the top of the chasm. She stared intently at the wall, forcing herself to move at the same steady pace to avoid overloading the questionable steps. As the distance to safety grew nearer, a pair of demons stepped forward to wait for her. Annin had spoken of escorts, but he'd also spoken of how much he hated Nessix. Kol wouldn't have willingly let her fall into harm's way so soon after her recent mistake—or at least that's what she hoped—and so she didn't fight these demons when they grasped her arms and hoisted her onto solid ground. They kept a hold of her as another pair stood by to assist Kol, but didn't prevent her from turning to look down into the chasm.

A detail of demon guards carefully sorted through the fallen bodies, gathering the weapons scattered about the carnage. Their presence kept the small number of akhuerai who had survived the assault tucked in their hiding spots. Nessix's heart wept for the lessons that had been slammed into her people, and she longed to uncover what had caused the disastrous event.

Kol's hand clasped the back of Nes's arm as he shooed the two demons away. "They'll be fine," he said, following her forlorn gaze. "Let's get you tucked away before my lord decides to come looking for you."

Nessix stayed in place a moment longer even after Kol began to pull her away. She scoured the bloody ground for some sign of movement, some proof that her people would recover as seamlessly as she had, until she remembered how badly she needed to please Kol. Feeling filthy, as though she was willfully abandoning her brave warriors to their brutal ends, Nessix turned quickly to catch up to Kol.

"I need answers," she said to him in her native tongue. "And you owe some to me."

Kol marched along in silence for several strides. Flanked by a guard of ten demons headed by Annin, Nes's demands didn't hold much weight. But that didn't stop Kol from realizing the truth in them. "There are many aspects about your creation that we cannot afford to let your people learn," Kol said after a long moment of consideration. "The revolt you just witnessed is a reminder of that—the more you know, the less you'll fear. And once you quit fearing us, that's when you'll quit obeying. In this, little one, I'm keeping you safe."

Nessix frowned tightly. "We are outnumbered and woefully unskilled for combat. That revolt you just witnessed is a resounding reassurance of that. I don't understand anything about the ways of magic, but I need to know the basics of how my people function. How are we alive? Why can't we die?"

Kol stared at Annin's back, chewing over his options. The oraku would not be pleased if Kol began explaining the process of raising an akhuerai, but he understood enough of Nes's yearning on the matter. She needed to know how to reassure her army that they were safe and explain to them why the demons were their masters. Kol could easily give her that information, if only he knew how Nes's tactical mind would use it. He'd routinely underestimated his prize's tenacity, and if he spoke these truths, he'd never be able to take them away from her.

"You are alive again," Kol started slowly, treading carefully to find a balance between indulging Nes's curiosity and protecting the entire operation. He frowned as Annin tipped an ear in his direction. "Because we reanimated you with the blood of demons who sacrificed themselves for you. You cannot die because we have placed permanent anchors on your souls, keeping them from departing for the divine realm."

Nessix gasped, her hand flying to the ring in her chest. Less than a second later, Kol's fingers caught hers to draw her hand away. She looked at him and saw his face grim and stony.

"I told you it wasn't smart to mess with that."

Heart thumping at the memory of Grell's fingers gripping the ring, hearing him growl about ending her, Nessix almost wished she wouldn't have asked. Maybe Kol was right. Maybe she was happier not knowing. A fresh bombardment of questions flew at Nessix now, but her courage was too shaken to seek their answers. What would happen if this ring was removed? Was her soul anchored to it or simply plugged into her body? Would removing it allow her to die, or would she be left living with nothing but demon essence powering her? That was the fate worse than death, she was sure of it. Nessix tugged her hand free from Kol so she could rub the chill from her arms.

Desperate to change the subject, she plucked at the next topic of concern. "So what about the dreams?"

Kol's brows furrowed. "This is the second time you've mentioned dreams."

Nessix frowned as it seemed unlikely she'd get an answer about this, either. "All of us have nightmares. Recurring ones, different for each of us, but all real enough that we wake in panics."

Annin turned his head again, eavesdropping more for the sake of scholarship than concern. Kol cleared his throat. It was the first time either of them had heard mention of this phenomenon, and Kol wasn't about to let the information pass him by.

"What do you dream of?"

"I wake up from unconsciousness in the middle of a battlefield. Thunder and lightning shake the ground, and I'm afraid to my very core. I try to get away from the danger, but my hip's broken and then a man with half a face comes to help me." She stared at Annin's back, deciding against mentioning any reference to his name. "He tries to drag me away, but then we both get struck by lightning, and that's when I wake up."

Kol's skin crawled and he watched as Annin nervously flexed his fingers. He knew what nightmare Nessix suffered from, because it was one that had haunted him for centuries. The color drained from his face and for a moment, Kol felt as though he'd faint.

"We all have different dreams," Nessix said, oblivious to Kol's issues with the content of her dream. After all, whims of the sleeping mind must be too petty for such twisted beasts to worry about. "But that's mine. Why do we have them?"

"I don't—" Kol cleared the catch from his throat. "I don't know. This is the first I've heard of them."

Nessix lowered her eyes, missing Kol's efforts to shake off his discomfort. She'd hoped that finding out why such troubles routinely found the akhuerai would give her a clue as to how to make them stop. There wouldn't be time to find a fresh approach to this dilemma, as Annin coughed and announced that they'd reached Kol's chamber.

In silence, the alar ushered Nessix into his room, secured the door behind them, then picked up her book from where Grell's tantrum had thrown it. Shoving it into Nessix's hands, Kol silently went to work putting his room back together and tried to forget the past.

TWENTY

Mathias left his meeting with Kenin carrying an emotion he'd feared had been lost to him. Hope. The fury and fear still boiled in his heart, but answers *did* exist, and they were within his reach. He hadn't yet summoned Ceraphlaks to take him to his next stop, largely in part because he didn't know where that would be.

He'd been absolutely certain that Azerick and Drao would have known more, and that the gods of natural forces would have felt something amiss. He'd expected Inwan to hear the cries of Nes's soul. None of the most obvious sources had provided Mathias with any notable insight. The fact that Kenin, a relatively ignored god, had heard rumors which hadn't even reached Etha threw Mathias's expectations completely off kilter. Visiting Kenin had been an impulse born of desperation to avoid a more unpleasant task, yet it had yielded the first nugget of information from the divine realm. There was no telling which of the other gods might know more. Mathias scratched his ear and suddenly became aware of footsteps crunching along behind him.

"Have you played around enough to satisfy your obstinance yet?" Etha didn't speak with malice, but her bluntness struck Mathias with a blow he didn't appreciate.

"You think I'm playing?" His question matched hers in terms of warmth.

Etha trotted ahead to catch up to Mathias and looked up at him. "Okay, maybe not playing. But you're wasting time."

He kept his eyes raised high down the path. "I'm being thorough. And safe. Kenin gave me new information, you know. No two victims from the same township, and the oraku bears no visible runes. Those are solid leads."

Etha rolled her eyes. "*That* is what you're overlooking Nes's inevitable suffering to obtain?"

Mathias winced and momentarily lost the rhythm of his steady stride. Etha frowned at how her reminder of the reason behind his quest hurt him, but it couldn't be helped.

"It *is* information," she granted. "And it'll be valuable once you're actually in the position to confront the demons responsible for it."

"And to find them, I have to keep searching," Mathias said.

Pouting should have been beneath the Mother Goddess, but Etha indulged herself a good glower. "So where do you intend to search next?" She knew well that it wouldn't be in the most logical place.

Mathias chanced a quick glance at Etha, regretting it the second he caught her stern eyes. The truth was, he didn't know where he wanted to go, though he had a very firm opinion on where he *didn't* want to be. Etha wouldn't wait for an answer long before heading down that road, and so Mathias spit out the first name that came to mind.

"Tebrim."

Etha wrinkled her nose. "Tebrim?"

"Yes." Mathias swallowed the nervous tickle in his throat, eyes focusing forward once more.

"The god of *commerce*?"

"That's the only one I know of."

The pair walked on in silence for several minutes, each crunch of a foot against the ground laughing at Mathias over his ridiculous proposal. Etha waited patiently for him to explain himself or rethink this plan, but the longer it sat in place, the more desperately Mathias clung to it. He knew it was unlikely to yield anything useful, but the ever-present optimist in him helpfully pointed out how Kenin shouldn't have known anything, either.

As it became apparent that Mathias had buckled down on this silly course of action, Etha darted in front of him. She turned to grab his wrists and forced him to a stop. His boots scuffed in the dirt, accompanied by an inconvenienced huff as his eyes rolled toward the sky. Neither aspect of his tiny tantrum fazed Etha.

"My laws regarding free will forbid me to force you to do my bidding, but my role as your mother and yours as my son demand you listen to a direct order. Go speak with Ceredulus. Now."

Mathias tried to tug his arms free but found them rendered immobile in Etha's grasp. Etha seldom abused her power over him in such a manner, and Mathias had forgotten how insignificant it made him feel to be overwhelmed by such a petite woman. Even if that petite woman was a goddess. "You already said he may not know anything."

Etha chastised Mathias with the jaded glower of any mother staring down her insubordinate child. "He'll know more than *Tebrim* would. What could that miser possibly have to offer you? That nobody's purchased souls lately? What currency do you suppose demons deal in when it comes to souls, anyway?"

Mathias flushed, abandoning his attempt to squirm out of Etha's hold, but that didn't loosen the rigidness of his jaw. "Ceredulus is untrustworthy."

"Untrustworthy or not, he's the god of the undead. He claimed his position in the heavens specifically for the purpose of manipulating souls. He may not know where Nessix is, but he'll have an idea of what the demons could be doing to her if anyone does. Use your brain, Mathias. Are you really going to let a personal grudge from centuries ago stand in the way of saving Nessix?"

As badly as Mathias wanted to accuse Etha of attempting to manipulate his emotions, the desperation in the way her fingers dug into his arms and the elevated pitch of her voice assured Mathias that she truly saw no other way to right the demons' wrong. She'd depended on him since the moment he climbed out of his grave, and nothing about that had changed. It was ironic that she'd raised him from the dead to thwart Ceredulus from doing the same to others, even more so that she now relied on that same evil god to help restore balance. Helpless against Etha's pleading, Mathias slowly met her eyes, his hatred for Ceredulus scolding him for doing so when he saw the desperation streaming back at him.

"I do not want to speak to Ceredulus," he said.

"I know you don't," Etha replied, voice small and gentle. "But the sooner you do, the sooner you can put it behind you. You told me you'd stop at nothing to fix this. Don't let your past with Ceredulus be the reason you fail."

Mathias thought back on Julianna's accusation, about how he'd rooted his intention to run off to learn about the stolen souls in selfish motives. He'd claimed Etha stood behind him at that time, and as he continued to protest every suggestion and demand his goddess made, he realized he was once again being driven by his own self-interest. Admitting as much to himself was a firm slap in the face, and Mathias frowned.

"You are aware that he swore to never let me to escape the Veil the next time I entered it, aren't you?"

Etha's shoulders sagged, a mix of relief and resolve settling over her as she allowed Mathias's wrists to slide from her grasp. "I am. But his powers are limited."

It didn't take any more than that bitter reminder to release Mathias's humorless chuckle. "By that logic, Shand's powers had been limited, too, and she did a fair job incapacitating me more than once."

Etha shook her head with a dainty sigh. "Not limited compared to *you*. Limited compared to *me*. I won't throw you into a situation you can't get out of."

Mathias stared at Etha and blinked mutely, wondering how much of the past she'd chosen to ignore to state that with such honesty.

She caught his skepticism and snorted. "Well, you *have* gotten out of every situation I've thrown you into."

He grumbled, refusing to admit the truth out loud since Etha already knew it. Rubbing his temples and closing his eyes, Mathias blew out a labored sigh. There was nobody in all of Abaeloth he hated arguing with more than Etha. "And if I go now, you won't ask me to again?"

Etha smiled, eyes glittering. "Not over this offense."

Mathias curled his lip. That was the best he'd be able to get. "Fine," he caved. "I'll go talk to him. This once."

Etha clapped her hands like a gleeful child. "This will be such an adventure, Mathias! Just like old times."

If not for the uneasy lump gumming up his stomach, Mathias would have smiled at her happiness. "Yeah," he sighed. "*Just* like old times." He resumed trudging down the road, Etha skipping along beside him.

TWENTY-ONE

Over the past few weeks, Nessix caught herself unwittingly enjoying Kol's company. Her foolish actions taken in his defense—and the equally foolish ones he'd made for her—reinforced the unlikely sense of camaraderie shared between them. She never let it slip her mind that she was shamelessly using Kol for protection and to leverage her path out of the hells, but she'd reached the point where she couldn't quite wish ill on him.

That was why the abrupt loss of his dry humor upon learning of her nightmares raised her concern. Never before in their unusual relationship had Kol been so stiff and businesslike with her, and when Annin checked in to pull Kol aside so they could bicker with each other in the corner, the alar's agitation grew even worse. Most demons suffered from the burdens of pride, and Nessix tried to attribute this shift in Kol's demeanor on his insecurity for not knowing everything about his creations. At least Nessix had opted against mentioning the coincidence of Annin's name in her dream. That would have been one more frustration for Kol to dwell on.

When Nessix returned to her studies, she refrained from asking Kol about the missing pages of demon history or what an unfamiliar word meant. He watched her through narrowed eyes, the swelling of his face draining courtesy of Annin's compress. Reading Kol had challenged Nessix from the start, but now his expression was simply blank. She couldn't decide if he was angry or pleased or curious; he held her only with a keen, steady stare that never lost focus. His intensity drove into Nessix, rattling her concentration. She hunched over her reading to keep from catching his eyes with the corner of hers and focused on her work.

Hours passed in this manner before Kol broke the silence at last. "You're done for the night. Get some sleep."

Pressing her finger to the page to keep track of her place, Nessix looked up into Kol's sharp eyes, regretting what she was about to say even as she spoke. "I'm not tired yet."

Kol stared at her a moment longer, then blinked and shook his head, eyes softening with that devious glint he so often wore. This was the Kol Nessix was comfortable with, but the rapid change in his demeanor brought tiny ripples of discomfort to the back of Nes's neck. "You will sleep. I suspect tomorrow will be a trying day for you."

Nessix swallowed her intention of asking Kol what he meant, daunted by his clinical nature. He hadn't reacted to her engaging Grell. He hadn't made any outward effort to hide his own injuries. He'd gone as far as to attempt to raise her spirits on the climb from the chasm. But Nes's mention of the akhuerai's dreams had launched Kol into a deep contemplation she didn't know how to face. Figuring Kol planned to watch her sleep so he could study signs of this new information, Nessix reluctantly abandoned her book on the desk and crawled onto her cot. She wouldn't fight this order, nor would she brood over what tomorrow's trials would be.

Nessix hadn't been sure when sleep found her or how closely Kol watched her in hopes of seeing her struggle through the horrors of that war. Much to Nes's relief, all she dreamt of was running through a meadow of lilies, chasing firehoppers. It was an unusually carefree dream for Nessix, but after surviving the previous day, she savored the peace it brought her, content to disappoint Kol this once.

A firm shove in the shoulder woke her in the morning and as the alar's face—now almost completely healed and smoothed free of worry—came into view, Nessix groaned. There would be no peace for her. She sat up slowly and wiped the sleep from her eyes as she yawned. Kol promptly left her side to begin sorting through her armor.

"Let's get you dressed," he said, his tone no longer hollow and absent.

Nessix hesitated. The last time he'd been so blunt and anxious about getting Nessix in her armor, it hadn't ended pleasantly for her. Last night, he'd warned her of today's potential for danger. Had the inoga demanded a trial for her behavior? Nessix studied Kol's relaxed shoulders and even expression and found that unlikely; he always wore his nerves openly when dealing with his lords was inevitable. She slipped from the cot and padded over to the demon.

"What did I need my rest for?" Nessix accepted the blouse Kol handed her, made a slight adjustment to her chest binding, and replaced the battle-worn shirt she'd slept in with the fresh one.

"Have you forgotten your assignment? You're going to train your army."

Nessix froze as she bent forward to put on her boots. "You... want me to put more combative skill on them?" In truth, she'd been afraid that the demons no longer trusted the akhuerai as weapons and would put an end to the entire operation.

"The army lacks discipline," Kol said. "They weren't unified enough to make a dent against their targets and aren't remotely ready to march in force. You've been the key to their progress, and you will finish the job." He smirked and began strapping Nes's armor to her. "Demons are a resilient bunch. We won't let a couple raging villagers daunt us."

Kol worked behind Nessix and so she allowed herself a brief, frustrated crease of her lips. She didn't know if she'd be able to get the akhuerai to stand in force after their recent massacre. Her greater reluctance, however, came from fear. The demons had raised this army with the purpose of striking the mortal realm, Nessix was certain of it. With Kol's assurance that chaos lurked within all akhuerai, the thought of them unleashed on the surface begged Nessix to refuse this order, no matter the cost.

Nothing else was discussed in the time it took Nessix to finish dressing. Her mind was too wrapped up in her fears over the changes in her army's collective mentality, and Kol continued to dwell on the fact that Nessix fought the Divine Battle in her dreams. Neither intended to discuss their concerns with the other, and so they finished securing Nes's armor and stepped into the hall.

A trio of guards had been posted outside Kol's door, and the pinch of security Nessix had lulled into herself fluttered away. The guards flanked Nessix and Kol as they walked toward the chasm, and an even greater surge of discomfort filled Nessix. Born of nobility, she'd grown comfortable with bodyguards—that had been Sulik's sole responsibility until she promoted him to commander—but they'd always walked alongside her as companions. These guards made no indication of casually hoping no danger sprang up. Their eyes darted constantly through the halls and they hung close to their charges, hands actively on their weapons. They anticipated trouble and, after the previous day's fiasco, Nessix couldn't pray hard enough that they'd be disappointed.

The gentle rumble of an active city comforted Nessix as they entered the hall leading to the pit. Her people *had* recovered. This happiness abandoned her as quickly as it arrived as Nessix faced the fact that she'd let them down. She'd been careful to make sure they understood the hazards of battle, but she'd also sworn to protect them from their demon captors. The revolt they'd attempted could have been a statement against her. In the first weeks of Nes's time with the akhuerai, rumors had spread readily that she was in league with the demons, and she'd recently been living with the one they all hated most.

As Kol and Nessix neared the drop off to the chasm, their guards backed away to grant their superior and his pet their privacy. The two of them gazed down as the akhuerai milled about their miserable existence, but there was a subtle difference between their previous trudging and the motions they went through now. Eyes were raised, unafraid to meet the glances of others. Shoulders were held erect with confidence. They still travelled in small groups, but it was with the warmth of camaraderie rather than the need for security. Nessix breathed out a deep sigh, her heart fluttering.

"Do you see what you need to fix?" Kol asked of her quiet gesture.

Nessix shook her head. "Fix? This is what I've been trying to find since you first tossed me in this hole."

"And it's what made them stupid enough to strike without guidance. Whether or not akhuerai come back to life, is that the sort of suffering you want for your people?"

Nessix snuck a glance at Kol, expecting one of his provocative smirks. Instead, she found a small, tight frown, his arms crossed. He'd been serious.

"There's already been talk about simply ending future troublemakers," Kol continued. "It'd be faster and easier for everyone involved, but I imagine you'd prefer not to go that route."

Nessix's toes curled in her boots as she forbid herself from squirming at this stoic side of Kol. "What if that troublemaker was me? Would you end me?"

Kol didn't turn his eyes to her, staring pointedly at the chasm's occupants. "Is that a threat, little one?"

"It was a question."

Kol heaved a weary sigh and turned to face Nessix, unfolding his arms so he could grip hers. "You are a smart woman, Nessix. It's what drew me to you in the first place. But you are a terrible liar. You'd never risk leaving your people unprotected."

"I will do whatever I must to protect them," she said, unflinching from his hold. "Even if that means putting myself in danger. If a time comes where I must make trouble for the guards, will you, Kol, let them end me?"

He frowned. The truth Kol couldn't tell Nessix was that he had no idea what ending her would do to him. He was the only demon to live through the role he played in an akhuerai's creation, and as such, there were too many unknowns to succumb to hastiness. Grudgingly, Kol admitted that Grell and Annin had been right about his foolishness. He couldn't risk Nessix uncovering this, and if he brooded over it much longer, she'd begin with her endless stream of questions as she tried to uncover what he was hiding from her.

"I told you from the start that I want no harm to come to you." *Or me...* "But the hells don't function based on my wants."

Nessix opened her mouth to press the issue just as an

exuberant exclamation shot up from the chasm floor. "It's our general! They've brought her back!"

All of Nes's fears melted away in a swell of pride as more voices were raised at the discovery. There was much she hoped to discuss with Kol to try sniffing out what she could get away with, but she'd have to wait on that. The relief and excitement from her army compensated for the inconvenience, and Nessix stepped forward so they could better see that she was alive and well.

Kol stepped up beside her and a cloud of curses spun through the greetings. He didn't bat an eye at the hatred thrown at him. "It seems they're pleased to see you."

Nessix nodded, smiling at the surge of dignity she hadn't enjoyed in quite some time.

"I don't expect much to be accomplished in terms of training today, but I do expect you to get them back on track."

Nessix bristled at Kol's judgement, taking it as a challenge to her skill as a commanding officer. She'd show him… "I won't rest until they've got their determination back."

Kol chuckled. "You're coming out of there tonight, little one. Be sure to forgive yourself if you don't meet your expectations."

"What?" Nessix breathed. "Where am I going to go?"

"Back to my quarters," Kol said. "You haven't finished your studies, but neither have they. Their structure fell apart without your guidance, so we're compromising."

"A compromise involves giving from both parties," Nessix muttered.

"I've given up enough for you already." A tinge of bitterness snuck through Kol's confidence. "You wanted to be with your people, and this is the best I could arrange after their display of disobedience. You'd be wise to warn them against acting out of line again."

As much lenience as Kol had shown her, Nessix doubted she'd sway him now, and so she silently submitted to his words. She was lucky to return to her army at all. "Fine," she said shortly. "But you and your colleagues and superiors will have to accept any shortcomings that may result in me not getting to stay down there."

"It's cute when you list your conditions so boldly." Kol's tone was flat, drawing Nes's glower. "We expect results. You're an experienced general and I trust you'll find a way to produce them."

Nessix rolled her eyes and muttered incoherent curses beneath her breath, eliciting another chuckle from Kol.

"They're growing impatient." Kol gestured to where a cluster of Nes's army stood staring up at them. "Would you like me to escort you to them?"

"Can your wings safely carry us both?"

"We won't know until we try."

Of all the responses Nessix had anticipated from her insulting question, jest hadn't been among them. She couldn't tell how serious Kol had been, but she didn't have the time to pursue the matter before he wrapped his arms around her and dove into the chasm.

Nessix had no fond memories from her previous experiences with this method of travel, and her belly leapt as they fell. Kol's wings proved reliable and he soared lazily through the air, keeping his descent slow. At first, Nessix thought he took his time as a reminder of the power he had over her, but as her stomach settled and she opened her eyes, she saw that the akhuerai had gathered in a fierce mob that followed Kol's flight pattern. Their cheers of jubilation had warped into fierce curses against the alar, and though he was stronger than a large group of them, they outnumbered him by a devastating margin.

"As soon as we land, you do whatever you must to force them to obey you. Understood?"

The thought of forcing actions onto anyone chilled Nessix, but she had no doubt that the akhuerai intended to tear Kol apart—and that they'd possibly succeed at doing so—if she didn't discourage it. Still confused over why she cared about the alar's fate, Nessix turned her chin toward Kol. "I'll do what I can." Her instinct to protect Kol still smoldered inside of her.

Kol didn't respond to Nes's compliance, raising his voice to address the masses below. "If any of you make an attempt on me, I'll drop her," he called. When several of the bolder men scoffed at what they viewed as an empty threat, Kol added, "As your creator, I can also be your destroyer. Do not make me make an example of your dear general."

That threat gave the mob pause, and their shouts dwindled into speculative murmurs.

"Now's an opportune time to make good on that promise," Kol said in Nes's ear.

She swallowed her reluctance and followed his instruction. "I beg of you, do as he says. This alar has proven himself honest so far. Please do not test him."

"Honest?" Kol chuckled. "I'm touched."

Nes's words effectively dispersed the mass, providing a wide clearing for Kol to land. Nessix suspected the army wouldn't have the tactical sense to coordinate an attempt to surround and jump Kol, and as he prepared to land, he seemed just as unconcerned. As Nes's feet safely hit the ground, the crowd shifted nervously, glancing between Nessix and Kol. He continued grasping her arms to ensure their good behavior.

"I will come retrieve you before dinner," he told Nessix quietly. "And I'll have oraku backup with me. I'd prefer to avoid calling on them, so convince your doting army to not complicate things."

Nessix sighed and cleared her throat. "I've returned to you unharmed. Please help me stay this way by allowing this demon's safe departure."

"I'll see him departed..." rose a sneer from within the crowd.

Kol chuckled deep in his throat. "Sounds like you've got your work cut out for you today. I'll leave you to it."

He departed with nothing else, leaving Nessix in the cloud of dust kicked up by his wings. Wrapped in the throng of akhuerai, guilt and self-consciousness pummeled Nessix. Their resentment for Kol was tangible, and she was faced with needing to defend him against their suspicions. The akhuerai may have rejoiced Nes's return, but there must have been a seed of bitterness lodged in them somewhere for how she had left them alone.

Silence pulsed through the chamber as they watched her, hopeful expectations in their eyes. They waited patiently on her orders, trusting her more than they trusted themselves. For the first time in Nes's life, this obedience weighed her down, grinding her enthusiasm into the dirt. How could she ask them to engage in combat ever again? Balancing all of the contending factors in her reality was becoming increasingly difficult, and Nessix longed for the days when she had Mathias to fall back on. Channeling his compassion and courage as best she could, Nessix took a deep breath. She'd keep Kol and his lords happy *and* support her people if it was the last thing she did.

"I understand if any of you want to quit training after recent events, and I won't fault you for that. The demons still insist on me developing an army, but I'll do everything I can to protect those of you who want to back out."

Amid a subtle commotion of awkward shuffles, a bold scoff reached Nessix. "*Back out?*" Auden shouldered his way through the crowd to reach Nessix, arms crossed and eyes glittering. "General, we're more determined than ever to learn how to fight."

Nessix appraised Auden's confidence, approving of how he'd come into his own during her absence. He was an honest man, a dedicated worker, and Nessix thanked Inwan—whether or not her god of old could hear her—that Auden had been selected as her second in command.

"Is this the consensus?" Nessix asked, raising her gaze to the crowd.

An enthusiastic response from the majority of the akhuerai answered, and in the back of her mind, Nessix heard the pounding of fists against shields, saw the glint of sunlight off blades raised toward the heavens. With her interests spread so thin—defend her people, build her army, please Kol, avoid Grell, decipher her dream, find Mathias—Nessix didn't know how much longer she could perform all of her duties without breaking. Inwan had made her a warrior. Her father had raised her a general. Kol had given her life unending. If anyone could find a way through this mess, it would be Nessix.

"Very well, warriors," she said, shoving her doubts and fears behind the banner of charisma she'd spent so much of her life parading with. "We'll start with discussing what everyone learned from this past battle, see what tactics we can develop from it."

The akhuerai, emboldened by the concept of mortality no

longer a frightful concern, readily shared the discoveries made through their combative actions. Nessix had worried about her newly minted soldiers reverting to terrified villagers, but their excitement as they spoke of the assault floored her in the best ways. Terminology was wrong more often than not and weak spots riddled their demonstrations of impromptu brawling efforts, but Nessix increasingly felt less like she was trying to coax bravery out of timid survivors and more like she was cozied up in a tavern, laughing off the troubles of the latest ogre raid upon her unit's homecoming.

Such nostalgic whims carried Nessix to their midday meal, and the ranks broke readily at the prospect of food after their engaging morning. Having grown used to a higher quality cuisine and proper dining ware, Nessix hid her disappointment in the fare behind a warm smile. After she retrieved her rations, she turned to find a seat when Auden caught up with her.

"General, I'd like a word, if you don't mind."

Nessix smiled. "Not at all." After spending so long in Kol's constant company, she hadn't looked forward to the idea of dining by herself. "There's a few things I wanted to discuss with you, as well."

Auden's features fell in an uncertain blanche and he hesitated briefly before falling in alongside Nessix. "If it has to do with the rebellion—"

Nessix held up a hand and shook her head, expression soft and forgiving. "We can address my concerns after yours."

He gulped down his anxiety and plopped down next to the wall. Nessix sat beside him, far more relaxed, and began to eat immediately. Her casual demeanor coaxed the same from Auden, and after he swallowed his first bite, he spoke.

"I don't think I can voice my concerns without addressing the rebellion, because my concerns are about you, and those are what launched the rebellion."

Touched and a little dismayed that the people who had despised her so strongly in the beginning had been concerned enough to strike the demons in her defense, Nessix shook her head. "Concern for *me*?"

Auden nodded, refusing to look at her as he picked at his food. "Look, we... we were nothing before you came. Our lives meant nothing. Our ambitions meant nothing. Our futures *held* nothing. You... you showed up and taught us how to hope again, General. You reminded us what it means to live and dream. When you were taken, I thought those virtues would be lost in that old misery, but they stuck. *You* did that for us. Then that alar came back, told us you were well and to keep training, and in your name, we did. And then he came again. And again. But never with you. He wouldn't answer when we asked where you were or when you'd be back, and we couldn't get anything out of the guards."

"And so you figured the best option was to *fight* them?" Nessix asked.

Auden worked his jaw slowly and lowered his food to his lap. "Better to risk physical torment than to fall into despair again. You gave us a reason to fight, so we were willing to fight for you. The demons... they *owe* us that much."

Nessix watched quietly as Auden hung his head, his eyes swirling with prideful disbelief in what the akhuerai had done. "Well, your actions worked. I'm back for now."

He looked up at her hastily. "For now?"

"I was taken to study. That alar has been teaching me demon history and lore, about their social structure. He's been teaching me about *us*. He's the only demon who's bothered to share information with me, so I'm investing everything I've got in keeping him happy. He says I've got more to learn, and I'm willing to believe him. The more I get, the more weaknesses I can spot. I'll be returning for daytime training sessions, but it's vital nobody protests when he comes to collect me at the end of the day."

Eyes wide, Auden gawked at Nessix. "He's just... *giving* you information?"

Nessix nodded.

"About *us*?"

She nodded again, eyes twinkling.

"And what have you learned?"

Nessix hesitated, taking a bite of her dream stop as an excuse to buy time. Auden was a good man. She trusted him in leadership roles, but didn't know if she trusted him enough to share that there might be a way for akhuerai to permanently die. Whether or not Nessix had given these people hope, she wouldn't be responsible for telling them that their horror could end, no matter how great a mercy it would be. Even the bit of truth she could tell was something she loathed to speak. Maintaining the akhuerai's trust and good will was as important as keeping Kol happy, and so Nessix delivered what she could.

She told Auden about the akhuerai's demon blood, information he accepted with a mortified blanche, but no debate. She told him of the nature of the dream stop as it tied to suppressing those vile whims inside of them. She told him all about how her report of the nightmares had startled Kol and Annin, adding that there might be some things their captors didn't know about them. And, in the aftermath of a massacre caused by her absence, Nessix reminded Auden of her intention to escape the first chance she had to petition for the Order's assistance in their plight.

Auden accepted all accounts with a weighty gulp and resolute nod. "Am I safe to spread the word of these discoveries?"

Had Nessix not spent the last year of her life fully immersed in the improbable realities of Mathias's magic, the demons' curses, and the irrefutable pull of the gods, she'd have taken this information with the same shock. To her knowledge, none of the akhuerai came from backgrounds that lent them a simple way of swallowing this information, but they deserved to know. She'd told Auden all of this having overlooked that he was a normal man who'd had duty thrust upon him, not an officer groomed through his youth to cope with such burdens. Struck by guilt once again, wanting little more than to fix all of the akhuerai's troubles, Nessix lowered her head.

"Reassure them that we'll all benefit from my studying and remind them of my plan to reach Zeal; I cannot support another rebellion, not yet. If you think they can cope with the rest, you can share what you feel is prudent." Nessix glanced away. "Forgive me. It was unjust of me to drop this burden on you." At least she'd thought better than to tell him what lurked behind those little metal rings.

Auden laughed. Not the nervous kind Nessix had expected after one received such a flood of information, but a wholesome, warm laughter that begged Nes's tension to ease. "I asked you for the information, General," he said. "If I wasn't prepared for the worst, I'd still be hiding behind the rocks and spitting curses behind your back. You're the one braving the demons' halls to bring us intelligence. Perhaps *I'm* the one who needs to beg for forgiveness."

Nessix smirked, giving a gentle chuckle of her own. "I haven't braved anything. Where Kol tells me to go, I go. There's no courage in that. I'd much prefer to stay with the army, you know."

The humor promptly fell from Auden's face, and he looked down at his hands. "That's another thing…"

Nes's heart stalled. What had she said?

"That demon does what he wants, regardless of what you're willing to do, doesn't he?"

"I'm a general, Auden," Nessix said. "I've done many things I don't *want* to do because I'm the first and last line of defense for those in my charge. I'm used to it and gladly accept the role to keep others from needing to face it."

"We were worried, you see, General," Auden stammered, awkwardly picking through what he meant to say. "We've all heard rumors of the way demons torture people… especially the confident." He swallowed hard enough for Nessix to hear a distinct gulp. "Especially women. Are you… Are you okay?"

Nessix laughed beside herself, regretting that she was the cause of Auden's flush. "The worst torture Kol's subjected me to is learning to read obscure text. He's made no actions to look at me in any other capacity, and his immediate companions are too disgusted by me to be interested in those forms of torture." She slapped Auden on the knee and pushed herself to her feet. "I'm not sure how much longer we have before Kol comes back to fetch me. How about we put these worries to bed and get back to training?"

Auden contemplated Nes's tone, extracting the hint of forced cheer she'd used for his benefit, and sighed. If their general was making the best of her circumstances, it would be shameful to not follow her lead. "Yes, General." He climbed to his feet, shoved his remaining food into his mouth, and wiped his hands clean on his pants.

Wondering if what she was doing was right, Nessix led the way back to the training grounds.

* * * * *

It had taken Nessix more pleading than she'd ever had to use before to convince her army that Kol only meant them harm if they refused to let him take her away. None of them—Nessix included—fully believed he'd return her the following day, but after a tedious evening of studying and a night of solid sleep, Kol and his detail of stoic guards escorted Nessix back to the chasm. This routine continued as each day passed and though the bulk of the akhuerai frowned at the schedule, Nessix returned daily to whisper bits of lore that might lead to uncovering the demons' weaknesses. Two weeks later, she was able to negotiate basic spear shafts from the demons to begin teaching the akhuerai to wield weapons. The army rallied around Nessix and her enthusiasm, and their performance finally began to gain the approval of those demons Kol tried so hard to impress.

And then, the nightmares came.

Kol's interest in the nature of her dream only raised Nes's suspicions that something of value hid within this world, and she didn't waste the time to tremble at the rumbling around her or brace for the pain that would follow. Proactively reminding herself that this wasn't real helped numb the agony that sought to cripple her, and Nessix rolled over to drag herself toward where her battered savior always appeared. She looked past the casualties and exotic weapons, tuning out the cries of despair and ringing in her ears. Bent on her mission, Nessix clawed her way forward, sheer determination holding her tears at bay. The shredded man came into view, staggering over top of fallen soldiers as he frantically scanned the battlefield. Nessix sucked in a deep breath, choking on the stench of burning flesh before she gathered enough to speak.

"Have Berann and Annin raised a barrier?" She felt foolish calling out the question, as she didn't know what sort of barrier to expect, let alone what Annin had to do with it.

The man's attention snapped to her, and he kissed his bloody fist and touched it to his forehead in a foreign salute. He hustled forward and wrapped his arms around Nessix to help her to her feet.

"They should be working on it," he said, hefting Nessix against his side. "Let's get moving before the next wave comes."

Nessix complied readily, stumbling along as effectively as her broken hip allowed. "Who are you?" she asked, prepared for his initial response.

Just as in her previous dream, the question jarred the man to a stop and he turned troubled eyes to her. Nessix beat him to voicing his disbelief.

"I was hit pretty hard and am dazed. You can talk while we run. Please, help me just a little more. Tell me your name."

He didn't resume walking, still gawking at her with wide eyes. "It's me," he said, voice rattling with regret. "Grellandier."

But that sounds like... A chill washed over Nessix as she did a double take at the grievous wound which nearly tore the face from this man. Following the jagged line from lip to eye, Nes's fingers went numb. She knew a demon with a scar that matched this injury. She just didn't want to admit it. Despite her best intentions to harvest all the information she could, Nes's single, functioning knee threatened to give out and Grell—if intuition spoke honestly—held her more tightly.

Too many coincidences charged toward her, and Nessix almost wished she hadn't searched for answers at all. And then, the last coincidence slammed between her eyes, carried by Grell's trembling voice.

"Kol, are you alright?"

Nes's vision distorted and between the shock of pain and this unexpected truth, she nearly threw up. Overwhelmed, she spun her gaze across the horizon, watching the lightning streak across the sky. In the distance, faint crashes of waves assaulted the mountains, shooting a furious spray past their peaks. The earth trembled beneath her feet, and Nessix understood.

She was reliving the Divine Battle, and she was doing it through Kol's memories.

237

"Sir, are you alright?"

Grell's plea reached out to her, slapping her across the face with the title of respect the inoga had never uttered toward anyone before. This wasn't what Nessix wanted to uncover.

"Kol!"

Nessix woke with a start, gasping sharply as she clutched the blanket around herself. Her heart raced just as fast as it had when her nightmare had been limited to mere physical terror. She pinched her eyes shut and forced herself to breathe out her tension. In one more beat of her heart, that terrible bolt would have torn Grell from her. She had seven more until the second would strike her—strike Kol—and begun creating a demon. Six beats… it was only a dream. Five beats… a dream rooted deep in history, a history part of her instinctively knew. Four beats… as long as she stayed calm and logical, she'd figure this out. Three beats…

Behind her from across the room, a pathetic whimper fluttered through the darkness. Two beats… Nessix opened her eyes. Kol sobbed audibly and in the relative silence of the room, Nessix heard the whisper of bedding being shoved aside, accentuated by Kol's panting. One beat. The bolt would have struck.

Nessix blinked, but kept her eyes open as she tried to process her discovery. Plucking at fingers of truth she was now deathly afraid of, Nessix missed the sound of Kol padding across the room, but she did feel the cot give to his weight as he climbed in behind her. Eyes widening, Nessix parted her lips to breathe through her mouth, fighting to keep her respiration rate steady as not to alert him that she knew he was there. His arm slid beneath her, wrapping across her chest as he pulled her closer, and then he buried his face against the back of her neck, hot tears tickling her flesh.

It was all Nessix could do to keep breathing at all. *This* was why Kol had been so patient with her. *This* was why she felt so drawn to him. All akhuerai were created from demon blood. Kol had given his to raise Nessix. It was a realization she'd have been far more content never making, but it was too late for that now. An overwhelming sense to ease the alar's pain consumed Nessix and she leaned against his chest, sharing her warmth through the thin blanket. The same radiated back at her, wrapping Nessix in a wave of serenity. Kol's breathing slowed, his tears ebbing to mere sniffles and, comforted by his nearness, Nessix fell asleep once again.

* * * * *

The warmth of a deep sense of security carried Nessix to morning. When she woke, she did so slowly, uncertain how to face Kol after the silent understanding that had passed between them. She didn't know what she'd say—what she *could* say—nor how he'd react to the weakness he'd shown her. Simply knowing she'd been bound to a demon had tormented Nessix from the start. Knowing Kol was the demon she'd been bound to pushed her to a pathetic discomfort she didn't want to acknowledge. And that didn't even scratch at the knowledge that Annin and Grell had always existed in Kol's life. And that fourth name, Berann? As powerful as the other three were, where did he stand in their hierarchy? Curiosity and an innate drive for survival convinced Nessix that she needed this answer, but if she hadn't met him yet… Maybe Berann was dead. That, Nessix told herself, would be for the best.

Needing to expel her nervous energy, Nessix carefully pressed her back toward where Kol had been curled up behind her. She met no resistance and shifted her arm to find that his no longer wrapped around her. She breathed out a sigh, but her relief didn't last long. Regardless of where Kol was in the room, she'd have to face him eventually. If only there was an obvious way to work this in her favor.

Nessix stretched and timidly rolled over to slide from the cot, a swarm of potential greetings tumbling through her mind. All of them fled her grasp as she looked into the room to discover Annin sitting alone at the desk.

"Where's Kol?" Nessix blurted, more self-conscious facing the oraku than the alar who had slept beside her.

Annin glanced up, lip twitched as though he'd wafted a foul smell. "He's out."

Nessix bit into a hasty retort. These elite demons were masters at hiding their intentions, but Annin never shied from displaying his disgust for her. This was the first time Nessix had been alone with him, and she hadn't felt this vulnerable since her first scuffle with Kol. She walked to her armor, keeping her eyes focused on her path, but ever aware of Annin's position. She'd have to dress herself today, but she preferred that to the alternative.

Silently, Nessix sorted through her armor and pieced it onto herself, trying to ignore the pressure of Annin's intense stare. She'd become so complacent, so comfortable with Kol until last night, that she struggled with how to use her diplomacy on anyone else. Or maybe that was the excuse she used to keep from admitting she was helpless against this particular demon.

Either way, the silence wore on her, the weight of Annin's disapproving glare scratching at her until she wanted to scream. Accepting that the demons had significantly more experience playing mind games than she did hadn't come easily to Nessix, and she folded before she cracked completely.

"Do you know if I'm still heading to my troops today?"

Annin heaved an inconvenienced sigh and stretched out his arms. "Is there a reason you shouldn't?"

Nessix blanched as she floundered for a reply that might sound halfway respectful. "Kol usually escorts me for safety, and you don't give a damn whether I live or die."

Annin shrugged. "I don't have to like you to want you functional. I have to do my job. Why shouldn't you do yours?"

His questions grated on Nessix, something a quick glance at his pale eyes proved he meant to do. Swallowing a fresh surge of loathing, Nessix continued donning her armor. "I'm happy to do my job, provided I can safely reach it."

Arguing with Kol had become a game to Nessix, a way to pass the time that they'd both seemed to find pleasure in. Attempting the same casual provocation with Annin wasn't even a remote possibility. There were no smirks from him, just a flat glare that spoke of how little he wanted to deal with her, and Nessix awkwardly shifted her attention away from him again. If the oraku had any inclination to give her more information, he'd have done so by now. All Nessix would get out of him was that Kol was gone.

She'd get no explanation for his absence, even if she found the nerve to ask.

Nessix finished dressing, and Annin wasted no time in ushering her into the hall. She spent the journey to the chasm contemplating who Annin was. Armed with greater insight than she'd expected, Nessix easily recognized Kol's voice in the tome depicting the Divine Battle, and Annin's initial reaction to Nessix reading that volume confirmed that it contained subjects he didn't want her uncovering. It had served the demons well that Nessix had been at their mercy to learn how to read their script; it had given Kol the opportunity to tactically hide their identities behind false names.

Kol had been the one who logged the tale of his people's service to the air goddess Kalina, evident now by the manner which thoughts had been recorded and the eerie echo of the mortal version of Grell calling him sir. As a mortal, Grell had been of a more even temper than the inoga Nessix was unfortunate enough to know, and she had difficulty deciding which of the other names she'd been taught was supposed to be him. What she'd gathered from her research suggested only that he'd been self-taught in warfare, just like the rest of Kol's unit. Only one magic user had been mentioned in Nes's reading, which left her with the same gnawing question.

Who was Berann?

There hadn't been so much as a passing mention of a second magic user in the text, though Grell had referenced this warrior clearly in Nes's dream. Kol had told her that the demons functioned more like tribes based on when they'd first been created, and as closely as Kol worked with Grell and Annin, they had to have shared a close past. One that every instinct in Nessix swore involved this missing man. So why hadn't he been recorded in their history? Where was he today?

Nessix seared her gaze into Annin's back. He'd never had the patience for Nes's prying, and she suspected he would be no more open to her questions now than he was in the past. For all Nessix knew, Berann had died during that war. It made no sense why she couldn't dismiss her curiosity and forget she'd ever heard this name, but her gut screamed that Berann was important. Frustrated with herself for being so hung up on such a trivial matter, frustrated with Kol for leaving her with Annin, and frustrated with Annin for being himself, Nessix trudged down the passage, gnawing on the inside of her cheek.

The akhuerai had quit causing grief for Kol when he escorted Nessix to and from the chasm, and though they watched Annin with leery eyes, they didn't present any problems for him, either. The oraku's rough hands hoisted Nessix by her armpits as opposed to the protective embrace Kol always wrapped her in, and he didn't bother to land before depositing her on the ground. Annin departed with none of Kol's playful snark or cool orders, and all the while, Nes's mind chased after Berann's identity.

She rubbed her forehead, internally scolding herself for her distraction as Auden approached her with Garrett and Pierson, two sturdy men who Nessix had recently begun grooming as officers.

"Good morning, General," Auden greeted with a warm smile.

"Is it?" Nessix cringed at her tired tone.

The three men stopped short, unaccustomed to anything other than fierce enthusiasm from Nessix.

"Is everything alright?" Auden asked cautiously. Nessix wouldn't be angered by the question, but flashes of the speculations that had circulated before the attempted revolt came back to him.

Nessix sighed and glanced upward, as if such a simple action would toss her petty concern over a missing demon from her thoughts. "I... yes. Everything's fine. Just have a lot on my mind."

Garrett and Pierson purposefully kept their eyes directed away from Nessix and awkwardly ran their hands over their practice weapons. The akhuerai had grown comfortable with Nessix and her authority, but few of them felt as though they could call her a friend. Auden was the closest to it, and his eyes pinched a bit narrower, scolding Nessix for the secrets she clearly kept.

She shook her head wearily. "It was a dream." Her simple explanation gained instant, understanding nods. "This one was real, though. Tangible. I was able to interact with the men in it."

Auden and Pierson gawked at her in startled disbelief, though Garrett looked as though he thought she'd gone half mad. Nessix was about to dismiss the entire discussion when a thought struck her. The history Kol led her through contained at least twenty names. If all akhuerai were tied to demons, someone else might have dreams of this elusive Berann, too. It was a long shot, but better than not taking one at all.

"Does the name Berann mean anything to any of you?" Nessix watched each of their eyes in turn, met by shaken heads and one mumbled apology. She blew out a huff of disappointment so sharply that it fluttered a stray lock of hair. "No bother," she said at last, cramming her fixation with this unknown man into the spider webs of her mind.

She'd get her answer eventually. For now, she had to raise an army.

TWENTY-TWO

Mathias stood just outside the Veil's boundaries, trying to ignore the brisk wind that beat against him. He'd chosen to skip returning to Zeal for luxuries such as cold weather gear. Outwardly, he claimed to honor Etha's suggestion that he speak to Ceredulus, but he'd dealt with enough fussy female persuasion lately and preferred to forego any further scolding from Julianna. He shivered, more from the thought of entering this forsaken realm than the chilly breeze that blew out from it.

"Oh, it doesn't look *that* bad."

Beside Mathias, Etha stood looking every bit the plucky adventurer. Dressed in rugged clothing and carrying a plump knapsack, the goddess's eyes glittered in anticipation of venturing out of her comfort zone. Around her neck hung both yellow scarves Mathias had been forced to purchase for her.

"It doesn't," Mathias granted grimly, and his agreement was true enough.

Beyond the knee-high rock wall that marked the Veil's boundary grew a peaceful coniferous forest. The path was well groomed, more passable than many others Mathias had traveled, and songbirds hid in the boughs, composing intricate melodies that defied what lurked ahead. The welcoming appearance was just one more of Ceredulus's tricks. Mortals could freely enter the Veil, but it took the escort of a lawfully aligned deity to see them out again. Mathias loathed to think of how many unwitting travelers and children badgered by their friends' dares had fallen victim to this façade.

Etha pouted at Mathias's persistent gloom and pulled one of the scarves from her shoulders. "I still don't see what you're so worried about." She stood on the tips of her toes and wrapped the scarf around Mathias's neck, giving the tails a tender pat where they crossed over his chest. "There's not one sentient being in the Veil who would dare to harm either of us, not with the way we can cleanse them."

That was Mathias's one advantage. Etha's blessing could purge the taint out of even the strongest of the undead, rendering them as fragile as a mortal. "I'm not *afraid* to go in there," Mathias said. "I just don't want to negotiate with Ceredulus."

"You're good at negotiating," Etha said helpfully. "Besides, this couldn't be any more in line with his interests if he'd come up with it himself. Time, my dear, is wasting."

Mathias grumbled and rubbed his chin. "You do realize all I do for you, right?"

"I do," Etha said. "But this isn't for me. Not this time."

That was the last reminder Mathias needed. Speaking to Ceredulus, while Etha's favorite idea at the moment, was likely a necessity to unravel the demons' scheme. Mathias and Ceredulus might not share the slightest mote of love for one another, but the foul god had always been willing to come to the table in the past. With Etha at his side, Mathias was confident Ceredulus wouldn't be able to delve into his mind the way gods liked to do, safeguarding the limited insight Mathias had and practically forcing Ceredulus's compliance. Mathias checked over the security of his sword belt and heaved a labored sigh.

"Fine. Let's get this done." He strode forward with firm purpose and Etha clapped her hands and darted after him.

Mathias had never entered the Veil before. He'd been inside when Azerick and Drao first raised it, pulled free from Ceredulus's claws by the good nature of the only gods he could rely on, and that experience had been more than enough to satisfy any desire to explore this cursed realm. Worse than the idea of his own imprisonment or torture by the likes of vampires and liches was the fact that it had been necessary to sink two townships of innocent civilians into this bleak cage in order to protect the rest of Abaeloth from the damnable scourge. It was a decision Mathias and Azerick had mourned once they discovered where Ceredulus had gone to ground, but Drao, ever the practical one, had contently signed those souls over to serve as nourishment for their new neighbors. As Drao had said, it would suppress the captives' unrest by providing them with their needs. To date, this theory seemed accurate. That did nothing to rid the sour taste from Mathias's mouth.

The Veil's creation had been a pivotal event in Abaeloth's history and the dark facts tied to its construction were well known to the Order. Nevertheless, Etha hummed a cheerful traveler's tune as they journeyed deeper into the reaches that made Mathias squirm even more than the hells did. They walked along, Etha humming and Mathias silently brooding over past weaknesses, until they stopped at a fork in the road. Both branches appeared equally inviting, besides the biting breeze that coursed through the clearing, and neither road was marked. Mathias wasn't comfortable enough to close his eyes in frustration and settled for rubbing his forehead. The last thing he needed was to get lost in the Veil.

"Hmm…" Etha peered down each pathway, narrowed eyes working feverishly with the all-seeing intelligence she enjoyed. "We should go that way." She pointed down the left path.

Still silent, Mathias obeyed. He'd trusted Etha enough to let her push him into the Veil, and he'd trust her to guide him through it. They didn't reach any signs of civilization and Mathias could only assume Etha had intentionally directed him away from one of the townships. Witnessing the souls he'd had a hand in condemning would have deteriorated Mathias's resolve, and that would have defeated the purpose of them entering the Veil in the first place.

The forest grew thicker, or maybe visibility had died down due to the general gloom that hunched over this region of Gelthin. A shiver brushed at the back of Mathias's neck, and he swatted at it like he would a mosquito, casting wary eyes into the thick woods around them. Not so much as a pine needle rustled, and none of the birds faltered in their songs, but Mathias could feel cold eyes watching him with a loathing so strong he nearly hated himself. He glanced at Etha, who gaped at their surroundings with a sense of wonder and awe, and garnered confidence from her casual approach to this most unsavory mission. At this rate, they'd wander through the Veil, stalked by vampires and their ilk for days. Patience and nerve depleted, Mathias stopped abruptly.

"Alright, Ceredulus! I know you know I'm here and I know you'd rather I wasn't. Come out, let's have a chat, and we can both pretend this didn't happen."

Three steps ahead of Mathias, Etha turned and parked her hands on her hips. "You expect him to answer you?" she scoffed.

Mathias shrugged. "You could try calling for him."

Etha rolled her eyes. "You expect him to answer *me*?"

Mathias hissed in frustration and stalked forward. He wouldn't dream of accusing Etha of leaving him hanging, but couldn't help but feel she had. Of course, with the shoddy state of his mental fortitude, Etha had ready access to those bitter thoughts he had regarding where he *ought* to be. Etha stood and watched the rigid swing of his arms as he strode away before sighing and scampering to catch up. An apology was due, but not until he'd completed his mission. Mathias wasn't one to be coddled and the moment she showed him her regrets, she knew he'd jump on them.

Thoughts stewing in a bitter loop, Mathias couldn't tell if minutes or hours had passed when the forest began to thin. Here, blood red roses peeked through the brambles of underbrush and a fresh shiver darted across Mathias's flesh. Not far ahead, the path opened to a clearing illuminated—but not warmed by—the sun. It had been lifetimes since he'd last been near this place, but not long enough for him to forget it. Even less forgotten was the willowy maiden who appeared on the path before them. Her long blonde hair fluttered effortlessly from beneath a wide brimmed hat, dancing on the breeze, and her dark eyes were too swollen with hatred to discern anything else in them.

"Oh, look! A guide!" Etha leaned forward to get a better look at the woman, gasped with recognition, and straightened sharply.

"*Oh.*" She glanced hastily at Mathias, tapping her lips as his eyes flooded with loathing. "Oh, dear. Mathias. Please remember we are guests in this realm. Please?"

Mathias worked his jaw back and forth solely to keep from clenching it. "If I must."

The woman continued her steady progress forward, painted lips peeling back in more of a snarl the closer she got. Mathias wondered idly if Etha's plea of playing nice would be waived if he was forced to defend himself. The woman halted her advance ten feet from the paladin and his goddess. She didn't offer any form of greeting, and Etha gently prodded Mathias's arm. He groaned, but dutifully shouldered the responsibility.

"Lizette." The woman's name snapped off Mathias's tongue.

"Mathias," she hissed back venomously. "My lord wishes to know what you want."

Mathias's lips trembled as he attempted to find words cordial enough to answer this cleansed vampire. Every aspect pertaining to the idea of actively seeking life unending disgusted Mathias, now more than ever before. Lizette had been the first vampire he'd encountered, and her army had devastated the mortals Mathias had been entrusted with. She'd been his first taste of this horror, and he'd been her last taste of the strength she'd obtained through blasphemy. She'd left Mathias with a pair of scars on his neck that had nearly faded to memories, but he'd left her with a gaping hole where power and terror should have been hers. Neither had forgiven the other for the damages they'd done and Etha, shaken by the intensity sparking between the two, grasped Mathias's arm to pull him behind her.

"Your lord's insight is needed on matters only he is qualified to answer," Etha said, authority ringing through the tension. "And you will take us to him so we can ask him our questions."

Lizette narrowed her eyes and cocked her head as she studied Etha's petite form. "Who are you to be giving me orders?"

"I am the one who gives your lord orders." Etha didn't use any grand displays of divine might to reinforce her words. With her power, she wouldn't have to. "Who else would have led Mathias this far into the Veil? You have two options right now, young woman. You can escort us safely to wherever it is Ceredulus frequents, or you can attempt that foolish notion brewing in your head and try to attack us. Mathias soundly defeated you once, and that was before he understood what my blessing did for him."

"*Your* blessing—" Lizette's eyes widened and she staggered three steps back. "I… Um. Yes." She sent a hasty glance at Mathias, no longer scowling at him from her fear of confronting Etha. "I will do what I can to secure an audience for you. Please, follow me."

Lizette backed a few more steps down the road before slowly turning to walk toward the clearing. She kept her shoulders hunched close around her neck, her short strides choppy. Etha turned to Mathias and grinned, waving him forward as she resumed walking. Less than convinced of Lizette's good intentions, Mathias followed them into the sunshine.

Mathias and Etha were led to Lord Sergulion Weliviel's manor, an impressive structure which Mathias had once marveled at. It stood every bit as pristine as he remembered, grounds immaculately groomed and the plain brick exterior scrubbed clean. In any other town, the manor would exude brilliance, but here in the Veil, it stood as a monument of corruption. During the rush to master necromancy, Sergulion had formed a pact with Ceredulus, a move which had benefitted both man and god in terrifying ways. It made sense that the god continued to reside in the manor's luxuries when occupying his mortal form.

Lizette escorted her charges into the building, leading them down a grand hall to an even grander sitting room. Furnished with lavish, overstuffed chairs and a gold embossed fainting couch, it was clear that the higher ranking members of the undead didn't want for mortal comforts amid the Veil's despair. There was nothing to speak of along the lines of refreshments, but eating was among the last things on Mathias's mind.

"Make yourselves comfortable," Lizette muttered, skirting close to the wall as Mathias and Etha entered the room. Her sneer had returned, but Etha's presence kept her timid enough to not seek trouble. "I will inform my lord that you are here."

Mathias frowned as Lizette scurried from the room. She

wouldn't need to tell Ceredulus anything—the god had likely known Mathias planned to intrude on his territory the moment he'd reached its border. If Ceredulus had any intention of cooperating, he'd have been waiting in the sitting room when they'd arrived. Well aware that his words and actions were being monitored, Mathias looked to Etha, who was methodically testing the comfort of each chair in the room. He sighed at her resilience, wishing he could wear the smile her endearing antics stirred up.

Goddess and paladin sat among silk and satin luxury and waited for a god who wanted just as little to do with them as Mathias wanted to do with him. Etha made several attempts at small talk, asking Mathias what sort of flowers he thought were hardy enough to blossom among the undead and whether or not he thought Sergulion's taste in color schemes was as pretty as she did, but his patience ran too low for him to waste on Etha's curiosity.

This waiting continued for hours. Mathias's stomach petitioned for nourishment but he refused to give in to its demands. More hours passed and a timid servant snuck into the chamber to light sconces and a fire in the hearth. Mathias glowered out the window as the outwardly young woman drew the curtains back. He hated dealing with vampires after dark.

All the while, Etha continued to chatter.

It was becoming difficult for Mathias to stifle his yawns, even more so to continue insisting that his groaning stomach didn't bother him. His eyes burned, his muscles ached with fatigue, and his need to relieve himself had nearly reached his maximum tolerance.

And Etha continued to chatter. "Do you think Ceredulus actually knows what—"

The goddess had stumbled upon the one topic Mathias forbid to be discussed. "Shh!"

Etha shook her head with a start before furrowing her brows. "Did you just shush me?"

"I did," Mathias grumbled.

She crossed her arms, too perturbed to delight in the fact that she'd finally got him talking. "May I ask why?"

Afraid of losing what little tolerance he had left, Mathias

leaned forward and sank his face into his hands. The way his eyes rejoiced at being closed and his body instantly relaxed startled him upright again. "Because," he groaned, "the mystery we carry is the only leverage we have to ensure Ceredulus shows up. If we uncover it now, we'll sit here until the end of time. You're the one who dragged me here. Don't ruin it for me."

Etha pursed her lips, delicate brows lifting in surprise at Mathias's boldness. She flopped deep into the back of her seat. "Fine. *Grump.*"

Too tired to react, Mathias rubbed his eyes and began anxiously tapping a finger on the arm of his chair. At least Etha had cast some good bait; Mathias was certain Ceredulus himself monitored the room's activities.

Sure enough, before the second time Mathias felt himself try to nod off, the chamber's door flew open to reveal a dapper man dressed in the finest suit Abaeloth had to offer.

"My dear, *dear* friend," Ceredulus gushed, pompously sweeping into the room. "Please forgive me for keeping you waiting—you must understand how busy I am managing my slice of paradise. Now, what matter is it you need to speak with me about?"

Mathias didn't bother to stand to greet the god. Even if he'd had the disposable energy to do so, spitting at Ceredulus showed him more respect than Mathias felt he deserved. Gathering up what remained of his wit, realizing how the devious deity had worn him down intentionally, Mathias started from the beginning.

"Have you worked out a way to speak to any of your brothers or sisters?" Mathias hadn't meant for the question to come out as an insulting slap, but was content to take credit for the furious flare in Ceredulus's eyes and the ugly scowl which flawed his dashing face.

The god flicked a glance at Etha as she watched quietly, and scoffed. "Only when they bother to come for a visit. It's not often enough, by the way. Might I trouble you with telling them that it's cold and lonely in my corner?"

"And risk you manipulating them into aiding you?" Weariness tugged at Mathias's smirk. "What sort of undead-slaying knight of the Order do you think I am?"

Ceredulus glanced at Etha once more, squeezed and released his fist, and looked back at Mathias, a poor attempt at a smile leveling his lips. "So this question? Assuming you've actually got one."

Mathias slapped himself on the cheek and blinked in rapid succession to try to rouse himself. The results of his efforts were lacking. "Were you aware that the demons have been harvesting souls with the intention of raising the dead?"

Ceredulus's jaw dropped, pupils restricting in shock and all of that cocky air flit away from him. "Without paying homage to *me*?"

The urge to chuckle at the venom used to hiss that question lodged in Mathias's throat. "I'll take it you didn't know."

Fury raged in Ceredulus's eyes, though he held himself back from advancing on Mathias under Etha's watchful gaze. "How *could* I have known?" he spat, voice ticking higher in pitch. "You've had me locked in this damned cage and now you've let the demons bastardize my art!"

Exhaustion had rendered Mathias more foolish than normal, and he shoved himself to his feet. "I can assure you, none of us *let* the demons do this."

Ceredulus chanced a single, stalked step closer to Mathias. "How are they doing it?" Neither desperation nor curiosity carried those words, but accusation did.

Mathias drew on the final remnants of his strength and squared his shoulders. "All I can tell you is that an oraku extracts the souls of the dying and they come back to collect the body later. This is far from my area of expertise. Etha had assumed you'd be able to fill in the rest."

Perhaps it was his fury of the demons' liberties, or maybe it was Mathias's intentional use of Etha's name that launched Ceredulus into an enraged sputtering a more alert version of Mathias might have balked at.

"They are operating out of my realm!" the god spat, red splotches marring his porcelain cheeks. "Out of my *blessing*! How am I supposed to fill in the rest?"

"Well—" Mathias leaned his weight against the arm of his

chair. "You *are* a god."

Those blotches filled the rest of Ceredulus's face and the moment he raised his foot to rush Mathias, Etha sprang to her feet.

"Enough!" Her shout shook the room, toppling a portrait to the floor from where it had hung near the door. She'd been a fool to bring Mathias here and expect a peaceful conversation. He'd done everything he could to warn her that this would happen, and she'd ignored it for practicality's sake. Elidae had taught her that Mathias wasn't able to engage gods on equal footing, but he was ever willing to try. His current state of exhaustion enhanced his fractiousness, and Etha was afraid of what might happen if he became incapacitated while inside the Veil.

"Ceredulus," Etha said diplomatically, striding across the room to be nearer her paladin. "I regret that we came bearing such alarming news, and if you agree to deliver any theories you might develop to me, I will work with you to bring the guilty parties to justice once they are located."

Mathias spun on his goddess, bloodshot eyes blazing with an indignant tantrum. "Those demons are—"

Etha held up a hand and Mathias's mouth snapped shut from the weight of her might. "We will be in touch, Ceredulus. Thank you for whatever help you may give Abaeloth in the future."

Before Mathias could push past Etha's charms and complicate matters, she grasped his arm and whisked him back to the safety of his chamber in the blessed security of the Citadel.

TWENTY-THREE

It had taken the bulk of Nes's concentration, but she managed to keep her mind away from the mysteries of Kol's past to put the growing army through its paces. Her troops worked diligently to midday and well past the time which Kol usually arrived to collect her. It was the alar's tardiness, matched with the lingering concern of his absence when she'd woken, that pulled Nes's attention away from the sparring soldiers. She quietly dismissed herself from the bulk of the army to fetch a drink and try to clear her mind.

Rapid footsteps clomped behind Nessix in an easy jog, and her nerves stretched closer to fraying. She'd removed herself from the bustle of the army for a reason, and suspected that Auden, no matter how good his intentions, wouldn't want to hear what troubled her.

"Why didn't you tell us you'd been given permission to stay with us?"

Auden's tone was light and cheerful, so warm that Nessix felt villainous just thinking about correcting him.

"Because I hadn't been," she said evenly as she reached the cistern. She ladled a cupful of water for herself and turned to face her commander.

His brows wrinkled in an endearing jumble and he cocked his head. Nessix swallowed her drink and rolled the coolness of its afterthought between her lips. Auden may have been her second in command and she valued his honesty and loyalty, but he was no more a soldier than any of the others. He'd routinely failed to understand the intricacies of wartime tactics, unwilling to entertain employing deception or engaging in political games. Nessix had managed to convert these civilians into soldiers, but had yet to see any of them evolve into true officers.

She leaned against the cistern and lowered her eyes. "I have asked a lot of you," she said. "The akhuerai in general, but you in particular."

Auden flushed and gave a little shrug. "You asked us to take a stand. I'm only doing the best I can."

Nessix looked into Auden's trusting eyes. They hadn't regained any of the innocence lost from when the demons had slain him, but they were soft with hope and faith. Nessix had returned those virtues to this man and he had helped spread it to the others. Maybe Nessix was wrong. Maybe Auden could be taught how to navigate political conflict. It was a chance she'd have to take.

"I'm going to have to ask a little more from you," she said.

Auden chuckled nervously and rubbed his chin. "General, I... I meant it when I said I was doing my best."

Nessix shook her head and waved a dismissive hand. "Not more skills at arms. That needs time and practice to develop. I need you to back me on a controversial matter."

As Nessix expected, Auden's eyes widened at the implication of unrest. "Not intending to argue, General, but I learned my lesson about inciting boldness—"

"I'm not looking for you to incite anything. Rather, I'm hoping you'll be able to pacify the army for me." When his brows returned to their confused furrow, Nessix continued. "If Kol hasn't come to gather me yet, I'm not sure he will." She squinted toward the top of the chasm, scanning the ledge for signs of movement and finding none.

"That's a blessing, isn't it?" Auden asked.

Nessix pressed her lips together, reluctant to share more than she already had. "When I told you about last night's dream and how real it was, I *knew* the men around me, and we were fighting in the

Divine Battle, the final stages that gave rise to the demons."

"Is that why you asked about that Belthane fellow?"

"Berann," Nessix corrected in stride. "I have a hunch he's more involved with—and more important to—the demons' history than I've been able to uncover yet."

"What makes you think that?"

It was a fine question, one which Nessix hadn't quite managed to resolve past the wriggly feeling in her chest at the mention of Berann's name. She shook her head slowly and chewed on her lip. "There've been… inconsistencies in what I've been reading, and everything in my academic training suggests that there's an important reason for that."

"Alright." Auden crossed his arms. "What can I do to help?"

Nessix sighed and pushed herself away from the cistern. "I need to figure out how he ties in to the demons' history, if for no other reason than to sate my curiosity."

"But if that alar hasn't come to get you…" Auden twisted his lips into a contemplative pucker and shrugged.

Nessix fully believed that Kol suffered the exact same dream she had, and wondered if he'd been avoiding her for the same reason she wanted return to her studies. The more she obsessed over this mysterious man, the more she knew she had to identify him.

"Then I'll have to go to them," Nessix said.

Auden's jaw dropped and he scooted closer to Nessix to keep his voice down. "But we *need* you!"

"You've fared beautifully these past several weeks without me spending my evenings here. I'm close to something vital, Auden. I just need to dig a little deeper."

"But what if the reason that alar hasn't come to fly you away is because they don't *want* you up there?"

It was a valid argument, especially when matched with Kol's absence that morning. Nessix studied the top of the chasm again. "If they don't want me up there, they'll catch me and toss me back down and then we'll know. But for now, I have to try. I haven't worked this long and hard to throw up my hands when the answer's so close."

Auden opened his mouth to try a fresh debate, but nothing came out. He *wasn't* a tactician. He *didn't* have a strong academic background, not remotely close to the likes of Nessix. And simply wanting her to stay here to take on the burdens that went with keeping the army happy wasn't an acceptable reason to challenge her motives. After all, Nessix was his general, and he'd sworn to serve and obey her.

"What duty do you have for me?"

Nes's heart warmed at Auden's pitiful compliance, but its charge couldn't quite make it to her face. "I'll have to climb out of here, meaning the army will see me choosing to return to the demons on my own accord. I need you to help reassure them that I'm doing this for our future. I need you to fight any accusations and criticisms that come from my actions. I've given the army strength and direction, and they respect me for that. But they've loved and trusted you for much longer. Keep them happy for me, at least until I get back and have time to tell them what I've learned."

A small frown creased Auden's lips. "Are you certain you'll be coming back? The pattern's already been skewed. What if there's some dangerous reason for it?"

That was a concern Nessix had avoided thinking about, and she took a moment to wonder if she might have underestimated Auden's tactical prowess. Either way, this was a chance she had to take. "There's a dangerous reason for everything the demons do. I'll come back, you have my word. We can't die, remember? Worst thing that happens, I know more than a few demons who would leap at the chance to launch me back down here. Give me a few more days. Please."

Auden still didn't like Nes's request, but what it all came down to was that she knew better than all of them. She knew how to fight and was armed with more skills than she'd be able to teach them in a lifetime. She knew how to manipulate at least one of the more influential demons and was prepared to wield that in their favor. She knew—or so she claimed—enough about the demons' creation to form a way for common folks like the akhuerai to stand against them. Nobody else had made it half this far, and to Auden's knowledge, Nessix had always been honest with them. He was opposed to the risks involved with her plan, but he was equally resistant to the idea of wallowing in this pit for the rest of eternity. He looked into Nes's eyes and met a steely courage he aspired to one day call his own.

"Very well, General," he murmured. "You find us our advantage and I'll keep faith alive."

Nessix allowed herself to smile at last, shoulders drooping as she relaxed. "Thank you, Auden. I'll do my best to not let you worry for long."

She slapped him on the shoulder and quickly strode off toward the chasm stairs, her choppy steps betraying her wavering confidence that her quest would be victorious. She addressed the guard at the foot of the stairs, glowing with enough authority that she didn't even need to twitch her fingers toward a weapon. Auden envied her bravery. The guard shrugged and flung a hand toward the stairs, and Nessix approached them with a rigid determination, not looking back. She truly was a woman to admire.

As Nessix began her climb, the first concerned shouts popped up from the army. Before they could grow into turmoil, Auden returned to the body of the army to explain their general's plan as best he could.

* * * * *

The climb was easier the second time, possibly from the comfort of having survived it once before but more likely because Kol wasn't breathing down her neck. Nessix shoved her thoughts of the alar into the same corner Berann lurked as she concentrated on each step. She waited for a shout from above to demand what she was doing, but all she heard was an initial surge of debate from below her, followed by Auden's calm voice bringing the army back to order.

Her skin crawled with the terrible possibilities of why Kol had abandoned her after how he'd held her so close, unable to shake the feeling that Grell had something to do with it. Even if the inoga had snatched Kol away, that didn't explain why Annin hadn't returned for her or, at the very least, why nobody prevented her from leaving the pit. Beginning to wonder if maybe Auden had been right with his suggestion that the demons might not want her back, Nessix reached the final stair and crawled onto the security of the ledge.

She refrained from looking down into the chasm, queasy at the thought of not having a pair of wings ready to catch her if she slipped, and allowed the sounds of her army easing back into their exercises settle her mind as she headed down the corridor.

Her worries had to be unwarranted. Annin and Kol had given every sign of being close to each other, and if Kol had been called to answer for her disobedience, the oraku would have made sure Nessix knew of it. Instead, he'd simply told her Kol was out. It wasn't a satisfactory answer, vague and well out of the routine Kol had established, but not implausible. Though Nessix had tried hard to feign sleep—and considered her efforts believable—Kol had displayed a vulnerable side of himself that Nessix wouldn't blame him for trying to escape. After all, she wanted to run from his nightmare, too.

The more Nessix contemplated the circumstances, the more relieved she felt. It didn't explain why she'd been left in the chasm, but it did convince her that Kol was still alive. Pleased with her conclusion, Nessix had all but forgotten that the relative safety she enjoyed while navigating the hells had been directly tied to that absent demon she'd charmed. This fact came rushing back to her as combative instinct prickled the hairs on the back of her neck. She was being followed.

Slowly stretching out her fingers, Nessix focused her eyes forward, allowing her remaining senses to methodically scan the hallway. At least three pairs of feet sauntered behind her, trailing by a solid half dozen yards. Along the walls, casual observers smirked and murmured brief statements to their friends. One of these observers—a stout demon armed with an entire belt worth of knives—peeled from his position on the wall to follow Nessix as she passed, his companion doing nothing to hide her snickering. Cursing her stupidity, Nessix swallowed the lump in her throat as she gathered her courage. This hall was packed with demons who wouldn't hesitate to attack the moment fighting started. She'd have to engage with care.

Her opponents tracked her fully aware of her combat expertise and with knowledge of how dirty she fought. The moment Nes's fingers twitched to draw her sword, they sprang into action. Focus trained on her blind side, Nessix ducked out of the crushing grasp of the demon immediately behind her. She abandoned drawing her sword to snatch two knives off her assailant's belt.

Nessix scanned a quick assessment of her opponents—all five of larger stature than herself, three in sturdy leather armor, one in plate, the last in a cloak of thick wool and a simple leather breastplate. In normal circumstances, Nessix would have aimed for the most formidable opponent first, but in these steep odds, she cared more about thinning the field.

Digging her feet into the ground, Nessix darted for the cloaked demon, knives braced for impact. Close enough to spit on him, she froze as the demon calmly raised his left arm and snapped his fingers in the narrow void between them. Stunned by the demon's lack of defense, Nessix looked up to see the faded traces of runes lining the lower lids of his eyes. Her head swam before her vision plummeted into darkness, and she cursed.

Blinded by the oraku's trick, Nessix lost precious seconds as her remaining senses reached out to gather intelligence. Unfortunately, the first insight to her opponents' locations came in the form of her forearm being grabbed. Nessix spun and slashed with the dagger in her left hand, the action effectively curling her into the demon's grasp. Her knife ricocheted off steel with a mocking clang, echoed by a throaty chortle. Kicking the demon in plate wouldn't hinder him, but his armor had joints she could exploit.

Swinging her leg upward, Nessix's heel caught her assailant's poleyn. She pushed her weight upwards and jabbed with her opposite knee, connecting with some part of the demon's face, evident by the soft give on the other side of her strike and the demon's enraged curses. Past experience tangling with the average demonic soldier gave Nessix a mere second before he flung her aside in fury, and she spent that breath commanding her muscles to relax for her fall.

Her stomach lurched to her throat as the anticipated swing began, flinging back into place as she sailed in an arc. Nessix breathed her residual tension out on a slow breath until an abrupt stop twice as fast as she'd expected pummeled the rest of it from her. A fresh set of arms wrapped around her torso and left arm, and as she groped at her captor's waist with her right hand, a second demon snatched her wrist and twisted it. Options rapidly depleting, Nessix tried to kick for freedom until her legs were immobilized by a third demon. She panted, frantically trying to blink vision back to her eyes.

"Now that wasn't so bad, was it?" one of the demons said.

A second spat and rumbled a testy reply. "The bitch didn't knee *you* in the face. I say we take what we want from her now and end her ourselves."

"Here in the hall?" a third asked, the swing in his voice suggesting the idea had already crossed his mind.

"Enough, all of you." That must have been the oraku; he was far too calm and enunciated his words too crisply to be an average demon soldier. "It's best we don't anger our lord more than he already is."

A gloomy chorus of muttered replies answered from the demons restraining Nessix and they lifted her off the floor and carried her down the hall. They moved with urgency, as though trying to avoid further complications. There had been several demons populating the hall before the scuffle began. Maybe there was someone who favored Kol over these brutes who was willing or interested in coming to her aid.

Nessix had always been proficient at making a commotion. Releasing a determined growl that grew into a shriek of fury, she twisted her hips and thrust her legs forward. The demon restraining her legs staggered ahead as he fought to keep his hold on her. Nessix twisted in the gap she created and bit into the bicep of the demon gripping her torso. He howled as her teeth sank into his arm. Success.

Her sense of victory was short lived as the demon supporting the bulk of her weight dropped her. Her armored body crashed to the ground, wrenching the arm held by her third captor. A flash streaked across her restoring vision, giving Nessix a slice of visual information at last. The demon at her feet hadn't regained an effective position, and Nessix jerked her right leg free. As he scrambled to catch it, Nessix wriggled her left free as well.

Vision creeping back and able to gather her legs under herself again, Nessix shouted at the top of her lungs, "You want a fight? I've got one for you!"

It was a weak taunt, but it served its purpose as it rebounded off the cavern walls. Her opponents shared curses and accusations of who was to blame for her will to fight. The demon at her feet rushed forward and grabbed her by the waist and Nessix grit her teeth and flung her head back. His nose crunched against the back of Nes's skull and though the impact dazed her, it sent the demon scuttling backwards, hands wrapped across his bleeding face.

"Who *is* this cunt?" he screamed, much less threatening with his voice so shrill.

By now, the demon twisting Nes's arm looked as though he no longer thought his prey was worth the grief she caused them, but he held her fast, no doubt more afraid of what punishment would await his failure than the pain this tiny akhuerai could dish out.

"She's that pet of Kol's that Inek's been after," the armored demon sneered.

"And our lord wants her—"

The oraku never finished his statement. His eyes rolled back in his head and he sank to the ground with a dull flop. Everyone else—Nessix included—gaped at his sudden collapse until something much more alarming than an oraku's mysterious defeat filled the hallway.

"Inek, *eh*?" Grell's deep voice drew out the last as if it was a challenge. "He's not supposed to touch my toys."

Nessix cringed closer to the ground, eyes widening in terror. Her arm dropped free from her final captor's grasp and, trembling, she turned her head toward the inoga's voice. She was terrified to meet Grell's eyes, his previous punishment vividly imprinted in her mind. Flanking the repulsive brute were Annin—who must have neutralized the offending oraku—and Kol, his arms crossed and a pitying scowl aimed at the demons surrounding Nessix. For the briefest moment, Nes's eyes stung with tears of relief, and then Grell spoke again.

"I think it's time I go have a talk with my old friend," the inoga growled. "Kol, I'll leave you and Annin to it. Do as you will."

Grell turned and stalked down the hall, and Kol's arms dropped to his sides as he stepped forward. He made a brief appraisal of Nes's condition before glaring at the offending demons.

"I warned you before. This akhuerai belongs to *me*."

Kol sprang forward with speed that defied logic, his hands wrapped around one demon's neck before his actions registered to the crowd. The three enemies still standing scattered to flee and Annin raised his voice in a harsh bark. A brilliant light flashed between Nessix and the oraku, a residual shimmer hanging like a curtain in the air. A pulsing hum deafened Nessix for a heartbeat as her foes were flung back toward her by Annin's barrier. Kol snapped the first demon's neck, drawing a thin, curved blade of iridescent metal as he turned to select his next target. Bearing down on the demon with the broken nose, Kol cut into him with the cold apathy of an executioner, his eyes blazing with a finely tempered frenzy that made Nessix doubt everything she thought she knew about him.

The demon in plate scrambled to his feet and sent a toxic glare first at Annin, then at Nessix, before bracing his stance to charge toward Kol. His remaining companion had scuttled away from Kol's madness, pressing himself as close to Annin's barrier as possible, but the armored demon practically glowed with entitled rage. Nessix had assumed her assailants' oraku, with his steady mannerisms, had been the leader, but as this last demon focused Kol in his sights, she realized he was the one in charge. Just as Annin worked beneath Kol, the offending oraku must have answered to this demon. Which meant he was as formidable an opponent as Kol.

Nessix scanned this demon's armor, searching for a weak

point she couldn't readily see—it'd be his throat or nothing. With Kol blinded by his bloodlust as he carved apart the unfortunate demon beneath him, the armored demon found his opening and leapt forward. Perhaps he had disregarded Nessix as a threat. Maybe he doubted that bizarre sense of loyalty she had for Kol. He couldn't have simply *forgotten* about her. No matter his reason for darting past Nessix without a second glance, he'd made a grave mistake.

The demon pushed off the ground with a powerful thrust of his right leg and the second he lifted his left to stride forward, Nessix grabbed his ankle. She slid on her back across the rough floor as he tried to extend his leg, but her efforts to slow him worked. Hissing, the demon shoved his leg back to try kicking Nessix from him, but she scissored his right leg between hers and he toppled to the ground.

Latched onto a man nearly twice her size wearing a heavy suit of armor, Nessix invested all of her strength and that which she borrowed from adrenaline in holding her opponent's legs. All she had to do was keep him immobile until Kol could tend to him. Nessix's back protested as the demon kicked his powerful legs to try ridding them of her, dragging her across the floor. Just as she thought his efforts would tear the usefulness from her muscles, Kol's booted heel connected squarely with the demon's face. His struggling ceased in the same moment.

Nessix panted on the ground and hefted limp legs off of her. Head swimming from exertion and the battering she'd taken, she sat up and watched as Kol stalked over to the final demon. The pathetic beast looked around himself frantically as if he'd be able to find a way out of Annin's barrier, his empty hands raised before him and head ducked low between his shoulders. He didn't stand a chance.

Kol crouched down before the trembling demon, the same as he had when he'd delicately explained to Nessix that he was going to kill her. He balanced his elbows on his knees and casually clasped his hands together. "Am I foolish to leave survivors?" he asked this demon, his voice so quiet and calm Nessix shivered.

The demon shook his head mutely.

"I'll credit Inek his tenacity and the boldness he's put in his underlings, but all of you need to work on your intelligence. You couldn't have possibly thought our halls weren't monitored."

The demon hunched his head lower, and Kol reached forward, grabbed his chin, and forced him to look up.

"You can keep your oraku and your commander, and I'll spare you your pathetic life. Carry back to your lord and your peers that this action has been considered a declaration of war. Remind your lord that Grell's got more loyalty and the might of an undying army behind him, and then ask him again if his petty hatred of my akhuerai is worth it."

Kol shoved the demon away and stood, lip curled as though he'd spit on the wretch, but that obscure honor of his prevented him from such a crude action. Annin's barrier flickered out in a puff of glittering dust that sifted lazily to the floor, and Kol spun on a heel to walk over to Nessix.

"Can you stand?"

Her legs ached, her head swam, and a sharp pain accompanied each of her inhalations, but Nessix stood without complication. She dove into Kol's orange eyes, searching for that fondness he had for her, unable to dig it out through their strictness. Nessix hadn't felt so thoroughly chastised since she was a child, and her gaze lowered accordingly.

"What were you doing up here alone?" There was no concern in Kol's voice, but neither was there reproach. As always, his question was built solely for the information he could pilfer from its answer.

The full truth wasn't something Nessix could express, so she stuck to the half of it she could safely share. "I came to keep studying, sir."

Behind her, Annin scoffed and grudgingly tramped away.

Kol's glare softened with a dull glow of surprised satisfaction, though his tight frown continued to convey his disappointment. "And you thought it was wise to travel by yourself?"

"I didn't have another option," Nessix said, her courage returning. "Where were you, anyway?"

Kol's lip twitched at Nes's forward tone, and he grabbed her by the arm to lead her toward his chamber. "I had some personal matters to attend to."

Nessix accepted the warning in his voice as her cue to quit prying and walked along with him in silence. Kol's demeanor had grown chilly but remained consistent to his character. His short reply, however, confirmed that the previous night's quiet breakdown had mortified him. Nessix bit her lip to keep from asking him her questions; it would benefit them both if Kol calmed down before she prodded the subject.

Word of the scuffle had travelled ahead of them and the halls were vacant on the way to Kol's chamber. By the time they reached their destination, his hand had relaxed its grip on Nes's arm and his strides had lost their snappy pace. He ushered Nessix inside as casually as usual, and waved at the desk where her books awaited her.

"Get to it." He turned from Nessix and strode toward the bathing alcove. As if struck with an afterthought, he stopped short of removing his shirt and stalked over to his wash basin instead. "I'll send for food once I get the stench of Inek's men off my hands."

Nessix didn't follow his instructions, rooted in place as she stared at Kol. His behavior was still off, evident by the fact that he felt he needed to exercise modesty before her. Neither of them could get more uncomfortable, and Nessix decided she had nothing to lose by asking for the information she was after now. Better to completely ruin a single day than drag this awkward tension on longer.

"You... you know about my dream, don't you?"

Kol's eyes hardened as he stared at his hands, scrubbing them with unnecessary vigor. "You did tell me about it."

On a day Nessix didn't feel quite so reckless, she would have backed away at Kol's blatant avoidance, but she'd quit caring about sense hours ago. Kol knew about her dream because he also had it. She would not allow him to escape facing her a second time.

"Who is Berann?"

Nes's question punched Kol in the gut and his brows flew up in shock before setting in strict declines. "Oh, little one..." he murmured, voice strained thin with an emotion Nessix almost labeled as grief. He quit scrubbing his hands, bracing them on the edges of the basin as he hung his head. "Why did you have to ask me that...?"

Nessix gulped. Kol had repeatedly shown that he cared about her in those odd ways of his, but had never expressed remorse of any sort. She shivered and crossed her arms. "Because I've heard his name mentioned several times now, enough to know he's important."

Kol looked up at her through the mirror, lips twitching. He clenched his fingers around the basin's edges, a wave of bitterness fleeting across his face. "There is no way you've heard that name down here."

Sensibility traipsed away from Nessix, and she disregarded this warning, as well. "I didn't hear his name down here. I heard it in my dream. Who is he?"

Embers stirred in Kol's eyes and he shook his head slowly. "You will forget you ever heard it."

"No," Nessix said. "You will tell me who he is."

All thoughts of wanting to ruin the day lost their validation as Kol whipped around and leapt onto Nessix, plowing her to the ground. Straddling her waist to hold her down, he struck her once in the face before she managed to grasp his wrists. Already worn from the night's interrupted sleep, a full day of training, and the trouble she'd barely survived in the hall, Nes's strength didn't stand up to Kol's and he pulled his hand free to strike her again. She abandoned the concept of fighting him and lifted her arms in front of her face to protect herself.

"We do not speak of him!" Kol spat, swatting her arms away. He grasped her gorget and jerked her bloodied face close to his bared teeth. "We do not *think* of him. Forget you've ever heard that name in your life."

Nessix stared into Kol's eyes as well as the starbursts in her vision allowed and saw, for the first time, fear in those raging fires. It was a fear greater than that of self-preservation or his desire to protect her. It was a fear rooted in survival at a much deeper level, as deep as the soul. And all it did was make Nessix hungrier for the truth.

Despite that longing, it was time for Nessix to back off the topic. She wouldn't be able to tolerate much more in terms of physical assault, and suspected another blow to the head would render her incapable of studying tonight. Her answer had to be in one of these books—around the torn pages if Kol's reaction to her request was any indication—and Nessix needed to preserve her ability to think clearly in order to figure the answers for herself. Grateful she'd waited to ask this question while alone with Kol, Nessix nodded timidly.

He blew out a great gust of a sigh. Closing his eyes to hide their flood of relief, Kol swung himself off of her. "None of this leaves my chamber," Kol said. "And even in here, it's never mentioned again."

Nessix slowly accepted the hand Kol extended toward her and stood with his assistance. "If that is your order," she murmured.

Kol sighed again and pulled Nessix into an embrace, arms trembling. "It is. I do not want to hurt you, little one."

She stood there as Kol regenerated his confidence. To merit such secrecy and violent reactions, Berann couldn't have just been a demon of the past. He must be pivotal to their demise. Nessix cursed her mind for craving the answer even more.

TWENTY-FOUR

Mathias slept a peaceful, dreamless sleep for the first time in months, wrapped in the comfort of plush bedding. Rest eased his tension, restoring the patience he'd lost while dealing with the more fickle gods and even the likes of Ceredulus and his manipulative ways. No amount of warm blankets could ease his fury with the demons, though, and after nearly a full day's recovery, that ire pulled him close enough to wakefulness that the rapid knocking on his chamber door chased the final notions of sleep away.

He groaned a feigned sob of frustration and pulled a pillow over his head, wishing he'd been given a bit more time to forget the world's troubles. The world's troubles, however, were his responsibility. Flinging the pillow from his face, Mathias stared at the ceiling as he attempted to patch up what remained of his resolve to deal with who was on the other side of the door. Julianna wouldn't give him that luxury.

"Mattie, I know you're in there!"

He winced. Her voice was unusually shrill and ticked with an instability she never let out in public. Any other day, this would have amused Mathias, but knowing *why* she was so irritable—and that he didn't have a reason she'd find satisfactory for running off—Mathias looked forward to talking to Julianna the way a novice horseman looked forward to being thrown by an unruly

269

colt. There would be no running or hiding from Julianna right now, and Mathias honestly didn't have the strength or motivation to try it.

"Julianna may enter," he murmured to the sacred chamber.

The door swung open.

"About time you—" Julianna burst into the room and froze when she didn't have her brother's face to glare up at. Performing a brisk survey of the room's sparse furnishings, she located Mathias laying in his bed, right where Etha had left him. "*Sleeping.* At a time like this!"

"Do you have any idea where I've been lately?" Mathias countered, voice even and giving no indication that he planned to make a game of the pending debate.

"I have *no* idea where you've been, and that's the problem!" Julianna stormed over to Mathias's bed and whipped the covers from him, depositing them in a heap on the floor. "You were supposed to be staying here in Zeal to help research. Instead, you went galivanting off—"

"Etha's quite literally the one who sent me down the road."

Julianna blew right past Mathias's deflection. "I had no idea if you'd gone diving back into the hells or *what.*"

Mathias pushed himself to a seated position and rubbed his eyes. "Did you bother to ask Etha where I was?"

"I did. And all she told me was that you were busy. Busy! Like I'm supposed to trust when you're *busy*!"

This was not the way Mathias had hoped to wake up, but he'd take it over being in the Veil. "Well, I was busy," he said, slipping from bed to begin preparing for the day. "While I was off... what did you say? *Galivanting* across Abaeloth, I snooped around Heiligate to see what news the demons of the surface had heard. I met Havoc while asking Inwan if he'd caught Nes's scent. I spoke to Azerick and Drao, Xiral and Thausch. Finally got confirmation of the oraku's appearance from Kenin—" Mathias stopped abruptly. Too abruptly.

Julianna arched her brows with strict patience. "And what else?"

As frantic as Julianna often got thinking about Mathias

traipsing into the hells, she couldn't possibly want to know that he'd entered the Veil to have a talk with Ceredulus. Mathias didn't even want to think about it, and he'd been the one to go. If Etha had wanted Julianna to know about that excursion, Mathias trusted she'd have already known about it.

"And now I'm home and recovering weeks of spent energy, drained patience, and constant worry." Mathias turned to face Julianna, meeting her spoiled glare with a steady challenge to criticize him for tending to such needs. "Now that you know what *I've* accomplished, what did you and your priestesses dig up while I was off playing?"

In an instant, Mathias's reminder of the reason he'd been gone and why she was so anxious in the first place rushed back to Julianna. She frowned and eased a step back to remove the aggression from her posture. "We've dug hard and deep and uncovered documents that appear to be accounts of the first wave of demons, including the first dozen alar. It may very well point to something important; two of that group became oraku, one an inoga." Her frown shrank into a petite pucker of trouble. "Mathias, it adds up… doesn't it?"

He nodded mutely, having not thought recorded history from that age existed. "The names Kol or Annin appear anywhere in that research?"

Julianna gasped and nodded slowly. "They were officers of a branch of Kalina's army. Kol was said to be their leader and close with a magic user named Annin. Mattie… do you think…" The idea of expressing hope that they were courting the truth still felt too far away, and Julianna was afraid to grab it in fear of another disappointment.

"It's the most solid connection we've made so far." Mathias shed the weariness of his aimless search from his shoulders and replaced it with the fresh burden of duty, something he could proactively work with. "All I have to do is locate this Kol, then. He should be where the rest of the answers lie."

Julianna hummed a stern reservation. "This Kol is likely well underground, provided he's still alive."

Mathias chuckled bitterly. "Oh, he's still alive."

He met Julianna's gaze with that confirmation, as set in his convictions as she was in hers. He was prepared to march back into the hells to complete this mission, but it was unlikely any force— Etha included—would be terribly compliant with him doing so. Mathias heaved a heavy sigh, expelling that rumble of audacity that ceaselessly nagged him to charge ahead, and sank on the edge of his bed.

"Have any of these findings been reported to the Council?" he asked.

Julianna released a gust of her own nervous breath at what appeared to be Mathias's surrender. "No, and they won't wait much longer before demanding to know what we're so urgently searching for."

Mathias sucked his teeth and lowered his gaze. "The second they find out, it'll either get buried under paperwork or they'll shoot at it haphazardly. If the first wave of demons is behind it, Jules…" He shook his head, eyes glazing over as common sense chimed in with what that could mean. He'd never imagined any of the original demons would still be alive, and if they were, they were likely more powerful than he'd be able to contend with. How could he even *think* of average knights marching against them?

"I know," Julianna murmured, her thoughts having mirrored Mathias's for days now. "I'll do what I can to keep the Council distracted, but it's only a matter of time."

Mathias blinked and looked up at his beloved sister, treasuring her gentle commitment to him despite all these years of putting up with his impulsive behavior. The idea of breaking her heart brought tears to his eyes. "If it comes to it, Jules, I'm going to go down there. You know that, right?"

It was her turn to lower her eyes. "I do."

"The Order is an arm of Etha's justice, and I am her shield. I cannot allow anyone else to enter that realm."

Julianna pinched her lips tight and nodded mutely.

Mathias sighed, feeling every bit the villain. "You keep the Council distracted. I'll do what I can here on the surface to see if there's a way to track where this Kol will show up next. You have my word that going back down there is among the last things I ever want to do."

His vow did little to reassure Julianna, but she knew his intentions were good. Pulling out one of the smiles politics had trained into her, Julianna looked into her brother's eyes, diving into his virtue and honor, his desire to protect and serve. "I'll let you get yourself presentable for public," she said at last. "When you're able, meet me at the temple. I'd like you to review what we've found."

Mathias agreed without a fuss and bid Julianna a gentle farewell. She saw herself from his chamber. One step closer. Mathias rose to prepare for the looming battle ahead of him.

TWENTY-FIVE

Auden Clement had been born a simple man, the son of a hardworking father. He'd made an honest living logging, just like most every other citizen of the town of Timberfall. He felt best after a hard day's work, he believed in the virtues of physical labor, and enjoyed the sound of laughter around the campfire at night. Timberfall's people had always looked after their own, with each resident's voice heard equally when it came to political disputes. For these reasons, he'd never figured out why Nessix had taken a liking to him, and as a detail of three heavily armed demons and a pair of oraku marched his way, he wished she never had.

Choking on his mouthful of food, Auden shot hasty glances at the akhuerai dining around him. Only a few of them scattered for cover as they once had, and those who tensely held their ground looked to him for instructions. That was something Auden was quite sure he'd never adjust to. Heart pounding, he stood, feigning the confidence he'd seen Nessix exude. A handful of his nearby friends followed suit.

The demons didn't balk as they approached.

"You Auden?" The demon at the head of the pack stopped two paces before the akhuerai commander and crossed his arms.

Auden couldn't recall a demon ever speaking to him in a cordial manner, and he hesitated. Looking over each demon in turn, the hairs on his arms prickled at their calm, dutiful expressions. Their lack of malice was out of character for the demons Auden had dealt with in the past and those prickled hairs raised in full with a foreboding chill of why the demons had come.

"Where is my general?" he breathed, gutted by the fears running rampant through his mind. He'd known it wasn't safe for Nessix to return to these overlords.

"She's occupied," the demon snapped.

The flood of relief that came from the coarse reassurance momentarily obscured Auden's reservations of facing demons. "But she's alive?"

"For now."

Just as easily as Auden's relief had made him forget the danger he faced, that crisp reminder that none of them were remotely safe flung straight back at him. This wasn't the first time he'd admired the courage Nessix used against their captors, and he was sure it wouldn't be the last. His mind worked frantically to figure out how to address these demons in a safe and respectful manner, but they weren't fond of patience.

"Your general's word and your past actions say these wretches are willing to follow you," the leader said. "Get them organized and let's get moving."

One of the first lessons laid into all akhuerai was to never question a demon's direct instruction. Though Nessix hadn't led by example in this regard, she'd insisted the same. All of that was before Auden had a plucky warrior maiden to consult with and the expectations of actual command. His heart rate sped faster as survival instinct questioned whether or not his peers had recovered from their past massacre enough to try again.

"Well?" the demon snapped.

Auden winced at the sharp question, unaware of how long he'd been quiet. "Where are we—" He cleared his throat and swallowed his apprehension. "I'd like to tell the army where we're heading."

The demon shifted his weight to one foot and scratched the side of his neck, sending an inquisitive glance back at his companions. They shrugged and grumbled a universal lack of concern. Vote complete, the leader dragged his attention back to Auden.

"We're taking you to the surface."

Auden's jaw sagged and the color drained from his face. This was what they'd been waiting for, the chance Nessix had repeatedly sworn would come, the time when the akhuerai would overthrow their guards and reach help and safety in Zeal. The prospect left Auden torn between excitement and terror; Nessix wasn't here, and his last attempt at inciting a rebellion hadn't gone as planned. He didn't have the knowledge or experience to know what to do once they reached the surface. Nessix would have slyly twisted this opportunity to her advantage, and Auden suddenly realized that the demons had separated her from the army for this specific reason.

Struggling to process what he was supposed to do, all it took was a glance at the impatient rise of the demon's brows to push Auden into action. *Especially* if the akhuerai hadn't recovered from their last encounter, he wouldn't let his lack of experience and confidence endanger them. He cleared his throat and lowered his eyes.

"I'll... I'll get them into formation."

The demons didn't so much as grunt in acknowledgement and Auden, last nerve fried, gave them a stiff bow in hopes of gaining their favor and clemency. Not one of their expressions faltered, and Auden gestured to the men around him, praying they'd assist in his first—and possibly last—official order to the army.

Soothing the tense, whispered fears of why the demons had come was the hardest part for Auden. He didn't have the charisma that allowed Nessix to alleviate such worries with heartening quips, and the mass's communal concerns proved that the devastating outcome of their failed rebellion was still fresh in their minds. Each strained speculation raised from frightened voices shook Auden's illusion of competent leadership, but he was too aware of the dangers of disobedience to fail his fellow akhuerai now.

Auden wasn't able to satisfy the questions about why the demons were sending them to the surface or when Nessix would join them. He ignored the speculations that their general was no longer alive, and those suspecting her of finally surrendering to

Kol's whims met quick reprimands. Nessix was too strong and stubborn, too bound to hope to simply roll over and accept that fate. She was fighting for them in the way only she could, and Auden would do all *he* could to ensure she could continue to do so.

The process of gathering the troops was expedited by the akhuerai's conditioned efficiency of spreading rumors and information. Auden had never been part of a military operation, had never even seen an army in marching formation, and had to assume the vaguely organized clusters of troops would satisfy the demons' desires. The men and women clutched their plain polearms. They looked to Auden with desperate eyes like he truly knew what he was doing. Pressure constricted Auden's chest, forcing his heart to beat in his ears and his breath to come in weak strains that left him dizzy. And then, the lead demon stepped up beside him, overshadowing and demeaning the authority Auden tried so hard to fabricate. He didn't attempt to swallow his fear, certain he'd choke on it.

"What's with them?" the demon asked, jutting his chin toward a group of several dozen akhuerai who clung to each other as they pressed against the wall.

Auden followed the gesture and cleared his throat. "They're ah… our, um… our noncombatants."

The demon raised his brows. "*Non*combatants?" He hefted his weight to silently consult with his brethren once again.

Unable to see their unspoken discussion this time around, Auden's heart raced nearly to the point of fainting. He worked his tongue through a dry mouth. "Yes." The confirmation came quietly and quaking with dread.

The demon heaved a great, inconvenienced sigh. "Have the guards round them up and see what Kol wants to do with them." As one of the other demons trudged off to carry out his order, the leader turned around to look over the pathetic army. He made no effort to hide his doubt. "This rabble's what you've got?"

Words failed Auden at a rapid rate, and he settled for a mute nod.

The demon scoffed his disappointment but didn't make a fuss over it. "Fine. Let's get moving." He turned and took three strides toward the crumbling staircase before calling over his shoulder. "Listening's all that's keeping you and your general alive."

The other demons followed their leader, taking with them a bit of the pressure which crushed Auden. He cast a helpless glance at the akhuerai who had asked to stay behind, fearful for their fates, as the guards prodded them into a tighter cluster and directed them toward the confines of the sleeping chamber. Would Nessix have trusted Kol to forgive them for their passive natures? Would she have bargained for their safety or rallied them to play the part of brave soldiers?

Auden pinched his eyes closed against the bite of self-defeating tears. It didn't matter what Nessix would do; he wasn't her. If he made a mistake, he'd have to live with it. He opened his eyes to face his peers, those strong and willing enough to try fighting. They watched him with timid obedience, no more confident that they'd come out of this than Auden was. Right now, these were the people he had to protect.

Murmuring a prayer, begging to channel some of Nes's experience or courage, Auden gestured for the army to follow him, and turned to approach the stairs. Still undisciplined, the akhuerai shuffled into motion, trusting Auden had gleaned from Nessix what he needed to keep these demons happy. They'd spent the past months learning how to brawl, unfit for organized combat, and their confidence had come from Nes's charisma and determination. Auden tried his best to imitate her, but his closed posture and reluctance to get within grappling distance of the demons, his lack of weapons and armor, limited him to a laughable shadow of her composure. Regardless, the army followed him, old habits resurfacing as they hid behind those already in the demons' sights.

They'd all witnessed Nessix navigate the crumbling staircase and knew it could be done, but that didn't make the climb any less daunting. The lead demon and one of his lackeys ascended first, leaving behind the two oraku and the stockiest warrior to prod the reluctant akhuerai up the stairs. Seeing the army to the upper level was a slow, tedious process, and by the time Auden's belly groaned past his ball of nerves, not quite half of the population had made it up. He snuck a glance at the pair of demons, afraid they'd be impatient with the sluggish progress, but the leader leaned against a wall, picking grime from under his fingernails, while his companion appeared to doze nearby.

Auden looked back at the staircase crammed with his friends and comrades as they bit into their fears and forced quivering arms and legs to carry them up. The portion of the army standing with him on the ledge slowly began to recover their composure, some of their terror dissipating as they stood on solid ground. Auden consulted his own courage, finding his heart, though heavy, now beat at a more reasonable rate and he could once again breathe without difficulty. With the army accounted for, he turned back to the demons.

His initial though was how the two of them were alone, drastically outnumbered by undying men and women filled with underhanded combat skills and nothing to lose. Killing two demons wouldn't do much in the grand scheme, but Auden imagined it'd satisfy him in the moment. The leader glanced up from his idle task and met Auden's eyes, as if offering up the chance to try throwing him into the chasm.

A shiver passed across Auden's shoulders, bringing that oppressive doubt along with it. Even if he was brave enough to charge these demons, they had oraku on call and reinforcements were likely nearby. Besides, reaching the surface had been Nes's sole objective. According to her plan, all he had to do was cause a scene big enough to gain the attention of the Order of the White Circle, and help would come. In order to cause that scene, though, he'd have to keep himself compliant to these demons. Like everything else, Nessix had made it look so easy.

Doing nothing to bolster Auden's resolve, the demon shoved himself from the wall, that bored frown still on his face, and walked over to him. "Have you got any other officers in this lot?"

Auden caught himself on safety's side of insisting that he wasn't even an officer. He trusted Garrett and Pierson at least as much as he trusted himself and would gladly call them whatever the demons wanted him to if that would thin his burden. He nodded.

"Good. Tell them to oversee the rest of the army's ascent and to keep everyone calm. Neither of us want to deal with the consequences of another riot, so don't give anyone ideas. Everyone else who's up here needs to move out."

Too afraid to ask about the reason for this change of command, Auden complied, locating the skeptical Garrett first. His hooded eyes and shrunken frown suggested he wasn't thrilled to accept the responsibility, but he vowed his loyalty to Auden and Nessix both, and turned to try his hand at reassuring the dismayed akhuerai that all would be well.

Feeling as though he floated through a ridiculous nightmare, Auden returned to the demon to await his next instruction.

"What's the hold up? Call them to order."

Auden gulped hard. How did Nessix always address them? Brave warriors? Stalwart survivors? Those titles came so believably from her tongue, raising the spirits of even the most downtrodden of the ranks. But simply *thinking* of trying to rally the army with such casual respect felt pathetic and insulting. Nessix had delegated several responsibilities to Auden and the men had always responded positively to him, even now, but he was a *friend* to these people, not their leader. The demon crossed his arms and shifted his weight to one foot, spurring Auden's urgency past his doubt.

The idea of addressing the army with authority and anticipation of their obedience—especially after the last time he'd convinced them to listen to him—brought an aching tremor to Auden's throat. Hopefully, the sight of this demon looming over his shoulder would help convey the importance of his message. Clearing his throat, finding that lump lodged firmly in place, Auden walked toward a boulder jutting out of the floor and rapped his staff against it three times. The sharp crack of hardwood striking stone echoed off the cavern walls and momentarily stunned the crowd, fulfilling the objective Auden's depleted confidence assured him his voice couldn't accomplish.

Wide, reactive eyes turned to him, waiting for instruction. Tentatively, Auden grasped responsibility and climbed on top of the boulder.

"We need to get moving," he said, voice shaking in the silence. "Our general's safety relies on it. Let's make her proud and do what we must to reunite with her soon. Garrett and Pierson will stay back to organize those still climbing. For everyone else, let's go."

No enthusiastic shouts answered Auden the way they'd roared from Nes's rallying, but she'd never moved them in force. What mattered was that the army gathered up what passed for weapons, grit their teeth, and attempted to fall in line.

The demon walked up beside Auden, one brow wrinkled at the akhuerai's shaky concept of authority. "Follow me. We've got a long march ahead of us."

Auden turned to obey, looking over his shoulder to wave the army along. Motion rippled through the ranks and pulled the troops forward. They marched to the tune of hundreds of clomping feet, joined by a larger unit of heavily armed demons just as Auden began to relax and revisit the odds of attempting to overpower their guide. The simple notion of even thinking about such an action was squashed firmly in the ground when the demon spoke next.

"For now, your general lives. If my men and I don't make it back alive, that won't stay the case. Got it?"

Damn Nessix for getting me into this... Auden bit into the inside of his cheek and stared ahead down the vacant corridor. "Got it," he whispered in reply.

TWENTY-SIX

The impulsive side of Mathias fussed about how reading through crumbling parchment and mildewed tomes was a grand waste of time. He had names and time frames, origins and a growing list of victims' identities. Replies from neighboring kingdoms and townships had been coming in, confirming details of missing persons. That foolish, heroic buffoon thriving in Mathias's ingrained desire to do good insisted he had enough knowledge to charge into the hells now. Fortunately for the part of Mathias that found pain unpleasant, he'd learned long ago how to contain such impulses with moderate success.

That didn't make him feel like his research was doing any good.

Mathias leaned back in his chair, swallowed his bored groan, and rubbed his eyes. As the ache of overuse left them, he glanced around at the young priestesses as they toiled over their assigned reading, jotting frantic notes as they found information of potential relevance. He couldn't fathom how they maintained their enthusiasm for such a tedious task, but as his eyes settled on his sister, he understood. They pored over this work in Etha's name because Julianna had declared it their goddess's will. Mathias had served Etha much more intimately than any of these young women would ever hope to, yet he envied their unflappable devotion.

Perhaps there were lessons to learn from them.

Blowing out his boredom from puffed cheeks, Mathias tugged his document closer just as the door to the library flung open. With it burst a compulsion so powerful Mathias cringed and turned to find Etha dressed in the robes of an Official's aide. She jabbed a finger at Mathias then swept her hand rapidly toward herself to signal him to come. Even if he hadn't been looking for an excuse to escape this drudgery, the pull of Etha's urgency launched him to his feet.

"High Priestess, you too." Etha's instruction clipped far shorter than was appropriate for one of the position she'd feigned, but none of the young priestesses in the room were experienced enough to know better.

Amid a cluster of concerned whispers, Julianna stood and gracefully crossed the room. "Keep to your studies, dear ones," she told her students. "I won't be gone long."

As soon as Julianna reached the other two, Etha spun and led the way out. Typically rational and a fount of calm for the siblings to draw from, Etha's distinct lack of such traits rattled Mathias and Julianna both.

"Is something—"

"Not in the halls."

Mathias clamped his mouth shut and plowed forward as Etha hastened her step, reaching a hand back to grab Julianna's wrist and drag her along. His inquisitive mind delved through the possibilities of what drove Etha's haste. His favorite theory was that Kol or Annin had surfaced for him to confront and, preferably, capture, but logic was quick to strike down that fancy. That sort of news would have excited Etha, not left her a storm of distress, and she wouldn't have sought an audience with Julianna—who would be obligated to file paperwork and deliver formal reports—if that was the case. This was something else, something the nauseous lump in the pit of Mathias's stomach said he didn't want to hear.

Or maybe, the struggling optimist in him suggested, *it's exactly what you want to hear.*

Either way, Mathias had to press a fist against his mouth to honor Etha's request for silence.

She led them briskly to an empty conference chamber down the hall from the library and ushered them in the moment Mathias pulled the door open. He secured the door behind them, took a deep breath to calm the flurry of anxiety racing in his heart, and turned to face the two women. Julianna's eyes were wide, her cheeks pale as she awaited the burden Etha prepared to drop on them. Etha's expression, however, was the one that made Mathias frown.

Over the ages, he had seen every fashion of humor and delight on the goddess's face. He'd seen her soft with compassion, glowing with mischief. He'd witnessed her rage and regret and remorse, but he'd never seen this sort of ghastly terror glowing in her eyes. The optimist inside him hid behind his blossoming fears.

"Your search can be over now, Mathias."

Etha's words were hollow and numb, murmured so they nearly ran together, and as Mathias felt his heart rend in two as tears welled in his eyes, a weak smile lifted his trembling lips.

"Has her soul reached you?"

The color drained from Etha's cheeks and she sent an imploring glance to Julianna. The priestess was overrun with questions of her own, but understood Etha's request and rushed over to support her brother. Etha hesitated, even after Mathias was safe in Julianna's hands.

"Nessix is still lost to me," she said, just above a whisper. "But those thousands of souls the demons have taken? They... they seem to have surfaced."

Mathias was too stunned by emotional whiplash to respond but Julianna, blunt as ever, took the report in stride. "On their own accord?"

Etha shook her head, mouth falling open as if to sob, but she never let it out. "They're being led by a unit of twelve demons. Led as an army. They've marched on a village, Braden, about sixty miles west of here."

Mathias shook his head as the report mingled with his memories of Nes's charisma. "As an army... no." His declaration was one of staunch denial. "Fighting under demon guidance? Attacking villages? That can't be... *No*!"

Julianna attempted to slide her arm around Mathias's shoulders, but he swatted her away to take a step closer to his goddess who had the answers.

"Nessix would *never...*" The woman who Mathias had loved would sooner die than see harm come to innocents. She'd risked her army's stability to shelter her civilians in her own fortress to protect them from demons. She'd fought Mathias passionately when he'd suggested those same commoners be taught to bear arms against their enemies. Nessix had been impulsive and feisty, but she would have never had any part of an unprovoked assault. Mathias shook his head so firmly he pulled a muscle in his neck.

"Mattie, you knew this was a possibility..."

"No!" Mathias spun and shoved Julianna away from him. "It isn't. It *can't* be..." A cold sweat sprung on his skin and suddenly, Mathias staggered through a pitiful dizziness he hadn't felt since he was a mortal. Julianna caught her balance just in time to grab his arm and ease him to the floor as his knees gave out.

Eyes glistening with fear and remorse, Etha knelt before Mathias and cupped his face in her hands. "I can't accurately identify any of the souls in that army—they're... fractured—but I didn't see anyone physically resembling Nessix among them. I don't know what the demons have done, but maybe Nessix is still fighting them, fighting their influence. I'm not willing to give up on her, Mathias, and you shouldn't be, either."

Julianna fit her goddess with a disapproving frown; raising Mathias's hopes when there was little to be had historically ended in hardship. However, Etha either believed what she'd said or was too committed to saving Mathias to care. He looked up into those amber eyes he knew meant trust, and the pain numbed enough for him to breathe evenly.

"Sixty miles from here?" he asked, carefully navigating his legs to provide him a solid base of support. Etha and Julianna helped him rise. "Ceraphlaks and I could make that in just over an hour. How large is the village?"

Etha pressed her lips in a troubled crease and glanced away. "Only a couple hundred human lives."

Mathias hissed, the force of the gesture spinning his head once again. "An hour won't be fast enough."

Teleportation via the divine pathways only worked when traveling to a familiar destination. Mathias had no recollection of ever visiting Braden, but Etha knew every foot of Abaeloth and she'd watched her son suffer long enough to bend the rules for him now. Clasping Mathias in her arms, Etha dropped them both into the heavens and deposited them on the streets of Braden.

The moment Mathias's feet hit the ground, he was running, sword half-drawn. By the time he'd taken his second stride, he threw his momentum back and staggered to a stop. Bodies of farmers sprawled on the ground, most bludgeoned to death and lacking the typical bloodshed common to demons' preferred methods of slaughter. None of the fallen men appeared armed, no hoes or scythes laying nearby to indicate they'd tried to fight. There were a few dozen structures positioned around a central well, and all of them stood with their doors flung open, as if gaping in horror at their dead inhabitants.

Etha walked up beside Mathias, silent as he struggled to soak in the scene while maintaining his slippery grasp on hope.

"Why didn't they fight back?" Mathias asked her, continuing to survey the dismal scene.

"I believe they did," Etha said. "Notice that there are only men on the streets. They must have stood in defense of their women and children."

Mathias shook his head. "They have no weapons. There's no enemy bodies. Even unskilled for combat, *somebody* would have landed a lucky hit."

Etha counted the bodies in the street. "There's only eleven men here. Even with the village's small population, this couldn't be all of Braden's men."

Mathias double checked Etha's observation and walked ahead. "Then where are the others?"

Every bit invested in this mystery as Mathias was, Etha turned a slow circle as she searched for clues. She couldn't answer why there were no demon bodies, nor Mathias's unspoken question of where their makeshift weapons were, but she could seek out any life that remained. Three quarters of the way around, a trio of frightened flickers reached out for help.

"Mathias," Etha called, pointing down a narrow footpath that led between two small homes. "There are survivors."

Mathias spun and returned to Etha, heart spilling over with gratitude. He dashed off where she indicated, and she followed close behind.

The path opened into a field pocked with haystacks. Here, the grass had been trampled flat and another half dozen bodies lay on the ground. Blood accompanied these men, though when Mathias crouched to investigate the first, he only bore signs of blunt force, same as the others. Mathias raised his eyes to scan the vicinity. With the amount of blood on the field, these men had fought back, likely with farming implements, but neither those nor their opponents' bodies were found.

"What value would demons find in looting farm tools...?" Mathias wondered out loud.

Etha shook her head.

Closing his eyes, Mathias looked past this odd discovery to hunt after those souls Etha had found. They were close, and when Mathias quieted his mind, he heard muffled sobs nearby. Standing, he looked around at the fallen bodies, certain they were all dead. The sob came again, this time followed by a sharp hiss to demand silence, and Mathias spun to face the sound.

Hay tumbled down the side of one of the stacks and when Mathias looked more closely, an indention two shades darker than the rest betrayed the fact that people had taken sanctuary in the only place they'd had. Mathias regretted that the stowaways would have to come out of hiding to witness the bodies of their friends and neighbors, but he was now strapped with the duty of helping these civilians and tracking down the undead force that had pulverized their village.

"I am Sir Mathias Sagewind of the Order of the White Circle. The area is secure. You're safe to come out."

A squeak sounded from within the haystack, followed by a larger cascade of forage, but nobody came out of it. Mathias sent a glance back to Etha, who had her eyes lowered in response to the fear and pain radiating from within the hiding spot. Without knowing whether or not his frightened audience was armed, Mathias was reluctant to remove them by force, and was left with the chore of coaxing them out with nothing but his words.

"I've been hunting the force that attacked you for some time now, but with little luck. I realize what you've gone through is terrible. I know you can't fathom that any of it will fade from your minds. I cannot force you to come out, but if you choose to, I swear you'll receive safe, guarded passage to Zeal where clerics and knights are waiting to keep you safe." The sniffles and shifting ceased, and Mathias prayed his words were making a difference. "Any testimony you can give me about who did this will help me track them down to bring them to justice. You can help me spare others this same fate."

That last was a gamble, as Mathias had seen his fair share of survivors who wished others to suffer demon attacks, if only so they wouldn't have to face the horror alone. He held his breath, but only for a moment before the stack of hay collapsed as a woman's arm swam through the coarse fibers.

"Thank you," he whispered to Etha and the woman both. "I'll assist you with climbing out," he told the woman, giving her a moment for the words sink in before he grasped her arm and hoisted her forward.

Hay fell from around her, sticking in her hair and out of her clothing, and she looked up at Mathias, eyes puffy and red, face swollen by tears. In her left arm, she cradled a child no more than three years old and she didn't stagger free from the hay due to weakness, but from an older child clinging to her plain skirt. Mathias wanted few things more than to pull them all into an embrace and lie to them that everything would be alright, but they had just survived a great trauma and had no idea who he was. It would take more than gently spoken words to gain their trust.

As the older child emerged, Etha rushed forward to block his view of the death around them, kneeling down and gently engaging him in mindless chatter. His teary face relaxed under her warm smile, and when Etha reached forward to brush the hay from his shaggy hair, clarity reached his eyes. A frown tugged at Mathias's lips at the fact that Etha needed to ease such anguish from one so young, but he kept his sorrow hidden to spare the mother, whose tears resurfaced as she frantically scanned the bodies in the field.

"Ma'am, please look at me," Mathias bid softly.

Her eyes flicked at him and her arm twitched with the possible intention of pulling away. Heart aching, Mathias reached his free hand forward and gently guided her chin so she faced him.

"There's nothing we can do for them, save honor their passing. Please. Help me stop those who did this."

The woman choked on a breath as she attempted to answer Mathias, and she settled for a hasty nod to convey her willingness to assist him. Mathias released her arm so she could cradle her toddler's face against her chest to hide him from memories nobody deserved to carry.

"The intelligence I received was that a troop of demons led this force. Can you tell me if that's true?"

Her attention compulsively drifted across the field again, but returned to Mathias as he raised his hand to block her attempt. She swallowed the phlegm in her throat and shook her head slowly. "I wouldn't know a demon if I saw one, m'lord, but these were evil, *evil* men and women, I can tell you that much."

Mathias kept his curses to himself. Whether or not this woman was familiar with demons, an alar would have stood out vividly. "None of them had wings?"

"W-wings, m'lord?" The woman's voice trembled as hard as she did and risked being lost in the short distance between them.

Mathias had hoped Kol had marched with the army he'd built. Discovering he hadn't complicated all of Mathias's preferred theories. "Don't worry about it," he said, storing his bitterness away to avoid upsetting the woman further. "You said it was a group of men *and* women?"

She nodded and her lips tucked in an ugly frown as tears welled in her eyes. "Men and women, m'lord. They came bearing wooden rods and their fists. We're simple farmers, nothing proper to defend ourselves with. Our men… they…" The tears poured down her cheeks and obstructed her ability to finish the statement.

Mathias couldn't bring himself to ask more, worn down by the woman's weeping. He'd carried his own hurt for so long, was so painfully close to what had to be the answer to his problems, that all he wanted to do was crumble with her. But he couldn't. He had to be the strong one. The beacon of hope. The brave warrior who fixed the world's problems. As the emptiness of the village behind him pressed against his back, it was all Mathias could do to keep from crying with this woman. He wiped his nose and looked down at Etha as she asked the little boy what his favorite animal was and if he liked to catch butterflies in the summer.

Mother, I need your help…

Etha stopped her pleasant discussion with the child and turned her gaze up to Mathias. The cheerfulness was gone from her eyes, but they overflowed with compassion and warmth. She lowered her head in the slightest gesture of a nod and turned her attention back to the child before he slipped out of the trance she'd placed over him. Etha's faith in Mathias warmed his core and refreshed his resolve. He'd begged for her help, and she'd confirmed he'd have it without so much as inquiring about his intentions. After the past months' tension as he and Etha scoured Abaeloth for information and argued over how to collect it, this trust soothed Mathias, and he felt as though this was the first time he'd been able to breathe in years.

"You don't need to speak, ma'am, but can you point for me the direction they came from?" He didn't bother asking which way they'd departed, assuming she wouldn't have survived long enough to tell him if she'd seen.

The woman sputtered on her tears and choked on her sobs, but she nodded and lifted a feeble hand toward the west. Mathias allowed his frown to come out this time. Heiligate was only a few dozen miles down the road. There weren't many other places in this realm that wouldn't have immediately reported this army's movement, and Mathias suspected tracking them would begin in the demon city.

Can you tell where the army went? Mathias asked Etha.

Her words to the child cut off abruptly, but just for a moment. *I cannot. There's something obscuring them, possibly an oraku. The only way I found out they were here was from the villagers' prayers.*

Mathias nodded slowly. His anger had hoped to storm ahead

290

and meet the army himself, but maybe this was for the best. This woman was too shaken to give a full report of what happened, and so his most plausible option was to return to Heiligate and peel more information from Mehalco. Patience had brought him this far. He was willing to see where a little more took him. Stuffing his sorrow and regret away in the places where it could only hurt himself, Mathias smiled at the woman.

"The priestess who is with me is well versed in combative magic and has the best clerical skills I've seen come out of Zeal. She will escort you and your children to the nearest city where you will receive safe harbor for the night. Trust me to track down the beasts who did this. Their crimes will not go unpunished."

The woman's sobs subsided as she looked into Mathias's eyes, her pathetic gratitude shining through the glistening of her tears. She mouthed the words "thank you" and hefted her toddler closer against her side. Etha stood at last, a gentle hand guiding the older child against his mother's hip as she led them away from their home. She said nothing to Mathias as she left, her silent trust enough to rekindle his fire. Mathias turned from where the women and children walked toward safety and marched toward Heiligate.

If Mehalco was as wise as he thought he was, he'd tell Mathias everything.

TWENTY-SEVEN

Ten days had passed following Nes's misadventure in the hall. Kol detained her once again, claiming she was safest not roaming public avenues, but he'd delivered his ultimatum with an unconcerned tone. If not for the opposing oraku's intervention, Nessix felt moderately comfortable that she'd have won the fight, but she wouldn't win debating this decision with Kol. And so she sat in his chamber and studied.

The missing pages and passages blotted out with dark ink taunted Nessix now, whispering delicious tales of how they held the details she was after, but the text always ended abruptly and picked up in a new spot, omitting what she so desperately craved. Twice over the first three days, Nessix thought she'd mustered the courage to ask Kol about Berann now that he'd calmed down, but when she looked up, mouth open to begin speaking, he stared at her with one arched brow, words of warning on his tongue before she started. As well as Nessix thought she knew Kol, it seemed he knew her even better.

Kol left twice a day with the excuse of finding them food, but he always remained gone longer than necessary for such a mundane task. Nessix took advantage of these times to scan through the other books on Kol's shelves, but the bulk of them were written in scripts she'd have to be led through, and those she could read had irrelevant titles such as *Taxidermy of Reptilian Species* and *Secondary Principles of Thanatology*. Frustrated, Nessix held back her questions about Berann, concentrating instead on her army. She'd promised Auden she'd be back the following day, and she'd been gone for ten. If Kol wouldn't compromise and let her return to them, she'd subtly irritate him over the matter until he gave somewhere.

"When do I get to see my army?" Nessix asked the moment Kol entered the room after his latest excursion.

Pleasantly surprised by the neutral nature of Nes's question, Kol kicked the door closed and walked forward to put the food he'd gathered on the desk. "I thought you wanted to study?"

"I do, but I had no complaints about our prior arrangement."

"The attack made on you cannot be ignored. You're safest here for now," Kol said.

Nessix rolled her eyes. "That attack wouldn't have happened if your stupid oraku would have come to get me like he was supposed to. Has *he* been reprimanded for his part in endangering me?"

Kol sat down across from Nessix and began eating, shoving the second plate over to her. "Oh, I'm the only one who cares that you were the specific target of that attack. Everyone else is concerned that the akhuerai are looking like a failed experiment, so we've decided to show them they're not."

Nessix froze as she reached for a piece of bread, Kol's vow of the attack on her being a declaration of war coming quickly to mind. "Show them how?"

Kol continued eating, unfazed by Nes's concern. "We've mobilized your army." He snapped off a bite of carrot and chewed noisily. "That's why I can't simply take you back to them."

Nessix narrowed her eyes and watched Kol closely. He was so casual and sure of himself, confident that whatever was actually going on was right. He'd played Nessix the same way in the past, prodding her over sensitive matters to see if she'd snap. This had to be one of those situations.

"You know what?" Nessix stood as she grabbed the roll from her plate. "I need a break from studying."

"Sit down," Kol said, drawing out the command on a humored groan. "You're not going anywhere."

Nessix kicked her chair back to squeeze out from her place. "I'm going back to my army and I'm *not* afraid to face a few of Inek's underlings to get there."

"You'll be disappointed."

"Why?" She paused by her cot to loop her sword belt over her left arm. "Have you arranged for all of that brute's peons to vacate the passageways? Just because I *can* fight them doesn't mean I'll be disappointed not to."

"It's not about Inek's men," Kol said. "Your army has been mobilized. You can return to the chasm if you'd like, but nobody worthwhile will be there. You will be disappointed."

Nessix stared at Kol as her heart hammered away in her chest. Gauging his honesty had always been a struggle, and as the truth crept up on her now, her stomach twisted sharply. Kol had sent her men, her ragtag group of mismatched civilians, to war. He had slain them, risen them from the dead, enslaved them, and left them helpless to their fears. And now, he'd sent them to battle without their general, with nothing more than the basics their pacifistic minds had picked up. Nes's blood boiled, the pounding of her heart driven less from fear as rage sweltered in her chest.

"You son of a bitch!" she growled through clenched teeth. Storming toward him, Nessix flung her food to the ground to draw her sword. "Did you at least have the decency to send them with steel? Or do you expect them to survive with those lousy sticks you've allotted them?"

Kol stood slowly, a wary eye trained on Nes's blade as he held his empty hands open in front of himself. "They're armed efficiently for the task at hand and have been sent with a reliable guard. Calm down before you do something stupid."

"Stupid!" Nessix snorted. "Like sending an army to war without its general?"

"War's a bit of an overstatement. It's more like… pillaging. And they're not without guidance; we've sent good soldiers along and that Auden of yours seemed to have a pretty good handle on relations."

His attempt at reassurance didn't do the trick. All Nessix could think about was the akhuerai's last battle, seeing them cut down like a fall harvest. That fear wasn't what hurt Nessix the most. "How could you do this without telling me?"

Kol crossed his arms, eyes lingering on Nes's blade a moment longer before drifting up to her face. "Because you'd have handled it just as poorly then as you are now, only the risk of you slipping from my grasp to rally your troops existed then." He picked up the roll from his plate and held it out to her. "By now, they've likely already made it through the Undersea Pass to Gelthin. Even if you managed to talk me into letting you go, you wouldn't catch them before combat began."

Through all of her fury and confusion, one word caught Nes's attention. *Gelthin*. Her army had gone to Mathias's homeland, proving Nessix would be able to reach it, too. She pulled her sword back and straightened out of her preparatory crouch. "You should have sent me with them," she said. "They're not trained well enough to hurt people who aren't demons."

Kol chuckled. "They are when we've withheld their dream stop for a few days and tell them the only way they can have you back is to obey us. This is just another phase of their training. Nothing to worry yourself over. My men will make sure yours return unscathed."

"Unscathed..." Nessix sneered. She narrowed her eyes and sheathed her sword, reaching forward to snatch the roll from Kol's hand. "I——" She clipped her words short, startled by and disgusted with how close she'd come to declaring her broken trust in him. "I will do you the favor of looking past your terrible decision to mobilize them without me"——she ignored Kol's chuckle and strode around the desk——"considering you must have thought I needed time to recover from the attack in the hall. But I will march with my army the next time you send them out. They *need* me, Kol."

Kol whistled, brows arched over laughing eyes. "You sound so sure of that, little one."

Nessix froze, realizing she'd lost herself in her outrage. Kol was being generous with his willingness to let her play for authority slip by uncorrected, and Nessix blanched as she sank into her seat. Through her captivity, Nessix had said several things she didn't want to, kissed up to the most vile creatures she knew. She'd cried to Kol for help, thrown herself into death's hands to prove her loyalty to him, but the one thing she hadn't allowed herself to do was beg him. Pride alone wouldn't protect her naïve troops. It wouldn't safeguard them from the atrocities of war or ease them into accepting responsibility for the deaths they caused. They needed their leader with them to lie and say they were doing the right thing, that there was good to be had through this horror. They needed *her*. Nessix sucked the sour taste of what she had to do next from her mouth and took a slow breath.

"What I meant to ask is what do I have to do to march with them on their next assignment?"

Kol's eyes glittered and he sat down across from her. "You keep doing what I tell you. Grell's still got a few hang ups about how trustworthy you are, but I'll see what I can do."

That wasn't the answer Nessix had hoped to hear. If her ability to reach the surface relied on Grell's opinion of her, she'd never see the sun again. Ripping a mouthful of bread from the roll to avoid gnawing on her cuticles, Nessix returned to her studying, trying to distract herself from the worries about her army as she sought hints at Berann's identity.

* * * * *

Kol left Nessix reluctantly that evening, and he regretted his decision to do so more with each step he took closer to Grell's quarters. The chamber had lost its door long ago to one of the inoga's typical bouts of anger, and nobody had bothered to replace it. Assuming Grell was present, there would be no hiding from him once Kol came into view. Still, he'd told Nessix he would find a way for her to march with her army and he longed to see his precious creation thrive on the field. All he had to do was convince Grell that sending her out into the mortal realm wasn't a bad idea.

Annin's voice floated smoothly through the doorway as Kol neared, delivering reports of the akhuerai's progress. Kol hesitated to eavesdrop. Few had succumbed to the withdrawal of their dream stop, but those who hadn't were swayed into obedience by threats to Nes's welfare. Hopefully, Kol could exploit this information to gain Grell's favor, and Annin's presence was bound to help keep the inoga on survival's side of cooperative. Kol resumed walking.

"I've come seeking audience," he called ahead of his arrival. Grell hated surprise visitors and had never been timid about making it known.

No verbal reply greeted Kol, but neither did a demand to go away, and so he cleared the distance to the doorway and stopped obediently. Both Annin and Grell looked him over, the oraku seeming more satisfied than usual and the inoga's brows resting in a neutral fashion that made him almost look approachable. *Good. They're in pleasant moods.*

Kol didn't wait for a proper invitation into the room; Grell's limited patience wouldn't tolerate dawdling. "I heard reports that the akhuerai are doing well?"

Grell grunted and turned to balance his hulking mass on an overstuffed stool, but Annin narrowed his eyes thoughtfully, hunting for clues as to what Kol was after.

"Better than our critics expected," the oraku said. A delicate line of challenge stretched across his words, and Kol gripped the bait firmly, with confidence.

"But not quite as well as we'd hoped?"

Annin chewed over the question, wary about engaging Kol, but equally unwilling to raise suspicion from Grell. Kol was a sharp man. If he'd had the talent to access threads, Annin suspected he'd never be able to keep up with the alar. Whatever came next was unlikely to go over smoothly.

"They're hesitant," Annin said evenly. "Perhaps frightened. Fighting isn't in their nature and drawing out their aggression is taking more coaxing than we'd anticipated."

Kol grimaced, though the intelligent glint never left his eyes. "We shouldn't have ended the soldiers we'd captured. They'd have smoothed the edges."

"Perhaps."

A grin flashed across Kol's face. That was the door he'd hoped Annin would stumble through. "We do have one natural combatant who didn't make it to the surface this time."

Annin hissed at his own stupidity and sent a hasty glance

toward Grell. The inoga raised his chin and leaned forward, resting his massive elbows on his knees.

"You *want* to part with the bitch?" Grell asked.

In truth, Kol never wanted Nessix out of his sight—and that was precisely why he felt he needed to distance himself from her, at least temporarily. "I want our mission to succeed. It's the reason we selected Nessix to lead the akhuerai in the first place."

"I thought it was because you were smitten with her."

Annin snorted at Grell's jab and Kol grit his teeth. This was not the time to be goaded into losing his calm.

"We all agreed that she was ideal for the job," Kol said. "We've seen that the akhuerai function best with her at their head. My proposal is that they'd be more effective on the surface if you'd permit her to march with them."

"No." Grell's answer came immediately after Kol's final word, no energy wasted thinking over the benefits this could provide.

Engaging Grell was the last thing Kol wanted to do, and he braced himself for the worst. "May I ask why?"

Grell raised his chin and stared at Kol through narrowed eyes. "Controlling that little pet of yours is the only way to ensure the akhuerai's obedience."

Kol instinctively reached up and pressed his hand against the slice of Nes's soul that hung around his neck. Its warmth crept into his flesh, burrowed into his heart. Kol frowned and his fingers clenched around the crystal through his shirt. "I've *got* control over her."

Annin rolled his eyes and his lips twitched as though he had something to add, but he remained silent.

"Kol…" Grell shook his head as if scolding an accident-prone child. "You're of the first wave. You've been around for a long time. You *know* prisoners like her are flight risks."

Of all the insults Grell had tossed at Kol, this comment bristled him the most. "She's not a flight risk."

Grell's brows shot up and his lips lifted close to a smile at Kol's willingness to argue. "Every one of our prisoners is a flight risk. We're *demons*, Kol. *We* don't even want to be here."

Kol's lip twitched with the desire to snarl and remind Grell that there had been a time when they could have escaped their current condition. Grell had voted against that option, and so had Kol. He wanted to taunt his lord with how close Nessix was to stumbling over that truth of the past, but he had a very legitimate fear for her life if he did so. Kol needed Nessix as far from their realm as possible for her own safety. And for his own. He swallowed the sourness from his mouth and clenched his fist at his side.

"She is safe to send out, my lord," Kol said, his voice deep, menace trembling to enter it. "She will not leave me."

"You think that, just because you've got half her soul? She's already learned she can function with what we let her keep."

Kol gnashed his teeth as Grell dug his finger deeper into the wound that was Kol's bond to Nessix. He'd never be able to explain the connection he shared with her, of how much comfort he drew from touching her, of how the sacrifice he'd made for her connected them at a level deeper than Kol had ever fathomed. He couldn't even confess to Annin—who would have at least been interested in studying the phenomenon—the unnatural pull he had to be close to Nessix. Not a day went by that Kol didn't scold himself for demanding to be personally involved with Nes's resurrection, and today, he hated himself for it more than usual. Through his own stubbornness and stupidity, Nessix had taught Kol how to trust again. Fire welled up in Kol's core and he couldn't keep himself silent any longer.

"She will *not* leave me."

The words hung in the thick stillness between the three demons, giving Kol the chance to take them back. It was an offer he ignored; he had no doubt in them. A low rumble resonated through the chamber and Grell launched from his seat and charged.

Kol didn't have much time to react, but neither did he have the motivation to. He was at peace with his stance, and no amount of Grell's temper would shake him. Perhaps that should have been his first warning that the situation had inched out of his control. Grell grasped Kol by the throat and propelled them both across the room. Kol's back slammed against the wall, wings protesting on the verge of dislocation as the breath gusted from his lungs on impact.

Grell leaned close to Kol's face, his breath hot against the alar's flesh and eyes burning wickedly. Kol held them calmly with a stony glare of his own. He didn't struggle.

"How can you not see it, Kol?" Grell growled. "*This* is what we were afraid of when you came up with that stupid plan to bind yourself to her. You are not capable of dominating her; she's dominated *you*."

Kol wheezed in the breath to speak. "She is completely subservient to me."

From somewhere behind Grell's brutish mass, Annin coughed, and Grell's heated glower suggested he doubted Kol's claim, as well. Their opinions on the issue didn't matter. They didn't know Nessix the way Kol did.

"She will not disobey me," he vowed, not the slightest flicker of doubt lurking anywhere in the statement.

Grell scoffed but slowly released Kol. "You sound more confident than usual. What makes you so sure of yourself?"

Kol straightened, standing before Grell at his full height. "Where else would she go? She knows nothing but structure and hierarchy. She has that here. Elidae has destroyed itself over the past year through civil war. This has become her home. The upper realms won't give her what she needs."

"Yeah," Grell grunted. "But *she* doesn't know that."

"Then let me show her."

Silence flooded the chamber and Kol braced himself for another one of Grell's attacks. Only this time, it never came. This time, Kol's statement brought a thoughtfulness to Grell's face which was equally as frightening as his temper. Getting Grell to think meant he was ready to invest in a decision—and any pitfalls that might come with it.

"You really think letting her lead them to battle would make a difference?" Grell asked.

Kol blew out his breath, though it didn't ease the tightness in his shoulders the way he'd hoped. "I do."

"And you know—not just *think*, but know beyond a doubt—that she won't try anything that might jeopardize your station or safety?"

"I wouldn't be here otherwise."

Grell squinted in contemplation before giving a slow nod and backing away. "Alright..." He glanced at Annin. "We've got a witness. Let her go take a look at her wasted homeland if you think it will make a difference. But if she runs—"

"She won't."

The squint of contemplation narrowed at Kol's interruption. "*If* she runs, it's on your head. Am I clear?"

"Absolutely."

Grell seldom tolerated Kol's confidence; it reminded him of a past he preferred to forget. This time was no exception. He'd enjoy humbling his old friend when Nessix did disobey. "Very well. Out with both of you. I've got other matters to attend to."

Annin and Kol departed without further instructions, marching down the hall with quick strides, relieved to be rid of Grell's presence. Several turns later, Annin eased his pace just enough to snag Kol's attention, and the alar slowed as his companion halted completely. Stopping, Kol turned to face melancholy eyes he hardly recognized.

"You are asking for your death, Kol," Annin said quietly. "Part of you, somewhere, must know that."

Kol frowned at the premonition, but he stood his ground. "If I was meant to die from my connection to Nessix, it'd be done by now."

Annin shook his head and pinched his lips in a thin line. "You have become so blind, friend." He looked up at last, resigned to Kol's fate. "I'm begging you, be smart about this. Just this once."

The warning chilled the doubtful parts of Kol, but he'd already convinced himself that Nessix wouldn't wrong him. She'd had plenty of chances to lead him to harm, and she had no reason to start now.

"All will be well," Kol said. "Wait and see. Nessix knows her place beneath me and only needs to see the truth now. In a week or two, you'll wonder why you doubted at all."

Kol waited for Annin to respond, but when all he received was a dubious stare, he shrugged and turned to walk on down the hall. As the alar's form grew smaller in the distance, Annin heaved a sigh and hung his head. No matter the outcome of this experiment, he doubted he'd ever understand Kol's motives.

* * * * *

Ever since the day Grell burst into the room and grabbed her, Nessix had dreaded the sound of the door opening. With the exceptions of a visit from Annin and a select few demon guards, her reactivity was pleasantly voided by Kol's familiar face. This time was no exception and, as her stomach grumbled at the promise of dinner, she looked up with anticipation. That, too, met disappointment.

"No dinner tonight?" Nessix asked, not bothering to hide her irritation. She might have skipped questioning it if Kol had at least brought food for himself, but he'd returned completely empty handed.

Cursing sharply, Kol spun to order rations delivered from one of the posted guards, then entered the room. He turned his back to Nessix and shut the door, placing both hands on its sturdiness, head bowed.

Nessix straightened slowly and glanced through the room, wondering what she'd done wrong. "Are you… Are you alright?"

Kol stayed quiet a moment longer before speaking, still facing the door. "We've come to know each other quite well."

Nessix cautiously pushed herself to her feet. "We have," she agreed.

"I've seen you give your life for me."

Nessix fidgeted with the pages of the book in front of her, uncomfortable with the direction Kol's words were heading. She'd never imagined a demon expressing gratitude, especially to one they clearly saw as inferior. She cleared her throat. "Are you going somewhere with this?"

Kol didn't answer immediately, and Nessix held her breath. Her alar had displayed strange behavior of late, no doubt tied to her connection with him and the sensitive questions that went along with it. She much preferred his annoying cockiness to this uncertainty. A shiver ran up the back of her neck and she reached up a clammy hand to rub it away.

"Have I done something to disappoint you?" she asked.

Kol raised his head, his shoulders lifting with a great breath. When he turned around, he wore his typical smirk to defy what his voice had previously conveyed. "Quite the opposite, little one." He walked closer to Nessix. "You've made me incredibly proud."

Nessix typically thrived off praise, especially from those who acted as her superiors, but she drew a trembling breath as Kol neared. His look was one of deep fondness and keen satisfaction of his possession of her. It wasn't the lusty leer she'd received from Veed, but lacked the protective warmth Brant had shown her. Not knowing what to make of this attention, she shifted a step backwards.

Kol stopped at her subtle retreat and cocked his head. "What's wrong? Don't you trust me?"

Nes's heart beat rapidly, echoed gently in her soul. "Probably more than I should," she said. "But I can't tell what you want from me." *And that frightens me…*

Kol flashed a smile, the nervous tremor of Nes's soul confirming his belief that disappointing him was the last thing she wanted to do. "And I trust you. Exactly as much as I ought to. Always remember that."

A gentle rap sounded on the other side of the door and Kol blinked, eyes resetting from that eerie depth to their usual, stoic glint. He retrieved the food brought for them, delivered it to Nessix, and urged her to resume her studies. Concentration came difficultly to Nessix and she found no pleasure in her food as she crawled her way through the text. That night, she slept with her dagger close.

TWENTY-EIGHT

The last time Mathias entered Heiligate, he'd received his normal welcome of sneers and shouted curses. There was a certain degree of comfort that came with those gestures, a degree of comfort which was devastatingly absent today. The guards weren't seated at their post, rather they'd been tasked with repairing their collapsed station. Property damage wasn't an uncommon sight in Heiligate, but Mathias had never seen entire structures pulverized as the guard station had been.

"What happened here?" he called ahead.

Both guards spun to face him, the first dropping his mallet to draw a short blade, the second brandishing his hammer with a certainty Mathias was in no hurry to test. Stumbling upon nervous demons was unusual, confirming his suspicion that someone in the city would have the information he needed. Before Mathias could draw a breath to request as much, the guards' eyes widened in horror. Mathias stopped and looked behind himself to see if some monster had snuck up on him. When he turned back, the hammer-wielder had bolted down the road to town.

"Good for nothin' waste 'a..." The second guard pointed a scolding finger at Mathias, though his eyes threatened to spill over with tears. "You!" Authority ached to frame the address, but that unusual flurry of nerves forbid it to make purchase. "Stay right there."

This demon, too, wheeled around and tore off after his companion, shouting curses at his back.

Mathias trusted the demons of Heiligate as much as he could trust any creature removed from Etha's grace, and he'd never been uncomfortable entering this town. Today was different. Confident in his strength and skill, and committed down to his soul to catch this army, he was half inclined to disregard the order given to him. His desperation for information from Mehalco, though, held Mathias in place. Something had attacked Heiligate and left her inhabitants squirrely enough to consider Mathias a threat. He needed what he sorely suspected they had and Mehalco would be disinclined to help if Mathias made a scene. If he was told to stay put, he'd do so unless circumstances demanded otherwise.

He didn't wait long for a mob two dozen strong to come tramping toward the city's entrance. Brows furrowing, Mathias pulled his shoulders back and glanced around himself once more. There *must* have been something else lurking outside this town. He kept his left hand on his scabbard, prepared to draw his sword if necessary, but commanded his body to relax.

"I've come with honest intentions and good will," he told the group of demons. They slowed as they got closer. "All I want is a word with—"

"All you *ever* want is a word with me," Mehalco groused as he shoved his way through the dense pack of bodies. He strode toward Mathias, wearing a patchwork of armor, a rusty serrated sword clutched in his hand. "So out with it."

Mathias glanced at the mob and back to Mehalco and heaved a sigh. They were buckling down for defense, likely against those who had previously attacked, but their trust in him seemed rather worn. Convinced he wasn't in danger from outside sources, Mathias unbuckled his sword belt and tossed it aside, holding his empty palms before him.

"Mind resting your soldiers and lowering your weapon first?"

Mehalco paused and swatted his free hand toward the mob. They grumbled and dispersed, but didn't venture far from sight, and Mehalco refused to lower his sword. Mathias swallowed his groan at the twitchy demon's lack of compliance. At least he'd gotten half of what he asked for.

"May I approach, or do you insist on us shouting this conversation?"

Mehalco spit to the side and muttered a colorful collection of expletives before marching up to Mathias in a bluster of self-doubt. When he stopped within striking distance, his cheeks were flushed and he wouldn't meet Mathias's eyes.

"Tell me what happened here," Mathias said quietly. Heiligate's residents might have been demons, but even Etha could see that they attempted to behave themselves.

"What does it look like?" Mehalco shot back on a harsh whisper. "We were attacked!"

"Not by mine, I hope."

"Of course not by yours, you fool! Nobody up here's stupid enough to risk trying you, especially now that word's gotten around about what you did to that witch goddess."

Mathias blinked, wondering which of the new children had gone gossiping on the mortal plane. Then, Mehalco's choice of words ran through his mind again. *Nobody up here...* It hadn't been a god that had come through Heiligate. As Mathias had hoped, the demons and their army of fractured souls had stopped here. Recently, if he could judge by the fresh construction only now underway. His plans were finally working out; it was a pity it took the loss of lives to get this far.

"I've only heard one report of demon movement on Gelthin in the past few months, and they weren't marching alone."

The color drained from Mehalco's cheeks and he glanced around the road as if someone nefarious might be eavesdropping. He scoffed and though Mathias had always known him to be shifty, Mehalco refused to let his eyes settle in one spot. "I wouldn't know what you mean."

Mathias crossed his arms and adjusted his stance to get more comfortable for what looked to be a long debate ahead of them. "Was there or was there not an army that marched through your fair city over the past couple days?"

"Well... We had some visitors." Mehalco tried unsuccessfully to match Mathias's posture and demeanor. "We might be demons, but we do want to keep our city standing, you know."

"I do know," Mathias said. "So why don't you help me out so I can track down this army for you and make them pay for the damages they caused?"

Mehalco's arms dropped to his sides and he scampered toward Mathias shaking his head fiercely. "Oh, no. You're not allowed to go chasing after these troublemakers, friend."

That was just as good as a confirmation. "I'm not *allowed* to? How do you suspect you'll stop me?"

Mehalco growled, a shrill noise that had never intimidated Mathias so much as it announced the demon's wavering self-control. "I'll stop you by asking you to be the decent man you always prattle on about being," he snapped.

Mathias squared his stance again so he could draw closer to Mehalco. The demon winced at his approach, but held his ground admirably. "I've seen the destruction this army is capable of," Mathias said quietly. "And it gets much worse than a couple of busted up buildings. I'm not judging you in the slightest when I say I understand that you're afraid—"

"I'm not—"

"They will slaughter all of you without a second thought if they find out you've been talking to me about their plans. Of course you're afraid."

Mehalco snarled at Mathias but clearly didn't have grounds to debate that fact. "*They* might slaughter us even without me talking to you."

Mathias cocked his head and jerked his shoulders back. The demons residing in the hells openly mocked the residents of Heiligate, but they understood the value of this city. With Heiligate's destruction, they'd lose their one safe haven on the surface of Abaeloth. They'd need a whole lot more than a grudge to want to see the town leveled. "Who is *they*?" Mathias asked.

"*That army.*"

A victorious smile flew across Mathias's face.

"You son of a whore!" Mehalco spat. "I can't... I *can't* talk to you about this."

"We could always step into the privacy of whatever building is most secure," Mathias suggested. "You can yell at me and threaten me, send all of your fiercest men at me, but I'm not leaving until you tell me who was marching with the demons."

"It's not a *who*," Mehalco whispered, leaning close enough that Mathias could smell his sweat. "It's a *what*."

Mathias's heart dropped at that ominous correction. Sense and experience both told Mathias that he knew those stolen souls wouldn't be normal when he encountered them. Etha's claim that they'd been fractured had reinforced that, as did Mehalco's refusal to acknowledge them as people. Hope of recovering any recognizable part of Nessix began to shrivel away. Mathias had battled demons and undead both, and the thought of them rolled into one being, dually removed from Etha's grace, struck him with a weakness that threatened to buckle his knees. Neither Julianna nor Etha were there to keep him from collapsing this time, and he broadened his stance to maintain command over his balance and the conversation.

"Last time I was here, you told me about an inoga who had tasked an alar to build an army for him. Was that the *what* which marched through here?"

"Damn it, you…" Mehalco shot twitchy glances around them again and pressed so close to Mathias that the paladin unconsciously leaned back to gain distance between their faces. "Yes, alright? That was the army that was here. They needed food and rest, said they were marching east for a training operation, that they didn't want any trouble. Can you leave now?"

Mathias ignored Mehalco's request. "If they didn't want trouble, mind me asking how your township took so much damage?"

"I *do* mind, you meddling gnat."

The demon glared at Mathias, attempting a savage snarl that his debt to the paladin prevented from coming across as genuine. Panic scratched just as fiercely underneath Mathias's skin and at the back of his eyes, but he'd spent lifetimes methodically learning how to overcome such raw reactions. He crossed his arms.

"Fine then," Mathias said. "I'm no longer asking. This army

you seem so keen on protecting is an active threat to Abaeloth. I doubt I need to remind you what happens to those who make it on that list, and those who aid them."

"I'm not—!" Mehalco reeled back two steps, waving his sword around frantically as he tried to dismiss the accusation. "There was no assistance given to them here! You have my word."

"By not assisting me, you are helping them," Mathias continued. Mehalco was in too frantic of a frame of mind to overcome a persistent attack of goading, and Mathias was too tired to let honor keep him from taking advantage of that weakness. "If you want to keep your slate with the Order clean, tell me what this army did to your township and why."

Mehalco flung the tip of his sword toward the ground, pinched his eyes shut, and pressed his fingers against his forehead. He'd never asked to govern Heiligate; he'd never been of quick enough mind or stout enough courage for the position. It was Mathias's fault that he had these responsibilities, and not a day went by that Mehalco didn't hate himself a little bit more for his one childhood mistake that had suggested to the paladin that he had a sliver of goodness in his heart. He groaned and gasped as though he was about to be sick.

"Like I said, they came by for food and rest. We don't have much along the lines of making unsavories leave, so we let them in."

"How sentient was the army?"

Mehalco shook his head, nose wrinkled at the absurdity of Mathias's question. "I'm sorry, what?"

"I asked you how sentient the body of the army was." The fact that the question seemed so ridiculous to Mehalco blew on the embers of Mathias's hope.

"I dunno," Mehalco snorted. "They were plenty sentient, I guess. Ate and drank and spoke just like normal people. Just like you. Only not blessed. You know what I mean."

The answer offered only a pinch of kindling to Mathias's hope, but that tiny bit was enough to catch. "And can you tell me what the leader looked like?"

"How could that possibly matter?"

Mathias glanced at where his sword lay just out of reach, wishing he still had its leverage. "Because it does. Answer me, Mehalco."

Growling his resentment, Mehalco decided he didn't care for the way Mathias's fingers twitched as though ready to attack. "I don't know. I don't make it much of a habit to ogle men."

A relieved chuckle snuck past Mathias's tension and fears. It wasn't a response either he or Mehalco had expected, and the demon furrowed his brows and shook his head, gripping his sword tighter.

"You feeling alright, friend?" Mehalco asked.

The truth was that Mathias felt awful, but knowing Nessix hadn't been responsible for the recent attacks allowed Mathias to sort his fear of what might have become of her one place lower on his current list of concerns. He didn't know or care about what types of women Mehalco was drawn to, but had faith that Nessix was notable enough to mention if she'd been there. As with speaking to the gods, though, Mathias wanted Mehalco to know as little as possible about Nes's value.

"I hadn't been, but I'm getting there," Mathias said at last. "So you said they claimed to not be after trouble. What made them tear up your town?"

Mehalco muttered what must have been curses beneath his breath and ground his fingers into his temple. "You do not let up…"

"Never have. You've known this since the day we met."

"Shoulda called for help then…" Mehalco sighed and his shoulders drooped in surrender. He'd already allowed Mathias to extract enough incriminating information out of him. It no longer mattered if any of the more vile demon ears were listening. "It was all just normal activity. One of the demons with them said he wasn't going to pay his tab, Bronte said he would. Instead of the normal brawl, though, the hell dweller turned to this quiet fellow and told him have the army make it right."

"And this quiet fellow was one of the normal-looking people?"

Mehalco nodded.

"You expect me to believe that an army of normal people ransacked Heiligate without any of your citizens standing in the way?"

"Oh, we stood. We fought, too. But it… it wasn't a battle we could win." Mehalco scratched behind his ear, mouth turned in a bitter frown.

"What do you mean, you couldn't win?"

"Exactly that." Mehalco grasped his elbows in a defensive shrug and pointedly looked away. "It was impossible odds. We couldn't fight them."

Mathias tapped his lips as he sorted through the pieces. "They outnumbered you?"

Mehalco's cheeks flushed and he grimaced shamefully. "No."

"Were the troops armed?" Mathias asked, recalling the woman's report that they'd come bearing nothing but rods and fists.

Mehalco spat and cast a glare at Mathias, through with his prying questions. "No, they weren't armed," he snapped. "They didn't even want to fight us. Seemed scared half to death just being in town."

Mathias shook his head in frustration. None of this added up to the destruction he'd witnessed in Braden, and he knew the most important details were being left out. Mathias crossed his arms. "Help me here, Mehalco," he said softly. "Heiligate has held her own against every threat to date. I'm not here to judge or ridicule, far from it. Why couldn't you stand against an army of quiet, normal-looking people who didn't want to fight you? What went wrong?"

Mehalco looked around them once more and lowered his head to shield his lips. "They fought, Mathias… scared or not. And they fought past death."

A chill blew across the back of Mathias's neck, his worst fears confirmed at last. "You're sure of this?"

Mehalco met Mathias's eyes, the honesty of fear wiping away his combative air. "I'm not sure of much of anything anymore. Not after that. Dead men, Mathias. Standing up and fighting. Can you believe it?"

Heart racing as he fought to deny this report, Mathias didn't answer.

"Bah. Of course *you'd* believe it."

Mathias licked his numb lips. "Did their deaths affect how they fought? Did they lose any part of themselves in this process?"

Mehalco shrugged. "What little confidence they had, maybe. Just because they were able to come back to life didn't seem to make them want to risk dying."

Mathias rubbed his arms and drew a deep breath. That was better than the normal patterns of instability that the typical undead foes suffered from. "Combat frightened them, so what kept them fighting?"

"I dunno. The demon that seemed to be in charge kept yelling at them about something like... ah... remember the stakes? Something about their general's life? I can't remember. I was a little distracted at the time, you know."

Mathias gasped sharply at the mention of a general's life, his hands dropping back to his sides. Against both his greatest fears and wildest dreams, that general had to be Nessix. The demons' obsession with her during the war on Elidae insisted as much. His fear for her fate once again moved up on his priorities and he hid his worries from Mehalco's inquisitive gaze by walking over to his sword belt. Releasing his surge of distress through another gutted gasp while his back was turned to the demon, Mathias bent down and retrieved his blade. Carefully, he drew the mask of confidence over his face and turned back to Mehalco.

"You've been of great help to me once again," Mathias said, no longer with the firm, impatient tone he used to intimidate Mehalco into compliance. "If I didn't have to chase after this force, I'd stay to help you rebuild."

The offer sounded genuine, but Mehalco's pride didn't allow him do more than scoff. "Yeah, well, keep poking around here with my brethren lurking about and there may not be a Heiligate for you to bother anymore."

Mathias lowered his head in the first sign of respect and apology he'd shown for Mehalco's troubles. "Stay safe, my friend."

Mehalco had never known what to do with Mathias's gratitude

and squirmed just as uncomfortably with it now as he had when he'd been a child. "We'll all be a lot safer without you around."

Mathias wished he'd been able to laugh at the jab, but was beginning to think that this time, Mehalco might have been more right than wrong. Besides, he now had evidence of a new wave of demonic aggression and potentially the best lead on Nes's fate and whereabouts to date. He needed to get back to Zeal to discuss it all with Etha and Julianna. Without a word of farewell, Mathias honored Mehalco's discomfort at last and departed for home in a flash of light.

TWENTY-NINE

Nessix tossed through the night, concentrating on Kol's breathing as he slept soundly. Rest came to her in brief glimpses, but she always jolted awake to the memory of Kol claiming he trusted her.

The night dragged on in this manner, and by the time Kol grumbled his way into the waking world, Nessix heaved a groan at how miserable she'd be through the day. She pressed her fingers against her eyes to stave off the fatigue scratching at the insides of her eyelids and muffled a whimper at the dull ache that lurked behind her forehead. Kol, on the other hand, clattered through the room, undoubtedly aware of how badly Nessix wanted him to be quiet. And then he began to hum.

Nessix lifted her hand from her eyes so they could fly open. She'd seen Kol humored before and enjoying jest at the expense of others. She'd seen him glow with pride and set at ease. But she'd never seen him genuinely cheerful. Confused and rightfully concerned, Nessix sat up.

Kol bustled through the room. The commotion he caused came from him sorting through Nes's armor and buffing the blemishes free from its surfaces. Nes's heart sank. He wouldn't have a reason to care what her armor looked like unless he was sending her someplace where she had to look good. Here in the hells, those places were painfully limited.

Catching Nes's movement from the corner of his eye, Kol continued working as he addressed her. "Good. You're up. I'll finish cleaning your armor. Start getting dressed. You've got a big day ahead of you."

Nes's lips pursed against her urge to protest. What Kol considered a big day seldom complemented getting a poor night's sleep. Regardless, she'd gone through this dance with him enough times to know she'd end up doing what he wanted anyway, and slipped out of bed to change her clothes.

"Mind me asking what I'm getting dressed *for*?" She shook her head irritably to hurry her mind along to full function. The alar's excitement suggested it was unlikely that this was the sort of day Nessix could afford to be anything but her best.

Kol looked at her and smiled. "I'd prefer to leave it a surprise."

He'd often deceived Nessix but had never invested the effort in blatantly lying to her, and she suspected the concept of acting was beneath the proud alar. As he cheerfully assisted with piecing armor to her, though, she began to wonder.

Had the recent pressures she'd dumped on him pushed him to madness? There had been a time when Nessix assumed all demons were prone to instability, but having gotten to know Kol as well as she had and learning of the past he'd survived, she could hardly imagine him snapping over a few intrusive questions.

Was this some sort of obscure test he was putting her through? He'd been able to talk riddles around Nessix to gain her compliance early in their relationship, but it had been weeks since she'd been unable to keep up with him. All Nessix could settle on was that Kol was up to something, and that frightened her on the deepest level.

Nessix obediently allowed Kol to manipulate her limbs as he secured her armor, silently letting the chipper demon work. It had been some time since she felt like Kol considered her his property, but when he grasped her by the shoulders and leaned back to look her over, that humiliating sensation returned. Contentment, as opposed to his usual slyness, illuminated his smile. Nes's eyes fought to water as Kol reached his hands forward to cup her face. He smoothed her hair back behind her ears, leaned forward, and kissed the top of her head.

"Let's go, little one." Kol turned from Nessix with the full expectation that she'd follow him as he fetched her sword belt from where it laid on his bed. He reached the door before addressing the fact that she hadn't moved. "This is not a day you want to let go to waste. Come on."

Kol's confidence had never rattled Nessix the way it did now. She longed to blame her lapse of composure on how little sleep she got, but couldn't shake the dread from her soul. Nessix stayed unusually quiet as she attempted to figure out what to make of the alar's perkiness, refraining from replying to his casual attempts at small talk. On any normal day, Nes's silence would have drawn snide comments from Kol, and the fact that he continued to chatter as they walked struck more blows to her resolve than any of his cruel remarks ever did.

They walked past the turn which led to the common grounds and Nes's tension grew as they approached the chamber where the inoga gathered for their dysfunctional meetings. She eyed Kol, searching for any of the tiny tells of discomfort that always accompanied one of these encounters. They passed the chamber, the absence of angry shouts and shattering furnishings from within implying it was vacant. Nessix curled her lips between her teeth as Kol led her to unfamiliar territory.

She'd never enjoyed the hollowness which uncertainty carved out of her gut and without the faintest idea of where Kol was taking her—or why—she particularly disliked it now. All she wanted to do was stop where she was and refuse to move until Kol explained where they were going and why he was in such a damn good mood, but the fear of not knowing where the inoga might lurk in this part of the hells kept her quiet and close to Kol's heels.

"Will you at least tell me if I should be frightened?" she asked at last, exhausted from battling the terrible scenarios she concocted in her mind.

Kol chuckled, a rich, genuine laugh Nessix seldom heard. It was the laugh he reserved for Annin when he thought Nessix couldn't hear him. "I wouldn't say you should be frightened at all. Guarded, but excited, should suit you better."

Nessix eyed her sword where it was clenched in Kol's hand. "Is it dangerous?"

"I don't know." Amusement ran thick in his speculation. "It shouldn't be, provided you've been honest."

Nessix shook her head, unsure what to make of Kol's reply but too mentally spent to ask. All of these anomalies sang of danger she wanted no part of.

When Kol greeted two remarkably plain demons a short distance farther down the hall, Nes's reluctance intensified. The pair was dressed for travel, the taller of the two shouldering a full pack and both of them adequately armed. They obediently filed in behind Nessix to prevent her from balking at her growing confusion.

"Are you taking me to my army?" Nes's drive for answers wholeheartedly accepted the risk of irritating Kol with her questions.

"Not quite." His answer was ten times more pleasant than Nessix anticipated. "The akhuerai force moved through the Undersea Pass. That leads downward."

Reinforcing Kol's statement, Nes's legs ached with a mild burn, indicating that they'd been climbing a gradual incline. The alar still avoided providing her with straightforward answers, and past experience told Nessix that further attempts at extracting information from him would do nothing more than cultivate her growing frustration. She bit down on the inside of her cheek and trudged ahead.

Kol led the way up the passage until it narrowed so it was barely wide enough to accommodate the span of his folded wings. Nessix followed silently, the two demons driving her along as they ascended toward the smell of fresh air. The crisp scent, devoid of the stagnant, musty stench of the hells, sang to Nes's senses, pulling her mind from its pessimistic fretting and toward the memory of a bliss she hadn't experienced since childhood. Suddenly, her reluctant trudging turned to an eager march and she had to restrain herself from pushing Kol to move faster.

Nessix didn't know how long they'd walked by the time sunlight leaked in through a portal ahead of them. Kol held a hand back to halt his modest entourage and breathed deeply. "Do you smell that?"

The purity of the air from the surface flooded Nes's lungs, refreshing her spirit in an instant. She closed her eyes for several greedy breaths before catching herself noncompliant to Kol's request. Her eyes shot open to meet a faint smirk and softened eyes from Kol. "It smells divine," she murmured.

Her word choice, spoken without full consideration, wiped the whimsy from the demon's face, but he didn't correct her. "Would you like to see more?"

Nessix hesitated. There was no way Kol would allow her to leave the hells this easily. Between this offer and his unusual behavior, there had to be some sort of hidden agenda in his plans. A breeze from outside filled the passage with cool, clean air, whispering to Nessix that it didn't matter what Kol had planned; it would be worth any sacrifice to enjoy this sweetness for even a moment longer. Nessix nodded mutely and restored Kol's smile.

"Then let's go."

He continued to lead the way, and Nessix busied her hands with one another to keep from shoving him out of the way so she could run ahead. She didn't know how long had passed since she'd last seen the outside world, and though she'd ached every day over how she missed it, she hadn't realized how badly until this moment. At last, sunlight flooded the entirety of their path and they stepped onto a rocky outcropping several yards up a mountainside. Nessix stopped short, eyes large and lips parting open.

"Are you taunting me?" she murmured.

Kol glanced at her, pleased she'd played into his plan so well. "I take it you know where we are?"

Shock delayed Nes's response until longing helped her whisper a single word. "Elidae."

"And do you miss it?"

What sort of question was that? "Dearly."

Satisfied, Kol smiled. "That talk we had last night about trust. I'm investing it in you."

Kol's words clamped down around Nes's heart, stealing the euphoria she so desperately wanted to savor. Despite how terribly he hid his fondness of her, Kol had never done anything for her benefit without an ulterior motive. Nessix straightened and cast her eyes across her homeland, praying this wouldn't be the last time.

"What do you mean?"

Kol nodded his head to direct the demons who followed them to step aside and walked behind Nessix to grasp her shoulders. He turned her to face the direction of her old kingdom and leaned forward to speak into her ear. "You've proven your obedience to me, and it's time you were rewarded for that."

Bitterness wriggled past the flurry of hope and longing, seeping off Nes's tongue before she could stop it. "And what do you want in return for this reward?"

Kol hesitated, taken by surprise at how well Nessix had learned his ways. Stifling the cautious voice that suggested Grell might have been onto something, Kol addressed Nes's concerns. "I brought you here so you could see what's become of Elidae. I know better than to think you'd believe anything I told you in this regard, so I'm giving you the chance to see it yourself. If Elidae's still the home you died for, we can discuss conditions to let you return."

Nessix stiffened against Kol's touch. Paired with the demons' ambitions, that sounded like an ominous promise. "Are you implying it might not be the same?"

"I need you to decide that for yourself. If it's no longer the home you loved, consider the structure and security I've given you as an alternative. Until your final breath, you will have a home with me. I want you to remember that."

Ominous, indeed, but a chance Nessix wasn't willing to give up. Elidae couldn't have eroded so badly after her death that she wouldn't still be respected. Of course, she was assumed dead, but if Sulik still idolized Mathias like he did before her death, he'd be able to break the news of her condition to Brant. She'd reclaim her station eventually. She'd have an army—*her* army—to lead against the demons while she waited for Mathias's aid. Elidae had survived one war with these beasts, and now she had an intimate knowledge of how they functioned. They'd survive another one.

"You'd let me leave, based off trust alone?" she asked slowly, searching for whatever it was that Kol was hiding from her.

"Well, not alone."

On cue, the two demons stepped up beside them. All that would watch over Nessix was the two of them and the weight of Kol's trust. She'd taken on more perilous odds in the past and with her freedom and the fate of her kingdom of akhuerai at stake, defeating them would be an easy feat.

"Can I go wherever I want to?"

"You will avoid the fortresses and the temple, but any township of your choosing is free for you to access. Remember, you're only here to get a glimpse of the state of the nation."

Nessix worked her jaw as she thought over where to go next. It was logical that Kol wanted her to avoid the fortresses—even with her complicated relationship with Veed, she had too many allies in them, and knowing what she did about how she'd been resurrected, Etha's temple didn't sound like the safe haven it once was. Kol seemed so sure that Nessix would be displeased with where Elidae stood that curiosity whispered that sleuthing for information before trying to sort out where her strongest allies were was the smartest move.

"How long do I have?" she asked.

"I'll give you a week. If you're not back by then, we'll march out in force to find you. I don't think I need to remind you what we did the last time we visited your country."

All of that patience Nessix had carefully cultivated for Kol began to wither away as freedom grew increasingly near. She'd find a way to escape. She had to. "If I've only got a week, let's quit wasting time."

Kol chuckled and released his hold on Nessix so he could turn to his minions. "Take her where she wants to go. Let her see what she needs to, then bring her home." He handed Nes's sword belt to the taller one.

The demons accepted their orders with curt nods, and Nessix spun around to face them, hardly believing that slipping away from Kol would be this easy. She briefly appraised the demon who held her sword. He was tall and lean, arms exposed to reveal average muscling, and his eyes didn't harbor any extraordinary wit. She'd be able to take him if she was quick, and once she had her sword, she'd worry about the other one.

Kol interrupted Nes's thoughts by ducking his head to meet her eyes. "I'm trusting you, little one. Make me proud."

Oh, she'd make him proud. She'd show him the fighter he'd always claimed to admire. Overcome with anticipation, thriving off the rush of the risk awaiting her, Nessix nodded silently. Kol smiled, caressed her cheek, and stood to his full height.

"Keep her away from the shade," he told the guards as the shorter one gripped her arm. "I don't think I need to remind you why."

The demons grunted their understanding and dragged Nessix down an overgrown path, leaving her to ponder Kol's final instruction. In order to reach any of the cities, they'd have to pass through forests. None of Kol's previous remarks about Elidae's current standing had concerned Nessix, but whatever this shade was, the demons knew it as a threat, and she didn't. That put her at a distinct disadvantage.

The guards didn't make an effort to speak to Nessix or even each other as they traipsed through the forest, giving her plenty of time to work over how she'd overpower them. Without wings or any grotesque deformities, they appeared as close to an average mortal as demons could, making them prime candidates for infiltrating civilizations on the surface. What stumped Nessix was how little they looked like flemans. Fair skinned, they both sported pale hair. They'd stand out on Elidae like an archer on the front lines. Kol was too sharp to make such a blatant oversight.

Marching through the forest, each step carried Nessix closer toward a freedom she craved. It had been so long since she'd allowed herself to entertain the idea of a successful escape that she was almost afraid to try it, afraid this was some grand trick. If she was to believe Kol, Mathias had left Elidae once the war ended, but Brant and Sulik wouldn't have gone. She'd have her old army soon, her disciplined commanders. And if Sulik had continued fawning over Mathias after Nessix had been slain, she had a hunch her loyal bodyguard would have means of contacting the paladin. All Nessix had to do was figure out how to slip past these guards.

"I'd like to head to the city of Reiton," she said, through with this silence. "It's always been the hub for rumors and is far enough from either fortress to avoid trouble."

The taller demon who walked in front answered with a disinterested grunt and they continued through the timber in silence. It wasn't until they reached a clearing that he stopped and turned to face her.

"Which direction is Reiton?" he asked, his voice soft enough to make Nessix shiver.

Perhaps she'd misjudged him. "I'd be happy to lead the way if—"

A deadly flash in the demon's eyes silenced Nes's guileful offer, and the second demon stepped up beside the first. Nes's eyes swept across her sword belt where it hung securely around the first demon's waist as the pair sized her up. This would be more difficult than she'd hoped.

"We'll have to take the road heading southwest." She pointed in the given direction. "Provided I oriented myself correctly after leaving the cave."

The demons exchanged apathetic glances, as though they both resented their orders to escort her.

"Alright. Let's go," said the first. He spun on a heel and stepped ahead down the trail.

Nessix sighed, flicking one more glance at her sword, and followed behind him.

* * * * *

Though part of Nessix trusted Kol and, by default, his judgement that her demon guards would deliver her where she wanted to go, she was relieved when Reiton's gates came into view without complication. Despite their ordinary appearances, her guards hung back, shackling Nessix with the open threat of entering Reiton to hunt her down if they suspected she went missing. Understanding their terms and unwilling to test them,

Nessix stepped out on her own and approached her city.

What struck her first upon entering Reiton was the amount of new construction. Boards innocent of age and the elements held up freshly thatched roofs, and the bricks of the main street were clear of chips and debris. It was a beautiful sight, but dismayed her nonetheless, spinning tales of how the war she'd given her life trying to stop had devastated her country. Equally upsetting was how many glares she received as she passed, citizens hastening their gaits to reach their destinations and slip into shops or vendors' booths before she reached them. Nessix wouldn't fault the people for not recognizing her, considering her circumstances, but the amount of suspicion thrown her way shouldn't have existed in the hopeful population she'd left behind.

The only people who didn't hustle away from her was a trio of middle aged women who swept the dirt and refuse off the street with stiff brooms. Praying they were good gossips, Nessix approached them eagerly.

"Already paid our taxes," the first woman muttered as soon as Nessix stopped before them.

The second woman grunted her agreement. The third gripped her broom tighter and swept more furiously, giving Nessix the distinct impression that she had not, in fact, paid these taxes the first had referred to. Instantly, Nes's heart rate quickened as the thought of Veed having absorbed the northern territories flickered to life.

"I'm not a tax collector," Nessix said, wading through the variables presented to her.

"You're wearin' tax collector lookin' garb," the first woman said.

"I…" Nessix looked down at her armor and shook her head. What had happened while she'd been gone? "I was lost during the war."

The first woman stopped her sweeping and propped her chin on the end of her broom handle. "Which one?"

"There's been—?" Nessix stopped her question. If she let herself dwell on how many wars had come and gone, she risked admitting that Kol's speculations of Elidae's condition might be

323

more right than wrong. She sighed and held her hands open to the women, approaching from a different angle. "Can any of you tell me where I can find Comm— General Maliroch?"

The broom fell from beneath the woman's chin and the other two promptly ceased their sweeping to spin around and gawk at Nessix. "You been livin' under a rock?" the woman asked. "The man was burned alive!"

"On his wedding night!" the second added.

"Poor soul," said the third.

"Poor soul..." the first agreed.

Numbness struck Nessix between the eyes and her armor suddenly felt dangerously restrictive. She wrapped fingers around her gorget, the metal biting into her joints as she tugged on it as if that would let her breathe more easily. After everything Brant had survived, how had he succumbed to something so pathetic? *Probably the same way I did...* A balmy heat washed over Nessix and she cast her distorted gaze around for someplace to lean her weight before her legs gave out from beneath her. Finding nowhere convenient, she staggered to catch herself from falling.

"I blame that tramp of a wife he took," the second woman said, ignoring Nes's failing composure entirely.

"That's ridiculous!" the third insisted. "The poor woman's still in mourning!"

"Poor woman..." the first lamented.

"Her brother took control before the general was even peeled from his bed. The woman's not mourning *anything*."

Nessix had gone into Reiton in search of gossip, but this was not the kind she'd expected to find. Her breath came shallow and quick, dizziness flitting behind her eyelids, and she could only think of one solution to any of this. "Where can I find Commander Vakharan?"

The women ceased their bickering and looked over to Nessix as though seeing her for the first time. "*Brother* Vakharan?" the first asked. "Rumor is he and"— she lowered her voice to a whisper— "*the Shade* ran off to the cave temple the day after the Mad General died to organize some sort of holy rebellion against the new government." She leaned back and planted her free hand on her hip. "Where *have* you been, lady?

"It's… it's not important," Nessix said, beginning to feel as though that was true. "I'll leave you to your work. Thank you for your time."

As Nessix dragged herself toward the city gates, imagining her beloved cousin's demise over and over again, she understood what Kol had meant. The demon war hadn't been the last one to ravage Elidae, and Nessix hadn't been gone much longer than year or so. Brant was dead, Mathias was gone, and Sulik and this mysterious Shade were planning a rebellion.

Nessix hadn't expected to be recognized, and almost preferred that she hadn't been. This wasn't the Elidae she loved, but one thing was brutally clear. If the demons wouldn't have taken her, none of this would have happened. Kol's trust meant nothing to Nessix. That internal longing to make him proud and keep him safe meant nothing. She had to escape and set the world right again.

THIRTY

Mathias and Julianna had both been through trials nobody deserved to face. They'd seen horrors and atrocities, blasphemy and hopelessness, yet nothing instilled in them the same overwhelming dread that Etha's contemplative silence did. The three of them sat in the privacy of Mathias's chamber—Julianna at the desk with Mathias and their goddess perched on the edge of his bed—as the weight of Mathias's report soaked in. As tenaciously as they'd chased after answers, none of them had fathomed how much happier they'd have been not knowing.

"Well?" Mathias asked after the silence persisted too long.

Etha sat immobile, staring ahead with eyes glazed over by thoughts far deeper than Mathias knew how to fathom. Julianna had picked the cuticle of her left thumb raw, head bowed. She opened her mouth to try speaking, but all that left her was a burdened wheeze of breath.

This wasn't what was supposed to happen now that the pieces had come together. They were supposed to have a sound course of action, a way to end this madness. Instead, Mathias had to cope with his own fears and those dumped on him by his two most trusted advisors when all he wanted to do was gut every demon he came across as retribution for their sins. He didn't delight in killing the way some men did, but the idea of watching the demons squirm and writhe in agony as he split them open and left them to suffer lingering deaths—

A warm hand wrapped around his wrist, putting an abrupt end to the morbid thoughts which threatened to corrupt him.

Do not become the monster, Mathias…

Mathias had made the same plea to Nessix after she'd witnessed the brutal fall of Sarlot, and now Etha made the same to him. Obedience and honor wanted Mathias to tremble at the cruel intentions Etha warned him against, but a darker, stronger emotion smothered his virtues into the dirt.

I cannot promise to not seek vengeance. Not this time, and you know it. They've gone too far.

Not even blinking, Etha slid her hand from Mathias's arm and laid it back in her lap. She wouldn't have this fight with him right now, not with his passion and obstinacy charging toward destruction.

Etha's disappointment formed a dismal aura around her, seeping into Mathias like a biting chill. He heaved a brusque sigh at the goddess's admonition and leaned forward, resting his elbows on his knees. "Sitting here staring at nothing isn't getting us any closer to stopping the demons."

"No," the goddess answered, voice hollow. "It's not."

Julianna flopped her hands in her lap. "But where do we start? We've found out the demons have raised an army, but we don't know nearly enough about what they're capable of to risk charging at them blindly."

Silence settled over the three of them once more, eroding what remained of their confidence. Talking things through, being sensible, following rules and protocol… all of that had wasted so much precious time.

Mathias slapped his thighs and hefted his weight to stand. "I'm going down there."

Without a word, Etha's hand struck out and grabbed Mathias, giving him a stout tug to deposit him on the bed again.

"*Why* is that always your answer for anything involving the demons?" Julianna demanded on cue. "It didn't work for you the first time you tried, and it won't work this time, either."

Mathias drew in a deep breath, inflating himself with that stubbornness that often carried him so far. "It *did* work for me. I found Sazrah and we escaped just fine."

"You escaped because I ran in after you!"

Mathias raised his voice to talk over the rest of Julianna's pending objections. "Nessix wouldn't stand for what's been happening. I need to find her so she can help me put a stop to it. And going into the hells to find her is the only way to get that done."

Julianna sighed the patient, motherly sigh she used when one of her students forgot an assignment. "Mattie, you're assuming she's still the same woman you knew."

That was Julianna's favorite excuse and Mathias's greatest fear, but the more he thought it over, the less he believed it was true. "If she wasn't, the demons would have had her up here with the army. She's an enthusiastic fighter and thrives off making scenes. They wouldn't let her skills go to waste. If nothing else, if they'd perverted her so she was no longer herself, they'd have sent her back to taunt me."

Julianna looked to Etha, an argumentative frown sullying her pleasant face, coming closer to demanding the goddess set Mathias straight than she ever had before. Unfortunately for the priestess's objectives, Etha would have to let her down.

"Mathias is right." She held a hand out to Mathias to keep him from reiterating her point. "Nessix was a force of nature and if the demons had succeeded in unshackling her from her morals, they'd use her until she could no longer function. I can't confirm it, but strongly suspect they've kept her back because they can't quite trust her obedience. If she still lives—and her soul hasn't reached the heavens, so I assume she does—I believe she's still more Nessix than not."

Lips tightening even more, Julianna crossed her arms. "Yeah, but you're both assuming she actually holds authority over anyone down there. Zenos said the demons have taken thousands of souls. Besides her connection to Mathias, what would make her worth it to the demons?"

"Mehalco said none of the soldiers were confident in what

they were doing," Mathias said. "That their general's safety was used to leverage their compliance. The demons are smart, Jules. If they had anyone more skilled than Nes, they'd have been that leader and Nessix would have marched through Braden."

Continuing this argument was becoming increasingly difficult for Julianna and she dug into one final stand with the best pout she had in her. "So this is what we're coming to now? Trusting Mehalco?"

Etha expelled a gentle breath, finding a faint smile at last. Consoling the tantrums of her children came much more naturally to her than attempting to quell a demon assault. "Now, Julianna. We've trusted him for some time now."

Julianna gaped at her goddess—wanting nothing more than to stomp her feet and call her mad—to her brother, and back again. Etha's eyes harbored a sagacious compassion that threatened to devour Julianna's objections; any assumption that the goddess enjoyed the path this predicament had taken would be woefully misguided. And, contrary to what Julianna's temper insisted, fine lines of worry etched uncharacteristic maturity between Mathias's brows. For the first time, she had to admit that he might not *want* to venture into the demons' realm. Julianna sat back in her chair, too humbled to pout or protest.

"What's your plan?" she murmured.

Etha looked to Mathias.

Though he'd been willing to go this route from the start, he hadn't wanted it to be his only option. Memories of his first capture by the demons and the tortures he'd endured while kept from Etha haunted him even now, constantly weighing whether or not experience had made him better equipped to handle it. What it came down to was that he did have Etha. He had experience. Nessix had determination and more courage than a young woman should have had to cultivate, but she'd only just begun to hold her own against the fallen. What Mathias wanted more than anything was to pull her free from the demons and set things right. As far as his plan went to get this done... he hadn't quite gotten that far.

"The second I set foot in their realm, the demons will know I'm there." Plan or not, Julianna wouldn't be satisfied with his silence, so Mathias began talking. "And they know the fastest way to hurt me is through Nessix. Even if they find me before I find her, I'm sure it wouldn't be long before they brought her out to gloat about what they've done to her."

Julianna pursed her lips, but kept herself from pointing out how the demons finding him first was a terrible option. "And if they do catch you and bring her to you, what then? How do you escape? If Etha can't reach you in the hells, teleportation won't work."

Etha hummed an abrupt agreement. "I doubt Nessix would survive an attempt at divine travel. If she's anything like the soldiers who attacked Braden, her soul's been fractured." Her blunt observation quickly smothered the room in another heap of dismay and she frowned, combing her endless knowledge for options. She brightened as one came to mind, though her enthusiasm quickly faded as she delivered her suggestion. "You could always try blood magic to open a portal."

Julianna gasped sharply, the color draining from her face, but Mathias's tight jaw and hardened eyes stated that he'd already thought of it. Blood magic, a technique developed by the first children gods to aid their mortal servants in escaping the sight of the other deities, was a seldom practiced and hazardous technique. Using one's own source of divinity to bypass notice of others required precision and, for feats as great as physical relocation, the risk of death. Mathias could not die, but he could bleed out, rendering him—and Nessix—helpless to the demons. It was a technique he wasn't particularly experienced with, but at this point, he was willing to pull from every resource he had.

"It's settled then," Mathias said. This time, Etha allowed him to stand and he stretched out his shoulders to alleviate his accumulated tension. "I'm going into the hells. The moment I get my hands on Nessix, we're either running or magicking our way out. After that, she'll be able to tell us what we need to know to stop this practice for good."

Mathias declared his plan so simply that it was hard for Julianna to doubt him. But somehow, she did. "I'll go task the priestesses with prayers for your safety and success." It was all she could say past her fear of begging him to come up with a different plan. She knew no other existed.

"Thanks, Jules."

Julianna envied Mathias his resolve and stood so she could rush out of the room before she changed her mind about complying with this madness.

Alone in his room with Etha, Mathias exhaled a slow breath and hung his head, exhausted from the front he'd used to fool his sister. Etha's warmth embraced him moments before her arms wrapped around his chest. She pressed her forehead against his back.

"You are the only man alive who can do this," she murmured, her words bolstering his heart. "Do not forget that while I cannot reach you when you're in the hells, your prayers reach me. I'll be watching. And I'll help you however I can."

Mathias didn't answer her, not knowing what was left to say. If he started talking now, he'd break down over how frightening it was to not hear her voice and how scared he was that Julianna might be right about Nes's fate. He didn't need to voice any of that. Etha already knew.

THIRTY-ONE

Nessix took her time returning to her demon guards, fighting to compose herself in hopes of avoiding their ridicule. Growing up, Brant had told her that he intended to die before her and after she'd put on the rank of General, it was a fact she'd silently accepted. That had been under the impression that he'd fall gloriously in battle, not to some underhanded assassination after he'd been shoved into her position. Guilt rode Nessix hard, telling her it might be best to return to the home Kol promised her so she could forget about this part of her life. She paused, drawing a sharp breath. What if that had been the cunning alar's plan all along?

Kol had given Nessix a week to investigate Elidae's current status, and she'd barely suffered through a single day. Hopelessness vied to take control of her determination, cooing to her about how much easier life was when Kol made all of the big decisions for her, but Nessix couldn't look past the fact that he'd sent her here knowing exactly what she'd find. The trust he'd asked for and that foolish notion Nessix had concocted about him caring about her flew from her mind at the thought of him and Annin sitting in the hells, laughing over what she'd just discovered. Yet Nessix still couldn't force herself to hate him.

Reflecting on Kol's flaws, remembering that he was a demon and not her benevolent guardian, settled the last of Nes's doubts.

Once she was able to think of her beloved cousin and hear his heartening laughter instead of his tortured screams, she stalked toward where the demons had told her to meet them with renewed purpose. They'd tucked themselves well off the road and by the time Nessix arrived, the sun had nearly set. A campfire, just large enough to loan the two of them a bit of warmth, cast its dancing light across their faces, the shadows left behind making their expressions all the more ferocious.

"Back already?" the first asked.

His companion cackled with the knowing tone Nessix had expected. "Had enough of Elidae?"

Would Kol have been so cruel to her if he'd been there? That thought punched Nessix in the gut and she slumped to the ground a foot beyond her guards' reach. Of course Kol would have been this cruel. Somewhere in her quest to dominate him, in that fondness she'd coaxed out of him and that damnable connection they shared, Nessix had begun to make dangerous excuses for his behavior. Humiliated, defeated, and rapidly succumbing to helplessness, Nessix found herself alone and adrift in the despair Kol had hoped she'd find.

The demons told Nessix they'd make camp for the night, and she rolled to her side, back to their smug faces as she tried to get comfortable between her armor and a cyclone of contemplation. Kol had known what she would find. He knew how it would hurt her. And he knew that her need to be valued would lead her back to him. He'd routinely outsmarted her, but the one place she outsmarted him was in how well she knew herself. It would have been easiest to run back to his arms, but Nessix respected the difficult route. Kol was waiting for her, but a sliver of Nes's ideal world still existed where Mathias waited for her. Unfortunately for Kol, Nessix preferred the paladin's mischief to his.

Sleep didn't come easily to Nessix as she toiled over her fears of what would become of the akhuerai without her, but already wearied by the previous night's restlessness and the day's emotional burden, exhaustion claimed her easily. The guards woke her when dew still clung to the groundcover and a chill lingered in the air. Nessix sat pensively as they gathered up their sparse belongings, unsure why she put off what she had to do. Giving in to impulse had never been a problem for her in the past, and the fact that Kol had set her up for this discovery made her resent the demons even more.

If she ran, the demons would come after her, but bitterness and repressed mourning was content with ushering panic to Elidae's new leadership. Let the demons come after her and flush out the country's corruption. Sulik was the last competent leader left on the island, and he was safe in the temple.

Kol had invested too much in the akhuerai to simply destroy them in retaliation, and Nessix consoled herself with the knowledge that escaping had been the plan all along. She trusted Auden and his dedication to the army. The akhuerai—and any mortal unfortunate enough to end up in the demons' sights—counted on Nessix reaching Zeal. If she didn't run now, she may never have another chance. Mind settled, Nessix stood and surveyed her surroundings.

"Where are you going?" the brighter of the two demons asked.

Nessix hadn't worked out the specifics of her escape, but her first step would be to separate her guards. "I have to relieve myself," she snapped.

The leader scowled and nodded to the second demon, who grumbled his compliance.

"Seriously?" Nessix repressed her urge to grin at the ease in which her objectives were fulfilled. "Can't I have some privacy?"

"You're not a princess anymore," the leader said.

Nessix wrinkled her nose and shook her head. "I never was."

The first demon ignored her correction, leveling his voice with dull patience. "Master Kol's orders surpass your concept of decency. Either Baul goes with you, or you go in your armor."

Nessix scoffed and spun to trudge off. She held her breath, not sure if she should expect an escort or an attack from her behavior, but heavy footsteps soon clomped behind her, and she methodically released the negative tension in her arms and legs. The demon following her was armed with a dagger and a short sword, an advantage over her, but better odds than she'd have against his companion. Nessix had spent a generous portion of her youth camping and hunting, learning how to use Elidae's environment to her advantage. Selecting a location for her assault was the only thing she could do to improve her chance of success.

She settled on an ancient tree with a trunk wide enough to conceal her body. A thick bed of needles covered the ground, as opposed to the noisier leaves and sticks scattered about other parts of the forest. This was the best location she'd find, and she halted the demon behind her with a firm glare as she swept behind the tree.

Nessix clanked around with the straps of her armor but kept each piece secure in preparation for the scuffle to come. The illusion of removing the plates bought her time to cycle her adrenaline in a positive direction, and once she was relatively certain her guard had grown bored, she peeked around the tree to find him staring her direction. Flushing at being caught, Nessix froze as she tried to adjust her tactics. Fortunately, the demon gave her an opening all on his own.

He dropped his arms to his sides and took a menacing step toward her. "Hurry up, your High—"

Doubt stifled behind an internal battle cry, Nessix launched forward and slammed her fist into the demon's throat. Silencing and crippling him in the same motion, she reached his dagger before he could and jabbed it between his fingers as they groped at his neck. Nessix released the hilt to catch his collapsing body before it crashed to the ground, the weight of his corpse nearly pulling her down with it. She glanced at his sword, a more practical weapon for dueling demons, but she'd be unable to conceal it. Tearing the dagger from his throat, Nessix wiped it as clean as she could in his hair. Flipping the blade to hide it against her forearm, Nessix headed back toward camp.

All that kept her confidently marching ahead was the knowledge that she couldn't die—and demons could. If she failed to defeat her guard, he'd drag her body back to Kol, giving her half a chance of being commended for her spunk. Even if Kol wanted to punish her for the display of disobedience, she'd been through worse than anything he'd do to her. But if she succeeded... Nessix pressed forward with increased purpose.

The demon looked up from where he'd been poking around the fire's ashes and frowned. "Where's Baul?"

Nessix gasped and threw out the first lie that came to mind. "There's trouble! Come quick!"

Brows furrowed, the demon cocked his head to listen for the sound of a struggle. Nessix held her breath, but the guard's curiosity overwhelmed what his senses observed and he strode past Nessix to peer deeper into the trees. Not quite believing her ruse had worked, Nessix jumped forward and sliced through the back of the demon's thigh. Roaring in shock and pain, he crumbled to the ground, granting Nessix an opening to plunge the dagger into his throat.

Heart hammering victoriously and flooded with an intoxicating rush she'd missed, Nessix stood where she was and laughed. All this time under Kol's heel, and escaping had been this simple? It seemed too surreal and a little bit daunting, and Nes's laughter came to an immediate stop. Kol was too smart to have allowed something like this to happen... Wasn't he?

Nessix didn't have time for doubts or hang ups about Kol's intentions. This was her only chance to run, she was sure of it. If she got caught before she reached substantial reinforcements, she'd never see another opportunity to slip free again. She knelt down and took her sword belt off the dead demon's waist, then hurried back to the campsite. Checking the demon's pack, she found what remained of their rations, including three large roots of dream stop. Cramming the stolen dagger into the bag of food, Nessix looked to the horizon to orient herself, and ran east. If Sulik was at the temple, that was where she needed to be.

* * * * *

Legs burning, Nessix didn't slow down until the temple came into view and even then, it took spotting the curious faces of two children peeking at her from between gnarled hedges at the cave's entrance for her to break from a jog. Donning a warm smile, Nessix waved at the children, expecting them to wave back. Instead, their eyes widened and they spun to bolt inside.

"Brother! Miss Shade!" they called ahead of their hasty retreat. "Someone's coming!"

Nessix froze, heart falling. She'd been so hopeful of her homecoming, had dreamt so passionately of Elidae's warmth and comfort. Before the past day, she hadn't fathomed the idea that it could have fallen apart as it had in her absence. The children's panicked reaction to seeing her warned Nessix against entering the temple on her own. Whether or not she belonged here, times were too unstable to act recklessly. More lost and alone than she'd ever been in the hells, Nessix waited for Sulik's calm sensibility to come and invite her in.

Struggling to settle on a way to explain what happened to her and how to prove who she was, Nessix hadn't expected the feral snarl of a red haired woman encased in plates of fierce black armor to greet her. Great sword drawn and brandished with the intent to disembowel, this human warrior didn't shriek with the aggression burning in her eyes, reserving her energy for a brisk charge. Nessix gaped at her rapid approach a heartbeat longer than she should have before darting to the side, holding her hands far from her sword belt.

"Stay back, hellspawn!" the woman spat, seamlessly advancing on Nessix. "These are hallowed halls!"

"I know," Nessix said, drawing upon what remained of her diplomacy to keep an even tone. "And I mean neither them nor you any harm."

"Like you could harm me!"

The woman sprang forward again, just in time for Nessix to catch a flutter of movement at the temple's entrance and the wearied strain of Sulik's voice shouting, "Sazrah, hold!"

This Sazrah didn't stop, following through with her lunge. Nessix slipped on the uneven stones of the cave's landing as she dodged. She flailed in an attempt to regain her balance, but ultimately fell to her side. Startled and more heartbroken about Elidae's state of affairs than before, Nessix pulled her blade free to defend herself. As she curled one leg beneath her to push back to her feet, Sulik reached Sazrah and grabbed her raised arm with both of his hands.

"This is *not* how we greet visitors," he scolded. "If we're ever going to find allies, you can't keep assuming all of Elidae's against us and attacking everyone who comes our way."

"*That*—" Sazrah spat, jerking her head in Nes's direction. "Is not an ally."

Tears welled in Nes's eyes and spilled free before she registered they were there. Sulik looked down at her with eyes colder than she remembered, twice as many worry lines, and no hint of the gentle smile she once knew. Had Elidae taken even her stalwart bodyguard from her? Desperate to prove herself to him, Nessix flung her sword to the ground with enough force to send it clattering to his feet.

"Sulik?" Nes's voice trembled pathetically through her tears.

Deep brown eyes looked down at the blade he'd known from happier times and his expression fell blank. Sazrah jerked her arm free from his hands, muttering to herself as she paced a slow circle away from them.

"Commander Vakharan?" Nessix tried again, rising to her knees. "Please talk to me."

Sulik raised his head to look at Nessix and in that moment, he recognized her tears of anguish. He'd seen them when she'd lost her father, praying he'd never see them again. "...Nessix?"

Sazrah spun around, eyes wide at Sulik's hushed question. Unable to control herself, pushing aside modesty and decorum, a sob escaped Nessix and she leapt forward and threw her arms around her old commander. He wrapped her close in his embrace, his own tears dampening Nes's hair.

"What happened to you?" he whispered.

Nessix was too worn from her trials to hold herself upright, but when she pulled away from Sulik to look him in the eyes, he grasped her forearms to hold her steady, as dependable as always. "There's too much to tell you, but I need to find Sagewind."

Sulik sniffed back his tears and set his lips in a dutiful grimace. "He left once we defeated Shand." The ripple in Nes's brow reminded Sulik that she'd never known the cause of the war that had taken her, about Inwan's return, nor Veed's demise or Mathias's role in the new war that raged across Elidae. Considering her request was for that same man, Sulik thought it best to omit those details. Shaking his head, he tried again. "He returned to Zeal to begin looking for you. How did you—"

"No." Sazrah's voice cut through Sulik's gentle question. "You cannot mean this demon is who—"

"I'm no demon," Nessix corrected, confidence growing now that she had a lifelong ally at her side. "But if I don't find Mathias, Abaeloth will ache in ways you cannot imagine."

Sazrah cocked her head and drew herself to her full height. "Is that a threat?"

"Not by me."

Sulik closed his eyes and blew out a quick sigh. If he'd doubted this was Nessix, that snipped retort would have corrected him. "Sazrah. This is Nessix. I'd known her all her life, and I know her now."

The red haired woman stubbornly shook her head, jaw set rigidly and lips peeled back with a disbelief that was painfully familiar to Nessix. Even so, Sazrah didn't argue with Sulik's testimony. Instead, she growled a burst of frustration and spun to disappear into the temple.

"Forgive her," Sulik requested softly, wiping away Nes's tears. "She was brought here by Mathias when he left and she was raised in combat even more severely than you were. After recent events..." Sulik's gaze lowered from Nes's. He'd never enjoyed delivering bad news, and he'd yet to fully adjust to Brant's death, himself. "Please, come inside. Get some rest and we can catch up on all that's happened." Sulik slipped his hand behind Nes's shoulder to guide her toward the safety of the temple, but she held fast.

"Sulik, I don't have time to rest or talk. I need to run. I need to get to Mathias. The demons brought me back to life. They didn't release me; I escaped. As in this morning. My keeper will come after me as soon as he realizes I'm gone, and I *must* reach Mathias before that happens. You can pray to his Etha, right? Get her attention so I can be magicked to wherever he is?"

Sulik stared at Nessix in silence, weighing her words and the desperation with which she delivered them. "Are you saying the demons will resurface?"

Nessix grimaced and looked at the ground. "I suspect they will." She raised reluctant eyes to Sulik's. "But from what I've seen and heard over the past day, that might be the sort of emergency Elidae needs to remember who she is."

Sulik looked over to where Sazrah had disappeared and sighed. "We've got ways to protect the innocents, just like you did. And better yet, we've…" He paused. Nes's words implied she knew about Brant's murder, though her reliance on Etha suggested she hadn't heard of Inwan's return. Trusting Nes's urgency to reach Mathias, Sulik made the hasty decision to keep secret the god's presence on the island. That confession would do nothing but complicate matters he didn't yet understand. "We've managed to open the seas. A transport ship sails for Gelthin tomorrow. I can see that you make it aboard."

The concept of traveling by sea was unheard of to Nessix, a suicide mission for anyone foolish enough to tempt the demon sea, Havoc. She looked into Sulik's eyes, still so faithful, still so honest. Though generations of her family line had known sea travel as a death sentence, Sulik told her it would be safe. Besides, few things could be more perilous than surviving in—and escaping from—the hells. "Thank you, Commander," she said. "And thank you for not asking questions."

Sulik creased his lips, wishing Nessix wouldn't have added the latter, as questions flooded his mind. Dutiful as ever, he'd honor Nes's unspoken request and simply enjoy having her home in the moments he could.

THIRTY-TWO

The air was crisp and fresh so high up the mountainside and birds sang their joys of freedom. Beyond the mountain range rose the steady rush of the ocean, insulating preoccupied minds from wandering thoughts. All things considered, the setting was peaceful and serene, a welcome reprieve from trials and feuds. Kol craved such peace now the way he craved Nes's soul.

"Perhaps we—"

A fierce look of flaming eyes silenced Annin's attempt to cut through the tension, and the gathering of foot soldiers waiting at the portal's entrance scuffed about as they shifted their weight. At Kol's left shoulder, Grell stood with his massive arms crossed, his expression unusually placid and patient as he watched the foothills for signs of movement. He glowed with an arrogant satisfaction, silently gloating to Kol about how right he'd been.

"Still think she's not a flight risk?" the inoga asked.

Kol, even with his history of reckless decisions and resentment of the title he'd lost, wouldn't dream of trying to silence Grell. Annin bit down on the inside of his cheek and refrained from a second attempt at diffusing the tension building beside him. Someone had to be the smart one.

It wasn't so much the fear of Grell's retribution that Kol quaked from. It was the intense burning of betrayal that held his breath captive and ached in his heart. The rage he'd expected to experience from Nessix running never manifested, replaced only with a soul-rending emptiness Kol longed to hide from. Prayers wouldn't work for a demon, but Kol wished they would.

"There… there must have been some sort of accident." He'd meant to deliver his excuse as a confident, valid statement, but all he managed was a tiny murmur. To his right, Annin heaved a knowing sigh and preemptively shifted away from him.

Grell's movement was slow—or maybe that was just Kol's perception of it—as he turned his head to look down at his long-time acquaintance. "I'd say there's been an accident."

The words struck directly where Grell intended. It had been an accident for Kol to scout out Nessix to begin with, an accident to be bold enough to claim her. It had been an accident to bind himself to her, to nurture her so obsessively, to let her charm her way past his sensibilities. Mortal emotions didn't strike demons often, giving them an intense impact that Kol had difficulty breathing through. He'd been genuinely fond of Nessix, had trusted her and the grudging obedience she'd shown him. Having that trust ripped away in this manner tore at Kol's heart and left him with an annoying burning in his eyes. Nessix wouldn't have done this to him. She *wouldn't!*

Kol kept his fist clenched in a poor attempt at preventing it from shaking as he raised his hand to his chest. He slipped his fingers around Nes's soul vessel and felt nothing but cold metal and stone. The pendant still harbored the glow of Nes's fractured soul, implying she hadn't been ended in his absence, but that ushered in a new wave of uncertainty.

What happened, little one…

There was no answer, no matter how desperately Kol wanted one, and when Grell clapped a heavy hand on Kol's shoulder, it was all the alar could do to keep from screaming in terror and throwing himself to the ground. His fist clenched tighter around Nes's vessel, silently begging it to give him even a flicker of warmth.

"You were the one who convinced me it was smart for her to go visit Elidae." Grell's words were somber and held a weight that crushed what was left of Kol's nerves. "You swore to me she wouldn't leave you."

Kol gulped down the lump that had kept him from speaking and forced out a weak reply. "She wouldn't." This conviction still made sense in his heart and mind, but it never made it as far as his voice.

A rumble shook Grell's throat, but Kol couldn't tear his pleading gaze from the foothills to appraise the inoga's expression to determine if it had been laughter or a growl. It didn't make a difference to Kol. Nessix was in the wind, and he was alone. In this moment, nothing else mattered.

"I can see by the weakness on your face that this worries you," Grell said.

Oh, it worried Kol in ways he'd never be able to explain to Grell. The inoga based his harassment solely on his disapproval of the relationship Kol had built with Nessix, but matters stretched far deeper than that. Nessix was the kind of woman who got things done. She was tenacious and smart, self-confident and keenly in tune with what was just. Whether or not she understood it, she carried with her secrets that could lead to the demons' downfall. And all of this sat on Kol's shoulders.

"I've invested much in her," Kol murmured, lips tingling with shock and denial. "Of course I'm worried."

Grell continued to stare at Kol, his eyes bearing down on the alar, shrinking this proud warrior into a pathetic lump. A tremble raced beneath Kol's skin, and he couldn't force himself to look at the beast beside him.

"What's the matter?" Grell asked, too friendly. "This entire time, you've been full of praises for your little pet. I haven't been able to *force* you to shut up about her, and now that I'm asking for information, you can't even squeak?"

Tears pressed harder against Kol's eyes.

Grell patted Kol's shoulder, each strike prompting a quick wince from the alar. "You're smart, my friend. You'll be able to make this right."

A suffocating silence spread across the three demons standing on that mountainside, Kol's heart hammering in his ears as his voice continued to fail him.

"*Won't you?*"

Accusation ran thick through Grell's words, doubting Kol's ability to reclaim Nessix and tearing at the last bit of his confidence. Grell did nothing to hide the fact that he knew Nessix wasn't coming back and that he looked forward to the punishment he'd deliver once he thought Kol had suffered from mental strain long enough. This threat should have motivated Kol to take action, to launch himself down onto Elidae and tear each door off every house until he found where Nessix was hiding. What should have motivated him and what actually did conflicted immensely.

Satisfied with the terror he'd injected in Kol, Grell turned and sauntered through the portal, a disorganized jumble of demons parting to let him pass. What remained of Kol's nerve registered the inoga's departure, telling him it was safe to relax, but the queasy grip crushing his insides nearly prevented him from breathing. Time contorted into an abstract concept as he tried to rationalize what had happened. Reports stated that Sazrah the Shade had brought the Order's demon hunters to clean up Elidae. They must have routed Nes's guards and taken her captive. Nessix wanted to come back to him. She needed him.

Every time Kol declared as much to himself, it cheapened the sentiment, weakening it until even his delusional side began to doubt it.

Beside him, Annin heaved a sigh, conveying all of his regrets with that single breath. He turned, but was stopped abruptly as Kol's fingers gripped his forearm. Unsurprised by his old friend's desperation, the oraku creased his lips in a frown and waited for Kol's pathetic plea.

"You have to help me…"

Annin could have lectured Kol of how hard he'd tried to do just that long ago, but all demons had surrendered to the fact that trying to change the past was a wasted effort. Ties of camaraderie told Annin the honorable course was to help Kol. Fear of what would happen to him if Grell were to execute Kol told him the smart course was to help Kol. He pulled his arm free from Kol's grasp and faced him.

"You don't really believe there was an accident, do you?" he murmured, quietly enough to evade the ears of those lingering demons.

Excuses flew to Kol's tongue, but impending dread weighed them down too much for them to make it any farther. Kol clenched his teeth on those excuses of Nes's innocence and loyalty, and he shook his head.

Annin hesitated a moment, letting the truth soak into Kol's mind before turning again. "Come with me. There's a way we can track her."

Kol drew a full breath of cool air at last and gave the landscape of Elidae a final glare. *I'm coming for you, little one...* He turned on a heel and followed Annin back into the hells.

The Afflicted Saga

Defiance

Tale of the Fallen: Book IV

DEMONS MUST HUNT THEIR LEGEND...

They'd searched for nearly two days when the smell of death put an abrupt end to their hunger pangs, and neither Kol nor Annin bothered so much as a glance at the other before following the stench to a peaceful bed of pine needles. The corpse their meager search party came across had bloated, juices of decomposition seeping from between the seams of its armor. Its face had been peeled clean by scavengers, one eye missing and the other ruptured and oozing over exposed bone. If not for the style of armor, the body's origins would have been unidentifiable.

Kol stared down at the remains of the dead demon, Grell's suspicions and Annin's terse warnings echoing in his mind.

"That one of yours?" Annin asked.

The alar processed the question slowly and nodded.

Annin sighed one of those reluctant sighs that conveyed just how much he wanted to go back in time to never get himself involved with Nessix or the akhuerai or even Kol. Silently, he grabbed Kol's hand to let more blood into his orb. It glowed to life and led them to the next demon's remains.

"An accident, right?" Annin asked.

Kol's lips were numb and the warmth was beginning to drain from his extremities. Based on the armor he wore, this demon had been the elite of Nes's two guards, the one who should have carried her sword belt. It was missing and none of the demon's weapons had been drawn. That suggested he hadn't fallen victim to any sort of organized attack—the only way a group of flemans or the few members of the Order of the White Circle here on Elidae would have been able to take out both demon guards—and that he had been taken down by surprise. By someone he'd underestimated. Someone he'd been assured was not a threat. Annin stopped beside Kol, silently staring down at the corpse as identical thoughts formed in his mind.

Kol turned his head toward his oraku companion, the demon who had stood beside him through all of his reckless theories and experiments, the smartest demon he'd known, and his last chance at being spared from the punishment Grell had been gleefully choreographing for him. Quietly, to himself, Kol had to finally admit that Nessix had chosen to run. She'd deceived her guards just as she'd deceived him, slain them, and now she was in the wind. Admitting this out loud, with witnesses, wasn't an option for Kol. He was an elite, an ancient. He didn't make mistakes, because no demon who did survived long enough to face them. Overwhelmed by a cold confusion he didn't understand, missing the rage that once came so naturally to him, Kol held his breath to wait for Annin's reaction.

A sensible demon would have been outraged. He'd have spun on Kol and knocked him out, shredded his wings, and bound him to be delivered back to his lord. A sensible demon would have found a way to appease this lord with gifts or distractions while he figured out a way to solve the greater problem. All his life, even as a mortal, Annin had been sensible—and powerful enough to execute the necessary requirements to keep himself safe. But as he met Kol's pleading eyes, that sensibility wavered, reminding him that he had told Grell that the akhuerai were the demons' vehicle to conquest, that Kol was reckless but not wrong to bind himself to Nessix. He hadn't spoken up when the idea of sending her to the surface was presented. All of those factors added up to his own hefty portion of responsibility for this catastrophe. And that didn't even touch the fact that he genuinely liked Kol.

The rotting demon at their feet told the tale of Nes's escape just as clearly as if she'd dropped from the trees to share it herself.

Kol and Annin were sharp and had gotten to know Nes's mannerisms well, but that advantage would only buy them a few minutes before the backup they'd brought along put the events together for themselves.

Kol hadn't been able to relax in the vaguest sense of the word after he'd first realized Nessix wasn't coming back, and had minded protocol as precisely as possible in an attempt to manage how far he'd fall for losing her. Spent in every fashion, the alar wasn't in an ideal frame of mind to make important decisions, and since Annin had foolishly let himself be drawn into this mess, it was up to him to initiate a solution. At least the six footmen they'd brought along had been meant to serve as decoys in the event of an ambush. If they didn't make it back, nobody would question it.

Annin knelt beside the corpse and carefully placed his orb in a bed of leaves, nestling it close to the dead demon's shoulder to protect the magical artifact from accidental destruction. He took a moment to gather his strength, closing his eyes to concentrate on the steady pulse of his threads and take into account how many he was prepared to cut. An oraku was considered too valuable for his mind to be kept fit for physical combat, so all Annin was armed with was a jagged knife reserved for emergencies. This met all his criteria. Hoping Kol's anxiety hadn't robbed him of his ability to provide backup, Annin leapt to his feet.

Nobody in the group registered what was happening the first time Annin reached forward and snapped his fingers, but the moment the first of the six guards gasped and stumbled backwards, frantically rubbing at his eyes, he quickly figured it out. By Annin's second snap, Kol spun around to see the startled soldiers scatter. By the third snap, he realized Annin was eliminating dangerous witnesses.

With three more of the soldiers left to immobilize, the oraku would risk depleting even the energy to stand and speak if Kol didn't assist. A strange sensation washed over Kol, a feeling he hadn't experienced since he'd become a demon. Gratitude, and the desire to act in Annin's defense as much as Annin was acting in his.

Without a word, recognizing the cold determination in Annin's eyes, Kol pulled his dagger free and rushed toward the demons who'd been brought to the surface to serve as his backup. He pushed past the three who Annin had blinded, shoving one to the ground in the process.

The three soldiers who still had their sight ran desperately to escape the effective radius of Annin's magic. Kol sprang forward and grabbed the nearest by the arm and plunged his knife into his target's side where his leather armor came together. The strike might not have killed the demon, but it did slow him down. Kol didn't wait around to assess the results of his attack as the other two demons actively gained ground away from him.

A gargling scream sounded behind Kol, and he hoped it belonged to one of the blind demons, rather than his friend, but that was a concern to tend to after he disposed of the two fleeing witnesses. He had an easy visual on one and the other revealed his position by crashing noisily through the trees ahead. In such thick cover, Kol wouldn't be able to track them through the sky, and they'd distanced themselves enough that he knew he'd never catch them on foot. Dusting off his deception, Kol ran from the scene and called ahead to the fleeing demons.

"Annin's lost his mind! Regroup to me! I know how to fight him!"

The demon in his sights slowed enough to turn and look back at him, but the strain of exertion and terror contorted his face too much for Kol to determine if he believed the claim. Up ahead, an abrupt rustle of dried leaves and snapping twigs—accompanied by a startled curse—suggested the other demon had tripped himself to a stop. Kol didn't have their compliance, but he did have their attention, and he could work with that.

"We'll be stronger and safer together," Kol shouted. "From Annin and the Order both. Do not forget they now have a presence on Elidae."

At last, sense penetrated panic and the demon ahead of Kol slowed to a jog, then a winded halt. Kol shoved his dagger back in its sheath and strode forward as the demon doubled over, hands on his knees as he panted for breath.

"We have to stay together if we want to stand a chance," Kol said, throwing his voice hard to ensure that it reached the last witness. "Annin's likely made quick work of those he blinded. Hurry!"

Moments later, the last demon staggered toward Kol, wild-eyed and face scratched from thorns. "You really know how to fight an oraku?"

"I know how to fight that one," Kol said, reaching an arm out to beckon the demons close. "I haven't worked alongside him this long without learning his weaknesses."

Seduced by Kol's certainty and conditioned to respect his authority, the soldiers nodded through their panting and flanked him with no further encouragement. Disappointed at how easy the general population was to manipulate, Kol's flimsy grasp on compassion pitied the two's willingness to condemn themselves. Taking them down wouldn't be a simple task, as they were already seized by adrenaline, but that experience Kol had just claimed to have working alongside Annin also declared that the oraku was counting on him. And in doing so, Kol was counting on himself.

Kol struck in a flash, popping his left wing open in a forceful snap and catching the scraped up demon in the head. The strike flung its target to the ground, adding a second blow to an already dazed head. He was managed, but only for a moment, and Kol spun to grasp the feistier of the pair by the wrist as he began to scramble away. Kol was strong and an experienced fighter, but the soldier's desperation and reactivity countered a great deal of that skill.

The soldier flailed at the end of Kol's arm, swinging his free hand to his hip to draw his sword. It was an awkward, unbalanced draw, giving Kol the chance to jerk his opponent forward to drive a knee forward into his abdomen. Protected only by hard leather armor, the strike didn't cripple the soldier, but it did succeed in driving the air from his lungs, and Kol's grasp prevented him from doubling over to gasp against the blow.

While Kol had acknowledged the risk of turning his back to the other demon, he hadn't anticipated retaliation from him until pain pierced through the webbing of his wing.

"You son of a whore!" the offending underling shouted.

A wave of agony followed the blade's path through Kol's

wing, cleaving a two foot long laceration through the tender membrane. Kol howled in pain, the cry contorting into seething rage as the demon's insubordination processed in his mind. He'd used up all of his excuses for disobedience on justifying where Nessix might have gone, and since he'd actively forbid himself to be angry at her for disappearing, still convinced there was a logical reason behind her actions, Kol spewed that raw emotion at this unfortunate outlet. Quickly ramming his knee into the first demon once more, resulting in the sword falling free from his hand, Kol spun on the second demon, slamming his good wing into his head again.

The soldier seemed better prepared for a tactical wing strike this time around and only staggered from the impact. Staggering was all Kol needed. Before his prey could shake off his daze, Kol swept forward and grabbed his arm, giving it a yank so stout that the limb pulled free from the shoulder with a satisfying pop. The bloody knife dropped from the demon's hand as he shrieked and tried to retreat, but Kol held fast to the dislocated limb and prevented his opponent from moving more than an inch.

A furious roar sputtered from behind Kol as the remaining witness found his footing, and Kol cursed his luck. Still confident he'd walk away from this fight, he was no longer certain he'd do so with grace. Locking down on the current demon's arm, he twisted around to fling him toward the oncoming attack. In flight, the demon wailed in agony as his tendons stretched from the sudden move, but his cries met an abrupt end as the charging demon's sword sank into his back.

With the odds now greatly balanced against him, the soldier swore viciously and jerked his sword free of the last ally he'd had. He continued his charge, eyes steeled over with a look Kol had once known well, the recognition that he'd likely never see the results of his actions. If sympathy still had a place in the alar, he'd have felt it now, but his own determination and the degree his morals had degraded prepared him to intercept the attack. That option never came, either.

Two strides from engaging, a choke bubbled in the charging demon's throat and he jerked to a stop. Throwing his shoulders upright, a massive tremor shook him as his sword slipped from his grip. Instincts interrupted, Kol struggled to comprehend what happened until blood seeped from the demon's eyes, nose, and ears. The unfortunate soldier sucked in a breath that instantly sputtered out as a mouthful of blood, and then collapsed forward, a puddle of red growing around his head.

"What weaknesses were you speaking of?"

Annin's voice was strained and weak, but Kol had never been so relieved to hear it. If not for the pain pulsing in his wing, he would have laughed. He turned to face his companion, meeting drooped shoulders and exhausted eyes to accompany the spent tone.

"Convincing you to overexert yourself seems to be one," Kol said. "The others? I wouldn't know."

Annin's worn gaze eased with what could have been a smug smile, but the expression never made it to his lips. He slumped to the ground to rest. "You made quite a commotion. How long do you suspect we have before some mortal comes to investigate?"

Kol grimaced and took a moment to look around. There were no signs of civilization within shouting distance, but he didn't know what sort of patrol schedule the Shade had established since taking up residence on Elidae. His grimace developed into a full-fledged frown as Sazrah crossed his mind. Neither he nor Annin had it in them to engage her in their current conditions. He crossed his arms, injured wing twitching.

"How long do you need?" Kol asked.

Annin shook his head and waved Kol closer. "Give me that wing."

Kol complied readily as Annin groped around a pouch at his hip to produce the tracking orb. As long as Kol was bleeding, they might as well take advantage of it. "We're not reporting what happened here." Kol flinched as Annin squeezed blood from his wound.

"Of course not."

They paused their discussion as the magic within the orb settled. Annin raised it into the air and slowly swept his arm until he found its strongest glow.

"Damn it all..." he growled.

Kol looked down at the orb, straightened, and followed the path it suggested they head. He, too, growled his dissatisfaction.

Though he didn't understand magic the way Annin did, Kol had learned to trust the results the oraku was able to achieve with his powers, and the orb suggested that Nessix had moved toward the temple after she'd taken out her guards. Kol had never doubted Nes's intelligence, not when it came to things she understood, and she knew Elidae better than anyone else. She'd gone to the temple intentionally. There would be no sanctuary for demons there, and that desperation Kol had forgotten in the heat of combat returned in a flood of anxiety. Unless they could find a way to lure Nessix away from the temple, she was protected from them. Kol glanced at the demons he and Annin had just defeated, wondering if silencing them so hastily had been a mistake. They'd have made useful scouts for this unpleasant task.

Annin looked up at Kol, and the alar silently helped his companion to his feet. "Even if we were both in fighting shape, that is not a place I wish to go." There wasn't the same warning Kol had gotten used to in Annin's voice, but there was a degree of ridicule, constantly reminding Kol that his desire and attempts to own Nessix had been terrible decisions.

Kol's heart beat heavily, still aching with the pain of Nes's betrayal and now enhanced with dread of what Grell would make of it. "We'll need fresh forces to go after her," he said, pleased to discover that his acclimation to panic had resulted in a greater degree of confidence in his voice.

"And what story are we going to tell?"

Kol looked around the scene, assuming what Annin had cleaned up behind wouldn't look much better. "We're going to say evidence shows that Nessix was rescued by her people," Kol said. "Both of her guards had been slain and she was taken. When we came upon the scene, we were assaulted by flemans and members of the Order, which is how our men fell. I've got an injury no sane alar would inflict on himself simply to bend a story in his favor. We'll be able to petition for a greater force with this evidence, one that will coax Nessix free from hiding."

Annin's frown persisted. "You're assuming that her remaining commander won't figure out who she is. With what she knows"—that was spoken with a heat Kol didn't appreciate—"she'll be too valuable for them to simply risk letting go. We can attack all we'd like, but the rebel army, the Order, and whoever Elidae's new leadership can rally will be the ones who march out, not Nessix."

Cursing Annin's practicality and logic, Kol rubbed the back of his head and looked toward the temple again, contemplating the ever-decreasing options at his disposal. "If we began to raze townships, she wouldn't let any number of knights or commanders hold her back. Strike her people, and she will come charging in their defense."

A bitter chuckle left the oraku and he shook his head. "The faith you have in that woman, Kol…"

"Yeah, I know," Kol seethed. "I understand that you think I'm a fool for it. And maybe I am. But you cannot deny that I know Nessix better than anyone else does."

"Not better than she knows herself," Annin said. "And she's got one advantage over you now."

Kol furrowed his brow and jerked his attention back to Annin. "And what's that?"

"She's got your memories in her, doesn't she?"

Those drawn brows wavered and tilted toward uncertainty. Annin was the only person Kol had discussed Nes's dreams with, an unavoidable circumstance given the way she disclosed that she suffered them in the oraku's presence. At that time, she'd been unclear what she was seeing, the one comfort the demons had enjoyed.

Over the following weeks after that disclosure, though, her dreams had become more vivid, had uncovered details she'd asked Kol about. Details he'd been unable to give her. She hadn't spoken outright that she knew she was living his past, but the degree of certainty she'd had when asking him to elaborate on the details she didn't understand confirmed it well. What was worse, this understanding had developed on its own accord, organically developing in Nes's mind as she continued to experience Kol's distant past. How long would it be until she was able to see past the terror of the Divine Battle? When would she find out about the demons' downfall?

"That's what I thought," Annin said, interrupting Kol's internal fretting and driving the point home all the better. He shook his head again, lips twitching as he held back his chastisement and curses at what Kol had caused. Venting such thoughts at the alar wouldn't accomplish anything; it hadn't any previous time over the past year and a half. "We have to get a hold of her before she puts it all together."

Kol wouldn't speak that he was afraid she'd already done just that. "I know we do," he spat. "That's why we're out here."

"I thought we were out here so Grell didn't skin you and force you to eat your own entrails."

Kol glared at his friend, wishing there would have been some amount of jest in those words. Instead, all he found looking back at him were stern eyes every bit as apprehensive as he felt. "That's an added bonus." He sent one more loathing glare in the direction of the temple, then turned to trudge toward their portal back into the hells. "But if we can keep our story straight, we can postpone judgement until we have time to find her. There's nothing Grell likes more than war, and any chance to launch one will overshadow even the enticement of torturing me. Are you able to travel?"

Annin stared at Kol for long moments, hating him for what he'd gotten him into. At this point, even if Grell wasn't holding Annin in part responsible for Nes's disappearance, he was certain he'd take collateral damage. Annin had committed himself to this path, a decision he'd reluctantly made when Kol first sourced himself for Nessix, a decision he'd continued to make as he went along with the idea of not ending Nessix when she first began to show signs of disobedience, and a decision he'd sealed now that he'd slaughtered his own warriors to cover up damning evidence against Kol. Annin was every bit as responsible at this point. He'd learned to trust Kol as much as demons ever trusted anyone, but it had been lifetimes ago since he'd relied on another so strongly. They depended on each other now more than either had ever intended to again.

"What choice do I have?" Annin asked. "You won't be able to

lift me anywhere with your wing like that, and the longer we dawdle here, the more likely our chances are one of the Shade's puppets shows up to finish the job."

Together, the two demons, born of mortal men who had served alongside each other in the most trying time in Abaeloth's history, set a resigned course back to the hells, reciting their story until even they believed it.

Keep up to date at www.katikaschneider.com

ABOUT THE AUTHOR

A lover of literary adventure and notorious breaker of writing rules, Katika Schneider's been an obsessive writer for most of her life. She started out writing for herself before surrendering to her characters' demands, and began pursuing publication in 2014. She's a firm believer that everyone has a story to tell.

Holding her degree in Animal Science, Kat planned on attending veterinary school until incisions started making her faint. She lives with her husband and their abundant family of critters.